# DEATH
# BEHIND THE
# HEADLINES

# A HAVELL HUNDRED MYSTERY
## JEAN CRITCHLEY

# DEATH BEHIND THE HEADLINES
## A Havell Hundred Mystery
## Jean Critchley

FICTION/ Horror
FICTION/ Mystery & Detective / General

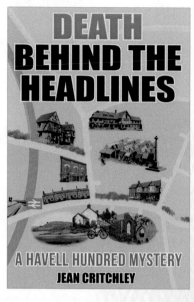

**PB** £10.99          9781528999694

**EB** £3.50           9781528999700

It is February 1986. Margery Moore, photojournalist and feature writer for the local paper, is unprepared for major news stories to unfold near her cottage, under the shadow of the mysterious and legendary Glebe Mound. When two of her acquaintances are found dying and historic documents go missing, Margery finds herself under suspicion. An eccentric recluse is arrested. Local gossip involves Margery's Russian 'fancy man'.

Two inquests explain everything, or do they? Margery's nosy neighbour is as perplexed as she is. Can it be down to the malignant spirits of the six witches of Havell-on-the-Marsh, who were hanged on the Glebe Mound four hundred years earlier?

Angry demonstrations in the marketplace against the cancellation of the traditional midsummer fair, proposals for a bypass and plans to build on the green belt culminate in a fracas after the Valentine's Ball. Can the detective from Scotland Yard enlisted by the mayor solve these mysteries? Or does his dismissive attitude to the provinces, legend and gossip blind him to the truth?

---

Please send me ...... copy/ies of
### Death Behind the Headlines
*Jean Critchley*

*Please add the following postage per book:*
*United Kingdom £3.00 / Europe £7.50 /*
*Rest of World £12.00*

### Delivery and Payment Details

| Format | | Price | Qty | Total |
|---|---|---|---|---|
| Paperback ☐ | | | | |
| Subtotal | | | | |
| Postage | | | | |
| Total | | | | |

Full name: ............................................................................................

Street Address ......................................................................................

City:................................................ County:.......................................

Postcode: ................................ Country: ...........................................

Phone number (inc. area code): ........................... Email: ...................

*I enclose a cheque for £.................. payable to Austin Macauley Publishers LTD.*

Please send to: Austin Macauley Publishers Ltd®, 1 Canada Square, Canary Wharf, London, E14 5AA

Tel: +44 (0)20 7038 8212, +44 (0)20 3515 0352
orders@austinmacauley.com
www.austinmacauley.com

## AUSTIN MACAULEY PUBLISHERS™
LONDON · CAMBRIDGE · NEW YORK · SHARJAH

Jean Critchley was born in North London, and went to school in the city. She now lives in Colchester. After training in retail, she moved to Essex. In creating this novel, she hopes to share the many interesting characters she has met, together with the intriguing, mysterious and amusing experiences she has had working in fashion, advertising, publishing and journalism. She has a BA in history and literature; she volunteers for two archaeological charities and works as a tour guide.

To all my family, friends and acquaintances, who have enriched my life and challenged me to write a novel.

Jean Critchley

# DEATH BEHIND THE HEADLINES

A Havell Hundred Mystery

AUSTIN MACAULEY PUBLISHERS™

LONDON • CAMBRIDGE • NEW YORK • SHARJAH

A CIP catalogue record for this title is available from the British Library.

ISBN 9781528999694 (Paperback)
ISBN 9781528999700 (ePub e-book)

www.austinmacauley.com

First Published 2022
Austin Macauley Publishers Ltd®
1 Canada Square
Canary Wharf
London
E14 5AA

Thanks to, Jim Connor, Trish Connor and Chrissie Scott for undertaking to read some of this in manuscript form and for their ideas, encouragement and support.

# Preface

The Havell Hundreds is an area about sixty miles northeast of London which is often overlooked. The market town of Great Havell is on the Cricklewater Estuary. The local authority is based in the town and is the largest landowner. To the north is the ancient walled cathedral city of Trincaster and to the south, the coast with its docks, nudist beach and seaside towns of Havell-Next-the-Sea and Sandy Reach. The great estates are the Manor and Trincaster Hall. The army is based at Grimpen Havell and the MOD owns a lot of the land nearby. There are many pretty villages in the area, Havell-on-the-Marsh, Havell cum Moze, Little Havell, Ashworth, Grinbury and Much Havell to name a few.

The dominant local media is the Gleaner, which manages to outclass its rival, Advertiser, in sales and revenues. Margery Moore, freelance photojournalist and feature writer works exclusively for the Gleaner. She sometimes submits her articles, for the attention of the features' editor Cheryl Francis, through the newspaper's front office. Here, she can gossip with Gill and Philippa. She also hopes to avoid the unwanted attentions of advertising director and brother of the mayor, Harry Grimes.

Margery lives in Priory Cottages under the legendary Glebe Mound with its tales of burnings, hangings and mysterious deaths. Her nosy neighbour, Alf, watches her 'fancy man', Margery's Russian lover Vladimir, come and go.

The Amicable Anarchist public house is the other side of Priory Street opposite the old priory ruins. Margery often meets up with her friend, the local librarian and historian, Jonah McKay, in his favourite corner, the snug.

Every year at midsummer, the Moyen Midden Fayre is held in the Glebe Park under the mound. This yearly tradition, it is firmly believed by local people, will rid the Glebe Mound of its legendary evil.

# Chapter I

## Great Event

**Monday 3rd Feb 1986**

'Hello girls!'

Margery Moore gave a cheerful greeting to the front office staff of the brick 1930s building which was home to the Great Havell Gleaner. They were only able to give her a smile and a wave in return. Both were deep in conversation on the phone.

Margery soon realised there was something afoot. She had stashed her feature copy on the recently opened Brass Monkeys Brasserie at the bottom of her tartan shopping trolley, hoping for a good old gossip with the girls whilst she fished around for it, sighing… 'I'm sure I put it in here last night when I finished writing it.'

Taking her glasses off, Margery gave them a polish on her tartan cape. She adjusted her hat and took a little hand mirror out of her handbag to refresh her lipstick.

'You'll never believe this!' exclaimed Philippa, slamming her trim phone down decisively.

Margery put her lipstick away, put her glasses back on, patted her golden-brown curls and looked at Philippa expectantly. She took a few involuntary steps forward as she received a gentle smack on the bottom and was greeted with a 'hello honey' by Harry Grimes, the Gleaner's advertising director. He walked purposely through the front office and took no notice of the girls, who were trying hard to attract his attention.

'The Birmingham band, Gary and the Fly by Night Boys are coming to Great Havell,' burst out Philippa, flicking back her long blonde hair and blowing her fringe out of her blue eyes before anyone else could interrupt or get a word in.

'My goodness, that's a coup for the town,' remarked Margery admiringly. 'When can we look forward to that?'

'They are playing a summer solstice concert in the Glebe Park,' replied Philippa, beaming, delighted to be able to be first with the news before Gill came off the phone.

'But the famous Moyen Midden Fayre is held in the Glebe Park every solstice.' Margery was surprised they hadn't thought of that.

'No one's going to worry about that if Gary is coming here!'

'Probably not, but I would love to have covered the concert for my "Pollux Theatre column",' sighed Margery, 'if he'd been booked to play there.'

'The Moyen Circle is furious about it,' said Gill breathlessly, running her fingers through her short light brown hair and putting her large dark rimmed glasses back on, which gave her elfin features an owl-like look. 'I've just had the chairman, Barney Cobbler, on the phone. The mayor is a cousin of Gary Hogan's and has invited him and his band to play here. Barney said he is trying to use his influence to get an extraordinary council meeting called to discuss it. He said he's not getting any support from the mayor. Everyone thinks it's a wonderful event for Great Havell. Local band Jollity will support the concert.'

'I'm due to interview Barney Cobbler for my next feature,' exclaimed Margery, delighted; her story might claim a bit more prominence in the Gleaner. This time she found her carefully typed article on the Brass Monkeys Brasserie easily in the shopping trolley, handed it to Gill and picked up a copy of the Gleaner. She glanced at the headline: "TWO-LANE BYPASS PLANNED FOR TOWN".

Margery decided to hurry home to make a start on her article about the Glebe Mound and the Moyen Midden Fayre. This was something she knew about; she could check her facts by ringing Barney up and arrange to meet him. Or she might even catch him on one of his daily walks on the Glebe Mound. She could make a start and the Gleaner would be ahead of the Advertiser with it.

There was no doubt the news about Gary Hogan and the Fly by Night Boys was being greeted with great enthusiasm at the Great Havell Gleaner offices, she thought as she negotiated her tartan shopping trolley out of the building. Her article on the opening of the Brass Monkeys Brasserie, which she had been rather pleased with, would probably hardly be noticed and there had been little of the usual friendly gossip exchanged with Philippa and Gill.

'Watch out!' called Gloria, one of the advertising sales representatives, as her red stiletto-shod feet stepped quickly from a Porsche outside the Gleaner offices, and she nearly fell over Margery's trolley.

The red car accelerated away, and Margery thought she recognised the driver as one of the local motor dealers.

She checked her apology to Gloria and thought the girl looked as if she had wrapped a tablecloth around herself in that straight red-check pattern dress. Gloria was wearing a bright red leather jacket over it. For early February, the weather was quite mild.

Margery wondered what Gloria's hurry was. She began to speculate she might be having an affair with the motor dealer. With this idea, she was in half a mind to go back for the gossip she had missed because of the excitement generated by the news of the solstice concert. She decided it could wait and instead she would go home via the Tastea Bite bakers and teashop in the marketplace. She bought a pasty for later, a loaf and some rolls to put in her small freezer. She was looking forward to starting her story, on the Glebe Mound and the fair, when she was home.

Margery walked up Priory Street, past terraces of Edwardian houses and the Amicable Anarchist in the centre of them. The publican had the door open, as he swept the floor, and gave her a friendly wave. She took the far turning into the wide marketplace, where many of the town's principal shops and business were. She bought her items at the Tastea Bite, where she was greeted by name and served with the usual civilities and remarks on what a fine day it was for February.

Margery walked the half mile from the bakers, which was on the west side of the marketplace, to her cottage. Her route took her back along Priory Street to the Amicable Anarchist pub, where she walked across the zebra crossing to the old priory car park. She was so deep in thought about the news of the concert and the cancellation of the fair, she nodded to, rather than greeted people she knew, as she walked through the extensive old priory ruins. She even greeted Sadie, absently, who was sitting on a low wall, drinking her favourite strong cider and smoking a roll-up, before she realised, she had been trying to attract her attention. Sadie had a home. She lived with Eric. They were both heavy drinkers and spent most of the money Eric's family paid him to live well away from them, on drink. Margery was beyond the railings of the priory ruins and in the lane, which ran in front of Priory Cottages before she realised Sadie might have wanted to tell her something.

Home for Margery was Number Four Priory Cottages in the middle of a terrace of seven timber-framed, tiled-roof cottages.

'Your fancy man has let himself in,' said Alf, her neighbour, who came out of his cottage door as she opened her garden gate. 'And I've shut your cat in my coal bunker,' he added. 'It was shitting all over my garden again. I'd half a mind to strangle it!'

As she negotiated her shopping trolley round Vladimir's bike and let herself into her cottage, Margery told herself to keep calm. Vladimir, tall, with light brown short hair and dressed, as he usually did, in a rather grubby vest and belted brown corduroy trousers, was pacing up and down in Margery's front room.

'Vlad, can you go over to Alf's and get my cat out of his coal bunker again please,' she said, as she took off her tartan cape, hat and boots and put her shopping trolley next to her desk. She moved to the small kitchen at the back of the cottage to fill the kettle up and turn on the stove. She put the loaf in the bread bin, the pasty in the fridge and the rolls in the little freezer compartment on the top, keeping one out for her lunch.

Vladimir took his short khaki army jacket off a peg by the cottage door and put it on. He put his feet in his army surplus boots and went out of the kitchen door. She could hear heated words between him and Alf almost immediately. Vladimir soon came back with the fluffy ginger tomcat, brushing the coal dust off his fur outside and making his vest under the open jacket even grubbier as he did so. He put the cat into the bathroom, which extended from the cottage next to the kitchen, shut the door, took his boots off and washed his hands in the small sink under the kitchen window.

'I have instructed that man not to do that again,' he said sharply. 'I said I might knock his teeth out if he does.'

Vladimir said he'd got a few hours off. Margery made a pot of tea and they had a mug each and sat in her front room. Margery was in her favourite button-back chair and Vladimir on the small settee opposite her under the window. He was sitting against the light and she could not see the colour of his blue eyes or the neat shape of his nose. She could see, or imagine, his roguish smile though. He was looking at her affectionately. It made her heart melt. After all, she was free to take a bit of time off with him, her article might have to wait.

By the time they had drunk their tea, Margery realised the phone call to Barney Cobbler would also have to be made later. They climbed her narrow wooden stairs, Vladimir treading heavily behind her with a "fuck" as he banged his head on the beam at the top. Margery smiled and wished he was wearing something other than his vest. He was so enthusiastic with the idea of them having some time together, she thought, he probably cycled over from Little Havell in his work clothes. She soon forgot about the grubby vest and everything else.

When Vlad called round these days, she thought, it was a good thing her elderly neighbour was deaf and used her hearing aid to listen to the radio, which was always on very loud and could now be heard through the lath and plaster dividing walls. Alf, on the other side, was usually out in his garden.

Margery's phone rang stridently downstairs. 'Take no notice,' said Vlad breathlessly. The phone was persistent and so was he.

'*Eto prekrasno*,' he said loudly enough, Margery thought, for Alf to hear. She guessed what it might mean. He had said it before. She tacitly agreed with him. She lay still, feeling almost sleepy. The phone had stopped ringing and, although she had plenty to get on with, she hoped they could lie in each other's arms for a little longer.

But no. He was standing up straight in an instant. He dressed and said, 'I have to go now.' She heard him clomp heavily down the wooden stairs. A little while afterwards, the front door latch opened and shut. He picked up his bike and the gate clicked as he left. She still felt relaxed and not inclined to move. The phone started ringing again. Margery got up reluctantly, pulled her dress on, over her head, and went down the narrow stairs to answer it. She reached over her Olympia portable typewriter.

'Margery?' said Cheryl from the Gleaner. 'Yes, Cheryl what did you want? I was in the front office only this morning.'

'I know, I've tried ringing before; I was expecting you to come in and see me. Where have you been? It's taken you an age to walk home.'

'I did a bit of shopping and my neighbour shut my cat in his coal bunker again,' replied Margery. 'I was just about to ring Barney Cobbler to make an appointment for an interview.'

'Well, you can't,' said Cheryl.

'What do you mean I can't?'

'He was seen walking on the Glebe Mound this morning as he usually does. He's been rushed to hospital.'

'What?'

'He's in hospital; I'm going to try to find out what happened and I'll pop in to see you to fill you in with the details.'

'But, Cheryl, he was giving Gill a hard time about the solstice concert on the phone when I was in the front office only this morning. Did he meet with an accident?'

'All I know is that he's been rushed to hospital,' said Cheryl and rang off.

*No rest for the wicked*, thought Margery, as she went upstairs to fetch her glasses. She looked in the mirror on her small dressing table, noticed the rosy flush on her cheeks and patted her golden-brown curls into place. *About time I had another perm*, she thought. She descended the stairs again to pick up the phone and make an appointment with the Hair Today, Shorn Tomorrow salon in the marketplace. She left her front door on the latch for Cheryl.

Before she sat at her little desk, between the stairs and the front door, Margery read the lead storey in that day's Gleaner.

"Great Havell is set to benefit from a two-lane bypass. Long overdue, the bypass will relieve the suburban roads, either side of the marketplace, which are currently being used as rat runs, giving the council concerns for the safety of children. The bypass will be financed by developers of the new homes planned for the Monks Thorpe estate. This development, which is still on the drawing board, will include slip roads to the new homes, a multi-storey car park and shopping complex for the town."

"The Gleaner asked Mr Denzil Bream of Bream Estate Agents about the plans for new homes at Monks Thorpe."

"'This is the most exciting news for Great Havell,' Mr Bream told the Gleaner in an exclusive interview. 'It should have been planned years ago. There will be a whole estate of top-class executive homes. These will be available only from Bream.'"

Before Margery put the paper down, she noticed another story on the front page. She had almost missed it. "Fair cancelled. The council has decided, for financial reasons, there will be no Moyen Midden Fayre this year. The event will be replaced by a pop concert. It will be headlined by Birmingham band, Gary and the Fly by Night Boys. They are excited about coming to Great Havell to perform their first open air concert in the Glebe Park venue."

Margery moved to her desk, sat down and started typing. She was thinking of Barney, who now seemed to be the latest victim of a mysterious menace which was associated with the Glebe Mound. She had a view of the east side of the mound from her kitchen window and often saw people she knew, including Barney, walking on it. Its gentle slopes were well drained and grassy. A variety of

15

flowers, plants and grasses grew on the mound, which Sadie had identified for her and a local watercolour artist. In those days, when Sadie was sober, she worked for the Root and Branch Garden Centre on the west side of the mound. Margery had an original watercolour of wild-flowers by the artist, who had lived at number seven Priory Cottages at the time. Margery's parents bought the picture for her framed. It had pride of place over her mantelpiece.

She started writing her article. "Will we ever overcome the apparent threat the Glebe Mound poses to the good people of Great Havell?"

Even if, her main source of information, Barney, had been taken ill that morning on his daily walk on the mound, she could at least make a start.

"Since time immemorial, this hill has dominated the local landscape."

"It had been the site of a gallows and gibbet in the middle ages. For years local people spoke in hushed tones of the horrors of the hangings and burnings meted out on the monks and priests of the priory. They had refused to surrender to the King's men in the summer solstice of 1538. They paid for their defiance with their lives. After that, the Lords of the Manor held a Glebe Mound Fayre every summer to raise money to build and maintain alms houses and an infirmary for the poor and the sick. Within a few decades, the six witches of Havell-on-the-Marsh were hanged on the top of the mound. In the summer of 1577, their thin pathetic remains swung in the summer breezes. There was no fair that year. Eventually, angry locals cut the witches down at dead of night and buried them in a secret place. It was widely believed the witches were interred deep inside the mound. It was thought their malignant spirits had the power to curse the living. Every sudden death or misfortune was attributed to the evil of the witches. Their destructive power would never die. At the time of the Restoration local people started to…"

At this point, as Margaret's fingers typed the story on the three sheets of copy paper, Cheryl, in a dark suit, her glossy straight dark hair cut in a bob, which framed her pretty face, burst into the cottage and said breathlessly, 'Margery! You are never going to believe this!'

Margery looked up expectantly.

'Barney Cobbler was found unconscious on the old priory railings at the foot of the mound near here. He was last seen at the top and stumbling down towards the old priory. He was taken to the General Hospital in an ambulance but pronounced dead there. They were unable to revive him. The Wicca group are out in the marketplace. They are claiming, to anyone who will listen, it's the cancellation of the fair which has unleashed the curses and evil of the mound. They also claim Barney was doomed from the moment it was cancelled.'

Margery was silent, taking it all in.

'So, Barney is dead. Does that mean you are not going to need the article?' she asked after a pause. 'And do sit down, Cheryl. We can't print superstition and hearsay. His death will be discovered to be natural causes, and everyone can put that silly curse idea out of their heads. After all, he had the stress of running the local inland revenue offices. My goodness me, if we are having a major star turn, like Gary Hogan and the Fly by Night Boys, performing in the Glebe Park at the summer solstice, we can't have potential visitors to the event put off by some ridiculous stories with no foundation in them.'

Cheryl seemed a little deflated. 'I suppose not,' she said slowly. 'I think, since the concert has been booked in the Glebe Park, we need to go ahead with the article on the Glebe Mound, without consulting our top local historian.'

'I heard from Gill, the mayor has booked the solstice show,' said Margery.

'Yes, Gary Hogan is a cousin of his family,' said Cheryl. 'It will be a great occasion. It should put Great Havell on the map and increase visitor numbers. It will be the first open air concert for the band. And, of course, we have our own band Jollity for a warmup act. They're already planning their set. We will want to have as many features and as much advertising revenue as possible out of this. Carry on with your article, Margery. If you can have it written by tomorrow, you could follow it up with a more detailed article on the witches of Havell-on-the-Marsh.'

Cheryl stood up again. 'I'll have to pop back to production now to sign off the features. I'm just hoping I don't have any problems this time. Last week, they nearly all walked out because I inadvertently touched a page on stone. The print unions are so sensitive and volatile these days.'

'I'll pop into the office tomorrow with my copy,' said Margery, wondering who she could consult or where she could find enough information about the Glebe Mound for a full-page article, without asking a local expert such as Barney Cobbler.

'I must stick to facts and not superstition,' She said to herself, sitting at her typewriter. 'No more interruptions. I'll have it written by this afternoon.'

After writing and breaking for a quick lunch of a cheese and celery roll and a pot of tea, Margery continued working, checking back her files for previous articles on the Glebe Mound. She avoided any mention of the suspicious deaths which had occurred on, or around, the mound during the Commonwealth. She described the unusual flora and fauna, which was unlike anywhere else in the area. The cache of medieval pottery discovered by an antiquarian in the 18th century was relevant. It was, she reflected, all fact, but extraordinary fact. The huge pit, where the pottery was discovered near the top of the west side of the Glebe Mound had been given the name the Moyen Midden. This, in turn, was used for a local charitable group called the Moyen Circle, which kept up the traditions of the mound, especially the annual Moyen Midden Fayre in midsummer. She wrote:

"When antiquarian Walter Wilkes was surveying and measuring the Glebe Mound in in the summer solstice of 1772, assistants from the Guildhall Museum witnessed him disappearing before their eyes. He had fallen into a sinkhole, full of medieval pottery. Clambering out of the hole, with some of the pottery in his hands, unhurt, he laughingly said 'I never expected to find a Moyen Age midden up here on the mound.' It was a local sensation and people have celebrated the event since by renaming their traditional Glebe Mound Fayre, at the summer solstice, the Moyen Midden Fayre."

After breaking to warm up and eat the pasty she had bought from the Tastea Bite and cooking some peas and potatoes to go with it, Margery carried on working. She finally put her story together late in the evening. She kept one copy to file, separated the other two copies with paper clips and put them in her shopping trolley. Remembering her cat, Growltiger, was still shut in the bathroom, she went quickly to let him out, only to find he had climbed out of a small window, which was slightly open, and disappeared. She called out for him, first from the front door and then from the kitchen door, but no cat appeared. The cat food had not been touched and there was no sign at all of her ginger tomcat.

It was dark when Margery read through her article carefully and listened to music on the radio for the rest of the evening.

She was weary when she went to the bathroom, changed into her dressing gown, washed and cleaned her teeth and went slowly upstairs to bed. She tossed and turned that night, dreaming of the mound, imagining her cat had fallen into the sinkhole. She dreamed of shadowy figures and forms moving in the breeze on the gallows on the top. She had been working too late.

## Tuesday 4th February

Shopping trolley in tow, Margery almost trotted to the newspaper office to deliver her article on the Glebe Mound. She had overslept and she'd been unable to find Growltiger. 'Good riddance!' Alf had said when she asked if he had seen him. She had no time to stop and talk to Sadie, who was sitting in her usual position on a wall in the priory ruins. Sadie waved her roll-up cigarette in the air and tried to attract her attention. Sadie would have to wait. She was on a mission.

She entered the front office as a customer was coming out, having bought that day's paper. Margery read the headline and had a sinking feeling in her stomach. It took a while for her to fully understand the implications of it. She picked up a copy from the front desk.

"DEATH CURSE STRIKES AGAIN" proclaimed the headline. She read on.

"Popular historian struck down on the Glebe Mound" was the subheading. Margery picked up a copy from the front desk, hardly giving herself time for a friendly nod to Philippa and Gill. She read on:

"'One minute I saw the familiar figure of Barney Cobbler walking on the mound on the marketplace side,' Derek Robinson, publican of the Amicable Anarchist told the Gleaner, 'the next moment, he seemed to be staggering and then he was gone.

"'I thought it was odd but, because I was quite busy, I could have imagined him being there, he is such a familiar figure. I see him every morning.'"

According to the Gleaner, market traders and customers had seen the well-known local historian taking his usual walk on the mound, the previous morning, shortly before he was found slung over the railings of the old priory by a member of the ramblers' club and his daughter, who summoned an ambulance from the public phone box next to the pub.

Margery wondered she had not seen Barney herself when she had been on her way home. Surely, if he was found on the railings of the priory, she would have seen something when she walked through. It must have all happened when she was walking home or shopping at the Tastea Bite. Deciding, not to see Cheryl, who might reject her copy as irrelevant, but submitting it through the front office girls, together with her invoice, she decided to see if she could find out any more from Sadie in the old priory and set off home that way.

Sadie was not there. There was no sign of her in the priory ruins, yet she had seen her on her way to the Gleaner, because she had been a little later than usual. Margery made haste, along the lane at the back of the priory to her home in Priory

Cottages. She glanced up at the Glebe Mound as she went. There seemed to be some activity at the top, but, seeing the figures against the light, she assumed the archaeologists were back and thought no more of it. She was disappointed at not seeing Sadie in her usual place and began to wonder what she had wanted to tell her. Was it something to do with Barney, perhaps? The phone was ringing as she put her key in the front door. It rang off as she picked it up. She sighed, took off her hat and tartan cape and hung them on the pegs near the door. She put the kettle on and switched on her electric fire to take the edge from the chill before she sat down at her typewriter. As Cheryl had suggested, she would follow up her article on the Glebe Mound with a more detailed one on the witches of Havell-on-the-Marsh.

"After the six Havell-on-the-Marsh witches were hanged on the Glebe Mound," she typed, "local people insisted on holding the fair, which had been established after the executions of the monks of the priory, always at the summer solstice. The inhabitants of Great Havell believed music, dancing and happiness would exorcise the evil of the mound. It was widely believed, because the mound had been a place of such cruelty and torture to the monks of the priory in 1538 and also to the six women hanged there in 1577, these horrible events had unleashed an intrinsic evil. The people at Great Havell planned to do as much as they could to rid the place of its dark, portentous reputation.

"In the reign of Elizabeth 1, at the time of the witch trials, Alice Keen of Havell-on-the-Marsh was in her teens. Many folks thought she was simple. Others thought she had the gift of second sight. She lived with her grandmother, Elizabeth, in a tiny wattle and daub cottage on the edge of the marshes. She was often seen in the Great Havell market. She sold bunches of sea lavender and samphire. Alice and her grandmother grew herbs in their tiny garden and local people were in the habit of visiting their cottage on the marshes for their medicinal brews and remedies. They sold cures at the yearly summer fair. At the time of the witch trials it was alleged, Alice and her grandmother, caused the death of some infants and children in Havell-on-the-Marsh, by witchcraft.

"At the Great Havell assizes the two women…"

The phone on her desk rang again and this time Margery answered it quickly.

'There are now two deaths!' announced Cheryl.

Margery felt her stomach churn at the news. Great Havell, she always felt, was a safe place, for someone like herself, to live on her own.

'I'm following up my feature on the Glebe Mound and the Moyen Midden Fayre, with one on the witches of Havell-on-the-Marsh as you suggested. Do you want me to continue with it?'

'I should say so,' replied Cheryl. 'This time, an unconscious person was discovered in the midden sink hole. The police haven't released a name, nor any details, just that someone was pulled out from under the grid covering of the sink hole, rushed to hospital in an ambulance and pronounced dead shortly after arrival. Hopefully, we can run with the story that there has been another death in tomorrow's edition. Since the body was found on the Glebe Mound, it will whet reader's appetites for more information on the story of the place. Put as much hearsay and legend as you like into it, Margery, people will be hungry for information. There's no need for accuracy and Barney Cobbler can't take us to task over anything we print now.'

When she put the phone down, Margery thought Cheryl had been a bit callous in her last remark, but nevertheless felt free to put down her own opinions on the witch trials, the mysteries of the Moyen Midden and the Glebe Mound.

She stood up, moved a few paces to the kitchen to turn the kettle off which was whistling. She put tealeaves in the tea pot and opened the back door to step outside into the garden and look towards the Glebe Mound, which she could see over the end of her garden, her bike shed and a bridle path. It dominated the view.

She looked to see if anyone was walking on the mound and spotted a lone figure, too distant for Margery to recognise. It seemed to be stumbling, stooped and bent as if looking for something. She regarded it for a few minutes. The figure was vaguely familiar, and it appeared to be wearing a long loose coat, fedora hat and scarf which flapped in the breeze. Then she realised who it was and looked harder to confirm. It was Sadie's partner, Eric. His rich London family paid him so much to stay out of their way, he could afford to live in a large house, Heathlands, which, as far as Margery knew, was full of rubbish and stuff of all kinds. Eric and Sadie were known to live in squalor. If something went wrong in the house, they didn't bother to get repairs done. They used the public toilets and showers at one end of the guildhall in the marketplace. They bought battery lamps for lighting. *No wonder Sadie spent most of her time outside*, Margery thought. She wondered, again, why she had not seen her.

The article could wait. If need be, she would stay up all night to finish it. She knew her facts. They could be checked with the accounts which she and local historians had written about the witches. These were in her files.

She decided to go and meet Eric on the mound, and see if he knew where Sadie was, if she could get him to talk to her. Margery locked her front door, put her hat, cape and boots on, left the cottage by the back door, locked it, went out of her back gate, crossed the bridle path, which ran between the cottage gardens and the foot of the mound, and started to look for Eric.

She had walked nearly all the way along the well-beaten path on the mound before she spied him. Eric was looking keenly on the ground, his old worn double-breasted great coat and long moth-eaten scarf were flapping in the breeze. He had a hand on his fedora hat to stop it blowing away. Margery called out to him, but he seemed not to hear, so she went up to him and repeated her greeting.

'Hello, Eric!'

'What the fuck do *you* want?' he said in his classy London accent and turned round quickly.

'I don't often see you when I walk up here; I wondered how you are,' replied Margery.

'I can't see it's any business of a nosy cow like you,' grumbled Eric.

Ignoring the insult, Margery said, 'are you looking for something? Can I help you?'

'Sadie's lost my Honey Monster watch,' he replied with a note of sadness in his voice.

Hoping Eric hadn't heard her impromptu giggle, Margery said, 'I'll help you look for it.' She started to scour the mound also.

'I had to eat six packets of the stuff to get it,' Eric was chattier than usual.

'We'll find it!' said Margery brightly. 'Where did you last see it?'

'Sadie had it and lost it. The fucking silly cow. She's hiding too,' grumbled Eric.

'It's likely to be around the old priory then, isn't it? She's probably down there and you can ask her what she's done with it. Let's go down and have a look.'

She started to walk down the narrow path towards the old priory ruins, looking for the watch as she went. Eric followed her slowly.

As they approached the priory car park, they could see a police car, its blue lights flashing, in Priory Street. The car turned into the car park at speed.

'There it is!' cried Eric, pointing towards the car park, as the police car screeched to a halt. 'Fucking bastards have driven straight over it!' Open great coat and scarf flapping around him and battered fedora hat still held on his head with one hand, Eric ran over to retrieve the watch, which had been squashed by the car, as two uniformed police officers got smartly out.

Eric was bent down over the watch.

'You, fucking idiots…you've ruined my watch!' Margery heard him shout as she approached.

Either side of him, the police officers hauled Eric upright before he could retrieve his watch. 'Eric Bolton…you are under arrest!'

Margery watched stunned as Eric was cautioned, handcuffed and pushed into the back seat of the car, which swiftly reversed out of the car park, running over the watch again, its blue lights flashing. It turned into Priory Street and drove towards the marketplace and the police station beyond the guildhall.

Left alone, Margery walked over and bent down to pick up the shattered watch, prising it out of the tarmac. Not sure what to do with it, she put it in her bag and decided to take it home, although she walked on to the newspaper offices first.

'No shopping trolley today?' remarked Gill in the front office as Margery walked in.

'I've just seen someone arrested!' she announced.

Philippa put her phone down. 'Who, where, when? Do tell!'

'I'm not sure I should, I think there's and embargo on publicising suspects until the police release the names, but I could tell Cheryl in confidence I suppose.'

Margery walked through to the newspaper offices and found Cheryl about to go out to the print works to sign off the feature pages for the following day's edition of the Gleaner.

'I'll walk with you,' she said. She waited until they had walked a distance from the Gleaner offices to tell Cheryl what she had witnessed.

'So, it must be the Barney Cobbler death Eric has been arrested for. Is that thought to be murder now I wonder? Or is it the body found in in the midden sink hole?' asked Cheryl.

'Even though I witnessed Eric's arrest, we cannot publish a name unless the police inform us. It could be for either or both the deaths. Shall I continue writing the history of the story of the Havell-on-the-Marsh witches?'

'Do, but you could also keep your ear to the ground and see if you can find out who the person found unconscious in the midden sink hole was and whether there was foul play involved in that. We could then get the story written, subbed and set ready for when the police decide to release details. That way we could run with it before the Advertiser.'

They parted company at the turning to the print works. Margery decided to treat herself to lunch at the Cosy Cafe nearby, which was on Priory Street near the turning towards the Cricklewater Estuary and the Quay Marina.

As she passed the Brass Monkeys Brasserie, she glanced in and noticed it was already quite busy with people at the bar. She could see Morris and Mack, the two institute catering graduates, who had just opened the restaurant, behind the bar chatting to customers.

The Cosy Café was a little further on. It was a typical teashop with lace-trimmed tablecloths, lace drapes at the windows and an assortment of teapots on shelves round the room. She was pleased to see Jonah McKay in there. He was a local librarian, historian, member of the Moyen Circle and good friend of Barney Cobbler. Asking if she could join him, Margery settled in for a long chat.

Jonah looked a bit upset and she did not receive the beaming, cheery welcome she usually had from him. He was a small man, smartly dressed in a suit, shirt and tie. He was a bit Pickwickian, Margery always thought. He wore his fair, thinning hair in a comb over. He was also a real ale connoisseur, which had given him a bit of a paunch.

They both ordered toasted sandwiches and a pot of tea to share. Margery, sitting opposite Jonah, realised she could not tell him about Eric's arrest. She asked him instead what he knew of something which had intrigued her recently. She had heard, his friend, the late historian, had discovered some old documents, hidden in the plaster walls in his Tudor home.

'What exactly were the documents Barney found concealed in the plaster walls of his house?' she asked.

Jonah, an asthmatic, always had a cheerful, enthusiastic, breathy style of speech.

'Actually, we think they were written unofficially by a clerk to the Great Havell assize court in at the time of the witch trials. He was there to make an account of them. Barney and I were studying them carefully. We were reading through them.

'We had discovered enough about them to realise they were the clerk's personal notes on the assizes, the people who conducted the trials and the witches.'

'That's fascinating!' said Margery. 'I'd be very interested to take a look at them.'

'Well, actually, you can't!'

'Oh! Why is that? Are they too delicate? Do they need to be kept secret for any reason?'

'No, in fact, they've disappeared!'

'Disappeared!? How? Why?'

'Barney was keeping them in archive quality clear files and cardboard folders. We were going through them meticulously after work most days. He kept them in his house. I keep a key for when he goes away. As soon as I heard he had been found unconscious yesterday, I thought I should pop in and collect them and take them home or to the library for safekeeping. I rang Brendon Dant, vice chairman of the Moyen Circle first, to let him know what I was doing. When I went to Barney's house after work, I looked in the filing cabinet where he had been keeping them, but I couldn't see them in there. I went all over the house, in case he had put them somewhere else, but I couldn't locate them anywhere.'

'Perhaps you missed them,' said Margery 'If you like, I'll come over to Barney's house with you and help you look.'

'Well, actually, the police may still be there fingerprinting everything. Because of this, I've requested a coroner's inquest on Barney's death. When I did that, I reported the disappearance of the files. The police wanted to know Barney's movements that morning. He was someone who had a regular routine. He was due to pop in the library to consult a book about early publications on witchcraft.'

'I'm writing an article for the Gleaner on the Havell-on-the-Marsh witches at the moment. Could I come back to the library with you and look at the book perhaps? Do you think it would be useful?'

'Yes, please do. I'm not sure the book Barney was going to consult would help, actually, but we might find a copy of the chapbook on the trials or a facsimile of it somewhere. In fact, it might save a lot of time looking for the documents Barney found and possibly save transcribing them when they do turn up.'

Jonah dropped his voice, 'You know, Barney was very opposed to the concert in the Glebe Park. In fact, all of us in the Moyen Circle are. Some of them even think that is why he is dead now. When I met Brendon Dant in the marketplace on my way here, all he could talk about was the cancellation of the fair.'

'I can't believe Barney's death would have anything to do with that!' exclaimed Margery.

'There is so much bad feeling about this pop concert, actually,' Jonah replied, 'and Barney was so very vocal in opposition. He didn't want traditions broken. He was trying to use his influence to arrange an extraordinary meeting of the council to have the concert date changed, so the Moyen Midden Fayre could go ahead as usual.'

'It still could,' said Margery. 'The midsummer solstice falls over a weekend this year. We could have the fair during the day and the concert in the evening.'

'Actually, the council has not only cancelled the fair this year but it has also said the tradition may not continue. That's why all of us at the Moyen Circle are so annoyed about it. After all, it is the whole point of the charity.'

'But I don't understand why or how they could have cancelled it for good.'

'They are saying the town is stuck in its past and it's time we all moved on from all that historical superstitious claptrap, and looked to the future.'

'I thought people come from all over the country to visit Great Havell at the solstice. The Youth Hostel is always fully booked and the inns and hotels. The campsite is usually over-flowing, and visitors even book overnight moorings at the Quay Marina for it.'

'That is why Brendon and I made an appointment to speak to the mayor about it when we first heard they wanted to cancel the fair this year. As Barney was likely to get angry with the council officers, we thought we would reason with him in a civilised manor. The mayor said we have to move on, away from all the medieval and witch curse stuff. He said it holds the town back and the fair costs the council more than it makes in terms of extra staffing, clearing the Glebe Park and policing. Apparently, we need to be building a two-lane bypass, a multi-storey car park and housing estates, to expand with new enterprises and businesses. The mayor said those old traditions could deter investors and house buyers wishing to locate here.'

'I read about those plans only yesterday in the Gleaner. The Grimes family own a lot of land around here, so I suppose they would benefit from these developments. I should think they could still go ahead with all that and keep the fair. The market traders and the shops in Great Havell would miss out on a lot if it didn't go ahead. After all it has to be a decision of the full council to cancel it.'

'I think they have already cancelled it.'

'How did that happen, without the Gleaner picking up on it?'

'Mayor Grimes told Brendon and me, councillors and the council officers had looked at the figures. The fair is too costly. He said he had been shown estimates and he could show them to us too. They prove the fair makes a tremendous loss every year. He said it is heavily subsidised by the council. He said the domestic rates would have to go up considerably in Great Havell to afford it, and that is more than they dare do. He said it would be political suicide to put up the rates, knowing how people in Great Havell will take to the streets and protest at almost any excuse. The pop concert, on the other hand, is expected to make a huge profit and appeal to a younger audience. The whole council realise the bypass is a necessity and they have been persuaded Great Havell needs more housing of all kinds, particularly executive-style family homes. Actually, I have to say, on paper, Brendon and I agreed, it all looks good. Mayor Grimes said it was evident it would all be beneficial to Great Havell. The new home development will be beyond the Thorpe Park on the north side of the town, with a slip road to the bypass, a few suburban shops and a new primary school. Outline plans are already in the library. I had a look at them.'

'I can't imagine a year without the Moyen Midden Fayre,' said Margery sadly. She thought she would prefer to go back to her cottage and complete her article on the witches of Havell-on-the-Marsh, rather than go to the library with Jonah. She also remembered she had put tealeaves in her teapot ready for a brew.

'Actually, I have to get back to the library now,' said Jonah. 'I'll have a look in the reference library to see if I can find any information about the clerk at the Great Havell assizes or a copy of the chapbook on the witches. If you are not coming with me, would you like to meet me in the Amicable Anarchist for a quick pint or a swift half when they open?'

'Yes, I would. Good luck with your search, Jonah. I am so sorry about Barney. I can't believe I won't see him walking on the mound anymore. People will make a big thing about the curse and I guess market traders, who benefit from the fair and its legends, will try to insist it goes ahead this year.'

Jonah held up his hand to the waitress. *'L'addition, si'l vous plait,'* he said to the surprised girl, momentarily forgetting which country he was in. He made a writing motion on his hand. The waitress glanced at Margery who mouthed 'the bill' to her.

Jonah was well known to nip over to France on the ferry regularly. He belonged to a local group called the Francophiles. He was eccentric enough to, occasionally, forget which country he was in.

As Margery walked home, she was thinking about her article on the Havell-on-the-Marsh witches. Their execution was the reason for holding a fair at the summer solstice, the time when the hangings took place. The fair always attracted visitors and stalls from all over the region and beyond. After the extraordinary find of the medieval pottery and other artefacts in the sinkhole on Glebe Mound in the 18th century, which was also around about the time of the solstice, that part of the mound had been called the Moyen Midden. The fair was still popular and also had a partly medieval theme, which was revitalised by the local arts and crafts movement in the 19th century. As Margery walked, she was thinking she wanted to go back to the stories of the witches, the trials and the executions. She needed to write about all the events, in fact, which had made the yearly fair such an important part of the local scene. She thought it had become bigger and more popular every year, attracting Pagans, Wiccas, Druids and all sorts of religious denominations, who all had some idea they could rid the Glebe Mound of its legendary evil and the pervasive haunting power of the witches.

Margery had written many features for the Gleaner, which carried subtle hints of the necessity of cleansing the spirit. The Little Havell spring water bottling plant was a regular advertiser in those features and also the Country Hotel, where Vlad worked. The hotel now had a gym, tennis courts, golf course and a spa. An attempt had been made to turn Little Havell into a spa in the 18th century and great Palladian towers from that time were still standing in the grounds of the Country Hotel. They were part of a complex which was never finished. These now served afternoon teas outside in the summer. If Great Havell had a bypass, it might have to cut through the grounds of the Country Hotel in Little Havell, Margery reflected. There could be trouble and objections from the village, she thought, as she opened the gate to her cottage, and realised she had not seen Sadie since the morning.

'No shopping trolley today, Miss Moore?' Alf remarked.

*He's trying to be pleasant, after shutting my cat in his coalbunker*, thought Margery.

'As you see,' she said, opening the door to her cottage and going inside. Growltiger shot through the door and followed her into the kitchen, where she put fresh food out for him. She put the kettle on and finished making the pot of tea she had started earlier. She had need of some. She continued with her work.

"Anne Baste and Cecily Robbins were widowed sisters in their 60s," she wrote, sitting at her typewriter after putting fresh copy paper sheets in it. "They had both married former priests from the Great Havell priory, where they had worked in the kitchens and refectory. They were reputed to be clever and were respected as they could read and write. The sisters were also good cooks and had written down and shared many recipes, herbal remedies and cures. It began to be rumoured they had used their knowledge of plants to poison their husbands, who died suddenly and within weeks of each other. Unable to bear the gossip, the antagonism and the accusations against them in Great Havell, the sisters moved to Havell-on-the-Marsh. They had similar skills in herbal medicine to Elizabeth Keen and her granddaughter Alice and became friendly with them.

"The two other women accused of witchcraft at the Great Havell assizes were unrelated. Janet Wilson was thought to be in her twenties. She lived alone in a former hermit's hut. It was rumoured she was a love child born to a local gentle-woman. She had been raised by a wet nurse. Janet had a squint. It was difficult, people said, to know who she was directing her gaze at. She also had a pro-nounced speech impediment. She emphasised the beginnings of words nasally. People often misunderstood her and thought she was insulting them or blasphem-ing, especially if they didn't know who she was looking at when she spoke. She and the woman who brought her up had a small market stall in Great Havell where they sold herbs and remedies. After her adoptive mother died, Janet started begging and was seen as a nuisance in Great Havell, so the authorities turned her out of the alms-house she had lived in with her mother. She found refuge in the hermit's hut at Havell-on-the-Marsh, near Alice, Elizabeth, Anne and Cecily. They all ensured Janet had enough to eat.

"Mad Molly also found refuge at Havell-on-the-Marsh. She had turned up there two years before the witch trials, wearing what had been very fine clothes and shoes. These were worn, ragged and filthy. The other women living there had no idea where Mad Molly had come from. She could not tell them, they thought she might have survived a shipwreck. The sisters, Anne and Cecily man-aged to persuade her to let them clean her clothes and wash her matted thick hair. They took her in. She made noises, rather than formed words and some thought she might not even be English. No one knew how old she was. Although there was no room for her to live in the hermit's hut with Janet, the two young women were friends. They were nearly always together and needed the comfort of hold-ing hands, wherever they went.

"The six women were not the only people living at Havell-on-the-Marsh at that time. There was a community of families who lived nearer the shore and had fishing boats. They also caught eels in the creeks and gathered shellfish for the market. The children of the marsh, if they survived infancy, were feral, sharp-eyed and sharp tongued. They were always on the lookout for anything and everything they could sell. They upset the little community of women by snatching up the herbs they grew and picking most of the samphire and sea lavender nearby, so the women had little or none to sell.

"People from Great Havell often walked the distance to Havell-on-the-Marsh to consult Anne, Cecily, Elizabeth and Alice on recipes and cures for ailments. The women were able to make a very modest living from this. Janet and Mad Molly looked out for each other helping the other women where they could, but visitors to the marsh were wary of them. Although the six women lived a few miles away from the town, they were often visited or seen in the market, by many of the local people, especially if they wanted to use Anne and Cecily's skills in reading and writing."

"In 1577, there was an epidemic of marsh fever and exceptionally high infant mortality among the marshland families. A swarm of bees had been seen around the cottages and hermit cell where the six women lived. Two of the marsh children got stung in the face when they were picking herbs from Anne and Cecily's cottage garden, where Mad Molly was taking refuge. Refusing any help from the women, the children, a sister and brother, ran back to their families and complained Anne and Cecily had bewitched the bees and forced them to sting. They said Mad Molly had put spells on them. This started a campaign from all the children on the marsh, who started calling all the women 'witches' when they came anywhere near them and followed them into Great Havell and along the shores of the Cricklewater calling out, 'Witch! Witch!'

"That spring, in the neap tides, two of the children from the marsh were found drowned in shallow water near where the little community of six women lived. The women were accused of cursing them. The families of Havell-on-the-Marsh spread rumours of witchcraft in Great Havell market and the women were no longer visited for recipes, herbal cures or remedies. The sisters were no longer consulted for their reading and writing skills. They all struggled to live on what they could glean from the marshes, the river and the estuary. The younger women, Alice, Janet and Mad Molly foraged for food, but it was clear to the others, this would not be enough to sustain them all especially after having barely enough to eat the previous winter. They now had no choice but to ask for alms from the parish. The younger women set out for Great Havell walking all the way to the marketplace. When they got there, Alice found many people, who she had known as friends and acquaintances in the past, shunned her and turned away from her. The odd speech and strange looks from Janet and the incomprehensible mumblings of Mad Molly were interpreted by the people of Great Havell as curses. The three women were hounded back to Havell-on-the-Marsh by groups of children, calling 'Out! Out! Witches! Never come back!' In absolute desperation, all six women returned to the town to ask for assistance. When they reached the guildhall, they were met by the town watch and constables who were under orders to arrest them."

Margery left the story there, put on her boots, hat and cape and went to meet Jonah at the Amicable Anarchist. It was dark, so she took her bike from the shed. She put the lights on and left from the back gate after locking the back door. She cycled along the bridle path which ran between Priory Cottage gardens and the Glebe Mound. It had been a green lane in Saxon times and was wide enough for a vehicle. Margery turned along a path at the end of Priory Cottages, turned left again and cycled along the lane which ran past her front garden. She was following a rut which had been made by a vehicle recently. It stopped abruptly outside the priory railings, where the lane came to a dead end and she stopped.

Taking the lamp from the front of her bike, she shone the light down on the rut, surprised she had not noticed it before. It was wide. Margery thought it was probably made by some kind of pickup truck or lorry. She decided it might have been made by the local authority, emptying the waste bins near the priory, although they usually accessed those through the car park.

Back on her bike, Margery made the rest of the journey to the Amicable Anarchist in a few minutes, secured her bike under an awning in the inn yard, picked up her bag from the basket and entered the saloon bar.

She found Jonah enjoying his pint in his favourite place, the snug, where he could read if he was on his own. 'What can I get you?' He stood up as she came in.

'I'll have a half of whatever you are drinking,' said Margery, knowing his taste for real ale to be good. Jonah went to the bar.

'I'll have a half of Falcon Old Priory for Miss Moore, please Derek.'

'Right away, Jonah, it's good to see Miss Moore in here again. She'll like this, it's a mild and not too strong.'

'That's what I thought. I decided try it first, otherwise, she'd have had her usual shandy. I'll have another pint too, while you are on that pump. It's not as pokey as the Cricklewater, but I rather enjoyed it for a change.'

Jonah went back to the little table in the snug, a beer in each hand, with a beaming grin on his face and sat down happily regarding his new pint and the remains of his first one, which he downed in one.

He held the new pint up to the lamp on the shelf above the table.

'Look at the colour of that, Margery, like polished rosewood…cheers!' Jonah clinked his glass with Margery's, closed his eye and tasted his new pint, putting it down on the table with a satisfied 'aaaah… that's really good actually'.

*They must be missing Barney in the Amicable Anarchist*, Margery thought. She mentioned it to Jonah.

'Eh? No! Not here!' said Jonah emphatically. 'In fact, not at all!'

'But didn't Barney always come in here after the Moyen Circle meetings in the guildhall?' asked Margery, puzzled.

Before Jonah had a chance to answer, a noisy group came in and Margery saw they were sales representatives she knew from the newspaper. They didn't see her in the snug. They all gathered around the bar and started arguing about who would buy the first round with their sales bonus. Each decided their individual bonus was not quite as high as they had originally boasted. One of them, who Margery recognised as Anthony Taplow, said he had already spent his on a new in-car tape deck and stereo. Then Margery saw Harry Grimes and a motor dealer following them in. The argument was settled by Grimes, who seemed to have a wad of cash in his wallet for the purpose. Margery hoped they would not see her in the snug and slunk further in the corner, pulling the little table over carefully, so as not to spill the drinks. Jonah, seemingly unaware of the noise at the bar, leaned forward confidentially.

'In fact, Barney made himself very unpopular in here only a few days ago,' he said quietly.

'I know he could be a stickler for facts,' said Margery, 'but I can't imagine him quarrelling with anyone; you surprise me, Jonah.'

'He did. It nearly became violent. He had a go at a member of the council over that pop concert. It was last Friday when the cancellation of the fair was first known about. He got very angry. He said would ensure the Moyen Midden Fayre would go ahead anyway. He claimed he had documents, only recently discovered, which would ensure the enduring rights of the people to hold the fair at

32

the solstice for perpetuity. He was really angry, shouting, in fact. I tried to calm him down and get him to go home.' Jonah took a long drink from his pint.

'In the end, Derek had to throw him out and tell him not to come in here again.'

'I'm shocked! I know Barney used to get angry over things, but not that angry. You really have surprised me, Jonah.'

'In fact, we had just been enjoying a quiet drink together. Barney had chaired the Moyen Circle meeting and we came in here afterwards. Actually, we were talking about the papers he had found stuffed in the plaster of his walls when a former mayor and member of the planning committee walked in. Barney left his pint on the table here, hardly touched, walked up to the bar and started sounding off about Mayor Grimes. He said the Grimes family would have the shock of their lives when documents recently discovered were made public. They would be compelled to think again about cancelling the fair, all their plans for Great Havell and the bypass.'

'How did the councillor react?'

'The planning officer put his hand on Barney's shoulder and said, "Look here, old boy." It was like a red rag to a bull… "Don't you dare touch me!" shouted Barney, shaking off the hand and making fists in his anger. But the councillor said there was nothing to be done about the arrangements for the summer; it was all booked. The Moyen Midden Fayre had been cancelled for good. It had all been organised and had been for months.' Jonah paused to take another long drink.

'Barney was furious and asked if it had been decided months ago, why the Moyen Circle had not been consulted? He asked how the council intended to compensate the local charitable institutions which were endowed from proceeds of the fair? Actually, I heard Barney order the councillor to convene an extraordinary council meeting about it. He said it was essential to ensure no one lost out. It was when the councillor said: "Look…old boy, it's all done, finished, done and dusted, nothing will change it now," I thought Barney was going to hit him.' Jonah was unconsciously showing Margery how his friend drew his fist back, ready to strike. 'He nearly did.'

'By this time, Derek had come round from behind the bar and caught Barney's fist before just before any injury was done. He escorted him to the door, pushed him in the small of the back and said, "Out! Now! … And don't come back!"'

'And you say this was only last Friday? You say the documents Barney was talking about have gone missing now?'

'Yes, the ones I've seen in the folders have. They are the only ones I know of. We had started transcribing them together. They were all about the witch trials and were written by the clerk of the court, probably for his own information. We think he intended to get them published in chapbook form for the popular market in London.'

'And were they?'

'Yes, and I have a facsimile copy here for you to take home and read. Barney and I had only just started comparing the hand-written notes with it.'

'Thanks,' said Margery and thanks for the drink. 'I'd better go home and finish my article. This will be really useful and complete it nicely.'

'Before you go,' said Jonah, very quietly, 'Barney and I noticed there were personal notes in the documents, which do not appear in the chapbook. We realised, from what we read, the clerk had noticed the trials did not go as he expected. All the evidence against the women was hearsay and gossip. Most of it was the testimony of children. It was all accepted as fact by the magistrates. It seems holding the Glebe Mound Fayre every midsummer in their memory was a sop to local people who may have been very shocked by the way the trials ended.'

'Interesting,' said Margery, 'I hope those documents turn up again, could I see the parts you have already transcribed?'

'I have them locked away in the reference section of the library. Please don't let anyone else know they exist,' said Jonah in a low, almost conspiratorial, voice.

'One thing puzzles me,' said Margery. 'If the council had decided the Moyen Midden Fayre was to be cancelled some time ago why has the Gleaner only just picked up on the story?'

'It was being officially denied, or at least councillors said nothing. If asked directly, they said they knew nothing about it. It was being kept quiet so the announcement of the pop concert, once it was certain it would take place, would eclipse the news of the cancellation.'

Intrigued, Margery left the snug and walked through the saloon, unable to avoid a 'hi honey' and a pat on the bottom as she walked past Harry Grimes, seated with the sales representatives, one of whom, Anthony Taplow, was in the midst of telling a particularly filthy joke, which was accompanied by a lot of swearing. She heard a chorus of sniggering and laughter and was pleased to get out into the fresh air and cycle home. Many people had been smoking in the pub and created bit of a fog in there.

She locked her bike in the shed, let herself in her back door with the key and locked it behind her. She put on the kitchen light and made herself a quick cheese omelette.

Afterwards, ensconced in her button-back armchair, she settled down to read the witch trial facsimile.

On the front cover was a crude woodcut print of the familiar figures of the six witches of Havell-on-the-Marsh hanged at the top of the Glebe Mound.

"The Six Evil Witches of Havell-on-the-Marsh" was the title on front of the chapbook and under the picture "A true account of how these six ungodly women did the work of Satan to kill innocent babes and children."

Inside was a picture of Elizabeth Keen and her granddaughter, Alice. Elizabeth was depicted with warts and a hooknose, Alice with wide staring eyes and a bat on her shoulder. Margery read the chapbook, moved over to her desk and typewriter and started to type. The chapbook gave her all the information she needed about the accusations and the trials. She finished her article.

"Elizabeth Keen and her granddaughter Alice had known a lot about herbs and remedies according to their trial but were said to encourage evil creatures such as bats and toads to do their bidding. It was alleged that one day they incited a swarm of bees to attack two children of the marsh, which resulted in the most horrible disfigurement of their faces. Had the marsh people not known how to treat bee stings, they would surely have died. It was said the two women had such a hold over the creatures of the marsh they could set tiny flies to attack small babies and cause their death. Many people from the marshes and some from Great Havell gave testimonies to the truth of these accusations at the midsummer trial. The two women were sentenced to be hanged and, according to the account, cried most piteously, claimed to be innocent and begged for their lives.

"Janet and Mad Molly were tried together. They held each other's hands. This part of the trial was short because neither could take an oath on the bible. A rosary was showing under Mad Molly's ragged fine clothes with which she seemed to be silently praying. She passed the beads through the fingers of her left hand whilst she still clung on to Janet's hand with her right. They were both accused of poisoning and putting spells on children and making them sick. Witnesses came forward to say they had heard them shouting curses at children with evil words which could not be understood, and they had caused to them to become so ill they died. As neither of them were able to say anything in their defence and no one came forward to speak for them or protect them, they were sentenced to be hanged."

Margery wondered if either of them had actually understood what they were supposed to have done or what would happen to them. It was even possible, she thought, they did not care.

"The two sisters were also tried together. Anne and Cecily took the oath with no problem, but the accusations against them were the worst of all. According to the families on the marsh they had taken two of their children into their cottage, so they were missed by their kin for days. They had tortured them, fed them a poisonous concoction which had killed them both and their bodies had been found face down in the marshes after a neap tide a few days later. There was no doubt, said the accusers, these women had poisoned the children and their brothers and sisters were prepared to swear it had happened. They had only escaped because they had run home over the marshes in fear of their lives. Not content with poisoning their husbands a few years earlier, these women had turned their dark arts on these innocent babes.

"All six women had nooses put over their heads after being found guilty of causing death by witchcraft and were immediately walked up the Glebe Mound and hanged on the waiting gallows on the midsummer solstice, to the jeers and calls of an angry crowd. A priest at the gibbet told them to renounce Satan and call on God for mercy on their souls. They were dispatched immediately."

*All the local people had turned against them and they had no chance*, thought Margery, *whether they were innocent or guilty*. She remembered Barney had told her of the immediate aftermath. She wrote: "The Justices of the Peace had ordered the women's cottages and the hermitage to be burned to the ground and the small holdings to be dug over. The Lords of the Manor put sheep on the marshes after that and managed a large part of the area for wild fowl. The marsh families worked for them. It gave them extra employment. The thin bodies of the six witches were left on the gallows, until local people were sick of the sight of them. The witches and the gallows were taken down at dead of night and buried in a secret unmarked grave, somewhere, it is believed, on, or under the Glebe Mound."

Margery paused. The Justices of the Peace and the Lords of the Manor, at that time, were all related by marriage. The manor house in its present form was owned by their descendants, the Grimes family. Mayor Walter Grimes and Harry Grimes were brothers; one the mayor, the other a director at the newspaper. Perhaps she would be diplomatic and leave that bit out.

"That should have been the end of the matter," she typed, "but it wasn't. No more accusations of witchcraft were ever made in the Havell Hundreds, but swarms of bees and other insects on the marshes continued. The marsh children also suffered with ticks from the sheep. Other children were found dead after neap tides and infant mortality on the marshes remained high. It began to be rumoured, in Great Havell and beyond, the women had been innocent, and their only crime was to be poor and friendless. It was agreed to hold the fair once a year in their memory, by the Glebe Mound, at the midsummer solstice. It would lift the spirits of the local people and erase the memory of something which was beginning to be perceived as a terrible injustice. It was also intended to raise money for the poor and to build and maintain more alms-houses. Refuges for the sick and needy were in demand since the priory had been closed decades earlier. It was even suggested, if the priory had not closed, it would have provided sanctuary and salvation for the women.

"So, it continued for about two hundred years," wrote Margery, "until the antiquarian Walter Wilkes fell through a sink hole on the Glebe Mound in 1772 and discovered a huge cache of medieval pottery, some filled with a few base coins, others with beads, but there was no indication of what it was or how it had got there. There was a potter's mark from a 13th century Great Havell pottery, which had been east of the market square next to the bell foundry in those days. There was nothing valuable found there. The antiquarian had decided it was a rubbish dump, for unwanted stuff and called it the Moyen Midden. The name has endured. Today, the sinkhole has a protective grill over it. Since the discovery the annual fair was renamed the Moyen Midden Fayre.

"From that time, unexplained deaths have occurred on or near the Glebe Mound. Together with claims of shadowy figures walking in the dusk and twilight, the legends of a curse began."

*Barney,* thought Margery, *had been very much against these legends and always insisted on sticking to facts. He was well known to become very angry about it.*

"The Moyen Midden Fayre thrived on the legends. There were folk songs and broadsheets published; about the monks of the priory and the witches who died on the Glebe Mound. The sudden appearance of the sinkhole, the many spirits seen, and the unexplained deaths ensured a steady stream of visitors to Great Havell, especially at the time of the Moyen Midden Fayre. The Moyen Circle was set up to organise the fair after the World War ll. it was deemed important to celebrate such English traditions at a time when the nation was recovering from the ravages of war."

It was forty-one years ago, now, reflected Margery, but included it her story.

Finally finished, Margery made herself a cup of cocoa and sat in her button back armchair. Her cat, Growltiger, jumped up on her lap. She'd had to keep pushing him off whilst she'd been working and he'd even jumped on her typewriter keyboard, so she had to untangle the mixed-up keys. Now he was keeping her warm, curled up on her lap and they both fell asleep.

She woke up with a start, drank the now lukewarm cocoa, picked up her cat, put him on his beanbag next to the boiler in the kitchen and went to the bathroom to clean her teeth. She also took a quick shower to remove the smell of stale smoke from the pub, which seemed to have lingered on her skin, and went to bed.

## Wednesday 5th February

When she awoke in the morning, Margery's first thought was, why were the gallows already set up on the Glebe Mound before the witch trials began? *Other people may wonder why the gallows had been erected before the witch trials when they read my article in the Gleaner*; she thought and wondered why it had not been picked up by historians or researchers before. She got up and had a breakfast of tea, toast and marmalade, glancing up, out of her kitchen window, at the Glebe Mound, which looked mysterious in the early morning light and watery sunrise. She kept a copy of her article for herself and put the other two copies in the shopping trolley to take to the newspaper. She fed Growltiger and put him out.

With her boots, cape and hat on, she pulled her shopping trolley out of her front garden gate and along the lane which ended at the priory railings. She walked through the old priory ruins, noting there was no sign of Sadie, crossed the road opposite the Amicable Anarchist and walked along Priory Street to the Gleaner Offices. She was quite unprepared for the greeting she would receive there.

# Chapter II

## The Mystery Deepens

'Cheryl wants to see you in her office NOW!' said Gill abruptly as soon as Margery was inside the door of the newspaper offices.

Margery made her way through the double doors towards Cheryl's office, wondering what she had done wrong.

Cheryl was on the phone and waved Margery in when she tapped on the glass door. She shut the door, cutting out most of the noise of the tele-ads and display advertising sales-people on the phones. Cheryl waved Margery impatiently to a seat. She had the feeling she had done something very wrong and waited.

'Lovely talking to you,' said Cheryl on her trim phone and slammed it down.

'Right Margery,' she said brusquely, 'I want you to write a feature on the Tanerife Tanning Salon, the Foo Kin Chinese Restaurant, Moonlight Motors and Girlie Curls.' Have you got that?' she snapped as Margery pulled her notebook and pencil out of her bag in her shopping trolley and wrote down the names hurriedly. 'I want you to start right away. You can ring from here to make appointments. Here are the numbers; I got the features' assistant to look them up for you.'

Margery rummaged in her trolley and took out her story about the witches, handing it to Cheryl with her bill. She had the feeling Cheryl was about to dump it all in her wastepaper basket, but she glanced at Margery first and put it in a drawer. 'How many copies are here?' she asked.

'It's all there,' said Margery, thinking of what Jonah had said in the pub the previous night and deciding to keep her own copy of the story. Cheryl locked her drawer without checking it and said quickly, 'Orders from above. We need revenues. Our figures are down. We must sell more advertising. I want these features in by the end of the week. When you see these clients find out if they have any other contacts, we could tap for ads. Two hundred and fifty words per story

39

please; forget the bill for any of that historical stuff you have written.' Cheryl gave the bill back to Margery.

'Orders from above,' she repeated curtly. 'No one is interested in those ancient traditions anymore. Oh, and by the way, we've heard there is to be an inquest on Barney Cobbler's death. The police are asking us to keep that development quiet for the moment. I understand it's because there have been two unexpected deaths within a couple of days. They don't want people to start worrying. There is a Scotland Yard detective on his way to help them with an investigation. Don't mention that to anyone though. We'll have to rely on press releases from the local police for information. Let me know immediately if you hear anything more. It is Mayor Walter Grimes who has asked for outside help to investigate the deaths because some of the Great Havell police officers belong to the Moyen Circle. They knew Barney personally. In view of the fuss about cancelling the fair, he thinks they might not have an unbiased view.'

Margery took all this information in surprise. So, in spite of the sales bonuses she'd heard about in the Amicable Anarchist, the revenues were down. It was a bit odd, but she hoped they knew what they were doing at the Gleaner.

She still had her bill in her hand and said: 'You might at least take this. I've done all the work you asked for. You were keen for me to do it and continue writing it when I queried if you still wanted it.'

'Oh, let me have that!' said Cheryl impatiently, snatching it out of Margery's hand. 'You've four features to write. I'll have to tag the payment for the historical stuff on to those, I suppose. Accounts will be none the wiser.'

Margery made her appointments and left the Gleaner offices with a heavy heart. Her friend, the normally cheerful Cheryl, had been irritable and snappy and all that hard work of the past two days would be spiked, shredded or go in the waste bin. But at least she had a copy of it all at home. She picked up a Gleaner in the front office desk and glanced at the headline: "SAILOR DROWNED IN MARINA".

Another death! That was three in as many days, Margery thought as she said, 'See you later, Gill and Philippa,' and left the Gleaner offices. She walked up Priory Street towards the marketplace for her appointment with Hair Today, Shorn Tomorrow. The salon was in the row of shops which backed on to the terraces of Edwardian houses and the Amicable Anarchist.

'My boys are the limit,' said Tina as she took strands of Margery's hair and wound them into rollers.

'Oh, yes?' said Margery, trying to sound interested.

'They pick up anything and everything from the street or the skips and make things out of them and draw and paint on them.'

'Isn't that rather creative?' asked Margery.

'Don't know so much of that! They make an awful mess in the house. We all have a go at them, but they don't take any notice of us. Some of the stuff they bring in smells as if it has been in kept in a toilet.'

'I expect you throw it all out then.'

'I would if I could get hold of it, but they've got furtive and I don't know where they put the stuff half the time.'

Tina put Margery under one of the huge conical dryers to set her perm. Margery looked at the front page of the Gleaner again and read:

"Expert sailor and member of the Cricklewater Sailing Club, Fenton Bradley, was rescued from the Quay Marina yesterday, after a sudden movement from the boom knocked him from his yacht into the water. He was returning to the marina from the estuary. Bystanders saw Mr Bradley in the water, buoyed up by his life jacket, but face down on the water. The sailor did not respond when a life belt was thrown to him. A sailing club member, who does not wish to be named, saw it happen, from his moored yacht. He put on his life jacket, jumped in and managed to haul Mr Bradley out of the water. Staff from the nearby Old Granary Hotel tried to resuscitate Mr Bradley. In spite of all efforts to save him the ambulance team, who attended the scene, were also unable to revive him."

Margery put down the Gleaner and picked up a Havell Hundred Life magazine. She looked at the glossy adverts in full colour. An advert for Girlie Curls featured power-dressed women, with big, crimped, hair, wearing bright tailored jackets with shoulder pads. An advertisement for Tanerife showed a scantily dressed, tanned, slender girl, side on, winking at the camera. Moonlight Motors had an equally scantily clad girl, spread out (very suggestively, Margery thought) over the bonnet of a Porsche. Underneath she read: "wide tyres, wire wheels and sports stripes make any car owner pull in the business."

*Well*, thought Margery, *I've made a head start on some of my next assignments.* The local laundry also had an ad… "We will not allow you to wallow in the shame of stains."

Margery smiled to herself as she read; she wished Vladimir would take his vests in there to be cleaned. She supposed he used a washing machine in his digs or a laundrette occasionally, but it was almost as if he didn't notice how grubby his vest was. She might even arrange to meet him and take him there. He wasn't the sort of person she could meet for lunch in the Cosy Café she thought. They wouldn't welcome him in there with his stained vest and army jacket, even if he was with her. Members of the Moyen Circle always wore jackets or blazers, shirts and ties over their neatly pressed trousers and would only wear corduroys, jeans, sweatshirts and casual jackets when gardening or rambling with the Havell Hundred Ramblers. Margery was a bit surprised to see an article about the Moyen Midden Fayre in the Havell Life magazine. It said little of interest about the fair, except it was an annual event and invariably held in the Glebe Park by the Glebe Mound on the weekend nearest to midsummer.

There was no reason, Margery thought, for the fair to be cancelled completely. It could either be held in conjunction with the pop concert or, on the previous, or following weekend. She really couldn't see why Barney had got so upset about it, to the extent, according to Jonah, that he was prepared to hit one of the councillors. She knew Barney could be a stickler for fact, but that sort of behaviour was unusual for him. She had one or two awkward meetings and phone calls with him in the past, because of features she'd written which he had decided were inaccurate, but he'd always been helpful in giving her the facts. He had even made her a cup of tea in his Tudor timber-framed house near the marketplace, whilst he sorted through his books and papers to find the exact details for her. He had been friendlier face to face than on the phone. He had rung her up on many occasions to complain.

Barney was not a popular person in Great Havell, Margery reflected, mainly because he was a local official for the Inland Revenue and used to run the office meticulously. He would chase up tiny amounts owing, with demanding letters, which annoyed people no end. Recipients of these letters carried on about the waste of government stationery and resources for such small amounts. So, the 20 pence owing would be paid grudgingly, and the costs of collecting it would be grumbled about for months, with Barney being named over and over again as the instigator. It was amazing how many people in Great Havell talked about either their own or a friend's experience of having to pay these tiny sums of tax owing. It was talked about so much, there seemed to be an epidemic.

Working as a freelance, Margery had always found Barney's advice on tax helpful. He would even advise her what she could and could not claim as expenses. She knew, however, anyone he had taken meticulous trouble with, to correct their personal tax owing, nursed a considerable amount of resentment towards him. The Gleaner had carried stories about the unusually large number of prosecutions for tax evasion in the Havell Hundreds. Although it wasn't mentioned, she guessed they were instigated by Barney. Sometimes she could detect who the culprit was, even though they were never named, because there would be a sale of antiques or property to pay the bill.

*There must be quite a long list of local people who resented Barney Cobbler,* thought Margery, as she sat under the huge beige conical dryer to have her permed hair set. Barney had probably made a few enemies.

*It probably wasn't just Barney's assiduity in chasing every penny owing to the Inland Revenue which would create resentment,* she thought, as she felt her hair tighten into curls around the rollers. He was often seen arguing with people in the marketplace.

One of the things Barney had a go at her about was an inaccuracy in one of her articles for the Gleaner about the sale of a local rectory. This was a fine brick 17th century mansion. Bream Estate Agents had asked her not to mention it was the former rectory in her article. She had omitted that from the historical details. Barney had been furious. He'd been angry and sarcastic on the phone, telling her the whole point of a rectory was its position near the church and the Glebe Mound was still part of a local rectory land holdings. He had reminded her the Moyen Midden Fayre was held beside the Glebe Mound, partly to raise money for the upkeep of the church chancel in accordance with a Tudor statute. He had made Margery feel a fool and hinted she was in Bream, the estate agent's pay. He even said they must have given her a backhander, so she would omit such a vital part from the history of the building. She remembered he'd almost had her in tears over it, making her feel humbled and foolish.

Cheryl, as features' manager, had dealt with Barney as best she could, telling him the property had been sold and Margery had written the article, from the information she had been given, in good faith. She had visited the house too and described it accurately in detail. But Barney had never let it go. He wouldn't let her forget it. For some months afterwards, he lectured her on the minutiae of ecclesiastical property rights and responsibilities every time he saw her, which was usually in the marketplace, where it was difficult for her to avoid him or get away. She also felt that Gleaner readers seeing, and even hearing Barney having a go at her, was bad for her reputation as a professional writer. She was invariably relieved when Jonah or Brendon Dant, were in the marketplace and took pity on her. They would make a point of talking to Barney so she could get away.

Margery did not argue with someone like Barney. When he criticised her articles for the Gleaner, as he had done on numerous occasions, the one about the rectory being the worst, she took it all to heart. She was inclined to lose confidence, rather than nurse any resentment against her critic. The commissions kept on coming, though, and as much as she was not relishing writing a number of short advertising features, she would do her best with them.

'All done now!' said Tina, coming over and releasing her from the huge dryer.

Margery's reverie was over, and it was time to chat with Tina again.

'What sort of things do your boys find in skips and rubbish bins?' she asked.

'I don't get to see much of it, these days,' replied Tina, 'but I think they are rigging up a game for this year's Moyen Midden Fayre with something.'

'I heard it's been cancelled this year,' said Margery.

'No! You must be joking! They'd never cancel that!'

'They have,' said Margery, 'you must have heard we have a pop concert instead, with Gary Hogan and the Fly by Night Boys.'

'Wow! Yes! I did hear something, but I didn't think it would prevent the fair from going ahead. The boys will be heartbroken if there's no fair to look forward to.'

'I'm sure something will be arranged,' said Margery comfortingly.

'I hope so. It's not just my boys, who look forward to the fair and we usually have music there anyway, don't we?'

Margery looked in the mirror, all the rollers were out now, and her head was covered in tight little golden-brown curls. Not for the first time, she wondered why she bothered with a perm, particularly as she usually wore a hat or a beret, but she had adopted that style and stuck to it.

Tina arranged each curl carefully in place with a small brush and Margery's hair began to look more stylish. Tina went to get some spray to keep it in place and Margery took the opportunity to freshen up her lipstick and make up.

'Thanks Tina, that's great,' she said, not daring to put her hat back on and spoiling the look.

'A pleasure, once again, Miss Moore. I'll see you again when you are ready for a shampoo and set,' said Tina. Margery paid her bill and left the shop. She decided to have a quick sandwich in the Tastea Bite cafe, before she went to her appointment with the Tanerife tanning salon. In the bakery cafe, Margery found her notebook and pencils in her handbag. The name of the person she was about to meet was Chardonnay Glossop. She knew nothing of tanning salons, so she persuaded herself it would be interesting to find out.

Chardonnay was expecting her. Margery noticed she was evenly tanned, tall, carefully made up, with long blonde hair and wearing what looked like a black cat suit with very high-heeled black shoes.

'Can I get you a tea or coffee?' she asked. Margery thanked her but said she'd just had one.

'Let me show you my tanning beds,' said Chardonnay, taking her through a door into the back of the shop, where Margery saw four wide shelves, one of which Chardonnay opened up and demonstrated.

'We have two more beds in the back salon,' she said, 'which are being used at the moment, so I thought I would bring you in here to show you how they work. Would you like to try one?'

Margery had not been expecting that. 'Just to lie on, thanks,' replied Margery, 'I don't really want a tan.'

'OK, try it for size.'

Margery slipped off her moccasins and hoisted herself up on to the bed. She found it surprisingly comfortable.

'So how long would it take to give me a tan on here?' she asked, lying down and holding up her notebook and pencil poised for the answer.

'Well, I'm guessing from your fair skin, you don't tan easily, so I would suggest only about ten or fifteen minutes to begin with, but you would need several sessions.'

'Would I need to turn over?'

'No, if I were to switch the beds on, they would tan you all over undressed. Excuse me, I have to go and make sure my friends in the back are off their beds now.'

Left alone, Margery decided to get off the bed, as much as she was enjoying the novelty of taking shorthand notes on her back. There was a burble of voices from the salon at the back. In a few minutes, a couple of tall slim girls, dressed in a similar way to Chardonnay, walked through, looking as if they had just come back from a Mediterranean holiday.

'Tracey and Babs,' introduced Chardonnay, 'my two lovely friends. I've only recently opened and I am hoping they will be able to show off their tans in Great Havell and drum up lots of custom. Let's all go through to reception.'

Margery realised she had already met Tracey at the Brass Monkeys Brasserie. She recognised her as Denzil Bream's dark-haired girlfriend. Tracey seemed to recognise Margery as well. She nodded but didn't say anything.

Chardonnay explained she had not any bookings for Margery's visit, so she could show her all over the premises. Margery was comfortably seated in the front of the shop. 'Are tanning lotions needed for sun beds?' she asked.

Chardonnay reached up for some bottles on a shelf. 'I would use this one for your skin, Margery, which is naturally fair, but Tracey has been using this one and Babs, who has a darker skin tone, this one.'

'Why would anyone want a tan at this time of year, in February?' asked Margery.

'Say your boyfriend gets tickets for a flight to Lanzarote or you decide to have a girlie holiday on the Costa del Sol, you get a tan before you go,' explained Chardonnay. 'Then you will look your best on the beach when you get there.'

'So why have you decided to get a tan, Tracey?' asked Margery.

'I bought a red dress to go to the Valentine's Ball with my boyfriend. It's really "glam", off the shoulder. It will look ace with a tan.'

'And you, Babs, why have you got a tan?'

'I've got a job at the Sylph Self gym. I treated myself to a load of new exercise gear. I decided, when Chards here offered us the chance to get a cheap tan in her new salon, to go for it! Thanks Chards…it's a real treat, we owe you!'

'This is going to go in the Gleaner, isn't it?' asked Chardonnay. 'When will it go in?'

'As soon as we can get it on a page with lots of advertisements,' replied Margery. 'I'll take a note of your sun bed and lotion suppliers and the sales team will see if they can sell more ads around it.'

'My boyfriend, Anthony, sells advertising,' said Chardonnay. 'He does really well. He's just had a bonus and bought a tape deck and stereo for his car. We can listen to our favourite songs when he takes me out.'

Margery knew who she meant. It was Anthony Taplow, the young man, with a repertoire of filthy jokes, she saw in the Amicable Anarchist the previous evening. But that pub was not likely to be Chardonnay's style. Margery guessed she would rather go to the Vin Rouge wine bar or the Brass Monkeys Brasserie than a pub.

She took her small Ricoh camera out of her bag, checked it had a film in it and asked if the three young ladies would mind posing for a picture or two in front of the sun beds. She also took a picture of them holding the tanning lotions and Chardonnay standing outside the shop. She knew enough about the tanning salon now to write 250 words.

It worked out that Margery would be a little early for her Girly Curls appointment, but she went across the marketplace to the salon anyway.

'Ah I see you've just had your hair done,' said the proprietress of the salon. 'Otherwise, we could have offered you a set and blow dry.'

'I only knew I was writing a feature on your salon this morning, when I made the appointment, and I'd already booked the hair do before then.'

'Well, next time maybe,' she replied. Margery noted she had what could only be described as 'big hair'. It was a mass of strawberry blonde curls. Margery wondered if it was all her own but dare not ask. She noticed that apart from hair styling, the salon sold curly wigs and hairpieces. Her assignments were all going well so far. She took notes of the suppliers and pictures of the salon and the staff.

She made her way to the Foo Kin restaurant. All her assignments were in or near the marketplace except for Moonlight Motors and she could use her bike to go there in the morning. At the Foo Kin, she was treated to some specialities and a pot of Chinese tea to try. She particularly enjoyed the seaweed she was offered. She had never eaten anything like that before. It was tasty. Margery took some pictures of the staff serving the food and a general picture of the premises.

*What a cheerful group of people*, Margery thought, as she checked through her notes at home later. She would like to try some more of their specialities. They sent their sons, they told Margery, to Hong Kong to learn authentic Chinese cooking, before they started preparing dishes at the restaurant.

Margery had decided to take the trip out to Moonlight Motors first thing in the morning, as she had arranged, and pop home to write her story. It could all be presented to Cheryl with her bill before lunch the following day.

She hadn't expected Vladimir to come in when she was hard at work.

'Look, Vlad, I'm busy, I haven't even time to make myself a cup of tea,' she said.

'I'll make one then.'

'All right, but I am really not to be disturbed.'

That didn't really work. It seemed Vlad couldn't do anything quietly and managed, as usual, to bang his head on beams and drop spoons on the floor. She just hoped her china would be safe.

Her china was safe apparently. Margery was presented with a rather strong mug of tea. She wondered how many spoons of leaves he had put in the pot and hoped he'd remembered to use a strainer. It seemed he had. Then she heard him rifling through her cupboards and fridge. It really was difficult to concentrate whilst wondering what he was doing, but she made herself do it. She had completed two sets of copy and was now writing up the Foo Kin. There was a smell of cooking, but she was used to that and thought it was one of her neighbours. She expected Vlad to ask her first before cooking. She didn't even know if he could cook.

She finished her copy and was splitting it up and putting paper clips on each story when Vlad opened the kitchen door and said: 'You come in now.'

Much to Margery's surprise, he'd had cooked pasta with tomato sauce, put it on plates, grated cheese on the top and it was all ready to eat on the fold down kitchen table. This was a surprise and treat indeed. When she sat down opposite Vlad and he took the apron off, which he had borrowed for cooking, she noticed for the first time, he was wearing a clean white t-shirt over his jeans. This was another surprise for her.

'Thank you, Vlad, this is a treat. When did you learn to cook?'

'When I was on the submarines. I cook at the flats too.'

With that answer, Margery realised how little she knew about this man. Which submarines had he served on, she wondered? Were they nuclear ones? British, American or even Russian? It would explain why he tended to stand to attention when anyone asked him to do something.

Margery had met Vlad on the rebound a couple of years ago. Her last boyfriend, Colin, had been an army officer, stationed at Grimpen Havell Barracks. He was often drafted abroad, and it was very much an on off relationship, but a good one when he was on leave and in the U.K. Then someone hinted to her that he had a wife and family in Germany. She was not sure what to do, whether she should confront him and find out if it were true. He had also started to become jealous of her time. If she was unable to see him, because she was visiting relatives or took the long journey to see her parents in Orkney, he would make her feel bad about it, as if she was letting him down in some way. In spite of this, she was shocked when he walked out and announced he was never coming back. Cheryl and her husband, Nigel, had been very supportive at the time. She had also spent more time in Orkney, staying with her parents that year and went to Havell-Next-the-Sea regularly to stay with her aunt and uncle.

She had been going to the Jazz and Folk Club at the Arts Centre regularly with Colin. She was planning to go, as usual, the week he left. Margery was very shaken by the split and quite angry with him. She took the decision to go on her own. She could have asked a friend, Cheryl even, might have come, as she often did, but on this occasion, she went alone. She knew most people at the club anyway. Jonah, for instance, would probably be there and she knew she could sit with him and enjoy a shandy if she wanted to. So, she did. She'd taken her bike and she could ride home safely at any time. She had been drinking a shandy with Jonah when Andy Clark of the Jollity folk group came over to their table. Andy ran the club and sometimes played clarinet with the jazz bands and guitar with folk groups.

He introduced them to a tall man with short light-brown hair, blue eyes and a roguish smile, who was wearing a white vest, jeans and a khaki bomber jacket. Andy introduced him as Vladimir and asked if he could join them, as he was new to Great Havell. Andy said Vladimir had moved into Little Havell recently but didn't know anyone in Great Havell. They didn't like to refuse. For a while, they all sat in silence until Jonah asked Vladimir if he could buy him a beer. Margery had looked away and smiled when he had asked for a cold lager and noted the look of disapproval on Jonah's face.

'What do you think of the music?' Margery had asked. Vlad had just shrugged, she remembered; she thought, *this is going to be hard work*. She and Jonah watched Vlad down his larger as if he hadn't had a drink for a long time. Watching him had made her think of the film, "Ice Cold in Alex."

After that, Vlad, as he became known, would often turn up when she went to the Arts Centre. His usual clothes were jeans or corduroys, a vest, an army jacket and army boots. He told her he had a job as an engineer, maintaining the spa and gym equipment at the Little Havell Country Hotel and also machinery at the mineral water bottling plant. He had his own flat there, but she had never seen it. A few more people got to know him in Great Havell and Margery became used to going to the Arts Centre with him. He began to leave his bike in her front garden and walk her home.

Last year, at the Moyen Midden Fayre, 1945 was being celebrated in various events. Margery got out her sewing machine and made herself a polka-dot wrap over dress to serve teas and wartime fare in a large tent, decorated with red, white and blue bunting. She was never quite sure how many teas and scones Vlad bought that day, but he couldn't keep away. She had been busy. His eyes were always on her, with the sort of look and smile which melted her heart.

Since then, they had gradually become closer. In many ways, it was very satisfying, except Margery was looking for a little more. Now that he had cooked for her, she was feeling spoilt indeed. Colin had never done that. In fact, as the memory of him faded, she realised how selfish he had been, although she had been very fond of him and was happy until he began to criticise her for staying with relatives. She was going away more often, once she heard he might be married.

'You've had a hairdo,' said Vlad.

'Yes, today, and I've been busy.'

'Shall I go after I wash up?' he asked.

'As you like,' replied Margery coolly.

'You need to work. I have something to tell you.'

'Can you tell me now?' she asked.

'No. It's quite a long story and it's best I tell you when you are not busy.'

Margery was intrigued. *What do I do?* she thought. *Does this man, who I had been intimate with for a few months want to stop the night with me? And if he does want to, do I want him to?*

'Should I worry about what you have to tell me?' she asked.

'No, not at all. It's about me and it is only fair on you that you know about it.'

She took a sip of the water Vlad had poured out for her. He'd found everything he needed, and the spaghetti was really quite tasty.

She decided to leave it entirely to him, whether he stayed tonight and when he told her whatever he had to tell her. She needed to wind down after working and they were eating quite late. There was not much of the evening left. She decided to have a shower to get rid of the tiny pieces of hair around her neck after the cut. Since he had offered to wash up, she could have her shower whilst he was doing that.

After the meal, Margery went into her front room. She finished separating the copies of the features. She put them in her bag, ready to take to Cheryl on the way back from Moonlight Motors; in fact, she thought, if Cheryl didn't mind, she could type that one up in the office.

'Would you like to use the bathroom before I have a shower, Vlad?' she asked.

He did and took a long time. This surprised Margery. He came out holding a toothbrush.

'I clean my teeth after every meal,' he explained and put it in a tube and into his back pocket.

*I see,* thought Margery. *Well, let's see what he does intend to do tonight.* She went in for her shower. The cap, protecting her perm, came well over her ears, so she could hear nothing else in the cottage and hardly the noise of the water running. It had been a busy day, and this was just what she needed. She put her dressing gown on rather than her clothes. When she got out of the bathroom, the kitchen was all neat and tidy. The washing up had been done and everything had been put away. The tealeaves had been put in the compost pot, ready to be taken out.

The phone rang. It was Cheryl.

'Margery? Sorry to ring you so late, I'm ringing from home because I'm under pressure at work. How soon can you have those stories written? I've been given a load more for you.'

'Tanerife, Girly Curls and Foo Kin all done. I've said I'll be at Moonlight Motors when they open at eight tomorrow. I've got pics and I will take the little camera.'

'Ace!' said Cheryl. 'The pressure is really on. It is all sell, sell, sell, at the moment.'

'Can I type up the Moonlight copy in the office?' asked Margery.

'Yes, but you'll find the reps and tele-ads are very noisy. When they are not on the phones, if they sell £500 of advertising, they all get up from their desks, stand in a circle, with their arms round each other's shoulders, dance round, kicking their legs in the air and sing "We are the Champions" loudly. I thought I ought to warn you.'

Margery giggled at the idea of it.

'All right, it sounds like a mad house to me. If you need the articles and the pics, it's going to be the easiest way to do it if I come in. I can pop the film into photographic on my way to your office.'

'Thanks, Margery. I knew I could rely on you.'

The cottage was quiet, so Margery, having put everything ready for the morning, folded up her clothes and put them on the stairs ready to take up to her spare room at the front of the cottage, which she used as a dressing room.

Then she put on her reading lamp and settled down to read a P.D. James she'd borrowed from the library. It was the only one she had not read. It was based, it seemed, on an actual murder. It was called "The Maul and the Pear Tree". Margery had not read far into the book when she realised it was co-written by another author, T.A. Critchley, whoever he was. She was a bit disappointed, but nevertheless persevered with it. She soon realised, the book was about one of the grisliest murders, which had ever been committed. She thought she was on her own in the cottage and had the knowledge that two deaths had occurred within a short distance of where she lived. She put the book down and looked on the bookshelves for some comfort reading, trying to get the images of the murdered Marr family out of her head. She needed something which would take her into a different world, different time… Thomas Hardy would do… "Under The Greenwood Tree" was ideal.

Growltiger jumped on her lap and Margery dozed over the book, dreaming of delivery carts and village bands.

The cottage was silent, but she woke with a start. She thought she had heard something, but no, all was quiet, and it would be a busy day tomorrow.

Still wrapped in her dressing gown and wearing her slippers, she made herself a hot water bottle, picked up her clothes and climbed the stairs, changing into her nighty in the spare bedroom. She turned off the light at the top of the stairs and groped her way into bed.

*Well, I never,* she thought, as she found herself wrapped in a pair of strong arms, *so Vlad decided to stay the night after all! I won't need the hot water bottle.*

### Thursday 6th February

Margery woke up and stretched across her bed to find her hand bitten gently by Growltiger, who proceeded to move over to her feet and curled up and went to sleep, purring loudly. Vlad had risen, taken his bike and left. It was 7.00 am. Still, she needed to get up and left Growltiger asleep on her bed. She found herself smiling to herself over Vlad's cheekiness. He'd decided to stay without telling her. The first time they had actually spent the night together and it had seemed quite natural. Growltiger, it appeared to her, was now claiming her back by coming upstairs and curling up on her feet, so she had to extract them gently. He usually slept on his beanbag near the warmth of the small boiler between her bathroom and her kitchen.

She went downstairs with her clothes. She found the kitchen was still all neat and clean and went through into the bathroom to wash, clean her teeth and put her clothes on. After a quick breakfast of tea, toast and marmalade, Margery took her bike out of the shed, packed her bag into her bicycle basket, locked the back door and set off from the back gate, later than she had intended to. She cycled along the bridle path between the back gardens of Priory Cottages and the Glebe Mound, turning left at the end of Priory Street. Moonlight Motors was on the corner of Priory Street and Station Road.

It was clear the garage had not been open long. The owner, Bill Walker's, Porsche was outside, and Margery noticed with amusement it had the wide tyres and the wire wheels she had seen advertised in Havell Hundred Life. *The ideal picture of the garage,* she thought, *with the Porsche showing off its sporty wheels outside.* She took the Ricoh camera out of her bag and took a picture which featured more Porsche than garage.

Bill Walker was surprised to see her so early. 'Miss Moore, I'm delighted to see you, my dear,' he said, shaking her hand. 'Let me show you round.'

Already, mechanics, in the grey overalls of the garage, with Moonlight Motors embroidered under the right lapel, were busy. They were changing the wheels on a sports car. It was jacked up over the pit. She got them to pose for a picture. Everyone, who could afford it, apparently, was changing their tyres and wheel hubs, putting sports stripes along their vehicles and having new paint jobs. The garage was very busy.

Bill showed Margery the paint shop through a window, his staff wore masks to do it. They offered every service there, said Bill. MOTs, body repairs, resprays, servicing, new tyres, wheel balancing and tracking. 'You name it,' he said, 'we have the skills to do it.' Moonlight Motors also sold all sorts of new and used cars of every type. They were neatly parked next to the garage with the prices in the windscreens.

'Have you thought of buying a car, Miss Moore?' asked Bill.

'Not really, I have my trusty bike and working for a local paper, I don't usually need to go far,' replied Margery.

'I've got the very thing for you,' said Bill, showing Margery a convertible Morris Minor. She had to admit, it was the sort of car she would like if she bought one. But, of course, there was nowhere to park a car near her cottage, except the car park by the old priory. She could borrow one of the pool cars at the newspaper if she needed one for an assignment.

'I'm very tempted,' she laughed, 'but I'll stick with my bike for the present.'

Just before she left, Gloria turned up, gave her an angry look and said: 'What are you doing here?'

'Miss Moore is writing a feature on my garage,' said Bill pleasantly.

'I wonder what they sent *her* for,' remarked Gloria dismissively, taking Bill's arm to steer him into his office.

'Thank you and goodbye,' said Bill over his shoulder, as he was propelled away by Gloria.

Margery, a little put out, put her notebook, pencil and camera back into her bag and into her bicycle basket. She got on her bike. She cycled along Station Road and turned into Priory Street to the newspaper offices.

She gave a cheerful greeting to Philippa and Gill before taking her camera down to photographic to have her film developed. She then went into Cheryl's office, where she sat down and handed her the features she had already written.

'Well, Margery, you've got a spring in your step and a sparkle in your eye this morning!' said Cheryl, taking the copy. 'What, were you up to last night?'

'You know what I was doing,' she replied, blushing and hoping Cheryl hadn't noticed. 'I was writing all these features for you. I've taken the film in to photographic to be developed.'

'Thanks,' said Cheryl, 'you can use the desk next to Gloria; she's out at the moment and there's a typewriter you can use on that one.'

Margery sat down to find the portable typewriter needed a new ribbon. She looked in the drawers in the desk, hoping to find one. Fortunately, there were two. One had black at the top and red at the bottom, the other was all black. She decided to put the red and black one in, thinking the typewriter might be used for figures and she made sure she had it on the setting to use only the black. It took up a bit of time, although she had her article finished and submitted within the hour.

Cheryl gave her four more advertising features to write after Margery submitted her copy. Before she left the office, there was a shout of £500! Everyone, who wasn't on the phone, stopped what they were doing, got up, put their arms around each other's shoulders and started singing in raucous voices: *'We are the champions my friends, and we'll keep on fighting to the end.'* Margery was quite glad she had finished her work. Once the singing had stopped, she used Cheryl's phone to make the new appointments. She'd be busy for the rest of the week.

How Harry Grimes managed to pat her on the bottom and say 'hello sugar' close to her ear, as she left the main newspaper office, she really did not know. She had no time to stop to talk to the front office girls; they were both on the phone anyway. She walked out of the door, put her bag in the basket and unlocked her bike.

'You, again!' said Gloria as she stepped out of Bill Walker's red Porsche and almost bumped into Margery as she wheeled her bike towards the road.

'My goodness me, you *do* get in the way!'

'Hello Gloria,' said Margery, crossing the road and mounting her bike. She was too surprised to make a retort and just said, 'I can't stop, I'm really busy!'

'As we all are,' Gloria called after her as the Porsche sped off.

Margery's assignments were fairly unusual, but sales staff had persuaded them they needed to be seen in the Gleaner as the major event in the summer would bring a lot of new business in the town. She thought about them as she cycled from the Gleaner offices up Priory Street past the old priory and turned left along the bridle path between the Glebe Mound and Priory Cottages.

Dewbury and Hicks, Margery thought, was an old-fashioned but large department store which dominated the market square in a palatial building. Customers went there from the whole of the Havell Hundreds. Most well-heeled inhabitants had accounts there. She also had an appointment with Sworder, Leigh and Runk. The firm was more than an off licence, Margery remembered. They were a well-established, well-respected wine merchant. They usually provided beers, wines and spirits for all major events in the whole of the Havell Hundreds. Trendy Tots, the children's clothing specialist and Root and Branch, the garden centre, were the other two assignments, Cheryl had given her.

She took her bike into the back gate and put it away in her shed which had been converted from an outside toilet. Whilst she was enjoying a tin of tomato soup and a roll for lunch on her fold down kitchen table, Growltiger came down from her bedroom, where he had been all morning, and jumped on to her lap. She let him stay there while she finished her soup, stroked him, fed him before she put him outside and went out again. This time she had her notebook, pencils and camera in her bag and no bike.

Tea with Mr Dewbury, the fastidious 85-year-old chairman of Dewbury and Hicks in his quiet wood-panelled office, was served in art deco bone china cups. These had been designed and made in Staffordshire exclusively for the store in the 1930s, Margery was informed. She sat opposite Mr Dewbury, who was behind his large, but mainly, empty desk. She noted the fresh deep red rose in his buttonhole which had been selected that morning from the florist department in the store's basement. She also noted the immaculate dark-grey tailored suit he was wearing, his white shirt with an old-fashioned wing collar and a red bow tie, the exact shade of the rose. She took a picture of him sitting there, with his permission. In his slow cultured tones, Mr Dewbury explained to Margery how the shop had its own exclusive china, tailoring, shirts and furniture, all manufactured to the store's specification. This had been the order of things from the time his grandfather had the building completed in Queen Victoria's reign.

Mr Dewbury explained the store had succeeded in delivering this principle for nearly a century now. Their reputation had been built up by word of mouth. 'We have never seen the need to stoop to doing something as vulgar as to advertise,' he said. Margery was at a loss to know what to reply.

'Why,' asked Mr Dewbury in his soft, slow, carefully enunciated way, 'would we need to advertise, when the whole population of the Havell Hundreds and beyond know Dewbury and Hicks can be relied on to supply and deliver anything they desire and everything they need?'

'Why,' he asked again, 'should anyone need to purchase anything elsewhere? Everything a household could possibly need is under our roof.'

She was, again, for a moment, at a loss for words. She finished her tea and the Dewbury and Hicks crisp shortbread biscuits, she had been given by Mr Dewbury's thin, smart, tall secretary. Miss Budworth looked, Margery thought, as if she could have retired at least ten years previously but chose not to.

'Marvellous,' Margery eventually exclaimed enthusiastically, 'I wonder if I could look round the store?'

Mr Dewbury picked up a small brass hand bell and rang it twice. It summoned his secretary from her office.

'Miss Budworth, would you be so kind as to show Miss Moore round the store.'

'With pleasure, Mr Dewbury,' said Miss Budworth, collecting up the tea things deftly and taking them out into her own office.

'Miss Moore, please come this way,' she said imperiously, as Mr Dewbury stood up and shook hands with Margery.

'Thank you, Mr Dewbury,' said Margery and followed Miss Budworth out of the office, along a corridor and through a private door into the store. They were met by a cheerful, young woman with large eyes and glossy dark wavy hair, smartly dressed in a fitted dark suit and white blouse.

'Thank you, Miss Budworth,' she said quickly. 'You may return to your duties. I will now show Miss Moore round the store.'

'As you wish, Miss Dewbury,' said Miss Budworth huffily. She said a clipped goodbye to Margery before walking towards the lifts.

'I'm Emma Dewbury, Mr Dewbury's granddaughter, please call me Emma. May I call you Margery?' said Emma, as soon as the lift door closed on Miss Budworth.

'Please do, Emma,' said Margery. She was relieved at the sudden informality after the uninformative interview she had just had. Emma showed her over the four floors of the department store enthusiastically at a brisk, energetic pace.

Hardly having time to take shorthand notes or even ask questions, Margery nevertheless saw there was more on offer than Mr Dewbury had suggested. Contemporary, even Avant Garde furniture, soft furnishings, and china on the top floor, near a dark panelled room with large windows, overlooking the marketplace, which was the cafe and restaurant. Here, she knew, one of the best treats was to order a buttered toasted teacake, which was served on a silver platter with a silver dome on the top. The waitresses wore black dresses, stockings and shoes, with white frilly caps and aprons which had Dewbury and Hicks embroidered on them in black silk. There were several customers enjoying afternoon tea on tiered plates with the store's own Jap cakes on the top. The store's logo was on the china and cutlery.

Toys, hobbies, cookware and gifts were on the second floor.

Dewbury and Hicks was still offering bespoke services, but in terms of alterations or personalising shirts, suits and designer dresses, on the first floor.

The fabric, dressmaking, florists and food department took up the whole of the basement area. Foods were exotic coffees, teas, snacks, confectionary, cheeses and the stores own selection of hand-made chocolates and tinned luxuries. Things to put in a food hamper for presents included boxed and tinned cakes and biscuits, baked locally to "secret" recipes, exclusive from Dewbury's. The store logo seemed to be on everything, even the model vintage delivery vans for sale. Margery decided to buy a tinned fruitcake for her next visit to her aunt and uncle, which Emma let her have on her own staff discount.

Margery was glad she had worn her black beret, with matching jacket, straight tailored tartan skirt and black boots. It was perhaps more elegant and less eccentric than the usual cape and brimmed hat she wore. It was more in keeping with the clothes in the store.

Emma took her around the whole of haberdashery, cosmetics and perfumery on the ground floor. She greeted the staff by their first names. She paused whenever she saw Margery take a long look at a particular hat, pair of shoes, scarf, gloves or handbag, which took her fancy. Emma probably would have sold the items to her if she had not been taking notes. She was enjoying herself. 'I've spent hundreds of pounds theoretically already!' she confided. 'You have a cornucopia here. Do you do much of the selection yourself?'

'We have many expert buyers and top salespeople,' replied Emma. 'We have weekly meetings to discuss our customer profiles, fashion trends and bespoke policies. Some of our staff trained in top West End stores but prefer to live and work in the Home Counties.'

'This would suit you.' Emma picked up a black leather bucket-shaped handbag, with the Dewbury label on it.

'It's lovely,' said Margery, 'but where would I put my notebook and pencil.'

'Ah yes, practicality before style. We cater for that too,' said Emma, selecting a bag with compartments, the right size for a shorthand notebook and slots for pens or pencils.

Margery laughed. 'As I said, I could spend a fortune in here, and I would if I could. I do buy all my cosmetics at the store.'

She asked Emma to pose for a picture with one of the salesgirls in the perfumery department at the front of the store. She wondered why Emma's parents were not involved in running the store but didn't like to ask. She guessed there had been a falling out. His granddaughter probably had more influence on Mr Dewbury than a son or daughter.

'I'll be back to do my shopping,' said Margery before she left, 'but for now, I must go for my next appointment.'

'Thank you for coming,' said Emma, holding open one of the brass trimmed double glass doors for her. 'Here is my card and phone number if you need to check anything.'

Margery stepped out of the store into the winter sunshine. She went into the marketplace and took a distance picture of the store.

Trendy Tots was in a side street from the marketplace. Here she interviewed a very enthusiastic young woman who had recently opened the store. Margery noted she had managed to translate the latest trends in adult clothing into miniature versions. She wasn't too sure little girls of four or five really needed to wear bikinis, but she didn't make any comments, just took notes. There would be no clash with the children's clothing department at Dewbury's, which was still offering sailor suits for the same age group, probably at Mr Dewbury's behest, and much loved by the local photographic studios for portraits of small boys and small girls. She took pictures of the outside and inside of the store featuring its enthusiastic young owner.

Her appointment with Sworder, Leigh and Runk was quite different. The wine merchant and off licence was situated on Thorpe Park Road, which led from the marketplace to the town's main public park. It too had a basement where there was a wine cellar. Margery learnt the firm had its own wine label.

'We are exploring the possibility of buying some land to have our own vineyard locally,' said Robert Leigh, as he showed her round the premises and took her into the basement, where the wines and fortified wines were stored.

'Although we are an off-licence, we specialise in wines. There are already a couple of vineyards in the Hundreds and we offer the local wines. They are white wines, but one vineyard is experimenting with a rosé this year.

'We have our own chateau-bottled French wine, which carries the Sworder, Leigh and Runk label. It is shipped over from France and we sell them to order by the crate.'

'Who would buy a crate of wine?' asked Margery.

'You might be surprised. Apart from local hotels and country clubs all over the county and beyond, a few individual customers, local clubs and bars will buy our wine by the crate. Of course, the wines vary from year to year, depending on weather conditions in the area where the grapes are grown. 1983 was a fine year for our label if you would like to taste some.'

Margery declined, thinking of her next appointment with Root and Branch, which was slightly out of town. She would have to go home for her bike so she could cycle there.

Robert Leigh insisted on giving her a bottle of Sworder, Leigh and Runk chateau-bottled claret to take home, so she added that to the Dewbury and Hicks bag with the fruitcake and decided to take both to her uncle's home when she visited at the weekend. Fired up with enthusiasm for the assignments she had done, she was keen to finish up with Root and Branch, so hurried back home with her bags to collect her bike. She noticed there was a slight dent in the surface of the priory car park where the police car had driven over Eric's Honey Monster watch and the tyre tracks by the priory had dried, but she could still see them.

'I've shut that cat in the coal bunker again,' announced Alf, coming out of his front door as she turned in towards hers.

Margery sighed. She put her bags down in her cottage and went through and out of her back garden gate into Alf's garden. He opened up his coal bunker and she extracted the cat. 'I'll take him now then.'

Growltiger had scratched her when she rescued him from Alf's coal bunker. She shut him in the bathroom and dusted herself down. She decided the garden centre wouldn't mind a bit of coal dust on her jacket. She locked the back door, picked up her bike from the shed and cycled off on the bridle path and joined the road south of the Glebe Mound towards the Root and Branch nursery. The nursery was on the edge of the Glebe Park and the 1960s Glebe housing estate. There was a stream running through it.

As it was fairly late in the afternoon, Margery decided to take her pictures before she started the interview.

Notebook and pencil in hand, she walked through the nursery, which was full of primroses and primulas in bud ready for an event in a few weeks. She met Ruth Baldock, the tall, well-built, tawny-haired and energetic owner of Root and Branch.

'There is still a demand for Christmas roses; they make a pleasant display with early flowering bulbs,' she said briskly.

'You probably think February is a quiet time for garden centres, but I can assure you we are very busy.' She gave Margery no time to reply.

'We are inundated with demands for bulbs in bud, as people make a mess of planting their own displays.'

'Of course, our primrose festival is early March, ready for Mother's Day; you'll need to order any pots of those, if you want some.'

Margery tried to reply but never had the chance.

'And, of course, we are still trying to supply orders for pampas grass. There is a great demand for that. God knows why! We've none at all in stock at the moment. I've an order book for it as long as your arm. They tell me they want it in their front gardens. They all want it on the Glebe Estate. They are all mad for it, you could say.'

'Come and have a look at our fruit trees. We're trying to preserve some of the local apple varieties here. We have a little orchard, not far from here, where we grow the apples. You've missed our last stocks of Little Havell Spice. There's a tremendous appetite locally for those. We kept them cool and sold the last three weeks ago. People were buying them for Christmas.

'There's also a demand for bay trees and we cultivate our own herbs. Come and have a look at the herb garden. We have our own selection sets of herbs called the "Glebe Mound Herb Collection". There are six plants in the set, and we use the names of the witches for our own particular varieties. It's a very popular collection. We do a tremendous trade at the Moyen Midden Fayre.'

'But….' started Margery.

'Look here you see… this one is the "Lizzy balm", a variety of Lemon balm we've grafted and adapted. Take a leaf in between your fingers, rub it and put it up to your nose….'

'Mmmmmmm,' said Margery.

'And here, this is the Molly Marjoram… it's fragrant…see.

'Look take these small pots, I can guarantee they'll grow well in the local soil. Take a set of them, plant them out at the weekend and let me know how you get on with them. The names of the herbs are on the pots. They are only tiny plants but should grow. Can you put them in your bike basket? Good. Sadie Petal helped me cultivate these varieties. It's a pity she left. She asked the wildflower artist draw the herbs for labels. You'll find the drawings on flags in each of the pots, so you'll know which is which. We have to close the store now, it's getting dark. Good to meet you, thank you for coming.'

Margery was shown out. She placed the herbs in her bicycle basket, put her bicycle lights on and cycled home. It was late afternoon. She glanced up to the top of the Glebe Mound in the fading light and thought she saw figures around the top, but it was what she saw on the top, which made her wobble to a stop on her bike.

The figures around the top of the mound were obscuring her view, but in the fading light, she thought she had seen a small gibbet, or gallows with some kind of figure suspended from it. *Surely not*, she thought, although, her stomach churned. What on earth was going on? Two deaths, she knew about, but only because Cheryl had told her in confidence, but what was this all about?

She peddled home thoughtfully. Had she seen a gibbet or had she imagined it. She found herself shaking when she went in the back garden gate, unlocked the bike shed and put her bike away, taking her bag and the herbs out of the basket.

Her cottage was in darkness. She left the pots of herbs outside the back door, opened it and switched the kitchen light on. It felt cold, so she put the electric fire on in the front room, put the kettle on, made herself a pot of tea.

Remembering the warmth of Growltiger on her feet on the bed that morning, she looked in the bathroom for him, but found he had climbed out of the window again. She opened kitchen door and called him expecting him come in, but there was no sign of him. Opening the front door slightly, she called out for him, but he did not appear. He'd come back before, so she should not worry. Because of recent events, Margery felt uneasy and almost wished Vlad would turn up and find Growltiger for her, but she had work to get on with. There were a lot of articles to write and she intended to finish them tonight.

She wondered how she would manage to keep them all down to 250 words; she had so much material for them all.

Switching the angle poise on over her desk and also her reading lamp on behind her armchair, Margery sat at her typewriter and worked for a couple of hours, getting up occasionally to call for Growltiger in vain. She would have everything finished for the morning to take into the Gleaner, no problem, but the quiet, very familiar to her normally, disturbed her. The moonless night with the low cloud, her inability to see the Glebe Mound from the back door, everything made her uneasy and she could not understand why.

Eventually, she decided enough was enough. She would complete her assignments in the morning before she took them to the Gleaner. She made herself a poached egg and beans on toast for an evening meal and settled into her button-back armchair to listen to some music and relax. Her eyes were too tired to read in the evening.

She rather hoped she might have Growltiger for company, but he never turned up. She could have gone next door and asked Alf if he had shut him in his coal bunker again but decided she didn't need another confrontation with him before bedtime.

She listened to a variety of music on her radio, starting with a programme on Mark Knopfler and Dire Straits, some jazz from the 1940s and later some popular classics to which Margery was almost falling asleep.

That night Margery's dreams took her to the top of the Glebe Mound among menacing shadowy figures. "Out! Out of here!" she was ordered, but, as in dreams, she could not move, and the figures moved about at the top of the mound and revealed the gibbet and the struggling shape hanging from it. *Only one small figure*, thought Margery, *not six*. She woke up with a start. She switched on her bedside light. It was only three o'clock and she felt wide-awake. Now there was a moon and she looked out on the Glebe Mound. Was there a shape at the top? She rubbed her eyes but could not see. Could she see figures there? She rubbed her eyes again, was it her imagination or had she seen them? This was ridiculous. She had work to do in the morning, but the feeling of dread came back. What could she do to help herself sleep? Read perhaps? What would help? She picked up "The Handmaid's Tale" by Margaret Attwood but felt she did not really want to return to that world, even if it was fictional. She picked up a paperback Cheryl had lent her. It was probably about time she read it. "A Crowning Mercy" by Susanna Kells; that would do. Margery began to read, the story took her back to the English Civil War and gradually she nodded off and woke up three hours later to find the bedside lamp still on and the book, in her hands and open, but on her chest.

## Friday 7th February

It was bright and early and there was still no sign of Growltiger. Margery finished off the Root and Branch story, using her recently researched knowledge of the Havell-on-the-Marsh witches to describe Ruth Baldock's Glebe Mound Herb collection. She mentioned the artist's sketches commissioned to illustrate the herbs. The Glebe Mound, what had she seen on it? She thought, getting up to look out of the kitchen window at it. It was still and lifeless in the early morning light. Perhaps she had imagined the figures on it. But where was Growltiger? She finished story and divided up the three copies with paper clips. She put them all in the shopping trolley to take them to the Gleaner and made herself some breakfast. After a shower, she dressed and put on her black jacket and beret, ready to go out.

She was about to do so, when, much to her surprise, there was a knock on her door. She opened it to find her Uncle Alec there with a very concerned look on his face.

'Hello, Uncle, I didn't expect to see you today; whatever is the matter?' said Margery in surprise.

'I'm fine, your aunt is fine, but I need to you sit down,' he said, coming into her cottage.

'It's only half past nine, I was just about to go out to the Gleaner.'

'I parked in the old priory car park and walked here. Look, Margery, I'm afraid something nasty has happened to Growltiger.'

Her stomach tightened, and she got up from her chair. Alec took her hands.

'Margery, he's dead; he was found yesterday evening, hanging from a make-shift gibbet on the Glebe Mound. I had to come and tell you, because it's on the front page of the Gleaner. Jonah phoned me last night; he heard it from Cheryl, but we thought it best to tell you in the morning.'

'Margery felt sick. She rushed to the bathroom and vomited into the basin.'

Uncle Alec followed her in.

'Because of the recent deaths and now this, Jonah thought I should come and tell you before you heard it from anyone else or even saw it on the front of the paper.'

Margery was at a loss for words. Her cat had been killed on the Glebe Mound. Her cat. Why? Who would do such a thing?

'I have to go to the Gleaner to take my copy and my bill in,' she gasped, as she retched again over the basin.

'I'll take you there in the car and come in with you.'

'Thank you, Uncle, I'm a bit shocked, I would be grateful for that.'

'But first, I'm going to get you to sit down and I'll make you some tea; it has been a shock for you. I can see that. Aunt Carrie and I would like you to come and stay if you don't mind. Just for the weekend. Your cottage will be safe. It will be a break for you.'

Margery's mind was in a whirl. Poor Growltiger. There was another knock at the door, Alec opened it.

It was Alf. He looked worried.

He came in, wiped his feet on the doormat, closed the door behind him and stood on the mat, looking at Margery, who was sitting in her chair, still feeling sick.

Alf took off his cap and passed it nervously from hand to hand.

'I want to say it is nothing to do with me,' he said. 'I'm sorry I shut your cat in my coal bunker. But it was always shitting in my garden.'

There was no reply from Margery or Alec. They both looked at Alf blankly.

'I heard you calling for that cat and I'd seen it hunting on the bridle path and on the Glebe Mound. I'm sorry, I should have told you when I heard you calling for it, last night.'

Both Margery and Alec were still at a loss for words. Then Alec said:

'Did you see what happened, Alf?'

'I saw people on the mound, but it was getting dark.'

'How many figures?'

'I don't know… two or three. I didn't see the cat after I saw it go off chasing after something or other. I saw it pounce and play and then pounce again.'

'Why didn't you tell me?' asked Margery angrily.

'I thought he would come back. I didn't know what would happen. No one could have guessed what would happen. Look, I'm really, really sorry, I should have said. I should have helped you look for him.'

'You should,' said Alec.

'I just came to say I was sorry,' said Alf defiantly and left.

Margery was still stunned with the news. She sipped the cup of tea slowly. The sickness had passed. Alec made her some toast.

'Take your time,' he said, 'and then we'll go to the Gleaner together.'

She rang Cheryl. 'I'm on my way with all the copy.'

'Ace,' said Cheryl, 'are you all right?'

'My uncle will bring me,'

'That's a good idea. Warn him about the dancing and singing when the sales-people reach their target, won't you?'

Margery didn't know how to tell Alec that. She was still stunned with the news of what had happened to her cat. Her cat! Why her cat? The very idea of such cruelty directed towards him or even towards her made her feel sick.

She was a bit shaky when she walked into the Gleaner offices with Alec. She introduced him to Philippa and Gill.

'Are you all right?' asked Philippa.

'Yes, fine,' she lied and took Alec down to photographic in the basement to drop her film in to be processed and collected film for her next assignments, before going upstairs through to the advertising and editorial offices. The sales reps and tele ads assumed he was a client as he was wearing a suit, as if he had an appointment, so he was able to wait outside Cheryl's office and no questions were asked whilst Margery handed over her copy and bill.

'Are you all right?' asked Cheryl.

'Yes, thank you.' It was Margery's turn to sound a bit sharp.

'Thanks for these and for writing them so quickly. Have a nice weekend and I'll see you with some more on Monday. Here's the Weekender Gleaner,' she said handing her a copy of the paper, folded so only the back page was visible.

'Thanks,' said Margery, not looking at the paper, but handing it to Alec who was looking amazed at the scene before him. Sales had reached the magic £500 already that morning. The reps and the tele-ads were in a circle, where there was a bit of space, arms around each other's shoulders, dancing clockwise, kicking their feet in the air and singing:

*'We are the champions, my friends, we'll go on fighting to the end.'*

She had not seen Gloria come in, who tapped Margery on the shoulder and put the print of a large glossy black and white photograph in front of her.

Margery's stomach churned at the sight of it, she retched and rushed to the Ladies toilet, which she managed to get just in time to be thoroughly sick. So, everyone knew it was her cat on the front page. The nastiness was directed at her. Gloria had got a large print of the photograph, especially to show her. She could not get the image out of her mind. Her poor cat, his eyes tightly shut against the world, strung up, suspended on gallows, made from two witches' brooms, all caught in the harsh light of a flash gun. Horrible.

# Chapter III
## A Stroppy Detective

Sipping from the drinking water tap in the Ladies in the Gleaner offices, Margery thought she would never see the hideous shade of shocking pink in those toilets again without feeling sick. She looked in the mirror, carefully wiped away any signs she had been sick, and she had been crying, refreshed her make-up, adjusted her black beret to a jaunty angle and went into the front office, where her uncle was waiting.

Unusually, she ignored Gill and Philippa, except with a nod in their direction, looped her arm in Alec's and said, 'Come on, let's go.'

His blue Vauxhall Cavalier was parked right outside the door. As she entered the passenger seat, Margery noticed a red Porsche with Bill Walker from Moonlight Motors in the driver's seat parked behind.

'We'll collect your things for the weekend, young lady. Perhaps you would like to take Bobby for a walk when we get home.'

'Yes, I'd like that,' said Margery quietly, suddenly wishing herself well away from Great Havell and the Gleaner. She could take a walk on the sea front with Bobby, her aunt's wire-haired fox terrier. A long walk, it would be cold, but the air would be fresh, blowing from the sea, and there was Aunt Carrie's home cooking to look forward to.

Her uncle, Alec Moore, had retired from his role as town clerk for Great Havell. He and his wife Carrie had bought, and moved in to, a semi-detached three-bedroom arts and crafts-style house in The Avenue at Havell-Next-the-Sea. There was a small upstairs study in the house, which could be used as an extra bedroom, with a camp bed, when Margery's cousin and his young family came to stay at Christmas.

Margery changed when she got home, keeping her black tights on and putting a pair of jeans over them for extra warmth. It would be bracing by the sea. She put on a jumper, a cardigan, a short green woollen jacket, tartan scarf and matching beret (a Christmas present from Mum and Dad, from the Orkney Islands). She packed her walking shoes, pyjamas, a change of clothes and underwear, toothbrush and make up bag in a small holdall.

Alec had parked in the priory car park. He carried Margery's holdall to the car. Margery had not once glanced up at the Glebe Mound and hardly noticed the drive to her uncle's house. Aunt Carrie opened the door to let her in, whilst Alec brought her holdall in and put it in her room.

Aunt Carrie's hug and concern was too much. Somehow, sympathy triggered tears and Margery hugged her back and went upstairs to her room. Carrie had put a bowl of crocuses in bloom on the windowsill and beyond them through the lattice windows, Margery could look out. The view was over her uncle's garden, his pride and joy. She looked over to the gardens and the backs of the arts-and-crafts-style houses which were in the road parallel to The Avenue. She opened the window a little, breathed in the cold breezy, tangy sea air and let her tears dry in the cool breeze. Her aunt had made the bed up for her with crisp white cotton sheets and pillowcases a woollen blanket and a paisley pattern eiderdown. She took her pyjamas out of her hold all and put them on the pillows.

A walk with Bobby would be just the right thing for her.

She took her walking shoes out of the shoe bag in her holdall and took them down to the hall. Bobby was in his basket near the boiler in the breakfast room and jumped up when Margery came in wagging his tail. He followed her into the hall. She put her walking shoes on, picked up his lead from the hook in the hall, attached it to his collar, put her jacket, hat, scarf and gloves on and took him out.

It was chilly along the sea front and she pulled her hat down over her ears. She kept to the greensward, looking out over the grey sea, but Bobby had other ideas and pulled her over to the steps down to the beach. The tide was going out and they ran together along the smooth sand, jumping over the groynes where they were low and climbing over them where they were too high. It was invigorating. When she reached the far end of the beach, Margery realised they would take something like three-quarters of an hour to get back along the beach. She persuaded Bobby to go back onto the greensward. They ran together towards The Avenue but walked sedately along the pavement back home. Bobby acted exhausted when he went back to his basket near the boiler. He put his head on his paws and feigned immediate sleep.

'Goodness Margery, you've worn poor that dog out, wherever have you been?'

'Not that far, Auntie, just up to the Palace Hotel and back.'

'Lunch will be ready in half an hour, would you set the table, please?'

Carrie's kitchen led into a breakfast room, where the three of them would eat lunch.

Margery took a Morris & Co willow leaf pattern tablecloth out of a fitted sideboard drawer and spread it on the wooden utility table Alec and Carrie had bought after their war-time wedding. Serviettes and the familiar mats with John Constable's pictures on and matching coasters followed. The knives and forks came from the canteen on the built-in sideboard.

'Shall I put spoons out at well?' asked Margery.

'Yes please,' came the answer.

They sat down to a lunch of fish pie and vegetables. There was rice pudding to follow. Margery savoured the home cooked food. Her appetite had returned after the walk, with Bobby, in the fresh sea air. The sickness that morning was forgotten.

The conversation over lunch was of holidays, books, her walk and the birds which were pecking away at the peanuts in the bird feeder hanging from the bare apple tree outside the window.

'On Sunday, the ramblers are going to walk along the sea front as far as the nudist beach and then inland to Havell cum Moze, across the marshes to Havell-on-the-Marsh and back here by lunchtime,' said Alec. 'Would you like to join us?'

'Yes, please,' said Margery.

'It will be an early start for a Sunday. It's an eight-mile round trip and we'll break for a drink at The Smuggler's Booty in Havell cum Mose. I don't think there will be many of us, winter rambles are not so popular. Did you bring your camera?'

'No, I never thought to bring that. Besides, I haven't got a film in it I can use.'

'We'll take my Retinette then; I've a slide film in it.'

'Make sure you are back in time for lunch, I've a rib of beef for Sunday?' said Carrie.

'We'll be back for that! No problem,' said Alec.

'I've been invited to a rehearsal of Priestley's "An Inspector Calls",' said Margery. 'I've to review it for my "Take a Pew at the Pollux" column for the Gleaner, the first public performance is a week tomorrow.'

'You'll have to return to Great Havell for that.'

'Yes, I must do that.'

'I'll come with you, Margery,' said Carrie. 'I haven't been to the theatre for some time.'

'It's a dress rehearsal, Auntie, is that all right?'

'Yes, I've not seen a play for a while. I shall enjoy going with you. What time is it?'

'We've to be there before 3.00 pm to catch the whole rehearsal.'

'Let's lunch at the Little Havell Country Hotel tomorrow. I'll drop you two at the Pollux theatre and pick you up later,' said Alec.

Margery collected up the dessert plates and started to wash up in the kitchen. Carrie supplied a couple of new tea towels and filled up the kettle.

Alec dried the plates and saucepans and put them away.

They all went to sit in the front room to have tea. Margery sat on the ottoman in the bay window. She put her teacup and saucer on the windowsill and stretched out, beginning to feel relaxed after the rush of work and the shock of recent events. Somehow, she felt cocooned from it all here. She was surrounded by familiar things, including her grandfather's collection of classic books in the built-in glazed bookcases, either side of the fireplace. The open log fire was pleasant to look at but did not give out much heat. Margery put her hand on the warm radiator behind the ottoman.

'I'm singing in the choir in a concert at St Luke's this evening,' said Alec, 'Would you like to come, Margery?'

'Yes, please,' she replied. She was beginning to feel more content. Somehow, the bad events of the past few days were becoming more distant, although they were constantly at the back of her mind. She picked up a copy of the Times and began to read it.

There had been arrests and injuries in a major clash between police and print union demonstrators outside the News International building in Wapping, where the Times was now based. There was a front-page picture of the violence.

Margery glanced out of the window. All was quiet in the suburban street which ran down to the sea front, she noticed. Trees were bare, except for the evergreens and in her uncle's front garden, there were snowdrops in bloom and crocuses in bud. It seemed a world away from London, where, she reflected, skilled men had been put out of work and replaced by computers. It was progress, she thought, but progress which, by building a fortress for the Times staff, who were still needed, had arbitrarily imposed a computerised system on them. The management could have introduced the computers gradually and phased out staff, if necessary. Perhaps they could have retrained them on a new system. Print workers had seven-year apprenticeships. It was a craft which required intelligence and skill. No doubt the Gleaner group would invest in this kind of machinery too, eventually. Margery wondered what would happen to the print works in Great Havell. The story was the Times version of events, written from within the heavily secured, ugly building. The violence of the demonstrators had resulted in injuries to two of the policemen.

Elsewhere in the paper were comments on the movement towards greater integration of the European single market with the agreement of the member states to form the European Union which would have a European Parliament, democratically elected by "universal suffrage".

Margery felt herself nodding off over this article, in spite of the noble aims which were being described as the future for Europe. She decided it was time to look at the Gleaner. After all, Gloria had already shown her a print of the front-page picture of her poor pet cat strung up on a make-shift gibbet, which had been crudely constructed with two trimmed inverted broomsticks, expertly lashed together, and secured into the top of the mound. The contraption had a thin wire noose hanging off it, from which poor Growltiger had been cruelly suspended. It was horrible in every way. Was she, in particular, targeted? Or was her poor ten-year-old cat just in the wrong place at the wrong time?

'I'll have a look at the Weekender Gleaner now,' said Margery, getting up and passing her empty teacup to her aunt for a refill.

'Are you sure, dear?' said Carrie, taking the proffered cup.

'I'm sure. I need to know any details. I'm over the shock. It's unbelievably cruel, but I need to know. So many disturbing events have occurred around the old priory and the Glebe Mound recently.'

Silently, Carrie handed Margery a replenished teacup and saucer with one hand and the folded Weekender Gleaner with the other.

Margery took them both back to the ottoman.

"CRUEL JAPE OR MOUND CURSE?" Ran the front-page headline with a large photograph of poor Growltiger suspended from the gallows, caught in the light of a powerful flashgun, with his eyes firmly shut and what looked like a thin wire garrotte under his chin. Margery gave an involuntary shiver and saw her aunt and uncle exchange a concerned glance as they watched for her reaction. She read:

"Neighbours of the old priory and the Glebe Mound are keeping their pets firmly behind closed doors today." Began the text, "One of their treasured marmalade cats, a tom, was cruelly killed and displayed on a gibbet on top of the Glebe Mound.

"The pampered moggy had been garrotted with wire and strung up on gallows made from two witches' broomsticks. These had been lashed together.

"Although most residents were in at the time, it seems not one witnessed the grisly event. The top of the mound is clearly visible from the row of cottages below, the terraces of houses opposite the Glebe Mound in Priory Street and the Amicable Anarchist. The pub was shut at the time local police were alerted to the bizarre spectacle.

"'That cat could be a nuisance,' said Priory Cottages resident, Alf Rudge, 'but we had all become fond of it around here.' (*Hypocrite*, thought Margery.)

"'I saw that going after something on the bridle path yesterday afternoon and I heard my neighbour calling after him in the evening, but by that time it was dark. It beats me, you know, I mean, who would do a thing like that to my neighbour's pet?' added Mr Rudge."

According to the article, other residents of Priory Cottages had been contacted by the Gleaner for comments and they were asked if they had witnessed any unusual activity on the mound, but it seems nothing was seen. Margery noticed the front-page solus ad was for the Pampered Pets grooming salon.

She wondered if she had seen something when she cycled back from Root and Branch. She looked up from the paper and mentioned it.

'I thought I saw something when I cycled back from the nursery.'

'What time was that?'

'I'm not sure, twilight or dusk; it would have been sunset if the sky had not been so overcast.'

'I was back in the cottage at about five. Thinking about it, I thought I saw three shadowy figures up there when I cycled by and thought I had imagined a gallows or gibbet, but as I cycled round the mound and glanced up again, I thought I was seeing things, the light was so poor. There are so many legends about ghosts and ghouls up there. I had a really bad feeling about it. I see the mound every day from my kitchen window and I don't, usually, have any feelings of threat or menace.'

'Sometimes you have to go with your gut feelings about things,' murmured Alec. 'I'm glad you didn't take it in your head to investigate; it would be just like you to do that.'

'There's more, Uncle. Jonah has said he has asked for a coroner's inquest into Barney Cobbler's death. He said there were sensitive archives stolen, which he and Barney were investigating. He said the local police are looking into that. Great Havell police have been encouraged by the mayor to enlist the help of a Scotland Yard detective, because people are saying the deaths, there has been another one, are linked to the cancellation of the Moyen Midden Fayre this year. The Moyen Circle runs the event every year. There are quite a few members in the local police force. They are angry with the mayor.'

'And what is your gut feeling about that, Margery?' asked Alec.

'I know there is a lot of anger about the cancellation of the fair. What I can't understand is why they don't hold it in conjunction with the concert or on a different date. I know feelings are running high about it, but I can't imagine anyone would stoop to bumping off a local historian. That's ludicrous!'

'Is the detective coming to look into both deaths? Will the body found in the former sinkhole be investigated too? I thought from the report in the Gleaner, the person had fallen in and died from hyperthermia, the weather being rather cold.'

'I suppose it's possible that has happened,' said Margery.

'I think you know more than you are telling us,' said Alec, watching her carefully. Margery sighed.

*He knows me too well*, she thought.

'I can only surmise certain things from what I have seen,' she said, picking up the Weekender Gleaner again to finish the front-page story and turning to page three.

'"It was when I walked by the Amicable Anarchist, when I had closed my stall,' said a market trader, 'I glanced up at the Glebe Mound and saw the gallows against the sky with something suspended from it. I hadn't the time to go up there and look, so I went to the police station and alerted the police.'

"A Great Havell police spokesman said there were two police constables on duty in the area at the time. They went to the top of the Glebe Mound and pulled the gallows out of the ground. It is being tested for fingerprints.

"The owner of the cat is invited to retrieve the remains of their pet from the station, as the police have some questions, they need answers to."

Margery read the last paragraph out loud.

'If you'd like to ring the police and make an appointment for tomorrow morning, I can take you both in the car, we could then bury poor Growltiger in your garden and have some lunch at your cottage, if you've got something in. After that, I can drop you and Carrie at the Pollux Theatre for your dress rehearsal viewing. How's that? We'll have to abandon plans for lunch at the Little Havell Country Hotel, but we can do that another weekend when you visit us.'

'Yes, I suppose it gets it all done. I wonder what the police want to question me about?'

'Maybe they think you did it yourself?'

'Oh dear, maybe they do!' Margery almost laughed at the idea, although she still felt a sick at the thought of what had happened to Growltiger.

Uncle Alec's bass baritone voice was sought after in choirs all over the Havell Hundreds. Margery found herself enjoying the visit to St Luke's that evening and the mixture of secular and devout music in the concert. It finished with Schiller's "Ode to Joy". *What an uplifting way to end the concert*! thought Margery, as the music of Beethoven's Ninth symphony filled the vaulted Victorian interior of St Luke's. It had been adopted as the European anthem, she reflected. The three of them walked home through the quiet streets of Havell-Next-the-Sea together and enjoyed bedtime drinks before bed.

## Saturday 8th February

The sun shone into the breakfast room when Margery sat down to an early breakfast with her uncle and aunt. The conversation was about Margery's appointment with the Great Havell police. Alec and Carrie decided to walk to the Cosy Café for morning coffee and they could all meet up in Dewbury and Hicks Restaurant for a light lunch at 1.00 pm. Her aunt and uncle wanted to look for a small sofa-bed to fit in the study for when Margery's cousin and his family stayed with them. Alec had been doubtful Dewbury's would stock anything as useful as a sofa-bed with their rather old-fashioned policies. Margery assured him the youngest generation of the family had brought the store more up to date.

Margery felt better about the drive back to Great Havell. She was in good time for her appointment at the police station and was shown into an interview room by Sergeant Taylor, who introduced her to Detective Inspector Barker of Scotland Yard. They all sat down. She felt she was being treated as a suspect.

'So, what do you mean by stringing up your cat, on makeshift gallows, at the top of the Glebe Mound?' was the first question from DI Barker.

Margery was, for a moment, at a loss for words. She looked at the detective for some clue as to his motive for asking such a direct and insulting question. She thought she detected a slight twitch in the corner of his mouth, although it could have been imagination. She took her time to answer, feeling her eyes filling up with tears at the reminder of the image of her poor pet.

Sergeant Taylor looked in alarm at DI Barker and then worriedly at Margery who answered the DI slowly and carefully as she blinked away the tears. She even felt herself flush with annoyance.

'What makes you think,' she said in a choked voice, 'I would kill my own pet cat in such a cruel and bizarre way?'

DI Barker seemed to relax with that reply. There was a pause.

'I didn't think you did, but I wanted to shock you into telling me something about it and the other deaths. I'm not here to investigate the death of your cat. Sergeant Taylor tells me you have a good local knowledge and contacts. I am new to the area. I've never been to this place before. I am looking into all these mysteries with an unbiased fresh pair of eyes. The body found on the Glebe Mound, in a sinkhole, which I understand is part of something which is quaintly called the Moyen Midden, was that of a local drinker, she was known as Sadie. Her partner was arrested for questioning.'

*So, Sadie was dead*, thought Margery, *that's the reason she hadn't seen her. Eric had been arrested in connection with her death and possibly Barney's.*

'Let's start with Barney Cobbler. Do you know if he had enemies?'

Margery's immediate impression of the DI, once she had recovered from his direct and upsetting first question, was of a man dressed a little eccentrically in a double-breasted grey suit with wide lapels, a blue shirt and a tie with an art deco pattern on it. Although he was seated, she noted he was a tall man with a slight frown on his regular features and receding dark brown hair.

DI Barker's direct approach reassured Margery. Yes, she did know both victims personally. No, she could not tell him anything of how or why they died or if they had enemies. No, she didn't mind having her fingerprints taken to compare with those on the broomsticks, the railings of the priory and the bottle of cider found near the sinkhole in the Moyen Midden pit on the Glebe Mound. No, she didn't think Eric Bolton was a dangerous murderer. Yes, she agreed, there was no harm in releasing him on the bail his rich family had put up. Yes, DI Barker could drive her to her cottage, and she would show him where she had last seen Sadie and where Barney used to go for his walk every morning. No, she had not seen anything which could give him a clue on how they had died. She only knew of their deaths from the Gleaner and that Barney's would have a coroner's inquest.

DI Barker's black BMW 3 series saloon car was powerful and smooth. When Margery was in the passenger seat in the police station car park, he started the engine and there was a burst of unfamiliar but cheerful jazzy music, which the DI immediately switched off.

'You've a radio in the car,' remarked Margery.

'That's a tape deck,' came the short reply.

'That sounded like something from a vintage film,' said Margery.

'I collect dance music from the 1920s and 30s,' said the DI curtly. 'Now tell me where to drive to the site where you last saw Sadie, where your cottage is, where your neighbour last saw your cat and where Barney Cobbler used to walk every morning.'

Margery directed DI Barker out of the marketplace, round the road by the Amicable Anarchist and to the car park by the old priory ruins.

'Is there any other way into the priory?'

'Yes, there is the track which runs in the front of Priory Cottages, where I live, and ends by the priory railings.'

Margery retraced the steps she took on the morning she had last seen Sadie. She explained Sadie had been drinking from a bottle of strong cider and she thought she remembered she had seen her smoking a rolled-up cigarette, as she usually did. She said she'd not had time to stop and chat, although Sadie had tried to attract her attention. She noticed DI Barker examining the priory railing fence and looking towards Sadie's familiar seat on the ruins. She then showed him the tyre tracks she had noticed, and they walked along the lane to Priory Cottages.

DI Barker had decided to walk to Margery's cottage rather than take his car round. She looked in her front window and sighed. Sometimes Growltiger had been sitting on the windowsill looking out for her.

Opening her front door, Margery warned DI Barker to mind his head, so he stooped to enter her cottage. He looked round at the phone, the angle poise and typewriter on the small desk, her shopping trolley, her chair and small settee. He stepped through into the kitchen taking care not to hit his head on the low lintel, after Margery's warning, and glanced into her bathroom. It was chilly in the cottage; she had turned her night storage heaters down low.

'What possessed you to live in a place like this?' asked DI Barker.

Once again, Margery was taken aback. The implied criticism, and his apparent contempt was obvious.

'I have everything I want and need here,' she answered slowly, flushing with annoyance.

Barker gave her a sharp look as he unbolted and unlocked her back door. He went into the garden and looked up at the Glebe Mound.

'Can you walk on that from your garden easily?' he asked.

'Yes.'

'What's in here?' he asked, trying the shed door.

'My bike,' she said, unlocking it and showing him.

Margery locked the shed and the back door. She decided her moccasins would do for the walk on the mound as it was dry. She led him through her back gate, across the bridle path which ran between the cottage gardens and the Glebe Mound and on the winding path which went to the top.

They were looking down on Priory Cottages.

'Who lives in there?' Barker was pointing towards 1, Priory Cottages, nearest to the old priory.

'It's rented by a couple of students.'

'What about next door?'

'It's a weekend cottage. Sometimes it's let out. Sometimes the owners stay there. It's often empty, which is just as well, because the students usually have their music on full volume. I can hear it when I walk by.'

'What about next door to you on that side?'

'That's Alf Rudge,' replied Margery. 'He was always shutting my cat in his coal bunker.'

'Why did he do that?'

'He said it was because my cat was always shitting in his garden.'

'So, he would rather it shit in his coal bunker?'

'Well, when you put it like that, I suppose he would! I hadn't thought of it like that.'

'What sort of a neighbour is he?'

'Very nosey. He is always out in his garden watching out for me to find out who is visiting me, or where I am going. I will guarantee he'll want to know who you are.'

'What will you tell him?'

'I'll tell him who you are?'

'So that's Mr Nose on that side, who is on the other side?'

'That's Florence. She is usually sitting in the window knitting when I go out. She has a large family. They often visit her and take her out shopping. Her grand-children play in her garden in good weather and she takes them on the Glebe Mound and into the old priory. They climb about on the ruins and play hide and seek in them. They are very noisy Alf never stops grumbling about them when they visit Florence and so do her other neighbours.'

'And what are they like?'

'I don't know the couple, but Florence does. They are always together, if they go out. They are always arm in arm and look carefully in everyone's garden and criticise and complain if they think there is anything wrong or if it is untidy. They got Florence to cut down her apple tree and it died. They keep trying to complain to their neighbour, Mrs Smith, on the other side, because the garden there is very overgrown, but she doesn't take any notice. They've even put weed killer or something on the plants near the fence, you can see where they've died, but she still hasn't taken any notice. She's a bit of a recluse. Keeps herself to herself. She has family visit, who do her shopping in a trolley. I noticed it because it is exactly the same as mine. When she goes out, she takes a taxi. It usually parks at the end of the terrace, so I don't see it, unless I am up here. She is rather bent and walks with a stick. I always say hello to her when I see her, but I only ever get a mumble in reply.'

'Now *that*,' said DI Barker, 'is interesting. Why on earth is such a fuss made of this place?'

Once again, Margery noticed the implied criticism and contempt in his question.

'Traditions and history,' was her short reply as she led the way round the mound to where there was a view of the Amicable Anarchist, surrounded on both sides by its Edwardian terraces of houses.

'From the top of the Glebe Mound, there is a better view of the town centre and part of the market square,' she said.

'How many people have died on this mound?'

'I don't know of many recent deaths, apart from Sadie. There may have been some. The local librarian or members of the Moyen Circle might know. Mainly it was the monks of the priory when it was closed, and the six witches hanged on the top. Those executions were more than 400 years ago.'

'So now there's an almighty fuss because there are two deaths on and near this place and some local fair was cancelled in favour of a pop concert. And I get dragged down here at the weekend to investigate them.'

Margery didn't reply. She showed the DI the view from the top and the route of the walk Barney took every morning.

'Do you think the poor blighter might have seen something that morning?'

'He might have, he took the same walk every morning before work almost without fail. You can see the roof of his house from here, look, it's that timber-framed house with the ornate chimney and a gable wing at each end. There's the turning from the Market Road and Barney's house is the second house in, next door to the insurance offices on the corner.'

'It's a big enough house. What did he do for a living?'

'He ran the local Inland Revenue office. He'd lived in the house all his life and inherited it when his parents died.'

'So why did he take drugs, or did he have any other sort of addiction which might have caused him to overdose?'

'Overdose!' This was new to Margery. Her surprise was obvious.

'Was he friendly with the man they arrested and is now out on bail?'

'He would be acquainted with him, as a lot of people were.'

'Can you explain what in the world a Moyen Midden is and why people bother to come to this place to see it?'

'I could,' said Margery, 'and I've just written and article about it. But it won't be published.'

'Why?'

'There's a panic on over revenues at the Gleaner, so I've been writing adver-tisement feature copy to try and drum up more advertising.'

'Any ideas why the revenues are down?'

'Not a clue,' replied Margery. 'I thought they were all doing fine and the advertising salespeople were spending their bonuses at the pub the other night.'

'What's the beer like there?'

'Good,' said Margery, 'it's real ale from the local Falcon brewery dispensed from hand pumps.'

Looking at DI Barker, she saw the ghost of a fleeting smile. He said: 'Have you a copy of your article on all this local stuff I could borrow?'

'I do, as it happens, although my editor doesn't know it. It was a lot of work to be spiked, so I kept a copy.'

'May I borrow it please, Miss Moore.'

Margery acquiesced. After showing DI Barker the view of the Root and Branch Nursery from the opposite side of the Glebe Mound, she showed him the padlocked grill covering the remains of the sinkhole where the medieval pottery had been discovered. She noted it looked as if some attempt had been made to wrench it off, it seemed to be damaged. She also saw DI Barker inspecting the two padlocks which held it in place. Margery led him down to her cottage and in at the back door. She put her copy of the articles Cheryl had rejected on the Havell-on-the-Marsh witches, the Glebe Mound and the Moyen Midden in an A5 envelope and handed it to the DI. He folded it into his breast pocket.

Margery was intrigued.

'Do you think these deaths could be anything to do with the cancellation of the fair?' she asked.

'I have no idea,' came the reply. 'I just want to read this stuff to find out what the inbred local people might imagine to be important. Thank you very much for your help, Miss Moore, I'm none the wiser for any of it. Goodbye.'

DI Barker left abruptly without offering her a lift back to the marketplace. She saw him from the window looking intently at all the cottages in the terrace and closely at the lane to the old priory as he walked back to his car in the car park the other side of the ruins.

Her cottage seemed empty without Growltiger, although he was often outside. Recently he'd been in the habit of jumping on her lap while she worked. She found it awkward with him there and often pushed him off. Once or twice, he'd jumped on the typewriter and locked some of the keys up, so she had to put him out of the way in the bathroom, take the cover off the keys and carefully put them back in position. She looked round her cottage thinking she would miss her cat. She found it hard to believe he would never come back. Margery locked up and was leaving from the front gate when Alf waylaid her.

'I'd like to know who that character was,' he said.

'DI Barker from Scotland Yard. He wanted me to show him the Glebe Mound.'

'Why? Is there something fishy about Cobbler's death?'

'Well, I don't know,' she replied, getting a bit irritated with Alf's questions.

'I'd like to know why they've got some detective from London snooping around here. I'd put him on to them Wiccan people and those weirdos who do funny things on the Glebe Mound.'

'You mean the Yoga Club?'

'Yoghurt, is it? Another stupid diet that makes them all fatter!'

Margery really hadn't got time for Alf deliberately mis-hearing her and moaning, so she said goodbye to him and walked off quickly. She went along the lane through the old priory and across the car park. She crossed the road to the Amicable Anarchist, walked along Priory Street and took the turning into the market square, where the Saturday market was in full swing. She walked briskly across to the other end of the square into Dewbury and Hicks. She took a lift to the top floor and joined Alec and Carrie in the panelled tearoom. They were sitting over a shared pot of tea in one of the windows which overlooked the market square. It was quite late, and Margery realised they had waited for her to have lunch. Although the weather was bright, it was a cold day and she was hungry. They all ordered bowls of soup served with granary bread. They had the teapot re-filled and the waitress brought a cup and saucer for Margery.

'How did you get on at the police station?' asked Carrie.

'I wasn't there that long. The DI from Scotland Yard took me home and wanted to look at the places where the bodies were found. He's very urbane. He seems to think we are all thick yokels round here.'

Alec looked amused.

'He's not going to get very far with that attitude,' he said.

'I don't know about that. He's asking some interesting questions, which is making me think. I really wasn't able to help very much, except with local knowledge. He resents being sent out to the sticks, as he put it, to investigate a couple of deaths.'

'I wonder why Mayor Grimes wanted someone from Scotland Yard to investigate.'

'Apparently, he thought the local police were too involved with people opposed to the cancellation of the fair to be able to take an unbiased view.' Margery laughed. 'I think our DI Barker is expecting to find the deaths are easily explained as self-inflicted and co-incidental and poor Growltiger was the victim of some superstitious children.'

'He's not taking any of it seriously then?' said Alec.

'I have no idea how he's taking it, he just objects to being sent here at the weekend, when he said he could be doing much more interesting things.'

'Well, it's all a rum business anyway. So, you've been back to your cottage?'

'Yes, I was quite glad to be back. The Moyen Circle has offered to bury Growltiger in the pet cemetery in Thorpe Park. I have accepted that offer. I thought it was kind of them. I think the whole sorry business will go into local folklore. Perhaps that was the aim of it.'

'Yes, that's a good way to think of it and I'm glad you can look at it that way. But I'm still pleased you are staying with us at the weekend. I can drive you in to the Gleaner on Monday, to collect your assignments for the week.'

*And then I can get on with some more work at home,* thought Margery. She was looking forward to getting back to her routine.

The waitress came to the table.

Would they like to order a desert?

Margery looked at her uncle and aunt, they all nodded to each other, they knew what they would like for dessert, a toasted buttered teacake each, served on a silver platter and kept warm under a silver dome. It was one of life's little pleasures. They had enjoyed them together before.

After lunch, they went to look at sofa-beds, selected one which would fit into the study and arranged for it to be delivered.

Carrie and Margery walked to the Pollux Theatre. It had been built in a grand style in the early years of the century. They arranged to meet Alec outside at 6.00 pm.

There were a handful in the audience for the dress rehearsal of J.B. Priestley's "An Inspector Calls." Margery had brought her notebook to review the play for her "Take a Pew at the Pollux" column, which would be published in the Weekender Gleaner on Friday, the day before the production opened.

Watching the play and sitting in one of the red velvet upholstered seats, in the ornate interior of the theatre, Margery immersed herself in the drama. Every character in the play was privileged in some way, although gradually, flaws in each of them were revealed. She found herself drawing parallels with people she knew but shook herself out of that line of thinking to admire the costumes, sets and acting.

Her "Take a Pew" column would recommend this production to her readers, although she did wonder how the theatregoers of Great Havell would like it. Priestly was highlighting a misuse of money, position and power in it. She doubted whether certain of the better off theatregoers would even recognise traits in themselves in the play. There would be audiences organised by the local theatre club, the Townswomen's Guild, The Women's Institute, the members of the Moyen Circle, students from the institute, the university, the grammar school and secondary schools, groups from Trincaster, the nearby cathedral city, and groups from the coastal towns and villages. This production was sure to be popular.

After the dress rehearsal, Margery introduced Carrie to the producer and director of the play and had a chat about the production. Had they been tempted to hint at the real identity of the Goole character? Was this Priestley's way of exposing the characters in the play? They discussed whether the name Goole was another spelling of ghoul and the play was about the family facing up to how they really were and not how they thought of themselves or expected others to think of them.

Margery looked up at the Glebe Mound as Alec drove them homewards. It was dark, and she could only see the shape of it. There seemed to be nothing on the top this time, although almost indiscernible shadows made by the moving clouds over the moon gave it an eerie presence in her mind and she thought of the executions, myths and legends associated with it. No wonder there were so many stories, with the way the shadows passed over it in the moonlight. She wondered if poor Growltiger would become a legend too.

Bobby came out of his basket, wagging his tail to greet them. Alec had been home to take him out whilst Margery and Carrie had been in the theatre.

Margery took Bobby out for a short evening walk towards the sea front and paused, for as long as he would let her, to look at the narrow silver liquid path of the moon on the sea. It was easy to understand how legends arose from moonlight and moon shadows she reflected, before she responded to the tug Bobby gave her on his lead, to head off back to The Avenue.


## Sunday 9th February

Sunday was cold and bright for the Rambler's Club walk. There were only five of them, apart from Margery. They were all about her uncle's age and talking about events at the golf club, plans for the summer theatre or planning the next ramble.

They stopped for refreshments at the Smuggler's Booty at Havell cum Moze, where the low beamed ceiling had yellowed from years of the regulars smoking in the pub. Margery noticed a lingering and not unpleasant aroma of pipe tobacco and beer in there. They all gathered near the wood fire to enjoy a dark winter special ale from the Falcon brewery which was on hand pump from the bar. The horse brasses, above the bar and on the bressummer beam above the fireplace, were bright, polished, and shone in the winter sunshine.

Refreshed and replenished, they rambled through the village. Margery noticed the little Victorian chapel she had visited for a feature, when it was sold for redevelopment, was now occupied. The large gothic window near the road had an equally large lace curtain obscuring the interior. Denzil Bream of Bream Estate Agents had insisted on taking her to see it, when it was for sale. He drove her there at speed in his Jaguar sports car. Unfortunately, Cheryl had given him her home phone number and he had been very insistent on picking her up and taking her to see it. She did not enjoy his driving, which, she felt, had been unnecessarily fast. He had been impatient with her questions about the property, which he couldn't answer and always seemed to take a long loud sniff, before he said anything. He'd also rung her up and objected to her article when it was written. She had been looking in the newspaper archives and found some interesting stories about the chapel, and the Havell cum Mose people, to write about. Denzil Bream had expected her to write what little he had told her, she reflected.

Once through the village, the ramble continued along a sea wall to Havell-on-the-Marsh, where Margery noticed the crossed brooms above the door of the Witches Cauldron cafe were missing. So that was where poor Growltiger's gallows had come from. She would go over there for a pot of tea tomorrow afternoon and ask what had happened to them. The site, where the old hermit hut and the witches' cottages of Havell-on-the-Marsh had been, could be seen in the distance. There were a few caravans on there now, used by city dwellers at weekends. One of them was a painted Romany caravan, which looked rather attractive and seemed to have a well-tended garden around it.

As they walked back to Havell-Next-the-Sea, the conversation turned to the new production at the Pollux, so Margery recommended the other ramblers see An Inspector Calls when they had the chance. The production design was set in the 1930s, she told them, which reminded her of DI Barker, his music taste and his wide-lapelled, double-breasted suit.

The conversation inevitably turned to the forthcoming productions at the summer theatre and the big names who were likely to come to the end of pier shows at nearby Sandy Reach. Margery mentioned the Moyen Midden Fayre had been cancelled that summer, but that Gary and the Fly by Night Boys would be putting on a concert there instead with local band Jollity supporting them.

The news was a surprise to the other ramblers, although Alec knew about it. She also mentioned the sudden death of Barney Cobbler, which was coincidental with the announcement the fair had been cancelled.

There was a lot of surprise in the group and one man, who knew Barney quite well, was very shocked at the news. 'But he was a fit man,' he said. 'Nothing wrong with him at all.'

'It's been suggested Barney had a problem with drugs or alcohol,' she said, without giving away the information DI Barker had given her.

'Absolute nonsense,' was the reply. 'I should know, I was his G.P. for years.'

'But you might not necessarily know, if he was taking something now,' persisted Margery.

'He was a blood donor,' came the reply, 'they'd have picked up on an illicit drug habit easily. It's a loss. Barney's blood group was quite rare, and the General Hospital often ran out. It would have to be helicoptered in when there was an urgent need for it.'

*So*, thought Margery, *Barney's death was definitely suspicious*. It was quite possibly murder. Perhaps she would learn more at the coroner's inquest.

She and her uncle said goodbye to the group at a bus stop and caught the bus to be back in time for lunch.

'I'll take the train to Great Havell tomorrow,' said Margery.

'I'll give you a lift to the Gleaner, no problem,' said Alec.

'I'd rather take the train, if you don't mind,' said Margery. 'There are a few things I would like to check out.'

'As you wish,' said Alec. 'Does that mean you'll not be staying here anymore?'

'Actually, it means I will be staying here, if that is all right with you and Aunt Carrie,' said Margery, thinking she would use her cottage for working in, as it was quiet, and she had everything she needed there. She could also go back to her old routine of taking her copy to the Gleaner in the shopping trolley, getting in some food for lunch, and, even, having a gossip with Gill and Philippa. Yes, normality was what she needed, but it would still be nice to go back to Havell-Next-the-Sea in the evening and perhaps take Bobby for a walk.

As they entered the arched porch and opened the front door, the delicious smell of Carrie's Sunday lunch greeted them in the hall, where they took off their walking boots and outdoor things.

Margery went straight to the kitchen and asked if Carrie needed help, but it seemed she only had to set the table.

'Little Neil is here,' said Carrie, 'so set for him too.'

Margery's young cousin was in the front room, happily playing with Alec's old Hornby clockwork train. The track was all over the place. When she had set the table, put drinking glasses and a fresh, water jug out, she went into the front room and got down on the floor to play with Neil. She had to keep pushing Bobby away, who wanted to sniff every piece of track, engine, trucks and carriages. He watched everything which was going round the circuit.

It was just what she needed, to get down on the floor and play with Neil for half an hour.

Lunch was roast beef, Yorkshire pudding, early spring greens, carrots, creamed swede and roast potatoes, followed by apple and blackberry pie and custard. The apples were from the tree in the garden and Margery had helped Alec pick the blackberries on an autumn ramble. They had been kept in the large chest freezer in the garage.

Carrie had no objection to Margery staying for as long as she wished. Little Neil was picked up and taken home by her cousin and she, her aunt and uncle went to Evensong at St Luke's, as Alec was singing in the choir. *It's all pleasant, comforting and familiar,* Margery thought, but she wanted a lot of questions answered in Great Havell and was looking forward to going back to her cottage, even if it was just to work.

## Monday 10th February

It took Margery about twenty minutes to walk from Great Havell station, turn from Station Road into Priory Street to the old priory and through the ruins to her cottage. As it was still fairly early, she noticed there was a light on in the Moonlight Motors office on the corner of Station Road as she walked by. She was surprised to see Gloria in there, wearing her distinctive red-leather jacket and leaning over someone sitting at the desk. It was only when she had walked past the garage, she realised it wasn't Bill Walker with Gloria. Although, she only glimpsed him from the side, she had the impression it was actually Harry

Grimes, in his pin-stripe suit. For a while it puzzled her, but then she dismissed it from her mind, thinking she must have made a mistake.

She decided to use the front door to her cottage but found it to be obstructed when she opened it. It was wedged. Margery pushed harder and found there seemed to be something caught in the bottom of the door, as she tried to push it open, so it became more wedged. She decided to close the front door and use her back door key instead.

She walked round the row of cottages to the lane in between the cottage gardens and the Glebe Mound and opened her back gate.

'You were out early this morning,' said Alf, who appeared out of his shed.

So, he had no idea she was not staying in her cottage last night, or Friday or Saturday night for that matter, thought Margery.

'Yes, I often take walk in the morning,' she replied, 'I'm surprised you've not noticed it before.'

'I've heard your phone ringing, but I think you've been out at lot this weekend,' replied Alf.

Margery was torn between liking the fact he was keeping a not particularly friendly eye on her and disliking his nosiness. All she said was, 'Yes.' Then she thought.

'Has anyone called round whilst I've been out in the past few days?'

'There might have been someone Saturday night. I think I heard the door-knocker, but I don't hear so well these days.'

Margery decided politeness and gratefulness was the best policy.

'Thank you, Alf,' she said and let herself in the kitchen door.

Everything was as she and Uncle Alec had left it on Friday. She went into the front room to see what was impeding the front door from opening.

It was a rag doll and lots of twigs, some of which were sticking into the doll. It had been wedged under the front door, from when she had tried to open it.

'What on earth?' she said aloud. 'Why would anyone want to shove a rag doll and a load of twigs through my letter box?'

She picked it up and gasped when she saw the face. Someone had painted and dressed it, to look like her. They had put glasses, some woolly golden-brown curls on the doll and a tartan beret and cape. It was clearly intended to be a sort of witch's doll. It had a few twigs sticking in it at various places. Who would be so mean as to make a rag doll, which crudely resembled her, and shove it through her letterbox? She went to a kitchen drawer and took a plastic bin liner from a roll, put on her rubber gloves, picked up the doll with the twigs sticking in it and put them in the bin liner. She pulled hard at a few twigs still wedged under the door and put them in as well.

She rang Great Havell Police.

'Could I speak with DI Barker please?' Margery looked at her watch; it was only just after 9.00 am. *Good, he probably wouldn't have gone out and if he was working from the police station, he would be there.*

'Who?' asked the duty sergeant.

'He is Detective Inspector Barker. I believe he's from Scotland Yard.'

'Oh, do you mean the bloke using one of the interview rooms as an office?'

'I don't know, it could be.'

'There's a phone outside, I'll see if I can get him to answer it.'

Margery heard another phone ringing. It went on for a long time. Then she heard the DI's voice answer, and some of his jazzy music playing in the background.

'I'll put the phone down now,' said the duty sergeant.

'Yes, what is it?' the DI sounded irritable, and she could just hear him over the music.

'I've found a rag doll and a lot of twigs inside my front door.'

'A lot of what? Hang on a minute.' There was a long pause and the music stopped.

Barker came back to the phone.

'Who's this?'

'It's Margery Moore, I've found a load of twigs, some of them stuck in a rag doll, inside my front door.'

'Twigs? A doll?'

'Yes, twigs and a doll.'

'What have you done with them?'

'I've put them in a bin liner for now.'

'Why are you ringing me up about it?'

'I think the twigs might belong to the trimmed broomsticks which were used to make the gallows my cat was hanged on. The doll's face has been crudely painted to look like me and it's wearing the sort of clothes I wear.'

'I'll be right over to collect them.'

'Thank you, I'll see you soon.'

DI Barker was at her cottage in ten minutes, parking his black BMW outside, with the jazzy music blaring from it. It stopped when he switched the engine off.

Margery let him in and handed him the bin liner. He looked inside.

'What's your explanation for these?'

'That they belong to the witches' brooms used to make the gibbet on Thursday evening. I think the doll was going to be hanged on the gibbet, but they decided to hang my cat instead.'

'You are very precise about that! Are you sure you didn't make the thing yourself?'

'Why would I want to do something like that?'

'Create stories for the local rag? You say revenues are down.'

Margery found herself getting angry with him. She went red with annoyance.

'You think what you like,' she said.

'I will,' was the reply. Without saying goodbye, Barker picked up the bin liner, turned round, opened the front door, bent his head under the lintel and let himself out.

Margery heard her door shut, the gate clicked, the purr of a powerful engine, some jazz music, and a receding sound from his car being driven in reverse down the lane to the road.

She began to feel both angry and upset.

The phone rang. It was Cheryl. Could she go into the Gleaner offices? She had a load more work for her. Margery said she would be on her way soon.

She changed out of her jeans and into her tartan skirt, black jumper and cape. She made herself up carefully, found her brimmed hat with the tartan trim, put her notebook and pencil into the shopping trolley and set off.

'So sorry about your cat,' said Philippa as Margery, shopping trolley in tow, entered the front office of Gleaner.

'So am I,' she confirmed.

'Who would do such a nasty thing?' asked Gill. 'I was really upset when I heard. Do you think it was some sort of prank?'

'You tell me,' said Margery, looking from one to the other.

'Well,' said Philippa, 'some of the reporters think it's funny and keep joking about it. But now all the talk is about the body found in the Moyen Midden pit.'

'I heard about that,' said Margery, thinking, they had not released Sadie's name.

'Yes, I expect you've seen the front of today's Gleaner. They've not said whose body it is; it might be medieval for all we know.'

'I'll take a copy of the Gleaner,' said Margery, glancing at the headline "DEATH AFTER GLEBE MOUND RESCUE" as she picked it up.

'People have come to the Gleaner to say they saw you coming from the direction of Priory Cottages and walking on the mound and going up to the top. It's being widely suggested you were party to what happened to your cat.'

Margery found herself getting angry again. She went red. What was going on? Had she made enemies in Great Havell? It didn't seem to be possible.

She was about to give a sharp reply, when she found an arm round her.

'Sorry to hear about your pussy, honey,' said Harry Grimes, who had just come into the front office and moved his arm down to her bottom and gave it a squeeze.

Margery was so annoyed, she felt like turning round and punching him in the face but moved out of his way, put the Gleaner in her shopping trolley, went smartly through the door and into the newspaper offices.

She walked straight into Cheryl's office, shopping trolley in tow, ignoring a scowl from Gloria when Cheryl nodded her to come in.

'Are you OK?' asked Cheryl sympathetically.

'Perfectly,' said Margery, still angry with Harry Grimes presumption.

Cheryl looked at her a bit apprehensively.

'Thank you for all that work last week, the reps are doing a fine job on selling around it. I've got a lot more for you.'

'Why are revenues down?' asked Margery 'Why can't you publish all the articles I wrote about the Glebe Mound?'

Cheryl was not used to Margery being so direct. She looked at her again, looked up to the ceiling and then said:

'I don't think it's any of your business, why revenues are down. You are not employed here, only on a freelance basis. You take the work I give you. If you don't want to do it, I can get one of the other freelance writers to do it. It's not your place to ask questions. We're not publishing that historic stuff. It's not what our readership wants any more. It's all ancient history. There is no interest in Great Havell for those tired old stories. We're a local newspaper. We report contemporary stories, not old ones and certainly not ancient ones. You can take the work I give you or leave it.'

'I'll take it then,' said Margery shortly.

Cheryl waited for her to say more, but no more was forthcoming, so she gave Margery a list with phone numbers.

Margery took it without even glancing at it.

'I'll make these appointments at home. I'll do them in my own time. I pushed myself to get all that stuff, on the Glebe Mound and the witches, researched and written. I worked hard on the interviews and to write up the eight advertisement features, you gave me. My pet cat has been killed. I've not got the patience to listen to excuses about how the Gleaner finances have been mismanaged. I am certainly *not* going to be bullied over getting work done to a deadline because of it. I've obliged up to now, but you might have to wait for these. You've had quite enough from me to be going on with.'

Cheryl looked at her open-mouthed. She considered Margery to be more than a colleague, a friend. Well, she had just lost her cat and she did live on her own. She was probably having a bit of a funny turn.

'I do appreciate what you do, Margery,' she said.

'You've sometimes got a funny way of showing it, Cheryl. I went to see the dress rehearsal of "An Inspector Calls" at the Pollux on Saturday. I haven't typed my review up, but that is the next piece of copy I will bring in. It will be in good time for the Weekender Gleaner deadline.'

Cheryl was silent for a moment; she didn't want to upset Margery, she was too good a writer and too useful to her.

'Where were you at the weekend?' she asked.

Margery was still angry; she felt a bit wicked.

'Lying low in case the police caught up with me,' she said.

'I had heard people are saying you organised that prank with your cat.'

'I know.'

'Well, did you?'

Margery found herself getting impatient with Cheryl.

'How long have we known each other?' she asked.

'About eight or more years.'

'And you really think I am capable of killing my own cat and stringing him up on some bizarre homemade gibbet?'

'No, Margery, of course not. I'm sorry, I'm under pressure here, everyone is. We're all being blamed for the fall in revenue.'

'And yet the salespeople were boasting of their bonuses in the Amicable Anarchist the other day. How come?'

'I shouldn't really tell you this, but there's a huge amount of advertising revenue missing, and no one knows where it's gone. The Gleaner has published as much display and classified advertising as ever, more if anything. But the revenues are still down.'

Margery was at a loss for words. There was a silence.

'Well, I never!' she said eventually, wondering if the Gleaner and therefore her job was on the way out.

'I'd best get on,' she added, deciding to do a bit of shopping and go home to make the appointments, but she wasn't going to rush these, she would take her time. She had things to find out and she knew exactly how she would do it.

Once she was home, with the shopping put away, the kettle on for a cup of tea, Margery sat in her chair and checked the list Cheryl had given her.

At the top was Bream Estate Agent, she hoped very much it was not going to be Denzil she would have to see there. He was bound to try and bully her into writing what he wanted, rather than an interesting angle for the readers. He had been at the opening of the Brass Monkeys Brasserie with his girlfriend, Tracey, who she met again at the Tanerife salon. Denzil didn't seem to recognise Margery at the Brass Monkeys. In fact, he never recognised her unless he wanted something. She'd noticed Denzil was very pally with the mayor's son, Berkley Grimes, and his girlfriend. They were also friends with proprietors, Morris and Mack. All of them had been knocking back quantities of champagne. It had been, Margery remembered, a very noisy evening. Morris and Mack stayed sober enough to be able to explain their ambitions for the brasserie. They intended, she remembered, the awning of the brasserie would shelter alfresco chairs and tables, when the weather was milder. In spite of the noise and celebrations at the opening, she had been able to learn enough about the restaurant for her article.

She made an appointment to visit the Old Granary Hotel and Grain of Truth Restaurant. *That would be an interesting one*, thought Margery, but she'd need her bike to get there. It was along the estuary, beyond the Brass Monkeys Brasserie and Cosy Café in Priory Street, near the riverside shops by the Quay Marina.

Great Havell Falcon Brewery was not too far away from the Old Granary Hotel. She hoped she might be able to have a tour of the premises and a sample of some of their ales. The last one on the list was a country clothing, gardening and an agricultural equipment supplier called William Fabb. This was a bike ride away as well. She made the appointments for the following afternoon.

Margery put her teacup and saucer on her desk, sat on her chair, ran through the list. She decided to arrange to go to Bream first, to get that out of the way. It was the one she was least keen to do. She made the appointment for after lunch. Afterwards, she could come back for her bike and cycle over to Havell-on-the-Marsh to find out when their broomsticks went missing and if they knew who took them. She typed up her review of "An Inspector Calls" and then had a lunch of baked beans on toast.

She picked up her bag with her notebook and pencils in and left from her front door for her appointment. She walked along the lane, through the old priory and the car park across Priory Street to the Amicable Anarchist, which was still busy. She turned into the eastern side of the marketplace, where she found the Bream Estate Agency near the corner. Margery took a picture with the E-type Jaguar outside.

Although she arrived ten minutes early for the appointment, and realised she would have to wait, she had not expected to wait half an hour.

Fortunately, there were plenty of magazines to read whilst she waited, but she nevertheless felt increasingly annoyed as the time went on.

Eventually, she was ushered into a back office by the rather miserable girl she had seen when she arrived earlier.

Denzil Bream was leaning back in a chair with his well-shod feet on the desk. Margery felt all the more annoyed. He didn't appear to have much to do and had kept her waiting because he wanted to. He didn't move his position, when she came in, or when she said a polite, 'good afternoon Mr Bream.'

He didn't bother to reply, but just nodded his head in the direction of the chair on the opposite side of the desk.

Denzil had shortish straight dark hair, brown eyes and Margery noticed, with increased annoyance, a bit of a knowing smirk on his angular face as if it had amused him to keep her waiting.

She sat down opposite him and selected a position in which his face was obscured by the leather soles of his shoes, so he couldn't see hers. She took her notebook and pencil out of her bag.

Denzil sniffed loudly.

Margery waited for him to say something, she wasn't going to make things easy for him after being kept waiting so long. There was a long pause and silence.

He didn't move or change his position, nor did Margery.

'What aspect of your estate agency did you wish to promote this month?' she asked politely, after what seemed like a few minutes silence. She repeated the question when there was no reply.

'(Sniff) New homes,' came an answer. Denzil did not shift his position and nor had Margery.

'Which particular new homes did you wish to promote?' she asked. This interview was proving to be hard work.

'(Sniff) The ones which haven't been built yet.' Margery became increasingly irritated, with him, after that answer.

'I made this appointment in good faith to write a feature which will promote your agency,' she said, getting up and realising she was flushing with annoyance. 'I take it you don't want me to do it.'

When she stood up and looked at him, Margery noticed he was grinning broadly. He still didn't change his position but looked up at her.

'(Sniff) If you're not going to do the job you are paid to do, I'll be making a complaint about you to the newspaper.'

'Do!' she replied, becoming angry. She put her notebook and pencil in her handbag and made for the door.

That got him up. '(Sniff) OK, OK, it's a new estate which will be near the new bypass when that is built.'

Margery took her notebook and pencil out of her bag.

'So, what is coming first? The road or the new homes?' she was still standing up and poised for an answer.

'New homes. There's some old farmer nearby objecting to the bypass and the homes. A bit of his land is needed. He can't hold out much longer.'

'Can you give me a map of the site and some details about the sort of homes you plan to have built? I'll write something on that,' she said, thinking she would go as soon as possible, before she completely lost patience with him.

Denzil sat down again and put his feet back on the desk. He reached forward and picked up his trim phone, dialling with the same hand.

'Janice, bring in the proposals and outline plans for the Monks Thorpe Estate and the designs for some of the houses to be built on it.'

There was a long pause whilst Margery and Denzil contemplated each other, neither wishing to continue a conversation. She was still keen to leave. She was tempted to take her camera out and take a picture of him leaning back in his chair with his feet on the desk, smirking.

Eventually, the unhappy Janice brought in two large glossy brochures and went to hand them to Denzil.

'Not for me, you stupid girl, give them to *her*.'

Margery noticed tears in the girl's eyes, who left as quickly as she could after she handed her the brochures. She followed her out of the door, glancing back as she closed it; Denzil had not moved.

Outside the estate agents, from that end of the marketplace, Margery caught sight of a bus going to Havell cum Mose which was being boarded. On impulse, she ran for it and was just in time to catch it. She decided she would get off at Havell-on-the-Marsh, go to the Witches Cauldron cafe to see if she could find out when their broomsticks went missing from the porch gable. They might even know who took them. Margery was on a mission. She paid her fare to the bus conductor and went up to the top deck to get a good view.

As the bus turned to leave the marketplace, she glanced towards an upstairs window of Bream Estate Agents and looked again in surprise. Seated at a desk, with his back to the window, was Harry Grimes. The bus had passed the building by the time Margery realised who it was and then she doubted what she had seen. He was wearing the pin-stripe suit and green shirt he had on, when she thought she saw him with Gloria in Moonlight Motors that morning and the same clothes when she had that annoying encounter with him at the Gleaner offices. What was he doing seated at a desk in Bream Estate Agents? Everything seemed to be a mystery these days. The bus turned towards the Cricklewater estuary and went past the Brass Monkeys Brasserie and the Cosy Cafe before turning towards Havell-on-the-Marsh.

The views were over the Cricklewater backwaters towards the harbour and the docks. It was a short journey, but Margery had a chance to glance at the glossy brochures Janice at Breams had given her.

One had a map on the cover with the proposed bypass in place and a slip road to the new Monks Thorpe Estate, with more detailed maps inside showing where the new homes would be built.

The other one had pictures of the proposed new homes on a particular part of the estate not served with the slip road from the new bypass. They were large, four, and five-bedroom houses, with double garages, described as "executive homes", which customers were invited to put deposits on.

Margery looked again at the detailed map on the first brochure, wondering how the homes would be accessed. There was a road, but it went to the council owned Home Farm. The executive houses, which were being offered for sale on deposit, were to be built on about a third of the Home Farm, which was, Margery thought, part of the green belt and council owned. How could that be? She rang the bell for the Havell-on-the-Marsh stop, went down the stairs and alighted from the bus. She walked along the road and into Marsh Lane towards the Witches Cauldron. After the difficult interview she'd had with Denzil Bream, she was completely unprepared for the hostile reception she was about to receive.

# Chapter IV
## Vlad's Story

The first thing Margery noticed, as she approached the cafe, was the crossed brooms, on the entrance porch gable, had been replaced. The large cauldron outside had been planted with crocuses which were beginning to show buds. Inside, the cafe was quite old fashioned. There was Lino on the floor, chintzy tablecloths and cushions on the dark wooden chairs. There were paintings by local artists on the walls, which mainly featured rural scenes, some of which were imaginary, with witches and wizards in them. She also noticed there were a set of six framed sketches of the varieties of herbs, Ruth Baldock had given her, which were named after the witches. She sat down and waited.

The young staff were ignoring her. They chatted quite happily to the other customers. Surely, they had seen her come in. She tried to attract their attention as they walked by, but they treated her as if she wasn't there. They were members of the family who owned the cafe and were studying catering at the local institute. She knew them as John and Joan, twins, but they weren't identical. In the end she stood up, wondering what to do, went over to John and waited until he had finished his conversation. But John turned his back on her, and she had to follow him to the door to the kitchen and grab his arm. He shook her hand off angrily.

'John!' said Margery. 'What is this all about? You know me, I come here sometimes for a pot of tea when I am walking on the marshes. I wrote a feature about the Witches Cauldron to coincide with the solstice fair last year.'

John turned round and glared at her and then looked at the brochure from Bream which she had put on the table she had been sitting at.

'Thinking of putting a deposit on a house which will be built on the Home Farm are you?' he sneered.

'Good lord, no!' said Margery. 'They can't build on there; it's council owned green belt.'

John looked at her for a moment, then at the brochure, then at her again.

'What are you doing with that brochure then?' he asked.

'I was given it by Denzil Bream, who I have just had great difficulty interviewing,' she replied, beginning to understand why the young man was angry.

'So, you are going to put it all in the paper, are you?' he asked.

'It's not my decision what goes in the paper. But I won't be writing about that estate, because it can't be right, whatever is in these glossy brochures.'

'Our uncle and aunt are the tenants of Home Farm,' explained John. 'Mum, Jean and I are very angry about this because these plans are worrying them and making them ill. They've not had notice to quit, but they've been told the council doesn't own the land after all. There will be nothing they can do when the real owners claim it back.'

Margery went to sit back at her table.

'That's appalling!' she said. 'Your uncle and aunt have been farming the land for years. I think, I hope, they may have long term tenancy rights to it.' She looked again at the glossy brochures for the plans and prototype houses for the Monks Thorpe estate. She put the brochures down on the floor, underneath her handbag.

'John, I don't understand any of this, but am not going to mention that estate is anything other than proposed in my article. I think it is completely wrong to offer them for sale when the land is council-owned and there are plenty of alternative sites for them to build on. But I would like a pot of tea, please.'

To her relief, the angry look left the young man's face when he smiled.

'Of course! I'm sorry! It was seeing you with those brochures angered me.'

Margery, relieved, wondered how she could broach the subject of the broomsticks outside, which had been replaced.

John brought her a pot of tea.

Whilst she was drinking it, Margery decided to look at the glossy brochures from Bream again. They were landscape format and quite large. She could not have put them in her handbag without creasing them, and she didn't want to do that.

There was a map on the front of one of them which showed where the development would be built. The housing seemed to spread over quite a large swathe of land belonging to the Home Farm. She could ask Uncle Alec about it when she saw him tonight. He'd know the legalities of it.

As she was looking, John came over to her table and asked if there were anything else he could get her.

'I'd like more hot water for the tea pot, please.' She was thirsty after the interview with Bream and her initial reception at the cafe. John took the pot away and filled it up for her.

He lingered by her table. 'Taking all that land from the farm for housing is a bleeding liberty!' he said angrily.

'I quite agree,' said Margery.

John looked at the brochure. 'Denzil Bream, Berkley Grimes, their girl-friends and Morris and Mack were all in here for coffee a few weeks ago. Bream was boasting his family had got a real property money-spinner. We realised afterwards this is what he was on about. He was taunting Berkley Grimes about new council housing to be built on his father's land, if the Grimes family were able to prove they had the rights to it.'

'Denzil Bream is a pain in the neck,' said Margery thinking this was a good time to broach the subject of the broomsticks. 'I noticed you've replaced the broomsticks over the porch gable with new ones. Was that because the old ones falling apart?'

'Nah. Some miserable blighter pinched them. Don't know why. Mum was really annoyed about it. She said she thought she heard something on Wednesday night, but she said she was too tired to get up and look out.'

*I wish she had,* thought Margery.

'I heard an engine that night,' ventured John. 'We don't hear many cars down here at that time of night.'

'What sort of engine?'

'It was a rumble.'

'What like a sort of throb?'

'Yes,' John brightened, 'yes, a sort of low throb, the kind of sound you are not quite sure if you are hearing.'

'It was distant then?'

'Yes, I guess, it must have been on the road, rather than down Marsh Lane.'

'Did it stop and start?' asked Margery.

'No, I thought someone in the village or in one of the caravans might have started up a generator. It was a cold night. I actually looked out, wondering if I would see some lights on, but everything was completely dark. I always have my window slightly open, even when it is cold, so I opened it a bit more and listened.

I heard nothing nearer, but then, if people were taking the broomsticks off the porch, I wouldn't necessarily hear them. They were only balanced on hooks and could easily be lifted, even in the dark, if someone knew they were there.'

'Was it moonlight when you looked out?'

'Yes, as a matter of fact, it was. While I was looking out, the noise of the engine seemed to get a little louder and then gradually more distanced.'

Margery was thinking hard. The people who took the broomsticks from the Witches Cauldron could have been in a sports car, which would make that kind of engine sound. One of them could sit in the car and the other could walk down the lane and unhook the broomsticks, take them up the lane to the car and they could drive off with little sound, except for the engine. As John suggested, it could be mistaken for a generator if the engine were kept running. Margery could imagine it all. She'd keep an eye out for someone with a sports car which had an engine which made the sound John described.

By this time, John's sister, Joan, had come in.

'I didn't hear anything,' she said, in answer to Margery's question. 'I sleep at the back. I didn't even hear an engine. Mum noticed the broomsticks were gone as soon as she opened up in the morning. We went to college, of course, and mum rang the college to give us a message. She wanted us to buy her replacement broomsticks before we came home.'

'Where did you buy them?' asked Margery.

'Root and Branch stock them,' answered Joan. 'They don't usually have them in the winter apparently, because they sell them for the events and especially at the fair. They said they would make two up for us. They make them for tourists coming to see the mound to buy for souvenirs. Mum went there and picked them up this morning and we've only just put the new ones up.'

Joan indicated the brochure. 'Can the Gleaner run a campaign to stop the developers taking all that farmland?' she asked. 'Our uncle rents that farm and he's going to struggle if he loses the land.'

'I have no influence over what goes in the Gleaner,' replied Margery, 'but I will mention it when I am next in the offices, which will be later in the week.'

Margery realised she had missed the bus she intended to catch. After she got off, it went through to Havell cum Mose and then on to Havell-Next-the-Sea, where it waited for half an hour, before it came back along the same route. She also realised she did not know when the next bus was, and didn't relish waiting for one as it was beginning to get dark.

She paid the twins for her tea and left the Witches Cauldron. She went up to the bus stop and into the red phone box which was next to it. Much to her annoyance, she found it had been vandalised. She was in half a mind to go back to the Witches Cauldron but realised there was another phone box outside a little group of cottages between Havell-on-the-Marsh and Havell cum Moze, so walked smartly in that direction. With relief, she found the phone in there was in working order and it would take her phone card, which had plenty of credit on it.

Aunt Carrie was in, Alec was out with Bobby, she said, but he wouldn't be long.

'I'm in between Havell-on-the-Marsh and Havell cum Moze,' said Margery. 'I've not got my bike with me.'

'Alec will come and pick you up, but he'll probably be at least half an hour; what will you do?'

'I'll walk back to the Witches Cauldron and wait there.'

'That's a good idea,' said Carrie.

Back in the cafe, which was about to close, Margery and the twins studied the brochures Denzil Bream had given her.

'Those houses will probably be very expensive, those executive ones,' remarked John. 'I wonder who will be able to afford them round here. I suppose we are in commuting distance of various other places, but we really need people who are going to live and work here.'

'There are some quite big employers in Great Havell and at Trincaster which is not too far from the site. As it is a walled cathedral city, there is a lot of restriction on development, more than we have in this area,' said Margery.

'I suppose so, but you can only have so many bosses in a firm. I can't see too many people affording big houses like that.'

'It would be daft to build large houses which couldn't be sold,' said Margery, 'and there are some smaller houses on the estate. I suppose they are aiming at families.'

'But these big houses are all designed to go on our uncle's farm… Well, it's not his farm exactly, but the one he rents. I know he's getting on a bit, but he and auntie really run that farm well. We loved going there as kids, didn't we, Joan? He's also worried about the affect the noise and fumes from the bypass will have on his animals.'

'I'll mention it when I'm next in the Gleaner. I'm surprised they've produced a brochure showing buildings on that land, but then, I suppose the council must have agreed to the development.'

'Now there's the sound of an engine,' said John, 'but it's nothing like the one I heard. And that one has been switched off.'

Within a few minutes, Alec, with an excited Bobby on a lead, had walked down the lane to the cafe.

In the car on the way home, as Bobby panted out of a, slightly open, back window, Margery told Alec about the proposed development which was going to take up quite a lot of the Home Farm.

Alec was puzzled. 'That's green belt,' he said, 'someone at the council must have made a mistake.'

Margery said that according to the house styles, the sort that would be built would be really expensive, gated, executive-style houses with double garages and large gardens.

Alec was surprised. 'I would expect green belt or farmland to be used if there was an urgent need and there were no brownfield sites in the vicinity. I am really doubtful councillors would have passed this through planning. You don't mind staying with us for a bit, do you?' he asked.

'No, it makes a nice change. With all the events recently, I'm quite pleased to be staying with you. I wonder if you know the answer to this one?'

'What's that?'

'I was having a drink with Jonah in the Amicable Anarchist the other day and a lot of the Gleaner advertisement salespeople came in boasting about their bonuses, but they were a bit shy of spending it in there. Then Harry Grimes the Gleaner's advertising director and Bill Walker of Moonlight motors came in. Harry Grimes took out a wad of notes and bought them all drinks.'

'Well, I expect he's better paid than the others.'

'He might be, but I think he has a family and a mortgage, the same as the others. Also puzzling me, the revenues at the Gleaner are so much down, I am having to write loads of advertisement features so they can sell more advertising around them.'

'How much down?'

'Seriously down, according to Cheryl, DI Barker was interested in that, I'm not sure why. Yet, the Gleaner is full of advertising every day. There are even letters of complaint about it. Too many ads and too little editorial. I cannot understand it.'

'Perhaps not all the advertisements are paid for?'

'That's a good point, we do have a lot of house ads.'

'Have you got a copy of the Gleaner with you?'

'No, I left it at home. I was intending to go home first, before I went to the Witches Cauldron, but then I saw the bus and decided I would catch that instead.'

'We might have a copy of the coastal edition of the Gleaner somewhere here. We can have a look at that and see how many house advertisements are in it. You could be right, there could be a lot of advertising which is not being paid for. That would explain why the revenues are down, or perhaps they are not charging enough for it.'

After a meal for the three of them in the breakfast room, Carrie rummaged in one of the scullery cupboards for old newspapers. She found a coastal Gleaner from a couple of weeks previously.

It seemed odd to be looking through a newspaper to read all the advertisements.

'There certainly are a lot of house ads,' said Margery. 'There is a big recruitment drive for advertisement salespeople.'

'Do they need a lot of salespeople?'

'I don't know. There are plenty of them working there at the moment, I haven't really noticed. Well, you saw it, there is a real push to sell advertising with them dancing round in the office singing "We are the Champions" every time a sales target of £500 is reached.'

'Yes, it was very noisy in there, with people on the phones and then dancing and singing. I was asked a few times if I could be helped, so I said I was already being looked after thank you very much.'

'Look! There is a specific advertisement for a property advertising sales representative. It's got one of those sketches of an executive house planned for the Monks Thorpe development. I've got the brochure with me, it's the same illustration.'

'Are those the houses planned for the Home Farm site?'

'Yes, I'll get the brochure. But obviously the advertisement is for recruitment, not new homes.'

'How much would the Gleaner charge for an advertisement this size?'

'I have no idea; what size is it?'

'I'll get a ruler from my desk.'

When they measured the advertisement, they found it was 15 centimetres by three columns.

'How much would that cost?' asked Alec.

'I don't know, but I suppose I could find out. I think those sorts of advertisement cost a lot more than the classified ones.'

Margery picked up the brochure from her bedroom and took it downstairs.

'There you are. This picture is of one of those artists' impressions of executive houses to be built on the Monks Thorpe Estate.'

'Let me look at the map on the front of the other brochure,' said Alec.

Margery passed it over to him.

'I see the development takes about a third of the land from the Home Farm, which is green belt. There must be some mistake. You say you have to write a feature about this development. It's going to be a difficult one, if there is no planning permission for parts of the site. I would be very surprised if the council would grant it to build on the green belt and farmland which is in use.'

'It does seem odd. I haven't read these brochures yet, but I see, from the back of this one, Bream have the sole agency for these houses and many of the other ones proposed.'

'Are you saying these brochures have been put out to sell the houses before they've been built? Or even have full planning permission?'

'Yes, I think so. You can put a five per cent deposit on a plot with Breams.'

'And they expect you to write this up in a feature?'

'Yes, I suppose they do. But there are no prices in the brochure, so anyone interested is going to have to contact Bream direct.'

'Goodness me! Would you put money down on a house that hasn't even been built?'

'I don't think I would and I'm not going to find writing this feature very easy.'

'Well, my girl, you always enjoyed a challenge, you can look at it like that!'


### Tuesday 11th February

Back in her cottage, after the short rail trip from Havell-Next-the-Sea to Great Havell, Margery found a bunch of daffodils in a milk bottle on her desk in water with a V and an X on a scrap of paper under the bottle. Vlad had been in. She smiled to herself. He was probably missing her. Never mind, she had a lot to do. Seated at her typewriter, Margery took up the challenge of writing a feature about the proposed new homes on the Monks Thorpe estate. She padded it out with a little information about the well-established family firm of Bream which would have sole agency for the homes.

That done, she made herself some tea and sandwiches and picked up yesterday's copy of the Gleaner to read: "DEATH AFTER GLEBE MOUND RESCUE." ran the front-page headline.

"A dog walker on the Glebe Mound discovered the unconscious body of a woman." she read. "The man, who does not wish to be named has revealed his story exclusively to the Gleaner. Less than a week ago, in the morning, he left his home on Glebe Estate and was walking by the Moyen Midden, when he noticed a woman's legs trapped under the grid covering the sinkhole. The rest of her appeared to be down the hole.

"Thinking she had got stuck, he called out to her and asked if she was alright.

"Getting no response, he thought he could try to pull the woman out, but realised she was unconscious and thought he might hurt her if he did. He walked his dog to the nearest phone box, by the Amicable Anarchist, and called an ambulance. The ambulance men together managed to manoeuvre the unconscious woman out of the sinkhole and from under the grill. They carried her down the mound and took her to casualty. She never regained consciousness and died soon after."

Turning to page five to continue the story, Margery found, opposite it, on page four, was a full-page advertisement encouraging local developers, builders and estate agents to advertise in the property supplement of the Weekender Gleaner. It featured the same map of the Monks Thorpe development, which was on Margery's brochure. It was a large free advertisement. No wonder revenues were down.

On page five, the story continued. "Great Havell Police have identified the woman and it is understood her next of kin has requested an inquest into her death. This will be held on Thursday afternoon. A Great Havell Police spokesman wanted to reassure the public. There is no need for the people of the town to be alarmed reading about the recent incidents on these historic sites. We are confident the inquests will reveal the deaths of the two persons concerned can be explained. Our mayor, Walter Grimes encouraged us to enlist the help of a Detective Inspector from Scotland Yard. Our ongoing investigations look set for success."

Margery was surprised to read the Great Havell Police spokesman was so vague about it all. Reading between the lines, she thought the local police were probably as baffled as she was.

There was an advertisement for Moonlight Motors on the same page "Our top-class services will take you all the way," ran the text. There was a picture of Bill Walker's red Porsche with a girl sitting provocatively on the bonnet and looking challengingly at the photographer. They are probably aiming at younger men, thought Margery. Putting the newspaper aside and washing up her plate and her cup, she got ready to go out.

She took her bike out of the shed, put the notebook, camera and pencil in her bag and into the basket and cycled along the bridle path at the back of Priory Cottages to Priory Street. She cycled across the marketplace, through streets of Victorian housing and an Edwardian one beyond. Her route took her through Thorpe Park and along the road, past the turning towards Home Farm and on to William Fabb, which had a regiment of tractors.

In contrast to Bream the previous day, the staff at Fabb were friendly and easy to talk to. They had not long started offering a range of country clothing, oilskins, tweeds, jodhpurs, riding helmets, wellingtons, riding boots and galoshes.

'This is the aspect of the business we wish to promote,' said Eileen Fabb, taking Margery through the new clothing department. Margery tried on an oilskin hat and bought it on the discount Eileen offered her.

Eileen showed her into one of the offices at the back, where, she explained to Margery, they took farmers who were buying or renting agricultural equipment, to discuss their requirements. The office had a large picture window looking out on farmland with sheep grazing on it.

'Is that part of the Home Farm?' asked Margery.

'Yes, it's nice to know we will always have our view from these offices at the back of the shop. As it is council-owned, we have permission to demonstrate, tractors, ploughs and drills there. In return we hire out equipment to the Home Farm at a greatly reduced rate.'

Fabb premises looked over countryside which was destined to be used to develop expensive executive new homes, thought Margery. She took a picture of the office with its view. She would mention the demonstrations in her article. It wasn't for her to say anything to Eileen about the about the plans for executive homes on the land Fabb was using for agricultural equipment demonstrations.

She cycled to the Falcon Brewery along the Cricklewater Estuary.

As she had hoped, the manager was able to show her over the works, the brewing vats, where the hops were added, the bottling plant and, yes, she was asked if she would like to try the beer. She was even given a couple of bottles to try at home. The barley was grown locally, she learned. The Maltings was owned by the brewery as well and situated alongside.

'Does more than one farm supply the barley?' asked Margery. I cycled past Home Farm on my way here, is that one of the local growers?'

'Yes, the Home Farm is one of the specialist farms which grows a particular variety of barley to be malted here and used for our beer,' replied the brewery manager.

*What would happen if that land was built on?* thought Margery.

The manager at the brewery proudly showed her their latest product. A home brewing kit, he assured her was now all the rage. Users of the kit could not fail to create a good brew, he said. The Falcon Brewery had worked out the quantities exactly for successful home brewing and the equipment could be cleaned and used over again. All customers needed to do was to buy more ingredients direct from the brewery. Their technicians were working on a variety of beers for customers to brew at home from pale ale to porter, he explained.

'Before you go,' he said, 'I'd like you to try some of this.' He selected a bottle from the shelves of the brewery shop and opened it up using a bottle opener attached to the counter.

He poured Margery a half pint of the amber liquid and asked her what she thought.

'Mmmm, refreshing,' she said, 'perhaps suitable for the summer.'

'Exactly,' he replied, delighted, and he showed her the label.

'This is our latest "Fayre" brew ready for the solstice.'

Margery did not have the heart to remind him the fair would not take place this year. It seemed the news it had been cancelled was not taken seriously at the brewery. They were assuming it would go ahead on a different date.

It was a short cycle ride to the Old Granary Hotel, by the Quay Marina and Margery took some pictures for her article before she went in.

The hotel had been carefully converted from a Victorian granary, the wide reception area was dotted with armchairs, sofas and coffee tables.

Margery announced her arrival to Debbie, a glamorous black girl at reception, who gave Margery a bright, welcoming smile.

Gail Cooper was a tall, thin, neatly dressed woman with short blonde hair.

Margery introduced herself and held out her hand to shake hands. Gail gave her a limp handshake.

'Oh, your hands are clammy! I must go and wash mine,' she said. Margery looked down at her hands in surprise as Gail walked off quickly. She glanced at Debbie, who rolled her dark eyes and shrugged her shoulders.

Margery did not know what to do, so she sat down in one of the arm-chairs and put her note-book and pencil on the coffee table in front and waited.

'Well, come on then,' said Gail.

She looked up in surprise.

'This way to my office,' said Gail standing over her impatiently. 'What are you sitting down for?'

She got up meekly and followed Gail into her office at the back of reception.

'Our busiest time is at midsummer, of course. Interest in the fair is growing and this year we are offering a package. Two nights' dinner bed and breakfast and with a discount for everything our guests purchase at the fair, including re-freshments. It's been really hard work tracking down all the exhibitors, but I've more or less done it and we are all set for the big event.'

Margery took notes in shorthand. There was no way she was going to be the one to remind Gail the fair had been cancelled this year and probably in future years too. Or did she and others expect it to be rescheduled on a different date? Perhaps businesses like the Falcon Brewery and the Old Granary Hotel were planning their own event. Margery asked for the names of as many of the exhib-itors as she could, perhaps the council would reschedule the dates if the Gleaner carried a large multi-page feature on the Granary Hotel and its plans, with all the local and visiting businesses, connected with the fair, advertising in it.

The fastidious Gail had a list of every single one of the exhibitors past and possible future ones. Margery asked if she could have a copy of the list. Gail called in Debbie and asked her to make a copy for Margery. She also asked Deb-bie to show Margery over the hotel, as she would know which rooms were vacant at the moment.

'And be sure to take Miss Moore into the Quay Marina bar, the Grain of Truth restaurant and the Clover Lounge where we serve afternoon teas,' said Gail. 'I will be in reception while you do that.'

'I'm sorry about the handshake business,' said Debbie, as soon as they were at the top of the main staircase and out of earshot.

'She does that a lot. She's always washing her hands. She's obsessed with it.'

'Like Lady Macbeth,' joked Margery. 'Perhaps she has a guilty conscience about something and thinks she can wash it away!'

Debbie laughed. 'She's a funny woman in that respect. You want to see her inspecting the laundry before the beds are changed! The chamber maids are terrified of her.'

Margery enjoyed her tour of the hotel. The brick Victorian granary had been built to accommodate grain which had been grown locally and was stored there before it was dispatched down river or abroad. The building had been designed to keep the stored grain warm and dry. It was an ideal building for conversion to a hotel, she thought.

She noted the clean white napery in the Grain of Truth restaurant, the polished wood tables in the Quay Marina bar, the comfortable seating in the Clover lounge, where she was invited by Debbie to sit down.

She was being treated to afternoon tea at the Old Granary Hotel.

Margery didn't fancy having it on her own, so she asked if Debbie could join her.

'I shouldn't really, I'll have to ask Gail.'

'Yes, please do.'

She waited for about ten minutes until a beaming Debbie joined her.

'She made a bit of a fuss and I can't be too long, she said.'

'That's fine,' said Margery. 'I have to cycle home in the dark, so I don't want to be too long either.'

Debbie was from Nigeria, Margery learned, and at hospitality evening classes at the institute.

Feeling thoroughly treated with her afternoon tea, she said thank you and goodbye to Debbie and Gail. She carefully avoided offering her hand to Gail again, but Debbie shook hands with her and winked. Margery left from the back of the building to look in the garden where she had taken a picture of the hotel earlier, rather than the front, which was too close to the Quay Marina to be able to get much in a frame. She went round the side of the hotel and noticed there was a section of the building which had not been refurbished. On the side were some double doors with no visible way of opening them. She tried pushing them, but they seemed to be firmly bolted from the inside. She looked up above the doors where there were large leaded light arched windows. They had been blacked out on every floor, except the ones at the top. She noticed the same with the windows round the corner. Intrigued, she went back to reception to ask Debbie what it was.

'There's a staircase behind there,' said Debbie, 'which goes up to a loft we use for storage. It's not really used for anything else. That end of the building was suspended over a cut from the river which has been filled in.'

'What is stored in the loft?' asked Margery.

'I've not been there. Only Gail and deliverymen access that as far as I know. It contains decorations for special occasions and events... Christmas, Valentines, Easter, Regatta Balls, all that sort of thing.'

'Can you access it from inside the hotel?'

'Yes, but I am not allowed up there. The door from the hotel has a key and a large, coded padlock on it. As far as I know, there is only Gail and one other member of staff with access to the key and who knows the code. There's no lift, everything has to be carried up the stairs on the side of the building. Special deliveries come through the double doors you saw at the bottom.'

'Can the doors only be opened from the inside?' asked Margery.

'Yes, I saw them open once when I came back from day release at college late, and I was walking back to the hotel from the bus stop. I noticed some lights in the marina, which is not unusual because sometimes people sleep on their boats. As I approached the hotel, there were a couple of dark figures, shining torches on the ground walking towards the hotel. They didn't see me, I was about to walk into reception, when I saw them go round the side of the hotel, so I thought I should have a look. I kept my distance, but I think I heard the bolts being drawn back from those double doors and the figures disappeared. Well, I was worried they were burglars or something. We've got a few valuable paintings and ornaments in the building. I tried to contact Gail but couldn't find her. There was no one on reception and she wasn't in her office. I thought she might have the night off, so I went to find the headwaiter in the restaurant. He said not to bother him about it and tell Gail in the morning. So, I went to my room and wrote the essay on hospitality for people with disabilities, the college had set me, and I forgot about it.

'I remembered to mention it to Gail a few days later and she said I must have imagined it. She said it was very rare they used those doors for security reasons and they only really kept them there for an emergency.'

Margery thanked Debbie, unlocked her bike from the rack outside the hotel, put the lights on and cycled home in the dark. She took the lane from Priory Street which ran between the Glebe Mound and the end of the row of Priory Cottages, so she could go in the back gate and put her bike away.

She noticed a light on in her cottage.

When she opened her back gate, Vlad came out of the kitchen door took her bike and keys from her to put it away in her shed and followed her into the cottage.

Where had she been? he asked. He had hoped to see her at the Arts Centre on Friday. He had parked his bike in her front garden as usual.

'Let's go and sit down,' said Margery. 'I've a lot to tell you.' With that, she burst into tears. He put his arms round her.

When she dried her eyes, she realised she would not have time to catch a train and stay with her aunt and uncle that evening. She phoned them to let them know.

'I'm late back from my assignments,' she said, 'and they gave me afternoon tea at the hotel, so I've had plenty to eat.'

That done, they found a large tin of winter vegetable soup in her store cupboard, warmed it up on the hob, folded down the little kitchen table and sat opposite each other to enjoy it with a couple of rolls they defrosted in her oven.

After they had washed up the dishes, they made a pot of tea and put the little electric fire on in Margery's grate, she sat in her chair opposite Vlad on the little settee under the window and began to tell him about her weekend. She told him what had befallen poor Growltiger, about her encounter with DI Barker, the difficult appointment with Denzil Bream, her visits to the Witches Cauldron, William Fabb, The Falcon Brewery and the Old Granary Hotel.

Vlad listened in silence.

'I know this DI Barker,' he said when she paused.

Margery was surprised. 'How come?' she asked. She felt her stomach tighten. Had he been in trouble? What would he tell her next?

'This is what I wish to tell you, Margery. I have wanted to tell you for a long time. I didn't know how to. I am Russian, but you know that. I am a defector. I was born in a village on the Techa River near Mayak in the Urals. You will not know the place. I do not expect you to and you would not know there is a big nuclear power generator there. There was a major disaster years ago in the 1950s. I was a child. I did not know about it until I was older. When I left school, I trained as an engineer. I had a job maintaining machinery in the local factories. One place I worked was in a poultry processing plant in my village. When I was in my twenties, I started to go out with Olga; she worked at the poultry processing plant and we got to know each other when we walked home from work together. We were married. We were young, happy and lived together in a little house in my village. Olga was only really well when I first knew her and when I married her. She was often ill. We thought, no, we hoped, she would get better. We saw the doctor in our village. She had tests and treatment in the hospital, but she did not get better. They were unable to cure her.

'I will never forget the look of hope in her lovely eyes when we went together to see a specialist. He had come from Moscow to see Olga and all the others in the village who were suffering. I now know it was radiation sickness. She died. She was 25 years old. I didn't know it, I have only found out since I have lived in England; it was most likely it was caused by radioactive poisoning from the nuclear generator leak. I was heartbroken. There was nothing left for me in the village. I didn't want to stay there. I left. I'd heard they were looking for recruits for the Russian Navy. I made the journey to Leningrad. When I was there, I re-trained as an engineer on the submarines and I joined the Russian Navy. They were building nuclear submarines, like the American and British ones.

'I was an engineer on one of these in the Baltic, when the engine developed problems. There was only so much I could do, whilst we were submerged, so we put in at one of the Swedish ports. It was apparent the sub had a major fault and would need complete repair. But we engineers could not agree how to do it. It was decided, because I spoke good English, I would travel to Barrow-in-Furness in the British Isles, where they make nuclear submarines to discover their engineering techniques. The Swedish mariners in the port strongly recommended it. They said I could have a free passage on one of their fishing boats.

'We Russians thought my visit there might not be welcomed and I would be arrested as a spy and not able to learn what I needed. I had nothing to lose and there had been problems in the port too. I was keen to leave. I took the passage on the fishing boat, which was in the port at the time, to the northwest coast of England. It was decided I would make it to the coast in an inflatable lifeboat and claim I was a shipwreck survivor.

'It was a stupid plan. I realised soon after I made it to shore. I was directed to the English coast guard. They knew there had been no shipwreck. There had been no gale force winds in the shipping forecast and no reports of any. I didn't know about the Royal National Lifeboat Institution, which is always sent out to rescue crew and boats in distress. They had not been called out. I was arrested in Barrow as a Russian spy. There was no way back.

'I am not a spy. Your MI 5 would not believe me. I was interrogated and imprisoned. I told them what happened over and over, and they thought I had been brainwashed into telling the story and it was not true. Eventually, I asked if I could defect. I asked if I could live in England.

'Everything changed after that. I was told if I did defect, if I was given permission to live here, I would have to report everything I was doing and everyone I contacted, and they would always need to know where I was.

'I had my Russian passport. It was the only thing I had to prove I was who I said I was. It was the only thing which proved I was telling the truth. I had no other evidence of my identity. With the Cold War, I could not get any.

'Your Home Office officials owned me in the sense I could not get a job or somewhere to live without papers. They were the only people who could provide me with them. In return I had to tell them everything I knew about life in Russia and everything I knew about Russian submarines and what they were used for. Not that I knew much. They found me an engineering job and a room for me in Little Havell. It was a quiet place, a village. People would get used to seeing me around, they said. They arranged for me to learn plumbing and electrical engineering at the Great Havell Institute. The room I have is in a building with a lot of other tenants. We are all trained in building maintenance, gardening, decorating and repairs. We all work for the Country Hotel, the Little Havell spring water bottling plant, the local letting agents and the tenants on the Glebe estate. There are other immigrants in the flats. I am not the only one. I think I am the only one who is a defector, but no one knows that.

'Before DI Barker came to Great Havell, he had to be briefed by the Home Office that I lived nearby.

'Now you know. I am Russian, a Soviet. I have lived in England for nearly three years. I am still getting used to a very different way of life. I do not know many people. There are my employers of course. The people I work with call me "the Rusky" or "the spy" or "the red" or "Vlad the Impaler". We laugh about it. The people I share a kitchen and bathrooms with, where I live, call me "Popeye" or "Ivan the Terrible" or even just Ivan.

'I have been very grateful to Jonah, Andy and other members of the Jazz and Folk club and especially to you, Margery, for accepting me into your lives. I am still learning the English way of life. It is very different from the life I was brought up to. The USSR is massive. There were huge open spaces in the Urals, where I grew up. There is nothing like that here. Although I have spent months confined under the sea, I was brought up in a place where there were vast wild areas, forests, mountains and lakes. Here, I can walk or cycle the short distance between towns and villages and take the bus or the train if I need to go further. I am still trying to get used to it. After being in a submarine, it was always a relief to come to the surface, to put into port and go on land again. Now, every day I wake and look at the sky and I know what kind of day it is. Even if the sky is grey or dull, I love that I can look at it.'

They were silent, each contemplating what the other had said.

'Losing a cat seems a small thing compared to all this,' said Margery in a soft voice.

'I am learning about the English. I am not only learning the language. As you know, I go to evening classes at the institute for that. I am also learning what it is like to live on an island. I am used to the sea, but I cannot serve in the navy here. I cannot really leave now. I cannot return to my old life. I must remain here because it is provincial, quiet and, in a small community like Little Havell, I can be useful. I can find a place. People have got used to seeing me and used to the fact I live there. They all know I am a Soviet, but no one knows where I am from or how long I have been here. I was born just after World War Two at a time when Russia and the British Isles were on the same side. I may never see Leningrad again, a beautiful city and where I was often based with the Russian Navy. I can never go back. I could never take you there Margery. Such is the Cold War we have to live with.

'England is both my haven and my prison. But we all make a life for ourselves. Yours is as a writer and photographer. You work hard, you have your own home, your books, your radio, your garden…how I like the English and their gardens…you have your bike, the Arts Centre, the theatre, the cinema, the library, the ramblers…they are all a part of your life, as your cat was. Of course, his loss matters to you in the same way everything I lost matters to me.'

Margery got up, sat next to Vlad on her little settee. All the pent-up emotion of the past week came to a head. She burst into tears. Vlad put his arms round her, holding her until she stopped crying.

'I tried so hard to keep going, but so much has happened and so many things puzzle me,' she said as she calmed down.

'I find life in England puzzling too. In Russia, I had many certainties. Perhaps it was just because I grew up there and I was used to the way of life. I knew I could get a job. I knew I could get a flat, I knew I could buy food and I knew Olga would be given best medical treatment the state could provide. I think, perhaps, it was the same for every Russian or that is what I was led to believe. The Home Office immigration officials said it would be the same here for me, but I would need official residency papers. Here things are very different and I must get used to it. I am getting used to it. I have to get used to it. I cannot go back to Russia.

'I will never forget my first visit to a supermarket in England. I had never seen so many different varieties of food before. I didn't know what to buy or where to find what I needed. I walked round and round looking at the shelves amazed. I didn't know which loaf of bread to have or what I should put on it. There were so many things, it took me weeks to understand what they all were. There are other immigrants where I live. They laugh at me when I ask what things are. Where they lived before, life was much the same as here, or so they tell me.

'What puzzles me most, Margery, is these recent events which have upset you. The sudden death of Jonah's friend, another body, I hear, has been found on the Glebe Mound. They cancel a popular fair here for the first time for centuries and the cruel, cruel killing of your cat.

'On the ships and submarines sometimes, there were quarrels and disputes between the crews and things could become nasty and violent. It was in the open. It was dealt with by the officers of the craft and we were punished, and it was all over. When we were on shore it was different. No officers to keep us under control. Perhaps too much vodka and too much…too much…making up for being confined for weeks on end. Here in England, these deaths, this cruelty, the detective from London. I cannot understand what could be behind it all. Perhaps I do not understand the English people enough.'

'Vlad, it puzzles me as much as it puzzles you, I think,' said Margery.

'I'm sorry I stayed the night with you last week without asking first. I did not know how to ask. No. That's not true. I wanted to stay with you. I was afraid to ask in case you said no.'

'Is that why you left so early, in case I was cross?'

'I didn't think you would be cross. I did not know what you would say or do. I knew I should have told you I was a defector when I first knew you. I was afraid to, I thought you might talk about me and tell someone who could make things

115

difficult for me. I thought it might go in that newspaper you work for. No, that's not fair, forgive me. I was afraid to do it, because I didn't know how you would react. I have become so used to keeping my background quiet and never talking about it. I did not know how to tell you. It's taken me a long time to do it, I know, and I'm sorry; it was not fair.'

'I suppose,' said Margery thoughtfully, 'living here after Russia and on the ships and the submarines must be very different. When did you learn English?'

'In the Russian Navy, we were away from home for months on end. One of the officers had language tapes and a couple of tape cassette players and we gambled with cards to borrow them. I won a month's use of the English tape. I still have a lot to learn, I know.'

*Well, here we are,* thought Margery, *two very different people, sharing parts of their lives.*

'I will not object, Vlad, if you would like to stay here tonight. I've not slept here since you were here last. I've been staying with my aunt and uncle at Havell-Next-the-Sea. I came back to work, and I have more work to do tomorrow. It's easier for me to work here. I have everything I need, and I can take it all into the Gleaner offices when it is finished. You can stay in the spare room if you like.' He looked at her silently and affectionately for a while. Then his expression changed into his roguish smile.

'It's cold in there; it's warmer in your bed.'

Margery smiled too. She tried to imagine his life in Soviet Russia in his village, on the submarines or on the ships, but it was all so very different from everything she knew and was familiar with. She extracted herself from his arm, which was still around her and stood up.

'Let's make a bedtime drink before we go to upstairs,' she said, kissing him gently and tenderly on the forehead.


## Wednesday 12th February

Vlad left for work, early again. Before he did, they had breakfast together. Tea, marmalade and toast. Vlad said next time he stayed he would make porridge.

Margery said if he did, he'd have to clean the saucepan out afterwards.

'Don't you have a double saucepan for porridge?' Vlad asked.

'No, I've never had one of those.'

'Maybe not next time then,' he said. 'Porridge is good, but a lot of English people have cornflakes for breakfast. I am still not used to seeing all the varieties

116

of cereals in the supermarkets. I would not know which to buy, so I always have porridge. You, I think, always have toast, marmalade and tea?'

'Not always,' replied Margery. 'I sometimes eat bacon and eggs at the weekend.'

'You never eat cornflakes?'

'No, but I know a lot of people who do. And some people buy packets of other cereals to eat them all up and collect tokens for things, like Honey Monster watches.'

'I don't think I understand what that is?'

'There's a man who lives in a big house, not far from here. His family bought the house for him to live in to keep him away from them, because he behaves badly and drinks too much. I was helping him look for his Honey Monster watch he had lost the other day.'

'This is a joke, Margery.'

'Indeed, it is not. We found his Honey Monster watch in the priory car park. But a police car ran over it and crushed it before he could pick it up.' Margery giggled at the memory of it. It made Vlad smile.

'How old is this man?'

'I don't know, about forty, he's probably about your age.'

'And he ate cereal to collect tokens for a Honey Monster watch?'

'Yes, about six packets of it.' Margery got up and fetched her bag.

'Here it is, crushed under the wheels of a police car, twice,' she said, taking the squashed watch out of her bag and putting it on the fold down table. 'I suppose I should take it back to him.'

'I think I should like to come with you and meet this man who drinks all day and eats a lot of cereal so he can have this watch.'

With no suggestion, he would come back that evening; after they washed up the breakfast things, Vlad set off to work at Little Havell on his bike.

Margery sat at her typewriter and wrote up her features.

After lunch, she put them in the tartan shopping trolley together with her little Ricoh camera. It was easier, she thought, for photographic to take the film out and replace it. She put her tartan cape over her black dress and wore the new waterproof hat from William Fabb, as it was drizzling slightly. She set out for the Gleaner.

As she walked down the lane to the old priory, she saw someone poking about. At the end of the lane, she opened the gate to the priory and noticed DI

117

Barker's BMW was in the car park beyond. She glanced up at the Glebe Mound but could not see him there, so she assumed he had just parked there to look round the old priory again.

She walked through the priory car park and turned right at the end towards the Gleaner Offices, after using the pedestrian crossing to the Amicable Anarchist.

As she was walking past the Edwardian-terraced houses on either side of the road, she was tooted up by Bill Walker in his red Porsche. She noticed he had Gloria with him as usual. Gloria would be in the Gleaner offices by the time Margery got there. All she needed to do was collect today's, and yesterday's papers and submit her articles and invoice for Gill or Philippa on the front desk to give to Cheryl. She could pop the camera into photographic to have the film taken out and replaced and go back to the marketplace for a bit of shopping, then catch an early train to Havell-Next-the-Sea.

'Hello girls,' said Margery cheerfully. She looked in her trolley for the features and her bill and said:

'I see Bill Walker dropped Gloria back here again, just now. I guess those two are quite close the times I see them together.'

'She's always popping out to Moonlight. I think they are respraying her car or something at the moment,' said Philippa.

'So that's the story,' said Margery. 'I never see her without Bill these days.'

'You might not, but if you think what I think you are thinking, our Gloria has other fish to fry, and she would be two-timing Bill.'

'Really?' asked Margery. 'Do tell!'

'Put it this way,' chipped in Gill. 'Our Gloria aims high.'

'Well, Bill's the boss of Moonlight, so I can't see how she could go much higher.'

'Sometimes people cannot see, what's under their noses,' said Philippa.

'Never mind, Margery,' said Gill. 'You stay in your nice cosy little world and don't worry about them others.'

A bit puzzled, Margery took her camera to photographic in the basement, where the film was taken out for processing in the dark room and a new one was put in whilst she waited.

The office door opposite the dark room was open. She noticed one of the features staff in there with a pile of green and yellow papers on the desk, going through them meticulously. *She's probably trying to find dockets for the adver-tisements which have been published and not charged for*, thought Margery. The dark room door opened, and she was handed her camera, complete with a new film.

Harry Grimes was in the front office.

'And how is my poor bereaved little feature writer,' he said, patting her on the bottom, as he usually did.

'Well, it was one of those things,' said Margery flippantly, knowing full well it was not.

Harry Grimes seemed surprised with that answer.

'Can I persuade you to come to our Valentine's Ball, my darling,' he whis-pered in her ear but loud enough for Gill and Philippa to hear.

'When is it?' asked Margery, surprised.

'On Saturday,' he said. 'You and I could have a romantic waltz!'

'Oh, what a pity!' said Margery. 'I have a prior engagement on Saturday,' she was thinking she would make sure she was staying with her aunt and uncle at least on that night.

'Off with some lucky bloke, I suppose,' said Grimes. 'Our little bird flies away again, as she did last weekend.' And with another pat on Margery's bottom, he walked into the Gleaner offices.

Philippa and Gill were open-mouthed at the exchange.

'He seems to know a lot about you,' said Gill. 'You're a dark horse, Margery. We'll have to keep an eye on you!'

Just then, her phone rang.

'Yes, Cheryl, she's just here. She'll bring her copy and bill in herself.'

Margery sighed. She'd been hoping to avoid going into the office. As she walked past Gloria's desk, she heard the word 'bitch!'

Margery went into Cheryl's office, handed her the articles and bill and stood there waiting.

'We're still under pressure here, said Cheryl. 'Your review of "An Inspector Calls" is great. It will go into the Weekender Gleaner. Shut the door, would you? Look Margery, I've had a complaint about you from Denzil Bream.'

'A complaint!'

'Apparently, you didn't interview him properly and he had to give you a couple of brochures in the end, otherwise nothing would have been written.'

119

'He had his feet on the desk the whole time I was there. I couldn't get any information out of him. I was tempted to get my camera out and take a picture of him like that. I've written a piece on Bream, it's here, but it's about the length of time the firm has been in Great Havell and the sort of properties they sell, their lettings and commercial arm. The sort of thing I usually write about estate agents. I've included a bit about the new homes proposed for the Monks Thorpe site.'

'I see. He wants to see the article before it's published. Look,' said Cheryl, extracting a copy and handing it back to Margery, take it round to him. 'We're using the story as a lead in the Weekender property supplement.'

'Is that fair on the other estate agents?' asked Margery.

'They'll get their turn,' replied Cheryl sharply. 'Oh, and by the way, it's not good form to refuse Harry Grimes' invitation to the Valentine's Ball. I hope you've a good excuse for not going. What *are* you going to do on Saturday night?'

Margery was astounded. She'd been surprised when Harry Grimes had asked her to the Valentine's Ball, but now, Cheryl wanted to know why she wasn't going to that, and where she was going on Saturday night. She thought quickly.

'Are you going to the Valentine's Ball, Cheryl?'

'Yes, Harry Grimes has given us all tickets for it. It's going to be in the Assembly Rooms. It will be good; they've got a live band.'

'I'm sorry I'm not going then,' said Margery, trying to sound genuine. 'It's all a bit short notice, isn't it?'

'Yes, that's what I thought.'

Margery looked at her watch quickly,

'I've a train to catch,' she said, turned round and went swiftly out of the office before Cheryl could reply.

She said a quick goodbye to the front office girls, picked up the two newspapers and left, realising she had not taken any more assignments from Cheryl. Well, she had to take her article on Bream into the agent's offices anyway, then she would have to go home before she caught her train, so if Cheryl rang, there would be no problem.

When she went into Bream, Janice, the unhappy girl who had supplied the brochures on Monday, was sitting at her desk outside Denzil Bream's office. Margery found an envelope in her shopping trolley, put the copy inside, wrote "for the attention of Denzil Bream" on the envelope and handed it to the girl.

She then left as quickly as she could to go home.

As she went out, an E-type Jaguar drew up outside Bream's and the powerful engine throbbed for a while as it idled and finally switched off. Margery had passed it before she realised that it could have made the sort of sound John at the Witches Cauldron had heard last Wednesday when the crossed broomsticks on the porch had gone missing. She turned round just in time to see Denzil Bream open the driver's door and step out. Glad he hadn't seen her; she popped into the Tastea Bite to buy some more bread and bought some apples from the greengrocery stall in the market. She went out of the marketplace into Priory Street, past the Amicable Anarchist, across the road towards her cottage.

She managed to let herself in to it just in time to avoid Alf coming out of his door and delaying her. She kicked off her shoes, put her loaf in the bread bin and sat in her armchair.

Her visit to the Gleaner Offices had been quite tiring, with everything that was going on there. There had been the usual buzz of tele-ads and sales reps on the phone. She wished Harry Grimes was not in the habit of patting her on her bottom and had not whispered in her ear in front of the girls. He had been pinching or patting her bottom, putting his arm round her shoulders for the best part of a year, ever since he was elevated to his present position of advertising director. Before then, he had been advertising manager and before that he was one of the sales representatives she used to see sometimes in the office. She thought it unlikely he singled her out especially and assumed he was like that with all the women in the office. Just then, the phone rang. It was Cheryl.

'Margery? I've just had Denzil Bream on the phone. He said the stuff you've written about his agency is utter drivel. He said he knew you weren't listening when he was explaining how the agency was run and what he'd done to bring it up to date for the 1980s. He said he's corrected it all and his secretary is typing it up and will bring it over to the Gleaner in time for Friday's Weekender Gleaner property supplement deadline.'

Margery was annoyed. Things could not be much worse at the moment, whatever would be next?

'Denzil is insisting you should be sacked. He said he would complain to the board of directors about you. I didn't tell him you were freelance. He said if we don't publish his corrections, he'll pull all his advertising.'

Margery was completely at a loss for words. She didn't know what to say.

'Margery, did you hear all that? Are you there?'

'Yes, Cheryl. I really have no comment to make.'

'I've got four more estate agents for you to visit. Berkins at Havell-Next-the-Sea and the Bodgers branches in Little Havell, Great Havell and Grimpen Havell. Do a good job on those and maybe they'll make up for the business we're likely to lose from Bream. Do you want to borrow a pool car for them?'

'I think I could do all those by bus, bike or train, Cheryl.'

'OK fine. No hurry, we need to have them done for future property supplements, as we can't feature one agent without giving the chance to others. And one other thing, I'd like you to cover the inquest into the two deaths tomorrow. They are to be held at the magistrate's court in the guildhall.'

'Wouldn't that usually be covered by one of the reporters? Or even the crime reporter?'

'Yes, but the MD has asked if you would do it for some reason. Oh! I know why, it's because he knows DI Barker has interviewed you.'

'Why would that make a difference?' asked Margery.

'I see you haven't looked at today's Gleaner yet,' replied Cheryl.

Margery decided to shut the cottage up and catch the next train to Havell-Next-the-Sea before it got dark. It was still drizzling slightly. She could read the Gleaner on the train and she would have a little time to take a walk along the sea front.

She picked up the Dewberry & Hicks bag to put the newspaper in, remembered there was the cake and a bottle of wine in it, so decided to take that with her too. She packed her notebook and pencils. She could go straight to the Coroner's Inquest from the station in the morning.

Seated on the train for the short journey to Havell-Next-the-Sea, Margery looked at the front page of her copy of the Gleaner.

"TOP COP SLAMS MOUND CULT" ran the headline.

Margery began to read.

"Top Scotland Yard Detective Inspector Barker cited local superstitions for the illusion, the two recent deaths in the old priory and the Moyen Midden sinkhole, are anything other than self-inflicted."

"'I've never come across anything like it,' DI Barker told the Gleaner.

"'The simple fact two people accidentally overdosed on cocaine within 24 hours, and within a short distance of each other, is claimed by these gullible locals to be the result of some archaic curse.'

"'Until I arrived in Great Havell a few days ago, I had never heard of the place. The sooner the people of the town ditch all this mumbo jumbo for the real world and recognise the deaths of these two sad drug addicts is an indictment on the state of their town, the better.'"

The article described Barney Cobbler as a well-known local historian with a hidden drug problem and Sadie Petal as a woman who lived with a partner in Great Havell but was known to social services. At the end of the article, it mentioned both inquests would be held at the guildhall courtroom the following day, starting at 10am.

Margery put the Gleaner back in her bag, got off the train at Havell-Next-the-Sea station and walked to her aunt and uncle's house in The Avenue, where she was greeted by them both, the smell of cooking and a very enthusiastic Bobby.

'You are lovely and early, dear,' Aunt Carrie opened the front door.

'It's great to be back,' said Margery.

'Were you alright alone in your cottage?'

'Yes, fine, thanks Aunt, I had a lot to do.'

'You look happier, I must say, they certainly keep you busy at the Gleaner,' remarked her aunt.

'I'll pop upstairs and change into my jeans if you don't mind,' said Margery and took the bag with the cake, wine and Gleaner upstairs with her.

She came down ten minutes later, bringing the bag with her. She put the newspaper in the front room. She and her uncle could look at it later together. She took the cake and wine into the kitchen, where her aunt was preparing the meal.

'Oh, that's lovely, Margery. I haven't cooked anything for dessert. I was going to open a tin of fruit. The meal is very simple tonight, we can have a slice of that each after it. Open the wine if you fancy a glass.'

'Yes, we could try it. I should have tried it earlier. I wrote the article, but I forgot all about it, with everything that's going on. It's imported exclusively for Sworder Leigh and Runk, you see, it says so on the label and it's chateau-bottled in the Cotes du Rhone region.'

'Ah French, dear, that's nice,' said Carrie absently.

Margery went into the back room where she knew there was a corkscrew, fashioned out of a polished piece of vine, on the mahogany sideboard. She had a bit of difficulty opening the bottle, but fortunately, her uncle helped and poured them all a glass.

They put them on a tray and sat in the front room to enjoy them.

'Cheers all,' said Carrie, raising her glass and looking at the deep burgundy colour. The wine was rich, smooth and aromatic. They all agreed they liked it.

'Sworder Leigh and Runk sell it by the case,' said Margery.

'I doubt we could afford a case,' said Carrie.

'I think it is hotels and clubs which buy them in that quantity,' said Margery. She showed them the front page of the Gleaner.

'It looks as if DI Barker wants to close the case on the deaths of Barney Cobbler and Sadie Petal, whilst simultaneously debunking any suggestion of foul play from people or even malign spirits,' said Alec, reading the short piece on the front page. 'I see there is also an article inside explaining why the town council has cancelled the fair completely this year.'

'Are they not rescheduling it?' asked Margery.

'No, the council spokesman is citing the reaction to the recent overdoses near the place and the nasty prank with the pet cat for good reasons to knock the event on the head for good and for all. It is also very expensive for the council to put it on.'

'That will upset a lot of people,' said Margery, taking a sip of red wine and enjoying its mellow, smoky notes.

'I guess it will. It's a bit much cancelling it without any consultation,' replied Alec. 'I see those full-page advertisements for motors and property sales executives are in again,' he added.

'Well, that's one way of getting free ads in,' said Margery.

'It would explain why the revenues are down if places like Bream and Moonlight Motors are getting free advertising integrated with the full-page Gleaner recruitment advertisements.

'The same images appear in other parts of the newspaper. Look, Margery it's got your by-line on this piece. There are a lot of advertisements around it from tyre firms, paint suppliers, motoring accessories, spare part suppliers, wire wheels, sports stripes and catalytic converters. I don't think they could have found any other advertiser to go in it. There's a large advertisement for Moonlight Motors too.'

'I'm guessing the short fall in revenues will soon be made up,' remarked Margery. 'I'm hoping so, because I enjoy my little job there. Are you singing anywhere on Saturday night, Uncle?'

'I'm not, but we are going to take Neil to the pantomime at the Sandy Reach theatre. He caught a cold when we bought tickets earlier in the season, so we had to change them. It's the last performance. Would you like to stay again on Saturday and come with us?'

'Yes please, if I may.'

'I'll see if I can buy another ticket,' said Alec, getting up and going into the hall to telephone.

Margery heard him on the phone.

'Yes, I'll pick it up and pay for it on Saturday, if that is all right? It is? Good, thank you.'

Alec came back into the front room.

'That's fine. A bit of luck, a few tickets next to ours have been returned, so I was able to buy one.'

Margery sighed with relief. She had a perfect excuse for not going to the Valentine's Ball if it was mentioned again at the Gleaner or by anyone else in Great Havell. But what was all that about Barney and Sadie being drug addicts? It wouldn't be a surprise with Sadie. Margery knew she sometimes put what she called "herbs" in the roll up cigarettes she smoked. She had always assumed it was cannabis, probably something Sadie had grown herself somewhere. Could she have taken an overdose of something? She thought in Sadie's case, it was possible. What she could not understand, though, was that Barney could have been a drug addict. DI Barker didn't know Barney. If he had known him, would he have been so keen to think he was a drug addict? But then, if Barney hadn't inadvertently taken too much cocaine to kill him, it meant someone had made him take it by force in some way with a view to discrediting him or even getting rid of him temporarily or even permanently. But why?

# Chapter V

## Coroner's Court

**Thursday 13th February**

Margery had an early breakfast with her aunt and uncle and they both accompanied her back to Great Havell in Alec's Vauxhall Cavalier, which he parked in the priory car park.

They walked to the marketplace and the courtroom in the guildhall. The guildhall in Great Havell is a long rambling building which has been built and extended over many centuries. Margery, her uncle and aunt walked past the public toilets at one end of the building, which had meeting rooms and art gallery space on the two upper storeys. They walked on, past the museum, to the far end of the building and climbed the stairs to the courtroom which is above the holding cells for the magistrate's court. The court, which takes up the two upper floors, has tiered seating and a vaulted timbered ceiling. It was already getting busy, even though the inquest would not start for half an hour.

Margery noticed some reporters she recognised from the Gleaner. She wondered, again, why Cheryl had wanted her to be there and report on the inquest. Maybe she wanted a feature length article on it, she thought. At least it was the sort of thing she had been trained for, rather than the seemingly endless advertisement features Cheryl had given her. There were going to be two inquests. One was scheduled for the morning, and the other for the afternoon.

Barney Cobbler's was the first.

By the time the coroner, who had served in the office locally for many years, came in, there was standing room only in the courtroom.

Wedged between her aunt and her uncle, Margery could only see the Gleaner reporters and people opposite, she could not see who was sitting to the side of her or behind.

The man who had seen Barney taken ill on the Glebe Mound was the first to give evidence. He had been walking on the mound with his daughter and they had seen Barney stumbling. He had called out to him, but there was no response. Then he saw a man go up to him, who seemed to help him down the mound to the priory, where Mr Cobbler appeared to be retching over the railings. He thought he was drunk and incapable, and he and his daughter went to the phone box next to the Amicable Anarchist to call an ambulance. The man who had been helping Mr Cobbler to the railings followed him to the phone box, but he had already made the call by the time he got there.

The coroner asked if he could identify the man with Barney, but the witness said he didn't really notice him except he was fairly tall and wearing a leather jacket. He said, as his daughter was with him and had the day off from school for an appointment with a specialist at the hospital, he couldn't stay. The ambulance turned up for Mr Cobbler pretty quickly. He felt he had done all he could for him.

Margery remembered Jonah had mentioned to her he had requested the inquest into Barney's death when he appeared next to give his testimony. He gave a character reference for Barney, emphasising his standing in the community.

'In fact, I do not believe my friend has ever taken drugs,' said Jonah. 'Mr Cobbler had been angry, actually, but not depressed a few days before he died. There was an incident on Friday 31st January. My friend, Mr Cobbler, was asked to leave the Amicable Anarchist. He had been especially angry with one of the local councillors. He had continued his daily morning walks on the Glebe Mound. He and I were researching aspects of Great Havell history together only a few days before. He was cheerful last time I spoke to him on the evening before he died.'

Brendon Dant, vice chairman of the Moyen Circle, introduced himself as a solicitor in the practice Lockhart and Upton. 'When I heard Mr Cobbler had died,' he said, 'I went to his house and collected the Moyen Circle records and meeting minutes which I now keep in a safe in my offices.' Margery knew Lockhart and Upton solicitors occupied a range of historic buildings, close to where the inquest was being held. Brendon Dant was of average height, with neat mid-brown hair and brown eyes. He was dressed very smartly in a dark-blue suit, blue shirt and navy tie. He had marked crow's feet above his nose, which gave his regular features a puzzled look. Margery remembered she always greeted him with enthusiasm when Barney had been 'taking her to task' as he put it in the marketplace,

127

because the solicitor took Barney's attention away from her. Brendon Dant used to come over and give her friendly a nod. He then took Barney by the elbow, engaged him in conversation and they would depart together. Now at the inquest, Brendon confirmed he had never known his friend and well-respected chairman of the Moyen Circle to take drugs or overindulge in alcohol. There had been that incident in the Amicable Anarchist last Friday, however. Mr Cobbler had been consulting him, because a councillor was intending to sue him for threatening behaviour.

Much to Margery's surprise, Detective Inspector Barker was called next.

The DI told the coroner he was new to the area and had been called in by the mayor to help the local police investigate this unexpected death. Barker said he had examined the mound where Barney was last seen walking. He had examined the priory railings where Barney had been found unconscious and he had been to Barney's home. This was where he saw a hole in the plaster where the late historian had found some historic documents. These had gone missing at the time of his death.

Asked by the coroner if he thought the disappearance of the documents had anything to do with Barney's sudden death, DI Barker replied it was possible.

Asked by the coroner if he thought Mr Cobbler's death could be anything other than suicide or self-inflicted, there was a positive gasp of amazement in the courtroom when DI Barker replied that it could. He said vehicle marks had been found close to the priory railings at the end of the lane by Priory Cottages. The local police were trying to trace the vehicle.

*Why then,* Margery thought, as she carefully took it all down in shorthand, *did DI Barker give that interview to the Gleaner?*

A pathologist from the General Hospital described the cause of death as a massive heart attack brought on by a large amount of cocaine administered by injection into the upper left arm. From his examination of the body of the deceased, Mr Cobbler did not have any evidence of heart disease or any other signs that he was suffering from an illness or a chronic health condition. He had consulted Mr Cobbler's GP, who had confirmed the deceased had been a healthy man.

'Was there a possibility Mr Cobbler had administered the drug himself?'

'Yes, it was possible. A dose that high, given by injection, would probably have had an immediate effect on his mobility.'

'Was it possible the cocaine had been administered by someone else, who then draped the unconscious Mr Cobbler over the priory railings, where he was found?' asked the coroner.

'There were only tiny marks on Mr Cobbler's body from the railings,' said the pathologist and he therefore had concluded the deceased had been helped there by a person or persons unknown.

The coroner closed the inquest and asked for the local police assisted by DI Barker to make further investigations into Mr Cobbler's sudden death and the source of the cocaine which had killed him. He said the inquest on Mr Cobbler would be reopened in a week's time.

The inquest on Barney Cobbler was closed for a week pending further inquiries.

The inquest on the death of Sadie Petal was scheduled for the afternoon.

Margery invited her aunt and uncle back to her cottage for some lunch.

They walked across the market square and into Priory Street, crossed the road by Amicable Anarchist over to the old priory. There were quite a few cars parked in the old priory car park and some people were looking over the site. The news of the death of Barney Cobbler had generated more interest in the Glebe Mound and the ancient priory ruins.

Margery led the way through her garden gate and into the front garden, noticing that, as well as the snowdrops, there were crocuses in bud. Alf was about to come out of his front door but seeing she had company, thought better of it.

Inside the cottage was chilly, so she switched on the electric fire she kept in the grate.

Carrie noticed the daffodils in the milk bottle on her desk.

'Who is V X?' she asked.

'A good friend,' replied Margery, going into the kitchen to open a tin of tuna to make sandwiches for them. 'Are you able to stay for the inquest on Sadie?'

'It's all very interesting,' said Alec, 'I see you are noting down everything, but we really need to go back to home for Bobby. We could not bring him with us. Do you mind attending the second inquest on your own? I'll come back and pick you up afterwards. When you are back home, you could give me a ring.'

That would be really kind of you, thank you,' said Margery.

'I have some more appointments to make for tomorrow too, one of them is at Havell-Next-the-Sea. I'll phone round now, if you don't mind, and make the appointments.'

The three of them ate their sandwiches in the front room by the electric fire and discussed the morning's proceedings after Margery had made her phone calls. She was only able to make one appointment for Friday, but, she reflected, she had really worked hard over the past week and felt she deserved to slow down a bit.

'Are you surprised there is to be a further investigation?' asked Alec.

'No, I thought there was something odd about it all,' replied Margery.

'Please come and stay with us tonight, tomorrow night and Saturday,' said Aunt Carrie. 'After what I heard this morning, I want to know you are safe.'

'Of course, I'll be pleased to. I'll put some extra clothes in your car before you go, if you don't mind. And you can take these bottles of Falcon Brewery beer which were given to me yesterday, we can enjoy them at the weekend when we've finished the wine.'

Margery popped upstairs and collected some more clean clothes for her aunt and uncle to take to Havell-Next-the-Sea for her. She put them in a duffle bag with the Falcon beer bottles she had been given. In her bedroom she noticed, or possibly imagined, a slight dent in a pillow where Vlad's head had been and smiled to herself.

She waved her aunt and uncle off from the old priory car park and walked back to the guildhall courtroom. Again, finding she was early, she sat in the same seat as before and was pleased when Jonah joined her. He looked serious.

'Are you all right after that business with your cat? In fact, I also heard local people are saying you did it yourself. There's a rumour going round, it has been done to perpetuate myths about the mound so the solstice fair will be reinstated. I am so sorry people round here can be very unkind and silly. It looks as if the national press is interested in these inquests, it's not just our local reporters over there.'

'I know what some people can be like,' replied Margery, 'although I have been surprised more and more recently. That business about Barney Cobbler being a drug addict, how on earth was DI Barker convinced of that enough to give an interview to the Gleaner about it?'

'Actually, I think he was briefed by a couple of council officers since the mayor was instrumental in bringing the Scotland Yard man in. It looks now as if he will have to stay longer than he intended to. He told me he thought he would be back in London after a few days with the case all wrapped up. Have you heard any of that music he likes?'

'Only snatches of it. It's quite an unusual taste. I thought it sounded like the sort of music you sometimes hear in old films.'

'Apparently, it's dance band music of 1920s and 1930s he collects and enjoys. He was asking if he might be able to pick up some 78 records in the local antique shops, so I suggested one or two. I recommended Havell-Next-the-Sea would be a good place to look. The bright young things of that era used to like it there. It's the sort music bands used to play at the Savoy Hotel. I went to talk to him about Barney yesterday after I read the Gleaner. I had already arranged for the inquest into his death. I heard Eric Bolton's family arranged for the inquest into Sadie's death too, once they had him released on bail. Clearly, if Eric was involved in it, the police need more evidence. Local people could be getting uneasy. In fact, I think the council were keen to suggest the deaths were coincidental and self-inflicted to avoid all that. It explains yesterday's Gleaner front page. I don't know if you noticed, but the confirmation of the cancellation of the Moyen Midden Fayre was on an inside page and very short. People will not accept it's been cancelled. Everyone thinks it will be rescheduled. The article re-iterates the current councillors' line of argument against the fair.'

'I met people yesterday who are still making plans for the fair and expecting it to go ahead,' said Margery. 'Did DI Barker ask to see you?'

'In fact, I went voluntarily for an interview with DI Barker,' Jonah replied, 'because Barney's death was being treated as self-inflicted. I could not believe that of him, knowing him as well as I did. Barker had those tapes of vintage music playing, in that interview room he's using as an office, all the time. I had the impression it was to keep anyone in the police station from overhearing what we were talking about. We went for a pint together in the Amicable Anarchist afterwards where anyone could hear our conversation. He took the practical line in there as he was quoted in the paper and we discussed music. In fact, he liked the local beer. He said he was finding a few compensations for having to work out in the sticks.'

'I'm glad you went to talk to him. It looks as if he will have to stay in Great Havell a little longer now,' said Margery.

They all stood as the coroner returned to the courtroom and opened up the preliminary inquest into the sudden death of Sadie Petal, which had been requested by her partner Eric Bolton.

It had been a dog walker from the Glebe Estate who discovered Sadie's legs protruding from the sinkhole. The rest of her had been face down and under the grid, which had been pulled partially open. At first, he thought she was an archaeologist who had forced open the cover enough, to enable her look at something, without bothering to undo the padlocks. He called out to her, but there was no response to this. He thought she was unwell and walked down the mound towards the Amicable Anarchist. Although the pub was not open, he saw Derek, the landlord, who notified the Great Havell police, whilst he called an ambulance from the phone box next door. He said he and his dog then went back to his home on the Glebe Estate, as he had done all he could.

One of the police officers called to the scene said they had raised the partially closed mesh cover as best they could, both of them holding it open whilst they tugged the woman carefully out. She appeared to be unconscious. When they gently manoeuvred her out, they recognised her as Sadie Petal who lived at Heathlands with her partner Eric Bolton. She was known to be a drinker and often sat on a low ruined wall in the old priory with a bottle of cider. The ambulance arrived soon afterwards and brought a stretcher up the mound, they also tried to bring the unconscious woman round unsuccessfully. They put her on the stretcher to carry her down the mound to the ambulance in the priory car park. The police officer said he had accompanied her and the ambulance staff to the hospital. He waited for half an hour before he was informed a doctor had pronounced Sadie dead soon after arrival and ordered a post-mortem to discover the cause.

The pathologist from the General Hospital testified that Sadie's heart and other vital organs were all found to be deteriorating through serious alcohol abuse. With her lifestyle of constant drinking, regularly taking cannabis and harder drugs, her death from an overdose was inevitable.

Asked by the coroner if there were any other factor causing Sadie's death, the pathologist replied that apart from the alcohol in her system, there was a large amount of cocaine.

Asked by the coroner how he thought the cocaine had been administered, the pathologist said it had been injected into the upper left arm. There was a murmur in the court. The two fatal doses had been administered in the same way.

A young woman from the local social services was called. She gave a detailed account of how she had tried to help Sadie, to conquer her addiction to alcohol and return to work, for more than a year now. She said Sadie had a wonderful knowledge of the local flora and was a good horticulturalist according to her former employer. Sadie could be seen spending her days drinking mainly strong cider, usually in the old priory. Before she started drinking heavily, she had worked at Root and Branch, the garden centre. About 18 months ago, she met and moved in with Eric Bolton, who had all the money she needed to spend on her addiction. She became unreliable at the garden centre and Ruth Baldock had reluctantly asked her to leave. Sadie had attended the local Alcoholics Anonymous, but could never be persuaded, nor could see any reason, to give up her dependence on alcohol.

The coroner then called Eric Bolton. He came into the courtroom accompanied by a police officer.

Eric confirmed his name and that he and Sadie Petal had been living together for about 18 months at his house, Heathlands, which was about fifteen minutes' walk from the Glebe Mound and the old priory.

There was a gasp in the courtroom when Eric first spoke. His accent was so measured, so cultured. If he had not been dressed in a stained great coat, long scarf and had long unkempt, greasy dark hair under a battered fedora hat, they could have been listening to a BBC radio announcer.

'Sadie's a free spirit,' he said. 'She's travelled a lot. She's visited many places. She looks after my garden when she's in.'

No one in the courtroom could fail to notice, Eric was talking about Sadie as if she was still alive.

'She borrowed my Honey Monster watch a few days ago. She said she needed to know the time because she was going to meet someone who wanted her to identify some unusual plants on the Glebe Mound.

'She never came back that day and I went to look for her and my watch. A woman from Priory Cottages helped me. I spotted the watch in the priory car park, but an idiot police car ran over it before I could retrieve it. I was having a go at them for ruining my watch and they arrested me.

'They tried to charge me in with the death of some man and also Sadie. I kept telling them she wasn't dead, but they insisted she was. I spent the night in the cells, but as soon as my family heard about it, they put up the bail and I was taken home in a police car. The local police still wanted to keep me in the cells, but the inspector said I should go home, and a local copper would see I kept the bail conditions every day. Sadie has never come back.'

The coroner told Eric that Sadie had been identified as the body found in the Moyen Midden sinkhole. He said she had been pronounced dead at the hospital.

Eric looked puzzled, confused and asked if he could go home. The coroner asked the policeman to take Mr Bolton home and they left the court.

The coroner wound up proceedings and ordered further investigation into the death of Sadie Petal and the source of the drug which had killed her. This would be undertaken by the Great Havell police aided by DI Barker from Scotland Yard.

They were to report back to the court for a second inquest in a week's time.

The proceedings were closed.

Jonah and Margery had a cup of tea in the Tastea Bite, then popped into the Amicable Anarchist. It had only just opened, and they chose the snug again. Margery insisted on buying the drinks this time and bought a pint of Old Priory for Jonah and a half pint of Falcon porter for herself.

'Well done for your testimony this morning, Jonah,' said Margery and raised her glass.

'Actually, I saw you, taking notes.'

'Yes, the Gleaner asked me to cover it, although I saw a reporter there. I think there may have been reporters from the national press too.'

'Can I join you?' asked DI Barker, coming over with a cup of coffee in his hand.'

Jonah and Margery looked at each other in surprise.

'Well, yes,' said Jonah, 'I did not expect to see you in here.'

'I thought I would pop in for a coffee, I'd like to have a beer, but I have my car in the car park.'

'I can't be long,' said Margery. 'I'm expected at my uncle's, for an evening meal in Havell-Next-the-Sea tonight.'

'What time do you have to be there?' asked DI Barker.

'I need to catch the 6.30 train from Great Havell station.'

'I'll run you over there. No need to catch the train. Would you like to come with us as well, Jonah?'

'I suppose I could, but I really need to get back home to cook something for myself.'

'Do they have fish and chip shops at Havell-Next-the-Sea?'

Margery smiled. 'It's not that sort of place, but there are plenty of chip shops in Sandy Reach, a bit further along the coast. Thank you, I would like a lift. And now perhaps you can tell us why you gave that interview for yesterday's Gleaner?'

DI Barker laughed. 'It was a bit of bad editing or poor reporting. I let it go, I couldn't be bothered to correct it.'

'Really? So, it's down to the reporters and sub editors?'

'Either of them, or the editor or even the management.'

'So, what *did* you tell the reporter?'

'I said that two people *may* have accidentally overdosed on cocaine.'

'So, the subs or the reporter left out one or two words?'

'Yes, but it changed the meaning. My goodness me, it's worse than the News of the World and they can be bad enough. I'm never allowed to give press interviews at the Yard. They employ a dedicated press officer there.'

'So, what else did the Gleaner leave out or change?'

'I called them "apparent" drug addicts, not "sad". I said more. I said the local people were more concerned about the cancellation of some archaic fair, than the fact their town had a serious drug problem, which had resulted in two deaths. They didn't like that and edited it down.'

'That's a point,' said Margery. 'Where is all this cocaine coming from?'

'That's something I intend to find out,' said Barker. 'It will be relevant to the inquiry. Problem is, people know me here now. But my superior officers want me to stay on the case, so I'm stuck with it. The only place they can give me as an office in the Great Havell Police station is one of their interview rooms, so I have to work in there. It was either that or one of the cells, but there is a phone outside the interview room, so I chose that. They haven't exactly made me welcome. They told me they are perfectly capable of handling the case themselves, but that was before the inquests and a further investigation was ordered.'

'A lot of local people are saying Barney was murdered because he would have insisted on having the fair this year, even if it was on a different date,' said Jonah.

'Well, why not?' asked DI Barker. 'I don't see any reason why they can't hold it on another date.'

'It seems the council want it cancelled for good. They say it's time Great Havell updated its image to be in keeping with the times,' said Margery.

'Well, I suppose they have their reasons,' said DI Barker dismissively. 'It's all petty small-town stuff.'

'A lot of local firms expect to benefit from the fair every year,' said Margery. 'Root and Branch garden centre for instance. They make broomsticks and have a selection of herbs named after the witches, which they nurture to sell to visitors every year. Falcon Brewery have a special brew for the event, the Old Granary Hotel are already taking bookings, so are all the other hotels in the area.'

The DI looked at Margery. 'It's all very parochial and small-minded, isn't it?'

'Not to them,' Margery was defensive. 'I don't see why the town council can't change the date.'

'When I arrived in Great Havell, I was briefed by council officers who requested someone from outside the town investigate the death of the historian. I had the impression from them they thought these traditions were holding the town back, rather than contributing anything to it.'

'Well, everyone seems to be very excited about the Gary Hogan concert,' said Margery. 'So perhaps that is the way forward.'

'By the way, here is the story you wrote on the legends, the history of the Glebe Mound and the Moyen Midden and the Fair. I think you had better have it back. I have read it. I can understand why they don't want to publish it, now the event has been cancelled. Did you find out why the revenues are down at the Gleaner?'

'I've been looking into that. When I was in photographic yesterday, I saw one of the feature staff, in a basement office, looking through piles of dockets. I think they are checking up to see if all advertising has been charged and paid for. Oh, and my uncle and I found a lot of house ads in an old coastal edition.'

'What are house ads?'

'Advertisements which promote the newspaper group and recruitment ads for jobs at the Gleaner.'

'You think there might be a lot of advertising which hasn't been charged for?'
'Could be.'

'Would that be the sort of thing the local tax office might be interested in do you think, Jonah?'

'Yes, that is a point, there is VAT on advertising.'

'Wasn't your friend Barney Cobbler manager at the local tax office and chairman of the Moyen Circle?'

'Yes, he was,' said Jonah. 'But surely no one would stoop to murder to cover up a tax dodge or suppress an annual event. It's unthinkable.'

'I agree,' said Margery. 'And anyway, Sadie died in the same way as Barney; we know that now, and she was nothing to do with the tax office, the Gleaner or the fair.'

'For whatever reason,' said the DI, 'the town council is keen to prevent the traditional event from going ahead for good. Drink up and I will take you to Havell-Next-the-Sea. Hopefully, you will join me for fish and chips at Sandy Reach, Jonah?'

Margery and Jonah followed DI Barker out of the Amicable Anarchist wishing a cheery good evening to Derek behind the bar.

They crossed the road to the priory car park and into DI Barker's black BMW. The music started playing as soon as he switched the engine on.

'Oh, I like that!' exclaimed Margery, who was sitting in the back. 'That's really cheerful, what is it?'

'Paul Whiteman, Wang Wang Blues,' said the DI. 'I'll switch it off.'

'No don't,' said Margery. 'I'd like to hear it. What else is on your tape?'

'More similar,' said the DI. 'I think it is mostly Whiteman.'

On Margery's directions, he drove her to Havell-Next-the-Sea and her destination in The Avenue. Jonah was then going to show him Sandy Reach and they intended to have a fish and chip supper in the car, listening to one of the DI's tapes along the sea front. Margery almost envied them.

'You are nice and early,' said Aunt Carrie, opening the door.

Margery, her uncle and aunt sampled the Falcon Brewery beer with their evening meal and chatted about the inquests. Margery explained Sadie had apparently been injected with a lethal dose of cocaine in a similar way to Barney. In view of what they had heard at the inquest, Alec and Carrie were pleased Margery would be staying with them that night. They urged her to stay on Friday as well as Saturday.

## Friday 14th February

Friday morning dawned bright and clear. Carrie had made them all porridge for breakfast and then Margery said she would walk to Berkin Estate Agents to interview them for a feature. After that she said, she intended to catch the train to Great Havell to write up her notes on the inquest and the article about Berkin. She had decided to stay in her cottage that evening, but she would be back in good time for the pantomime tomorrow.

'We would really rather you stayed here tonight, let us know if you change your mind and Alec will come and pick you up. We've booked tea at the Sandy Reach Grand Hotel tomorrow,' said Carrie. 'Neil will be staying the night with us. He's going to sleep on the new sofa bed we got for the study. He's very excited about it.'

It was a pleasant walk, along sunny suburban streets to Berkins. The agency had been adapted from a detached house in a street parallel to the greensward and the sea front. The sun was streaming in the door which was open.

Mr and Mrs Berkin were both in there waiting for her. Mr Berkin was seated behind a well-polished wooden desk and Mrs Berkin was sitting on a chair opposite the door in the sunlight, knitting something pink. The room smelled of lavender polish and baking. Margery asked if they would like her to shut the door.

'If you are not going to be cold, dear,' said Mrs Berkin, 'please leave it open, I think you should be warm enough in that nice tartan cape of yours.'

Mr Berkin stood up to shake hands with Margery. He introduced himself as Ralph and his wife as Nancy and set a chair for her opposite his and at an angle to allow her to talk to them both. She thanked him and contrasted his greeting with Denzil Bream's earlier in the week.

'What would you like to know?' asked Mr Berkin. 'We advertise in all editions of the Weekender Gleaner every week. It's a good package and doesn't cost much if we guarantee to take the space for a year.'

'Do you only sell properties in Havell-Next-the-Sea?' asked Margery.

'Almost exclusively. We have a few just outside in the suburbs of Sandy Reach and we also have some of the country properties, in the rural hinterland towards the marshes and the docks, when they come up for sale. People know us. If they want or need to sell a house here, they come in and tell us. We feature it in our weekly advertisement and it always sells quickly. People know to look for our advertisement in the newspaper if they want to buy something here. We know our market; we only sell properties, we don't get involved with new homes, commercial properties or anything like that. We don't let or sell beach huts as the other agents do and we are not involved in lettings. We are not looking to make vast amounts of money. We don't spend much on advertising. We always make a modest profit on sales, enough to tick over.'

Margery realised she was going to have difficulty making a story out of all this and asked how long they had been running their agency.

'It started with Nancy's parent's house when they moved away. They wanted us to move into it, but we were happy here, so we put it on the market through the Weekender Gleaner property supplement. It sold in days and we did the conveyancing ourselves. Word went round about it and other local people asked if we could do the same for them. That's really all we do, sell houses for people.'

Margery managed to get a little bit of information about the couple. She found out that between them they had a lot of relatives in the area and always someone to knit for, although Nancy Berkin explained she also belonged to the Ladies Knitting and Sewing Circle.

Margery was given a cup of tea and a homemade ginger biscuit. She had the impression Nancy Berkin was always either polishing, knitting, sewing or baking. Margery thanked them both and left feeling very relaxed. She didn't have much to write about them. She took plenty of pictures including the sea front with her Ricoh camera and walked along the front to turn in past St Luke's and along the main shopping street.

As she neared an antique shop, she was surprised to see DI Barker, with a square brown paper package tied up with string under his arm, leaving the shop. He spotted her immediately.

'Hello young lady, what are you doing here?' he asked cheerfully.

'I've been interviewing an estate agent for a feature.'

'Working hard as usual. Can I buy you a coffee in the Tastea Bite over the road?'

'I haven't long, I've to catch a train home to write up the coroner's proceedings. I'll see you in there. I'm going to pop in the newsagent to buy the Weekender Gleaner.'

'How do you like your coffee?'

'White, no sugar please.'

'Would you like a doughnut?'

'Thanks, I would, if you are having one.'

When Margery sat down opposite DI Barker in the Tastea Bite, they were served with their coffees and doughnuts, which Margery noticed with amusement were in the shape of teddy bears. She had forgotten they were a speciality of the Tastea Bite branch in Havell-Next-the-Sea. Since her uncle and aunt had moved to the coastal town, she hadn't much reason for going to the cafe.

She put the Weekender Gleaner on the table so he could see the headline.

"BARKER UP THE WRONG TREE"

DI Barker glanced at it without even raising an eyebrow and bit off the head of his teddy bear doughnut releasing a gush of red jam onto his plate.

'I see the Gleaner promises a full report on the coroner's court on Monday. I suppose you need to get that written and into the office today. I'll give you a lift back home.'

'Thanks. How did you enjoy your fish and chips at Sandy Reach?'

'Excellent thanks.' DI Barker wiped up the jam on his plate with a teddy bear leg. 'I almost wish I was based here or at Sandy Reach. I think I'll come back with the family when I'm not working.'

Margery wasn't sure if he was joking or not. She was itching to look at the paper to find out whether her article on Bream was in there.

'Bream wanted me sacked for the article I wrote on Tuesday.'

'And why would that be?'

Margery told the DI about the interview with Denzil Bream, inadvertently, she imitated his manner, including the sniffing.

'Is that how Bream speaks? Does he sniff a lot?'

'Yes, so it seems. He's rather annoying. He wouldn't tell me anything, just gave me a brochure on new homes, some of which are to be built on Home Farm, which is rented from the council. The farm grows barley for Falcon Brewery and is used by Fabb, the farm equipment people, for demonstrations.'

'So where would I find this article?'

'It will be in the Weekender Property Supplement in the middle of the paper.'

Barker extracted the supplement and showed the headline to Margery, who gasped; she was very near to swearing and checked herself.

DI Barker looked amused.

'Buy a touch of class off plan, by Margery Moore,' he read, 'Exclusive to estate agent Bream, executive new homes are set to be built bordering Great Havell Thorpe Park and open countryside. They will be a ten minutes' drive to the railway station along the soon to be built Great Havell bypass. Four and five bedroom brand new family homes will have double garages and ensuite bath-room in the master bedroom. Secure yours for a five per cent deposit… and so it goes on.'

Margery went red with anger.

'That's a load of bloody rubbish! I write articles for the Gleaner, not adver-tising copy.'

'It's got your name on it, so you must have written it.'

'I know! I'm beyond angry. What on earth is Cheryl playing at, letting that go! It's too much! The land where these so-called executive homes are to be built is council owned. It's green belt, part of the Home Farm.

'Who owns the land where the rest of the new homes are to be built?'

'It's the Grimes family estate.'

Margery didn't want to look at the offending article, although he offered it to her. Instead, she picked up the rest of the Gleaner and looked for her review of An Inspector Calls, which she saw had been printed exactly as she had written it. She was about to put the paper down when a small headline caught her eye.

"Party man in coma"

"Denzil Bream, who celebrated his 28th Birthday on Wednesday night, was rushed to hospital yesterday morning when his girlfriend, Tracey, 24, was unable to wake him.

"'We had a wonderful time, partying with friends for Den's birthday,' said the distraught Tracey. 'At first I thought he was pretending to be asleep, but then I realised he was unconscious.'"

"Mr Bream's family was unavailable for comment."

Margery handed the paper to DI Barker, who read it.

'That fits,' he remarked.

'What do you mean?' she asked.

'The silly bastard has snorted too much cocaine. Where are they getting this stuff from? Is there a lot of smuggling around here?'

Margery was silent for a moment.

'You mean people sniff the stuff up through their noses, like snuff?'

'My dear Miss Moore, where have you been? I suppose the cosy little world you live in at Priory Cottages insulates you from the hard drugs' scene. You've docks around here, haven't you?'

'There's a container dock, but it's very strict security.'

'I suppose you've been round it and written an article?'

'Yes. It's not all containers yet. There's a rail spur which runs from the dock to join the line beyond Little Havell. There's also a road to the dock. You might have noticed the turning and signs when you brought me here yesterday.'

'I did. I'll notify the drugs squad at the yard. If we could identify where the stuff is coming from and who is importing it, we might be able to find out who used it to inject Cobbler and Petal and where young Bream was getting it from.

Look Margery, we'd better get you back to Great Havell to write your articles. Are you coming back here tonight?'

'I think by the time I've written my pieces and delivered them to the Gleaner, I shall probably stay in the cottage tonight.'

'How do you fancy meeting up for a drink at the Amicable Anarchist later? I'll ask Jonah if he'd like to come too. What do you think? I'll leave my car at the station. Jonah and I can walk you back to your cottage and make sure you are all right.'

'Do you think I'm in danger then?'

'No, but that business with your cat may have been meant as some sort of warning to you. And that rag doll, with face, hair and clothes, which were obviously supposed to resemble yours; with the twigs from the broomstick stuffed through your door, suggests someone wants you to take notice or involve you in something. Come on, the car's just up the road. Here's your property supplement. Let's hope I'm barking up the right tree now!'

With a grim smile, Barker got up, picked up his records, paid the bill and led Margery up the tree-lined shopping street to his car. Opening the passenger door for Margery, he put his package of records on the back seat, before he got in the driver's seat, started the engine and drove smoothly off towards Great Havell, with one of his dance band tapes playing all the way. There was no conversation.

Barker parked his BMW in the priory car park. There were people shouting outside the Amicable Anarchist and there were crowds of people in the street. The DI and Margery looked in surprise as Derek pushed a couple of angry lads out of the pub and shut the door firmly against them.

'Let's go back to the marketplace and hassle Bream again,' they heard.

Without consulting each other, Margery and Barker crossed the road and followed the crowd round the houses and into the marketplace, where there was an angry demonstration going on outside the estate agents, which had been completely closed and shuttered up.

There were placards "SAVE OUR GREEN BELT!", "STOP THE LAND GRAB!", "SAVE THE FAIR!", "HANDS OFF HOME FARM!", "NO! TO BY-PASS". There was a lot of angry shouting and a chanting, someone had a guitar and protest songs could be heard. From what Margery saw and heard, hundreds of people were demonstrating about the cancellation of the fair and also against the plans published in the Weekender property supplement, which had her by-line on it. She might be recognised and even attacked. It was clear feelings, about it all, were running high.

DI Barker clearly had the same idea and steered her out of the marketplace as several uniformed policemen came from the direction of the police station to attempt to contain and even disperse the demonstration.

They walked quickly to Margery's cottage, where DI Barker left her and said he would be back later with Jonah, if he was available, and they could all go for a drink in Amicable Anarchist.

Margery switched on her electric fire to relieve the chill of the empty cottage.

She decided to start with her report on the inquest. It was just a case of typing up her shorthand. She found she was using a lot of copy paper and hoped she would have enough for everything.

She broke for a quick lunch and realised she would only just be able to get her copy in to the Gleaner before her 5.00 pm deadline. There would be no time to write the article on Berkin.

She rang Cheryl.

'I'm on my way, Cheryl. I'm going to need more copy paper please, if you can have that ready. I booked my other appointments for Monday and Tuesday, so I'll finish the film in my camera then. What did you mean by putting my name on that utter crap in the Weekender Gleaner? I could have been attacked by the mob in the marketplace. My name is known locally.'

Cheryl sounded unhappy. 'I'm sorry, Margery, it wasn't my decision. If you like, I'll pop over and pick up the copy. It will save you coming here and rushing, I'll explain more when I see you. Everything is being made very awkward for me here.'

'Awkward for *you*!' exclaimed Margery. 'That's a bit rich! I'm the one they will be targeting. I'll see you soon.'

Margery left the door on the latch for Cheryl, who turned up in a few minutes, which surprised her, because she had only just separated her articles out and put them in paper clips.

Cheryl stayed at the door. Margery could hear a car outside with its engine running.

'I can't stop, one of the reps brought me and will take me back. We can get this subbed and set for Monday. Thanks for doing it. I'm sorry about the Weekender property supplement; it was out of my hands.'

'Whose hands was it in?'

'It was Harry Grimes. He insisted. He had the last word. He said the Gleaner could not afford to upset Bream. The article you wrote was all set to be published and we were close to deadline. I didn't realise your name was still on it and even if I had, production might have refused to take it off at the last minute; it was all such a rush. We had to use a lot of influence and persuasion for them to take the replacement article Bream provided. I wouldn't have been allowed to touch the page. It was one of the property team who got the revised editorial in. They wouldn't have known to take your name off it. They would not have known you hadn't written it.'

'You know there have been angry mobs in the marketplace, demonstrating and shouting outside Bream and the town hall? You can still hear them from here.'

'Yes, I heard and saw them, that's why I got a lift here. Fortunately, the mob haven't had the idea of demonstrating outside the Gleaner… yet! Hopefully your factual report on the inquest for Monday's Gleaner will calm things a bit. Have a nice weekend and I'll see you on Monday with the property copy and pics. By the way, if you have a chance, read the two pages of letters in the Weekender. The directors are furious about them.'

'Did you remember the copy paper?'

Cheryl looked in her briefcase.

'Of course, I did. Look, I've got to go. I just wanted you to know I'm sorry. Are you going to be all right here on your own tonight?'

'I've got a couple of friends coming over and we're going out for a drink.'

'That's good, but make sure you bolt your door, just in case someone gets it in their head to harass you about that article on the Monks Thorpe development. I am just so sorry; I don't know what else I can say except I wish you were coming to the Valentine's Ball. I need moral support at the moment.'

With that, Cheryl left the cottage abruptly, got in the car, which reversed swiftly down the lane and was gone.

Margery felt uneasy. At lot had happened in the past two weeks. She wished she had asked Vlad if he would come and stay. They usually arranged between them when they would see each other, but she had not thought to ask when they had breakfast together on Wednesday.

She cooked herself some pasta and mushrooms and took the Gleaner in to the kitchen to read it while she ate.

The two pages of letters were angry objections to the cancellation of the fair. Many were in praise of Barney Cobbler, as a local historian, and an acknowledgement of all the volunteer work he did for the Moyen Circle. There was an obituary in there for him as well. A lot of letters expressed shock and outrage about the treatment of her cat. There were others demanding the fair be rescheduled, if it could not be held at the solstice. There were letters from religious groups, historical groups and archaeologists. Some people claimed the cancellation of the fair had released the curse of the mound, as evidenced by the two recent deaths on and near it. Others claimed supporters of the fair had been cruel to Margery's cat deliberately, to try to get it reinstated by suggesting both deaths were down to a curse. There were also a couple of letters complaining the Gleaner was all advertising and should be distributed free. Margery wondered why some of the letters, which were so rude and critical of the mayor and the Grimes family, had got past the editor. It had seemed to her, until she read them all, the Grimes family had everything their own way. Perhaps, with today's demonstrations, which had probably been going on all day, they might start listening to local people.

Maybe, when the drug squad had found the source of the cocaine, which had killed Barney and Sadie, according to the coroner's inquest, there could be some kind of solution to it all. The drug seemed to be readily available in Great Havell.

Who? Margery asked herself, would kill Barney and why? Were the Tudor documents found in his walls connected with his death? Or was it his unique knowledge of local history, which could have questioned the land rights? Why were homes being advertised for sale before they were even built?' Margery supposed, with all the sales of council homes in the locality, since the beginning of the decade, there was an unprecedented demand for home ownership, which needed to be fulfilled. Had the developer, agents and landowners hoped Barney's death would be dismissed as a drug overdose and self-inflicted by spreading it around he was an addict? But then, perhaps he was. The most unlikely people could take drugs on a regular basis. Friends from school and college had tipped her off about local doctors, dentists, solicitors, accountants, even magistrates who 'enjoyed recreational drugs' in their words, on special occasions and earned enough to afford the "best stuff". Until meeting DI Barker in Havell-Next-the-Sea, she had thought Denzil Bream's annoying sniffing was just an irritating habit.

The front-page story pointed out the inquest had ordered DI Barker and Great Havell police to make further investigations into Barney and Sadie's deaths. It said the detective inspector, who was invited by Mayor Grimes to assist police in their inquiries had, so far, got it all wrong. There would be a full report on the coroner's inquest published in the Gleaner on Monday, it concluded.

Still musing over it all, Margery washed her dishes and walked into the bathroom for a shower. She went upstairs in her dressing gown and put on her spare pair of jeans and a red Guernsey jumper. She took her duffle coat out of a wardrobe in her front bedroom and took it downstairs to put it on the peg near the door. Shortly afterwards, there was a knock on the door.

She was pleased to see Barker had enlisted Jonah for their evening in the pub. Jonah was wearing a light-blue hand-knitted jumper under his sports jacket and corduroy trousers, whilst DI Barker's long legs were in jeans and he wore a black roll neck jumper under his brown suede jacket.

The Amicable Anarchist was very busy, not just with people who had been demonstrating in the marketplace, but also the Friday night regulars. DI Barker insisted on buying the first round. Margery decided to stick to a half pint.

The snug was already occupied, so they had to hunt around for somewhere to sit. There was a buzz of animated conversations about the demonstrations and about the plans for Monks Thorpe. They eventually found a corner in the public bar, they could squeeze into, with stools to sit on.

Margery noticed she was receiving a few hostile looks, from some people, even from Derek behind the bar. It was disturbing. She was rather hoping she would not be noticed without her usual tartan cape and hat or black jacket. Did they think she had killed her own cat and written that crappy article about the executive homes on the Home Farm greenbelt land? They probably did.

Barker was asking about the Quay Marina. Could Margery show him round there at the weekend? She regretted she couldn't. Was she going to the Valentine's Ball in the Assembly rooms? Regrettably, she wasn't. Barker seemed to be quite pleased about that. 'Back to Havell-Next-the-Sea for the weekend then?' he asked.

Jonah was interested in all the different factions demonstrating in the marketplace. 'They were a motley lot,' he said. 'Your article about the new homes on the front page of the Weekender Property Supplement has upset a lot of people.'

'It wasn't my article.'

'Pardon?'

146

'It wasn't my article,' repeated Margery and gave them an account of her interview with Denzil Bream. She explained he had given her the brochures and told her to use them for the article. She said she had seen a bus to Havell-on-the-Marsh afterwards, caught it and met up with the niece and nephew of the tenants of Home Farm. She explained how later that evening, she and her uncle had tried to understand how an estate agent could try to get deposits on expensive homes, which had not yet been constructed, and were designed to be built on green belt, council-owned land. She also related how they had noticed the pictures from the brochures had been used for Gleaner recruitment advertisements. She told them about Fabb's use of the land, the variety of barley which was grown there for the Falcon Brewery and her discovery of a hidden loft and staircase on the side of the Old Granary Hotel. She noticed DI Barker was particularly interested in that.

'Does the hotel have a restaurant?' asked DI Barker.

'Yes, it's called the Grain of Truth.'

Both Barker and Jonah laughed.

'Do they do Sunday lunch?' asked the DI.

'Yes, it has a carvery.'

'Capital! I think I'll book and see if I can persuade my wife to come down here at the weekend.'

'Did you not have an invitation to this Valentine's Ball tomorrow, Margery?' asked Jonah.

'Harry Grimes tried to give me an invitation, but I am going to a pantomime. Are you going to the ball, Jonah?'

'Actually, I shall be there. In fact, I shall be with a couple of other members of the Moyen Circle and their wives.'

'You know Cheryl Francis of the Gleaner,' said Margery, 'You'll recognise her from the Jazz and Folk Club. Look out for her if she seems a bit lonely. She's not looking forward to this for some reason. I guess she feels obliged to go and her husband doesn't want to go and probably isn't keen for her to go. It seems Harry Grimes has bought a lot of tickets for the do and is giving them away to Gleaner staff. She loves her job and dare not refuse.'

'So, Harry Grimes is the big spender,' remarked Barker, 'yet the revenues are down.'

'Actually, that was just what I was thinking,' said Jonah. 'If you didn't write that article in the Weekender Property Supplement, Margery, who did?'

'I had to take a copy for Breams. Denzil Bream put exactly what he wanted to go in there and then threatened to pull his advertising if it wasn't published. Apparently, he wanted me sacked, but they can't do that because I'm freelance. They could, if they wanted to, not give me any more assignments. They should not have left my by-line on that article, because it was changed completely. I hadn't written it. That's what makes me really angry. Cheryl thinks someone from the property sales team was the last person to check the page. They didn't notice it or may have thought I had written it. If Cheryl had seen it, I hope she would have taken my name off but, apparently, she would not be allowed to touch a page on stone. It may have already been checked when the editorial was changed. She would have to ask a union member to do any further alterations. They would probably refuse if the advertisements and editorial on the page had been signed off. Ask for too much and the staff might all walk out, and nothing would get published. She says they are all very touchy these days.'

'Well, so it's all down to the Bream family, and it looks as if they have enough trouble on their hands at the moment. I see from the letters in the Weekender Gleaner, the Grimes family are not too popular either,' remarked Jonah.

Margery told Jonah and Barker that Cheryl had come round to pick up her copy on the inquests. She had apologised profusely because her by-line had not been removed from the article. Margery said she had to admit she was still really angry about it and she was also angry and upset by the suggestion she had killed her own cat.

'Is there any connection between Bream and the Grimes family?' asked Barker.

Denzil Bream and Berkley Grimes, the mayor's son and their girlfriends were drinking champagne together at the opening of the Brass Monkeys Brasserie, the other night,' replied Margery. 'I think they are also very friendly with Morris and Mack, the owners. They all go out as a group. They were in the Witches Cauldron too, a few days ago,' she added.

They felt it was time to talk of other things.

They all had an interest in music. Margery and Jonah told DI Barker about the Jazz and Folk Club at the Arts Centre on a Friday evening, the sort of bands who played there and the variety of music they played. Barker suggested they went there later, but neither Jonah nor Margery were keen to go after the anger and disturbances in the town centre that day, especially since some of the musicians, who played at the Arts Centre regularly, were in the marketplace, playing and singing protest songs.

Derek was calling time when they left the pub. They had all brought torches with them and walked with Margery back to her cottage. She had left the curtains drawn and a reading lamp on. Vlad's bike was in her front garden, so he had probably gone to the Arts Centre.

All was quiet, both her neighbours' homes were in darkness. The students, who rented the end cottage near the old priory, were up and music could be heard faintly from the end of the terrace as they walked past. Jonah and Barker came into the cottage and accepted her offer of coffee or cocoa. It was well past midnight before they left together after making sure the cottage was secure.

Margery washed up the cocoa and coffee cups, made herself a hot water bottle and cleaned her teeth. She was about to go to bed when she heard a gentle knock on the door. Vlad's voice came through the letterbox.

'Margery, are you there? Are you all right?'

She went to the door and opened it. He came in quickly and closed the door. He had a small rucksack with him.

'My bike is outside. I didn't like to use my key so late in case you had gone to bed and were alarmed. I've been to the Arts Centre. it was a good evening. I was hoping I might see you there. I called in earlier, but you were out, so I walked around the cottages and saw Jonah walking away with DI Barker.'

'I was in the Amicable Anarchist with Jonah and DI Barker.'

'I know I caught up with Jonah and walked with him to his house. He said they had seen you safe back to your cottage.'

'I would like you to stay,' said Margery, 'It will be good to have you staying here tonight. It's been a difficult day and I would feel safer, if you were here. I'm going to Havell-Next-the-Sea tomorrow.'

Margery noticed Vlad was taking a pair of shorts and a tee shirt out of his rucksack to sleep in. That was a change she thought. She noticed he'd also brought a clean vest for tomorrow.

That night, Vlad wrapped Margery in his arms until she fell asleep. She felt safe.

They were both disturbed by a massive bang on the front door in the early hours of the morning. They heard the sound of something being pushed through the letterbox.

Vlad got up and went downstairs. Margery imagined her door had been broken and waited in alarm. She was glad she was not on her own. She heard Vlad switch the light on and listened as he moved around downstairs. She expected to hear voices, but there were none. She was relieved he was there, but she still had a feeling of dread in her stomach.

Eventually, he came upstairs and switched on her bedside lamp.

'This is all I found,' he said.

It was a large red envelope with her name in capital letters on it.

Margery opened it slowly and carefully. She'd heard of letter bombs, but understood they were more likely to come in padded envelopes than one like this.

It was an invitation to the Valentine's Ball at the Assembly Rooms.

## Saturday 15th February

Margery awoke warm and comfortable and stretched out in the bed. Everything was calm after the disturbance in the night. Neither of them needed to go to work, they could have a leisurely breakfast.

They had toast tea and marmalade again for breakfast. Vlad asked Margery if she knew why there had been so many protests in Great Havell yesterday. He said even his workmates at the Country Hotel had asked for time off to go.

She explained, as best she could, about the plans to build on Home Farm green belt land. She said the houses were already being offered for sale, although they had not been built, people could put a deposit on them. She said Bream was the only estate agency which was able to sell them. She explained to him the agency and only that agency would make all the profits from the sales when they were built. She told him her article had been re-written by Denzil and her name had been left on it, though she hadn't written it. She explained local people were upset about the plans for new homes and about the cancellation of the fair. The demonstrations were about that, outside Bream and the Town Hall. Great Havell, she said, had a tradition of non-conformity, of protests. 'It didn't take much,' she explained to Vlad, 'for local people to become very angry about certain things, which they didn't agree with or they didn't think fair. They would demonstrate in the marketplace.' They liked to go out and make their feelings known. It was a local tradition in the town.

Margery had to explain it to Vlad several times before he understood it. Protests were outside his knowledge. It was not something he was aware of. But what he did understand was that Home Farm was not privately owned. It was rented from the council. It wasn't exactly like collective farms he said, which had been the way of life in Russia. A type of collectivism, he said, was one of the reasons he liked his job at the Country Hotel. He couldn't be fully employed there as a plumber, electrician and engineer as there was not enough work. This was why he and his flat mates were on call with the local letting agency. At the Country Hotel, he could also work with the gardeners and groundsmen on major projects as a team. It was working together as he was used to in Russia, he said. Vlad could understand the concept of land rented from the local authority. He also understood, eventually, that a cartel of, commercial agent, landowner, developer, builder and estate agent, who were all poised to take publicly owned land and make money from it, incensed local people enough to get them demonstrating with placards, outside the town hall and the estate agents. He had heard about it all from the people he worked with, he said. He had been to have a look in his lunch hour. There were a lot of signs and placards waved about. There was a lot of shouting and fist waving. It was mostly outside the estate agents and the town hall. Some people were making a point of marching in between the two buildings, holding up the traffic and the buses along that side of the marketplace. According to people he'd spoken to it had been going on all day as people heard about it. Students from the institute and university joined in. There was a folk singer with a guitar singing protest songs and spirituals, even a calypso, especially composed. These were mostly about the fair which people were shouting was their tradition and right to have. People were buying food and drinks in the market. Except for the anger, some people were enjoying themselves, especially after the pubs opened and when they were singing.

Margery said she hoped the anger was not directed at her. She showed Vlad the article in the Gleaner which had her name in it.

'Why did you write that?' he asked.

'I didn't. As I tried to explain to you, I wrote something different and took it to Bream because they wanted to see if before it was published. There is no similarity between that and the article I wrote. Apparently, Denzil Bream wanted me sacked for what I had written. I suppose it was close to deadline and his so-called corrections were printed instead of my article. My by-line would have been on the original article on the page, so the printers left it on there. Cheryl or one of the sub editors should have taken it off when the text was changed so much. She told me she didn't see it and it was too close to deadline to do it. The unions won't allow editorial staff to touch the pages once they are set and signed off.

When they check them, a union member has to make any changes. Denzil Bream was threatening to pull all his advertising unless his version of the article went in. What I object to is having my name on it.'

Vlad was quiet. He didn't really know what Margery was talking about but could understand enough to realise it made her look as if she was supporting the people who were keen on building expensive houses on council-owned land.

'Do you wish to go to this Valentine's Ball?' he asked.

'I can't. I am going to stay with my aunt and uncle, and we are taking my young cousin to the pantomime at the Sandy Reach Theatre.'

Margery could see Vlad was looking relieved. She never saw him in anything but a vest or t-shirt and army jacket, so she imagined he would have to hire clothes to go to a ball. Besides, she didn't really want all the gossip and questions from the staff at the Gleaner, particularly Gill and Philippa, if she turned up with him at a ball, even if he smartened himself up.

'Let's go and take Eric's Honey Monster watch back to him,' she suggested, and Vlad brightened up. He was obviously keen to see what sort of person ate his way through packets of cereal just to get a novelty watch.

Margery put on her duffle coat and boots and Vlad put on his army jacket and army surplus boots and they walked together to the end of the lane outside Priory Cottages and onto the wide grass verge along the road towards the docks and container port. The Glebe Mound was on their right, a series of allotments, market gardens, greenhouses and potato fields were on their left, behind hedge-rows. After about half a mile, the road forked to the right round the Glebe Mound, but Vlad and Margery took the left fork, where the terrain changed to scrub and heathland, with heather and gorse. They turned left along an unmade cart track, which was signposted "Heathlands" with high unkempt hedges on either side. The path, which was wide enough for a vehicle, was sandy and well drained. After about a quarter of a mile, it led to a large classical house with a slate roof and a wide porch with columns either side.

There was an old-fashioned bell pull outside and Margery pulled it. The bell was loud and made her jump. It seemed to echo into an empty space, but no one came. She pulled it again and looked through the letterbox; she could see all sorts of stuff on the floor of the wide hall. Piles of newspapers, books and lots of circulars which had never been picked up, together with official looking letters which hadn't been opened. She could hear a piano being played somewhere within.

Vlad was looking round the side of the house and Margery rang the bell again when Eric came to the door; he opened it as much as he could with all the stuff behind it, peered out through the gap and said:

'What the fuck do you want?'

'I rescued your broken Honey Monster watch from the priory car park. I thought you would like it back.'

'What the fuck did you do that for?'

'I don't know, I supposed you would want it. You seemed to be upset.'

There was a long pause. Vlad returned to the porch, having had a look round the back.

'Eric, I've got a friend with me. His name is Vladimir, can we come in?'

Margery heard Eric grumbling.

'Bloody, fucking, nuisance. I suppose you had better come in.'

It was cold in the house. There was a lot of stuff in the hall.

Margery and Vlad followed Eric into a large room at the back of the house which had shelves filled with books. Armchairs and a sofa were covered in books and magazines and there was a grand piano with a cornucopia of things piled up on it. There was nothing on the piano stool. But there seemed to be a lot of clocks which, if they couldn't be distinguished among all the other things on shelves, tables chairs and sofa, could be heard ticking. One chimed. It might have been on the hour, the half hour or even the quarter hour. Margery did not know which and didn't like to check by looking at her watch. They kept their jackets on.

God! I'm fucking missing Sadie,' said Eric and burst into tears. 'What did the silly woman need to know the time for?'

They couldn't answer that.

'I'll make tea?' Vlad asked.

You might find some coffee in the kitchen,' said Eric. 'You'll have to clean mugs if you want some.'

'I'll do that,' said Vlad and took himself off.

When Vlad had gone into the kitchen, Eric said again 'God! I'm fucking missing Sadie,' and Margery noticed tears running down his cheeks.

He turned abruptly on the piano stool and started playing… Gershwin, Cole Porter, Scott Joplin, blues, popular classics. Margery was amazed.

She pushed some books and magazines over to one side of the long low dusty settee and sat down, finding it a lot lower and less supportive than she had expected.

When Eric was in the middle of Fig Leaf Rag, Vlad came in with an ornate tarnished silver tray with three steaming mugs of black coffee on it.

She looked around for somewhere Vlad could put the tray, in vain. Every surface in there was covered in something.

'I could not find milk or sugar,' said Vlad, 'but I found a kettle and a camping stove.'

'The fucking electric is cut off,' said Eric turning from the piano, getting up abruptly and picking up a half full bottle of single malt whisky from the mass of bottles on the sideboard. Some were empty, some nearly empty and one or two half-full.

Vlad had put the tray of coffee mugs on the floor. Eric topped up each one with whisky and invited them to help themselves, which they did.

Margery found the stuff undrinkable, but Vlad didn't seem to mind. He stood up drinking his coffee, even saying, *'Za zdorovie'*. Eric raised his mug, said, 'Cheers, mate.' He moved over to make room for Vlad to sit next to him on the broad piano stool.

Margery looked at them thinking what an odd pair they were, sitting there drinking black coffee and whisky together. Vlad was in his clean vest, army jacket and corduroy trousers, his light brown hair cropped short. Eric sat next to him, with his long unkempt dark hair, a thick woollen jacket over two or three thicknesses of threadbare jumpers, a scarf wrapped around his neck, fingerless gloves on his hands, a grubby pair of trousers covering his legs and old leather wool-lined slippers on his feet, the uppers coming away from the soles.

Margery could not drink any of the black coffee with the whisky in it. She took her mug into the kitchen, pouring the contents down the sink, when she could find the plughole. She went back into the room to find them still in the same place. Eric looked a lot happier.

'Vlad, I have to leave to change and go to the station,' she said.

'I'll come with you,' he said, getting up and draining his coffee mug.

'You are not fucking going?' said Eric. 'You've only just come!'

'I'll come straight back on my bike,' said Vlad immediately.

Margery gave Eric his Honey Monster watch from her bag. She went back into the hall and Vlad came with her. Eric followed them to the door and stood watching them as they walked down the lane to the road.

They couldn't see him when they turned into the road to walk back to Priory Cottages but both waved, nevertheless.

'I saw the sadness and loneliness in his eyes,' said Vlad. 'I thought, you are going to Havell-Next-the-Sea, I have no plans for the rest of today. I found a chess set in that kitchen. I'll go back and have a game of chess with him or cards. We played a lot on the ships and the submarines.'

'It's good of you,' said Margery. 'Don't you mind the smell in there?'

'I liked his piano playing. I thought, if he plays the piano, I could start to clear the place up a bit.'

'That's really good of you,' said Margery. 'That's even noble.'

'What do you mean "noble"?'

'I suppose I mean you are acting like a top gentleman or landowner who is very good to his people.'

Vladimir laughed. 'That is really funny, as if I could ever act like a landowner!'

'Well, perhaps a better way of putting it, is behaving with high principals and benevolence. It's very, very good of you. The man is a mess. He's a drinker. If his family had not bought him that big house to live in, he would be on the streets.'

'I don't know what he would be, Margery, but he is a human being. I like him.'

'I must admit I'm surprised, I never expected you would want to go back there. His partner, Sadie, who was found dead in the sinkhole in the Moyen Midden last Tuesday, used to sit in the old priory every day, drinking her cider and smoking her roll-ups to get away. At her inquest, he said she used to tend his garden. But you might have noticed, when things go wrong, he does not get them fixed. They used to go to the public baths for a shower and the lighting is by battery lanterns. I think it was Sadie who used to go out and buy them and everything else they needed.'

'I'll buy some food from the market before I go back,' said Vlad.

Margery could not get over her surprise that he would go back to that house; she was glad to get out of the mess, the chaos and the drinking.

When they got back to Margery's cottage, Vlad picked up his bike to go to the market and to cycle back to Heathlands.

He said he would be back to stay with her on Sunday night. Margery changed into a black dress and jacket, tartan scarf and beret. She had kept a pair of boots at her uncle's and wore her moccasins to walk to the station. She made herself a sandwich to eat on the train.

She noticed, as she walked up the road towards the station, there were a lot of people about. Fortunately, there was no one she recognised or who recognised her.

All the activity seemed to be in the marketplace and she walked briskly past the turning to it, past shops, businesses and speeded up past Moonlight Motors, where she noticed a customer was looking at the Morris Minor convertible which Bill Walker had suggested she might buy.

She had a short wait for a train and arrived at her aunt and uncle's, in The Avenue, Havell-Next-the-Sea in under an hour of leaving Priory Cottages.

# Chapter VI

## A Storm Brews

Once back inside her aunt and uncle's Arts and Crafts semi-detached house, the outside world and all the pressures were in the distance. She couldn't help contrasting their orderly hall with the chaos she had encountered that morning at Heathlands. Neil was on the landing, looking out for her through one of the heart-shaped holes in the dark wooden balustrade. He was very excited. They had been waiting for her to arrive to start out for Sandy Reach. They planned to park along the sea front, which was never difficult in February, take Neil for a walk along the pier and then go for tea at the Grand Hotel Tea Rooms.

Margery and Neil took Bobby for a walk on the greensward before they set out. Bobby was keen to go on the beach, but they managed to dissuade him by taking a ball for him to fetch. The happy group almost ran together back up The Avenue.

Bobby was content to go to his basket near the boiler in the breakfast room and did not object when they all left in the car for the 20-minute journey along the coast to Sandy Reach. Alec easily found a parking space along the sea front. They all went for a walk along the pier, looking back at the resort as the lights along the Marine Parade were switched on. Walking up from the end of the pier, they passed the amusement arcades and the shops to the Grand Hotel which overlooked the pier and the sea front.

The tea rooms probably hadn't changed for decades. The long windows were palatial, and the lighting was by chandelier. Neil was amazed and delighted. Alec had booked a table by one of the windows, which looked out on the pier and the Marine Parade with its strings of lights in dipped arcs suspended from lampposts. Margery could see Neil was enchanted with it all, the white napery, the gleaming teacups, the green velour upholstered gold painted chairs.

Tea at the Grand was a series of treats. It started with warm, homemade sausage rolls, sandwiches and salad. Then they had toasted teacakes and finished up with a selection of homemade cakes, and in Neil's case, a lavish ice-cream sundae called a knickerbocker glory, which, when he heard the name, it made him giggle. Carrie looked at him with concern, just hoping all the excitement was not too much for his stomach. She also wondered he had room for that after everything else.

The pantomime was in a seventy-year-old theatre which was contemporary with the Pollux in Great Havell and was designed by the same architect. It wasn't quite as palatial as the Grand Hotel, but also had chandeliers and interior decorations picked out in gold. They took their seats at the front of the circle. Margery was glad she didn't have to write a review; she could just sit back and enjoy this production of Cinderella. They all laughed at the slapstick antics of Buttons and the ugly sisters.

'They've got very deep voices, Margery,' Neil confided to her.

They sang with gusto along with Buttons, hoping to be chosen as the loudest part of the theatre. They were enchanted with the glittering clothes and the magical glass coach. Neil never stopped talking about it all the way back to Alec's car. He was late to bed but wouldn't have to get up early in the morning. His final treat was to sleep on the new sofa bed in the study.

When Neil was in bed, Margery, Alec and Carrie finished the wine she had brought from Sworder Leigh and Runk. They sat in the front room and Margery kept them up to date with the events in Great Havell.

Alec took the advertising of homes to be built on council land very seriously. 'The Grimes family can do what they like with their own land, but they can't take publicly owned land and build on it,' he said. 'Before I retired, I noticed a big rise in demand for housing, but try as we might, we couldn't build enough council houses to keep up with the sales of them. The finances and resources were not there to do it. There was no compulsion on councils to spend the money from the sale of the council stock to build new ones. It was just not possible. Every young couple would like to own their own house, so it is understandable the Grimes family is planning to cash in on that. What is harder to understand is why they are supporting development plans on council land. I am not aware the couple who rent it are ready to retire, or, indeed, have any other home to go to. My guess is Home Farm's tenants would have the right to buy, at least their house, if they could afford to. It could be they have indicated to the council they wish to move. We can't jump to conclusions here. If that were the case, then it would be for the council to build on the land or let it. It could even become a country park, an extension to Thorpe Park. It would be needed if a lot more of the land in that area is to be developed.

'Whatever the council decide, it would not be for the Grimes family, or the Breams for that matter, to determine how it would be used in the future. Is there any connection between the Grimes and the Bream family, Margery?'

Margery explained to Alec she had seen Berkley Grimes and Denzil Bream together with their girlfriends drinking champagne at the opening of the Brass Monkeys Brasserie a couple of weeks previously. She also said the same group had been in the Witches Cauldron and were known to frequent the Den nightclub near the Quay Marina.

Her aunt and uncle were concerned her name had gone on an article which blatantly advertised new executive homes at the Monks Thorpe development planned on green belt on Home Farm. They were even more worried when they heard about the angry demonstrations in the marketplace, outside Bream and the Town Hall. Margery explained DI Barker and Jonah had made sure she was safe in her cottage and she'd had a friend to stay. She blushed inadvertently when she mentioned that.

'Would you like to stay here tomorrow night as well,' asked Aunt Carrie, 'or will your friend be able to come and stay again?'

Margery replied she thought everything would have calmed down by then, or at least she hoped it would and she thought her friend could stay again. She noticed her aunt and uncle exchanging glances and blushed again.

Alec was thoughtful. 'The Grimes and the Breams are very respectable families. I can't imagine they would be involved in evicting the tenants of Home Farm. My guess is the whole business of advertising these executive new homes to be built on Home Farm has been a mistake. Neither family is short of money. Then we have the two deaths. They died the same way apparently. In this case there might be an open verdict on both of them when they come before the coroner again next week. Have you any ideas about that, Margery?'

'I do, as a matter of fact. I think Barney had discovered something which would have caused trouble for someone. Some Elizabethan papers he discovered in the walls of his Tudor home went missing when he died according to Jonah. But I don't really see how they could cause trouble. It's all too long ago. Unless there never were any witch trials and the whole thing was made up. I don't think that could be the case. I think, because he was found drooped over the railings of the priory, Sadie, perhaps, saw something. She was really keen to tell me something on the two occasions I saw her. Perhaps she was given, or encouraged to take, a fatal overdose because of it. But with Sadie's record, it's likely she took it of her own volition.'

'Have you any idea who may have done this?'

'I don't know who actually carried it out, but I think it is connected with the delivery of the large batch of cocaine.'

Alec thought for a while and then said: 'Although the Grimes and the Bream families are respectable, if any of the younger generation has a serious drug habit, that might put a strain on the finances. Or it could put them in touch with some dodgy people, criminals even.'

Margery mentioned Denzil Bream was in a coma after a party. They agreed it was probably from too much alcohol or drugs. She said she'd had a bang on the door and something through the letterbox the previous night.

Aunt Carrie and Uncle Alex looked at each other in alarm.

'What had been put through the letter box?' asked Carrie.

'An invitation to the Valentine's Ball at the Assembly Rooms.'

'And when is that?'

'I should think the last dance will be in about an hour from now,' replied Margery, smiling.

'Ah! That's the reason you were so keen to come to the pantomime with us.' Alec smiled.

'You have no idea what a sanctuary you are providing for me here,' said Margery.

She explained how Cheryl had come round to apologise for putting her by-line on the lead article in the Weekender Gleaner property supplement and that she had still seemed to be under pressure. There was also the shortfall in advertising revenues and pages of letters in yesterday's paper included complaints the Gleaner was too much advertising and too little editorial. 'My account of the inquests on Monday should take up most of a page. I expect they will use pictures of Barney and Sadie in them, now Sadie's name has been released.'

'Do you think the deaths are due to some unhinged reaction to the cancellation of the fair, or do you think it's something to do with the supply of cocaine?' asked Alec.

'I think it's the cocaine. Perhaps the plans for the developments are connected in some way too. I guess Barney was wanted out of the way because he would have insisted on keeping the fair, which the town council has been persuaded is a money loss and therefore has to be cancelled permanently.

'I'm also beginning to think he may have found out something else, perhaps connected with drug smuggling or large amounts of untaxed money. He was like a dog with a bone for getting facts right. If he found out something they were trying to hide, they would definitely want him out of the way, or at least discredited in some way. With his knowledge, he could probably oppose the development effectively and maybe he could have given protestors, and anyone in opposition, enough ammunition to get those executive homes on the Home Farm scrapped completely.

'Barney had an argument with a councillor in the Amicable Anarchist because he said he had evidence which proved the council had no right to cancel the fair. He also claimed the Grimes family did not own all the manor land and particularly the area the new homes and the bypass would be built on.

'I think Sadie died because she saw something. She tried to tell me on the two occasions I last saw her, I wish she had. But then she must have seen Barney every day she went to the old priory, if she was there early enough. I walk that way most days and I usually saw Sadie and also Barney sometimes on his way back from his walk, if he was walking down the mound on the market side. I used to avoid Barney though, because he was always 'taking me to task' as he called it, for things I had written, that, as far as he was concerned were inaccurate. He was always having a go at me about some bit of minutiae I had missed out, which he considered should go in. I kept an eye out for him in the morning, so I could avoid him. I can't imagine Sadie or Barney would have much to say, if they did ever speak to each other. Sadie was a horticulturalist. She knew a lot about plants and all the unusual ones which grew on the Glebe Mound. It's possible she and Barney had a conversation about those at some time.'

'I'm glad Sadie didn't manage to attract your attention when you walked through the old priory,' said Alec, 'But I am still concerned there could be other people who think she had told you something they would rather you didn't know. It could be what happened to Growltiger was a warning to you.'

'Cheryl had the same idea,' said Margery. 'I wonder how everyone enjoyed the Valentine's Ball,' she added.

161

'I might write up the copy for Berkin Estate Agents tomorrow afternoon when I am home, so I can go into the Gleaner after popping into the laundrette on Monday and find out all about it from Gill and Philippa.'

## Sunday 16th February

They all gathered in the breakfast room on Sunday morning and watched the birds on the feeder which hung on the bare apple tree outside the window whilst they ate their poached eggs on toast and drank their tea or coffee.

Neil, Margery and Alec took Bobby for a walk along the sea front as far as the Palace Hotel and let him off the lead on the beach, where boy and dog went running along by the waves and jumping over the groynes. Margery and Alec discussed the situation in Great Havell. They were inclined to think DI Barker was on the right track and that both Barney and Sadie died by the hand of some drug dealer, smuggler or addict. Both were hoping he and the drugs squad would tie up the case quickly and life would return to normal.

The developments and the anger about the cancellation of the fair were another matter. They both thought they were not connected with the two deaths, but there could be a link with the cruel display of poor Growltiger. It was a nasty disturbing thing to happen and there seemed to be no reason for it, unless it was to warn Margery off probing into the cancellation of the fair or, in case she had seen something. Alternatively, perhaps, it was a bizarre way of trying to focus on the necessity for reinstating the fair. It could have been done to discredit her in some way. Although, as Alec said, it was the sort of thing bored and thoughtless teenagers could do without considering the consequences. It was a mystery.

Back home in The Avenue, Neil asked to play with the Hornby tin plate train set, which Margery found for him under the window seat in the back room. He was allowed to play with it again in the front room.

Margery helped her aunt prepare the Sunday lunch, trimmed the sprouts, sliced the carrots and peeled the potatoes. She set the table for them before they had roast chicken and vegetables followed by rhubarb crumble and custard.

After helping her aunt and uncle wash up, they had a cup of tea. Margery gathered her things together into her duffle bag and holdall to take the train back to Great Havell.

Her uncle and Neil saw her on to the train for the short journey home.

'Be sure to come back if you need to and let us know if you have any concerns whatsoever,' said Alec, when she boarded the train. Neil ran along the platform keeping level with the train until the end of the platform. She looked out of the window and saw him waving. It had been a lovely weekend, she thought, as the train made it's twenty-minute journey to Great Havell Station.

Carrying her holdall and duffle bag, and wearing her jeans, jacket and beret, Margery did not attract any attention as she walked the half mile from Great Havell station to her cottage. Moonlight Motors was all shut up. There were plenty of people in the marketplace, she noticed. They were in little groups. It looked as if the noisy protests and rowdy, angry demonstrations of Friday were over. The Amicable Anarchist was really busy, with a group of people crowded into the street door. It looked as if there was a queue at the bar too. Crossing the road over to the old priory, Margery noticed there were more visitors to the ruins than she had seen since the last fair. There was even a snack and tea van in the car park. It had its generator running to heat up food and water and plenty of cars were parked.

The lane from the back of the old priory, which ran along the front of Priory Cottages was quiet. Alf was in his front garden looking out for her.

'I hear there was trouble in the marketplace on Friday,' he said.

'Yes, so I heard,' said Margery.

'I don't know what our council is thinking of, cancelling our fair,' said Alf.

'Yes, I don't know why they did that.' Margery had her key in her front door.

'There was a bang on your door on Friday night again,' said Alf.

'Yes, I know, someone put an invitation to the Valentine's Ball through my door.'

'They woke me up.'

'Yes, I'm sorry, Alf, I don't know who it was.'

'Who was it?' asked Alf.

'I've no idea,' replied Margery.

'Been away, then, have you?'

'Yes, I'm back now.' Margery was still hovering in her open door.

'So, did you go to that Valentine's Ball?'

'No, I was away,' replied Margery patiently.

'I hear there was trouble afterwards.'

'Oh dear, sorry to hear that.'

'People got hurt and taken to casualty.'

'Really!?' Margery was surprised. 'Was it that bad?'

'Yes, all that trouble on Friday in the marketplace, police coming from all over the area to keep order, more people out there on Saturday and then a fight outside the Assembly Rooms.'

'It looks as if I have missed all the excitement then. Thank you for telling me, Alf.' Margery went into her cottage and shut the door.

It was chilly in her front room, so she plugged in her electric fire and switched it on. She hung her jacket and beret on the pegs near the door, took her boots off and put her slippers on. She went into the kitchen to put the kettle on and ran upstairs for a cardigan. When she came down again, the kettle boiled, and she made herself a pot of tea.

Writing up the Berkin article would not take long. She had pictures in her camera and would finish the film the following days, at her other appointments. It wouldn't stop her going into the Gleaner on Monday, after she had taken her washing into the laundrette. She wanted to find out more about the disturbance after the ball. She was intrigued to know what it was all about.

It was late afternoon by the time she finished. She put her washing into a bag and into her shopping trolley to take to the laundrette in the morning. She put the Berkin copy into a back pocket. It would be easily found and there would be no excuse for looking for it whilst she chatted, although she felt sure Gill and Philippa would be only too happy to talk about the ball and its aftermath. She switched the radio on, made herself a sandwich and settled in her chair to read. She could hear Florence had her radio or television on loud. She was beginning to wonder if Vlad was actually going to turn up when she heard his key in the door.

Was he hungry? No, but he had a lot to tell her.

Intrigued, Margery put the kettle on again, made some more tea and Vlad sat on the little settee under the window opposite her and began.

'Eric talked a lot about Sadie and what she had been to him. After I picked up my bike from your garden and bought some food in the market, I cycled back to Eric's, prepared the food for us both and made some more coffee. Eric put whisky in it again. I let him. It seemed to please him. I managed to find some plates, cleaned them and put the food out after I made space in the mess on the kitchen table. I had to use a small camping stove to cook on, but then I was used to cooking on small stoves in submarines. I couldn't get Eric to drink any water, but I had some; it watered down the coffee and whisky.

'I found a chess set and we played a couple of games of chess, then we played cards. Eric wanted to gamble. I told him I had no money to gamble. He found some notes from inside one of his books on the bookshelves and gave them to me. They were inside one of the really old books, it had a leather cover. It had some of the front pages cut out and there was a lot of room for all the money he keeps in there. Eric said I had to gamble with the notes he gave me. He won them all back. I told him he had enough there to pay his electricity bill. He could have the electric put back on. He said he didn't care about electricity. I made some more coffee and we finished the whisky bottle. Eric started to talk about Sadie. He said he missed her. He had never expected her to die. He cried a lot. He said he still couldn't believe she had died and would not come back through that door again. On that Monday, Eric told me, Sadie had come back stinking of that strong cider, but she was upset about something. At first, he didn't listen, he thought she was really drunk and making it all up. She said she had seen a lot of people she saw regularly. She said she saw you go out and come back again.'

'That's odd,' said Margery. 'I only saw her once, when I returned.'

'One man, Sadie told Eric, she saw nearly every day. He was an older man, who walked on the mound every morning and she had seen him walking there that morning with another one she saw regularly. She thought he had finished his walk and come down from the mound. But then she saw him again bent over and holding his back. The man went round the side of the mound beyond the priory and she could not see him anymore. Then she saw a younger man supporting the older man who was bent over. She told Eric she couldn't see the other man clearly, but he held himself like a soldier. She didn't think she had seen him before. She saw them coming round the mound and down to the old priory. She was drinking her cider as she watched them. The younger man had his arm around the older man and when they got to the railings, the older man bent over them. She thought the other man was going to tip him over, but he left him suspended there and walked fast through the car park and across the road to the phone box near the Amicable Anarchist. She said he soon came back again and disappeared into the old priory ruins. He, or someone else, must have called an ambulance. When the ambulance arrived, the older man was more or less carried by the men into the ambulance which was parked in the car park. She didn't see them again. Eric said Sadie had seen some people walking through the priory, including you.

'Then a smartly dressed man, who had been looking round the priory ruins, came up to her and asked her if she would identify some plants growing in there, which she did. She had seen him before, she said, but didn't know who he was. The man said there were some plants at the top of the mound he would like her to look at, but he hadn't time to go up there then. He asked her to meet him on the top of the mound at 9.30 am the next day. Sadie said the man had a posh accent like Eric's. Sadie had no watch and wanted to take one of Eric's clocks with her on to the Glebe Mound so she could be there at the right time. Eric takes pride in his clocks. He winds them up every day, although I don't know how he finds them in that place. Reluctantly he lent Sadie his Honey Monster watch, with strict instructions to bring it straight back again. She left, holding it in her hand, but never came back. He went to look for her, but never found her. He looked round the top of the mound. There was no sign of Sadie or his watch. Then, he said, you helped him, Margery, and together you decided to look for her in the old priory ruins, in case she had dropped it there.

'As you walked together to the car park, he spotted it just before the police car ran over it. It was because we took it back to him and he felt lonely, he was happy for me to go back to play chess and cards and talk with him.'

'Did he say what he was arrested for?'

'Yes. Eric said he was arrested in connection with the death of Barney Cobbler. The person who called the ambulance had described him and Sadie as being on the scene at the time, which, of course, he wasn't. But as he was alone at his house, he had no one to speak up for him. He thinks, after hearing what was said at the inquest, he would have been arrested again, but he said the London policeman, Barker I think, believed him, contacted his family and they put up bail for him and he went home, expecting Sadie to come back. I think he is expecting her to return, in spite of the inquest. After they took him home in the police car, a police constable came every day to check he was keeping the terms for his bail. He was told he would be called to give evidence at the inquest and the policeman, who checks on him, came with him to the court, as you may have seen.'

'Thank you, Vlad,' said Margery. 'I never expected you to find out so much from Eric. I've never known him to be talkative or even companionable. I find it odd if someone saw him around the old priory about the time Barney Cobbler died. I also find it odd that Sadie saw me when I went to the Gleaner. I didn't see her. I only saw her when I was on my way back. I wonder where she was earlier, if she saw me. She was trying to attract my attention when I returned, I've regretted ever since I didn't stop to talk to her.'

'I've only just left Eric again today. I cycled home on Saturday night and promised to go back there. I'm sorry, Margery, I probably smell of whisky; he drinks the stuff all day. I couldn't make a hot drink without him putting whisky in it, but I managed to have some drinks without whisky in them, by pretending to put it in myself.'

Margery moved over to sit next to him on the settee and sniffed. There was the familiar smell of the carbolic soap, he used, with strong spirits added and she caught a slight aroma of Eric's house.

'You don't smell too much of whisky,' she said, 'but I think you might like to take a shower. I can smell his house on you! I wonder why Eric didn't tell the court what Sadie had said about Barney's death. I suppose because he wasn't there and he hadn't seen Sadie since she told him about it. Eric probably didn't understand what she was talking about and, as you say, he wasn't really listening. I can guess he wouldn't be too keen on talking to the police.'

'I'll have a shower now,' said Vlad. 'I think the man Eric has described is probably the man the police are looking for, at least in connection with the death of Sadie.'

'Yes, I think so too,' said Margery.

## Monday 17th February

Margery woke up to find Vlad had left without breakfasting and his bike and rucksack were gone. He hadn't even left any clothes for her to take to the laundrette as she had suggested. She had rather hoped he might have left one of his stained vests, but he seemed to have taken all his things and it was still early.

She got up, showered and had her usual toast and marmalade for breakfast before taking her washing to the laundrette in the marketplace and leaving it there. She paid for the manageress to put it through the drier, so it would be clean, dry and folded when she had finished at the Gleaner. Margery was expecting to hear all about the ball and its aftermath. She decided to leave the Berkin copy with the girls, there was no need to go into the offices to see Cheryl.

Margery with shopping trolley in tow, left the marketplace and walked into Priory Street. She passed the Amicable Anarchist, walked past the terraces of Edwardian houses and entered the Gleaner offices.

167

Gill and Philippa put the phones down quickly as she entered, glanced at each other and both smiled as she greeted them with a 'Hello, girls.'

'Good Morning, Margery,' Philippa answered her rather formally and cautiously.

Margery found the article on Berkin in the pocket of her trolley and handed it to Philippa.

'This is for Cheryl,' she said. 'How did the ball go?'

'It was good,' said Gill. 'Some of the reporters who went, got drunk and so did a lot of other young men, and some of the girls, which spoilt it a bit.'

She dropped her voice. 'Harry Grimes was flirting with all the tele-ad girls and his wife, Rita, was getting really annoyed with him. He was dancing with anyone and everyone. They didn't like to refuse him because he'd given them the tickets. Apparently, he has hardly been home recently. Bill Walker from Moonlight and the guys from the Brass Monkeys came, Morris and Mack, they prepared the banquet; it was really good. Mayor Walter Grimes, Harry's brother, his son Berkley with his girlfriend, Bodhi, and the rest of his family were all there. The mayoress, Agatha Grimes, looked really glamorous. The Breams were there except for Denzil. He is out of the coma, but they have packed him off to one of those health-farm retreats for a month. His girlfriend was there though. She looked wonderful, very tanned. She was with a young man and Audrey Bodger from the Little Havell estate agents. We thought they probably came with Tracey, as Denzil was in rehabilitation. They were sitting with Clark and Veronica Bodger and a couple of really good-looking men we hadn't seen before. One of them was dancing a lot. We were trying to catch his eye, hoping he might come over and ask us, but it didn't happen.'

Margery picked up a Gleaner from the front desk and read the headline.

"BALL BUST UP MAYOR HURT"

She looked up. 'What is this all about, girls?'

'It was after the ball was over. We had said goodbye to everyone and were leaving with our husbands,' Gill said. 'We went to get our coats.'

Philippa continued: 'We could hear a row going on outside and we thought we would steer clear of it. We thought it was another demonstration going on. The ones on Friday had been really unruly and some people were back, in the marketplace, making trouble on Saturday. We thought they had returned to make trouble for the Mayor. We could hear it from the cloakroom.'

'What was it about?' asked Margery.

Gill and Philippa looked at each other.

'There was a lot of shouting,' said Gill slowly. 'We could hear that from inside the Assembly rooms, so we decided to leave by a side door. When we looked round the front, we could see all the Grimes family and a lot of their friends in the centre of something. We thought some demonstrators and protestors in the marketplace had come to have a go at the mayor over the cancellation of the fair or about the bypass and the new developments. We've heard there have been arguments in the local pubs about it already, and sometimes, violence. People have been thrown out of the pubs. Then someone told us the mayor had been kneed in the balls, was given a black eye and had been knocked out.'

'What!' Margery was quite shocked.

'We couldn't really see who was involved, there were so many people crowding around the mayor,' stressed Philippa. 'But apparently the man who attacked the mayor was that Russian who works at the Little Havell Country Hotel.'

'What!' said Margery again, this time she was very shocked.

'It's all round the Gleaner offices and Great Havell,' said Gill. 'People are saying he is a Russian spy and the Grimes family have caught him snooping about. Apparently, he's been seen in the marketplace and around the old priory a lot and now they are saying he was something to do with the deaths on the Glebe Mound.'

'But how on earth...' Margery began, her mouth dry, with shock... she didn't know what to say.

Gill and Philippa looked at each other.

'No one knows much about him in Great Havell,' said Philippa. 'Little Havell folk seem to know him. Since he was involved in the fight in Saturday night, people are now saying he was probably on the Glebe Mound at the times when Barney and Sadie were taken to hospital. He hasn't been arrested or anything. We've also heard, he's knocking off some bird, who lives near the priory.'

Margery was at a loss for words. Her mouth was still dry with shock. She felt like asking for a cup of tea but sat down instead.

'You say you only saw the Grimes family among the crowd. Did you see anything of the fight?' she asked slowly.

'We all sneaked a peak,' said Gill. 'Ron, my hubby, got a bit nearer to see who was involved. He said the mayor was in the thick of it. He didn't think he saw the Russian, but then he wouldn't know what he looked like. It was the

Grimes family he saw and a few others. Harry and Rita Grimes were having an almighty argument and Bill Walker from Moonlight was trying to intervene and sort things out. The mayoress was standing near her husband and Berkley, who were shouting at each other. Morris and Mack had a hand each on Berkley's shoulders. They were all closing in on each other angrily as far as Ron could see. When he told us that, we all went nearer to see for ourselves. The next thing we knew the group around the mayor were all stepping backwards, and he was on the ground. The mayoress went back into the Assembly Rooms to call an ambulance. We all decided to leave at that point, didn't we, Phil?'

'Yes, the mayor's fall seemed to shock everyone into soberness. Friends and family were consoling the mayoress. The police came, but there were no arrests. We heard the ambulance which took the mayor to casualty. It wasn't until yesterday we heard the Russian had been involved. Can we get you a cup of tea Margery? You look a bit shocked.'

'Yes, thank you, girls. I would like a cup of tea. I am a bit shocked. Have you heard how the mayor is?'

Philippa went off to get Margery some tea.

Gill carried on the account, 'apparently, Mayor Grimes was concussed when he fell to the ground. They may have kept him in hospital, we haven't heard any more. The Grimes family are not talking to reporters. The mayoress has been quite rude apparently. She said if the reporters at the ball hadn't got so drunk, they might have been able to report on the whole incident and would have seen what really happened. We don't know any more.

'One of our reporters claimed he had seen the mayor's glasses broken, and he had a black eye and that the mayoress seemed to have been hurt as well. The town hall is keeping strictly to the line that reporters from the Gleaner were at the ball and saw the incident for themselves but had been drinking too heavily to be able to report it accurately. Harry Grimes has said to the editor it was a "domestic" and no one else had been involved. Considering he was having a row with his wife as well, Phil and I thought it was a bit rich for him to say that.

'As Phil said, we only heard about the Russian involvement yesterday. It was Derek from the Amicable Anarchist, where we went for Sunday drinks, who told us. We thought we could find a bit more about it there, because it wasn't far away from the Assembly Rooms and someone was bound to have gone in and told Derek all about it. Derek said it was one of his regulars who said he saw the Russian there and that this Russian was snooping round the Glebe Mound and the old priory area a lot. It was also from this man Derek heard the Russian had been found out as a spy and was knocking off some local bird. Derek said, when he heard about it, he had to admit he had seen the Russian that day, but until he had a description of him, wearing a khaki army jacket over a white vest and jeans, he hadn't realised he was Russian. Derek said that he had seen the Russian around and about the old priory a lot, and he thought he had seen him the day Barney died.'

Margery was quiet, taking it all in.

'Maybe this Russian was at the ball. You say there were no arrests on Saturday night.'

'No, the police came, we saw them. Don't forget Ron had reported it all back to us and then we went to see for ourselves.'

Philippa came in with the tea.

'Are you all right, Margery?'

Margery took a grateful sip of the tea.

'Yes, thank you for this. These past two weeks have been a bit of a shock.'

She looked down at the Gleaner to avoid their gaze and turned to page two to find her report of the inquests on Barney and Sadie had been published and with a by-line she was pleased to note. At least she knew that had actually happened as she had reported it.

Still looking down at the Gleaner, she said as casually as she could, 'I think I know this Russian.'

Philippa and Gill exchanged glances and looked keenly at Margery who kept her eyes firmly on the Gleaner, turning the pages without actually seeing anything much.

'Andy Clarke introduced Jonah and I to the Russian at the Arts Centre when we were at the Jazz and Folk Club a couple of years ago. Cheryl Francis knows him too, because she goes there and chats to him as well. We all meet up with him regularly there. He bikes over from his flat in Little Havell and leaves his bike in my front garden, so he can walk me home from the Arts Centre. He works as a plumber, engineer and handyman at the Little Havell Country Hotel, the spring water bottling plant and for Bodgers Letting Agency. He's only been in this country for about two and a half years.' Margery looked up at them both, as if emphasising the veracity of what she had just said.

'Oooh, do you think he might be a spy? What does he look like?' asked Philippa.

171

'He's tall,' said Margery, 'with very short light-brown hair. He usually wears a not very clean white vest under a short army jacket. He also wears corduroy trousers or jeans and army surplus boots. In fact, he probably thinks of the Army Surplus Stores as his tailor. (Margery noticed the girls grinning at this) He'll wear a t-shirt or a sweatshirt if he goes to the Arts Centre. I think it's his idea of smart. He probably doesn't own a suit, or a shirt, or a tie, unless he really is a spy and he's leading a double life. He goes everywhere on his bike. I think, if he were a Russian spy, he would probably drive a car, don't you?'

'Yes, I suppose he would,' said Philippa thoughtfully. 'How well acquainted are you with this Russian, Margery?'

'Well enough to think the story about him assaulting the mayor has been made up. As for the idea he is involved in the deaths of Barney or Sadie, I would dismiss all this as so much gossip.'

'Harry Grimes is denying there was any family row after the ball now,' said Gill. 'I asked him when he came in this morning, and he got quite angry about it. I didn't dare ask him any other questions or even suggest he'd been arguing with his wife, although Ron and the rest of us saw them at it. I know he likes to be everyone's friend, but I've seen his nasty side this morning. And some of the reps and reporters don't seem to have sobered up yet. Gloria is very touchy. You can't even say, "good morning" to her.'

Just then, as if on cue, Gloria came through the double doors from the offices. She was wearing a fox fur coat. She glared at Gill and Philippa, mouthed the word "bitch" at Margery and walked out of the building banging the door behind her. Gill got up quickly, went round the front office desk, opened the front door and watched her go. She was some time at the door.

'What kind of a tart does she look like in that coat?' she asked, returning to her desk. 'I've just seen her pick up her company car from the car park and drive off in the direction of the quay. Did you know she keeps a load of soft toys at the back of that car?'

'Really?' said Margery, still sipping her tea. 'I wouldn't associate soft toys or fur coats with Gloria. She usually wears those check dresses and that red leather jacket.'

'Well, she's swanning around in a fur coat now,' said Gill. 'I wonder who she moved heaven and earth for, mostly on her back, to get that, eh Phil!'

'Yes, I wonder!' said Philippa, in a tone which suggested she knew, and laughed.

Margery got up to go. 'I have to collect my washing from the laundrette,' she said, 'and I've appointments this afternoon.'

She finished her tea, said goodbye to Philippa and Gill and set off for the marketplace and the laundrette deep in thought.

Had Vlad been involved in a fight outside the Assembly Rooms? Surely, he would have told her last night or had bruises somewhere, which she would have seen. Was she the "bird" he was knocking off? Margery was in a daze and felt sick with anticipation of…she was not sure what. Would Vlad come over tonight as he had promised, she wondered? She picked up her dried folded items from the laundrette, put them in her shopping trolley, and walked home, across the road at the Amicable Anarchist, across the priory car park, through the old priory and into the lane at the back, where Alf, was looking out for her.

'I hear your fancy man was in a fight outside the Assembly Rooms on Saturday.'

'Yes, I heard that too,' said Margery. 'I'll ask him about it when I see him.'

'He's in serious trouble now,' said Alf.

'Yes,' Margery agreed wearily, 'I reckon he is.'

'Expecting him, are you?' asked Alf.

'I've work to do,' said Margery. 'I must get on.'

She unlocked the door to her cottage, pushed the shopping trolley in and shut the door. She sorted the washing and put it away. She was not in the least bit hungry. She noticed the daffodils Vlad had left for her were still on her desk in the milk bottle with the note beneath them. She had arranged an interview with the Great Havell branch of Bodgers that afternoon. Afterwards, she planned to take the train to Grimpen Havell for her appointment with another branch of Bodgers. She had decided to do the Little Havell appointment on Tuesday morning and write them all up on Tuesday afternoon. She had pushed herself a lot in the past two weeks and she felt, in view of the embarrassing story with her name on it in last Friday's Weekender Gleaner, she could take her time over these. She did not feel like making herself some lunch, so decided to collect her notebook, pencils and camera and put them in her bag. She could treat herself to lunch at Dewbury and Hicks.

Unusually, Margery did not see anyone she knew as she walked into the marketplace, through the market stalls, past the guildhall, the library, the Assembly Rooms, the police station, the shops around the square to the large imposing department store at the far end.

As she went through the store, she had a look at the things which had caught her fancy when she was shown round the store by Emma Dewbury. She took the escalators up to the third floor. One of the waitresses took her to a table for two next to the window and gave her a menu.

Margery ordered a ploughman's lunch and a pot of tea. She wished she had brought a book, but then realised she had her notebook and decided to make shorthand notes about the events of the past two weeks. It was exactly two weeks since she had been writing her articles on the Glebe Mound, the Moyen Midden and the Havell-on-the-Marsh witches. Cheryl hadn't given her a cheque for all her recent work too, she reflected, and began to be concerned about the company's finances. It was unusual, because she was paid fortnightly on a Friday and picked up her cheque when she went in the office, either on the Friday or on the following Monday. Cheryl hadn't brought a cheque with her when she came to collect the coroner's inquest report on Friday afternoon, she reflected, but then she had been in a hurry and perhaps forgot it. She had enough in her current account to tide her over, but wouldn't be able to afford any unexpected expenses.

Margery's reverie was broken by a man's voice saying, 'Hello, young lady, what are you doing here?'

She looked up in surprise to find DI Barker in the restaurant.

She remembered this had been his rather unusual, but pleasantly polite greeting in Havell-Next-the-Sea. She felt reassured to see him and invited him to join her. He sat down.

At that moment, the waitress came over to serve Margery with her ploughman's lunch and tea things and went to fetch a menu for the inspector.

He studied the menu and Margery asked him if he would like to share her pot of tea. He said was keen on trying the Dewbury and Hicks own blend of coffee, which would be ground up for him and served in a cafetiere. Barker liked the look of Margery's ploughman's and ordered the same.

She then asked him what he was doing there. The reply was very noncommittal. He was exploring the town and thought he would try it out.

'I took Janine to the Grain of Truth at the Old Granary Hotel, for Sunday lunch yesterday,' he said. We had a good look round the Quay Marina and the hotel grounds. I was going to spend the weekend at home. After I met you and gave you a lift back to Great Havell on Friday, I rang Janine and asked her if she would like to come down and see the area. We decided to ask the grandparents to look after the children on Saturday and Sunday. I booked us into the Palace

Hotel at Havell-Next the-Sea on Saturday night. Janine likes it round here. We even went to Trincaster and St Ethelburga's cathedral. To be honest, Janine went into the cathedral, I went junking and found some market stalls, antique and second-hand shops, full of 78 records. If I had known the area would be such a good place for 78s, I would have visited years ago. I think Janine enjoyed it and she'd like to come down for another weekend, if I'm still here.'

'I was in Havell-Next-the-Sea again on Saturday,' said Margery.

'So, you didn't go to the Valentine's Ball at the Assembly Rooms?'

'I went to the pantomime at Sandy Reach with a young cousin.'

'Did you hear about the scrap after the ball? The local police were called.'

'Yes, I heard the mayor was taken to casualty. Was he kept in do you know?'

'Yes, the deputy mayor will be doing all his engagements this week. I heard the mayoress has a black eye or a bruise on her face as well.'

This was news to Margery. Mayor and Mayoress Grimes were always such smart, well-turned out people. She couldn't imagine them being in the middle of a disturbance or with facial injuries.

'There's a Russian who lives and works at Little Havell, who was accused of assaulting the mayor and all sorts of other things,' said DI Barker, looking at Margery keenly.

Margery was about to convey a forkful of salad to her mouth but put it down and blushed.

'Yes, Vladimir, I know him well. I heard all the gossip about him. I can tell you he was at Heathlands with Eric Bolton on Saturday night, drinking whisky playing chess and gambling with cards.'

'Yes, I know, he was helping the police with their inquiries this morning. Local people don't know his background, and he prefers it that way. Fortunately, he could account for, and had witnesses, for all his movements on Saturday night, so we know he wasn't anywhere near the Assembly Rooms. There are others who live in bed-sits in the same building as Vladimir. There are people who work at the Little Havell Country Hotel who know him. They all share a kitchen in the bed-sits. They could confirm he had returned by the time the fracas took place. They were happy to do so. Berkley Grimes had insisted the Russian was arrested for assault and Morris and Mack, who run the Brass Monkeys Brasserie, identified Vladimir as the mayor's assailant, but he and others could prove he was at home in Little Havell and there were other witnesses, which the local police checked out. Taylor, the station sergeant, was a bit reluctant to make a statement to the press over it, but since I was there, I insisted he had to. I don't think the local police like to contradict members of the Grimes family or their coterie of friends. Vladimir had been seen in the Arts Centre on Friday night. Your neighbour confirmed his bike had been in your front garden, until he picked it up on Saturday about lunchtime. He said he also saw you and him walking in the direction of the market gardens and the docks, presumably to go to Heathlands earlier in the day.'

'Yes, Vladimir came with me to return Eric's Honey Monster watch to him,' said Margery, pushing the remains of her ploughman's lunch away. She had lost her appetite.

'Have you visited the Gleaner offices today?' asked Barker as the waitress served him with his ploughman's and coffee.

*The fresh coffee smelled absolutely delicious*, thought Margery.

'Yes, I picked up a copy to ensure my report on the coroner's court had been published.'

'And how did you find everyone there?'

Margery looked at DI Barker. She remembered Vladimir had mentioned he knew about him as a Russian defector, so she guessed he had dismissed his involvement, in anything he was investigating, as so much local gossip. She decided to confide in the inspector.

'I'm a bit miffed, because I haven't been paid yet,' she said, 'which is unusual. On Friday night, there was a loud bang on my door in the early hours of the morning.

'Someone had pushed an invitation to the Valentine's Ball through the letter box. It was a bit frightening. I was glad I was going to Havell-Next-the-Sea the following day. My neighbour Alf is nosy, as you know, but in a funny way, he keeps his eye on me. My neighbour on the other side is rather deaf, but I can usually see her sitting by her front window knitting. It would be very unlikely she would have seen or heard anything in the early hours of Saturday morning.'

'The local police have interviewed everyone who lives in Priory Cottages,' said DI Barker. 'What puzzles me is why they haven't been to see you.'

'That's a good point,' said Margery. 'I wonder why that is.'

'I thought it might be because they have contacts at the Gleaner and staff at the Gleaner are able to confirm where you were when the unconscious Cobbler and Petal were discovered.'

'I suppose they might,' said Margery slowly, 'and Cheryl's brother-in-law is in the police at Grimpen Havell. But it still seems odd, doesn't it? And something else odd too. Someone claims to have seen Eric Bolton on the Glebe Mound the morning Barney had an overdose there.'

DI Barker's next remarks were a surprise.

'They didn't interview you because the local police know perfectly well where you and, also for the record, where Vladimir was too at the time of the murders and also at the time of the fight outside the Assembly Rooms.'

'You mean I'm being watched?'

DI Barker laughed. 'No, Miss Moore, you are not being watched, but the local police will accept what the Grimes family tell them. All this stuff about the mayor being assaulted by the Russian from Little Havell is just small-town gossip, probably invented by someone there at the time to deflect blame from themselves. The root of these rumours seems to be members of the Grimes family and their friends and acquaintances. What they don't know is that Vladimir keeps the Home Office informed of his movements as part of his agreement to remain here. The Grimes family don't know he is a defector any more than anyone else does. Vladimir was advised to tell you about his background, which I presume he has done, (Margery nodded) because it was only fair on you and it was also apparent you were being targeted for some reason.

'That business with your cat indicated that someone wanted to get at you or involve you in something in some way.'

'So, whoever put the invitation through my door wanted me to go to the Valentine's Ball with Vladimir so he could be accused of assault afterwards? It doesn't seem possible! Surely not! What you are suggesting is, excuse me for saying this, ridiculous. It means the assault on the mayor was planned in advance. Why would anyone do that?'

'Desperation perhaps?'

'Desperation? Why? I really don't get it.'

DI Barker laughed.

'I don't get it entirely either, but I'm hoping to tie it all up before too long. Did you hear anything, or did anything happen at the Gleaner when you were there this morning?'

'One of the salespeople walked out in a fur coat and a huff and drove off in the car they provide for her with a load of soft toys on the back windowsill.'

DI Barker laughed again.

'Now that is interesting. So, the revenues are down but the salespeople receive big bonuses and wear fur coats, and you don't get paid!'

'I'm sure I will be paid,' said Margery, feeling she needed to defend Gleaner. 'You are going to have to excuse me, because I have an appointment with Bodgers in about twenty minutes.'

'Let me pay for your lunch,' said DI Barker. 'You really have been most useful to me.'

'Have I?' said Margery. 'Well, thank you, it is very kind of you.'

'And Vladimir tells me you have a most comfortable spare room,' he added with a cheeky smile.

Margery blushed again and almost laughed. 'Well so I do, thank you very much indeed, Inspector.'

She walked down the escalators in Dewbury and Hicks and left the store to take a quick walk to Bodgers in Station Road. It took her a good fifteen minutes through suburban streets, and she was only just in time for her appointment.

She took her Ricoh camera out of her bag and photographed the outside of the building. She was met by Clark Bodger, the managing director, immediately she arrived. He was impeccably dressed in a perfectly pressed and fitted dark suit, white shirt and blue tie. He came out of his office door, shook hands with her, asked her how she was and invited her to sit in a comfortable chair in his office, next to a coffee table. He took the seat beside her.

'It's good to meet you, Miss Moore,' he said. 'My wife, Veronica, and I follow your "Take a Pew at the Pollux" column in the Gleaner. We enjoy the productions and always like your recommendations. I was surprised when I received your phone call for an appointment. We don't usually contact the Gleaner for anything other than our domestic property advertisements. What would you like to know about our agency here?'

Margery blushed when she mentioned the article about the executive new homes Bream were selling off plan, which had her name on it in the Weekender Gleaner. She asked him if he intended to sell any of the proposed properties.

Clark Bodger looked at her for a while without saying anything. She felt embarrassed and uncomfortable. Then he said, 'Are you claiming you didn't write that article in the Gleaner, Miss Moore?'

Margery was thinking it was a blessing she was freelance and didn't have to cover up for the Gleaner, but she would have to be careful with her words. Clark

Bodger, she thought, apart from being well dressed and good looking, was an intelligent man. She didn't want to appear to be a fool in front of him.

'I had an interview with Denzil Bream last week,' she explained. 'I had difficulty finding out enough information for the article I had been commissioned to write by the Gleaner. I put in a bit about the family business, the lettings and the commercial aspect, in which I included plans for Monks Thorpe. Mr Bream asked to read the article before it went in. He rewrote it entirely, but unfortunately, when it was published, it still had my name on it.'

She noticed Clark Bodger wince at the mention of Monks Thorpe, although she was surprised when he said: 'The family business is involved in the Monk's Thorpe development. We will be selling most of the land to developers on behalf of the Grimes family once the plans for the road are finalised.'

'Does that include the land on Home Farm?' asked Margery, before she realised, she was being a bit impertinent.

Clark Bodger looked at her for a while. She began to expect he would terminate the interview. She was about to apologise for suggesting Bodger's would consider selling land on Home Farm, when he said slowly and deliberately,

'No, it most definitely does not, Miss Moore. I want to talk about our agency, which here in Great Havell is almost entirely domestic. New homes would be a departure from our normal business for us. We are not involved with the Monks Thorpe development or new homes at the agency here. Talk to my brother Grant at Grimpen Havell. If you are interested, you can find out more from him.'

'I have an appointment with him later this afternoon,' said Margery.

'Good. We can close that matter in our conversation here,' said Clark decisively. 'Grant will fill you in with all that. I am not involved, unless any of the land or property on it is to be auctioned, in which case I will be the auctioneer.'

Margery made shorthand notes.

'I also have an appointment with your Little Havell branch tomorrow morning,' she said.

'Oh, that's good,' said Clark. 'You will see my sister Audrey there. You realise we have all been named after film stars, don't you?' he asked, visibly relaxing.

'Oh yes, I suppose you are,' said Margery, pleased to find an angle on the story which might interest the Gleaner's readers and noting it down. 'And why is that?'

'Our parents, who started the agency in the 1940s, when they married, were both film enthusiasts. They went to the Regal every week after they met. Our grandparents were builders. There was a building programme which started in the 1930s and continued after the war and still goes on, as you must be aware. We have cousins in the civil engineering and construction industry.'

'When your parents started the agency, did they sell the houses your grandparents were building?' asked Margery.

'No. You may be aware, there was a council house building boom after the war and, of course, they were all commissioned by the local authority. They were financed by the council, but not for sale at that time. The houses my parents sold through their agency were the houses which my grandparents and great grandparents had built in the last century and early this century. You would have walked by some of them to reach your appointment here, assuming you did walk.'

'Yes, indeed, I did walk,' said Margery.

Once they had changed the subject from the Monks Thorpe estate, Clark Bodger gave Margery more than enough information on his Great Havell estate agency for her to write about. Could she include all the branches of the Bodger agencies in the article? she asked.

She would have to ask his brother and sister about that, was his reply. He would leave it up to her and them.

'As you are a land and property auctioneer,' said Margery, 'I would be interested to hear more about that.'

'Auctions are unpredictable. Perhaps you would like to cover one for the newspaper when we hold the next one?'

'I would find that interesting,' replied Margery. 'What sort of buyers do you have at auctions?'

'All sorts. There are always builders looking for a bargain, either to demolish or refurbish and make a profit. They will be bidding against developers, who will want to use every square foot as profitably as possible. Landowners may take an interest if they feel a new development would intrude on their estates. If the property has an interesting history or a large garden, individuals may be keen to secure it. There are also speculators and investors. They could be from any part of the country or abroad.'

Margery took notes and asked Clark Bodger to pose at his desk for a photograph with a smartly dressed young woman who worked for him. They looked together at some house details and made a good picture, she thought.

She reluctantly declined the offer of some tea. She had been charmed by Clark Bodger. She walked through the Victorian terraced streets towards Great Havell Station and thought, how pleasant he had been and well mannered. He was older than Denzil Bream. The interview had been a complete contrast to the one at Breams last week.

The children from the local school were walking home when Margery walked to the station. Some were in little groups, others with a parent or grand-parent. There were one or two of the older generations Margery recognised. They were nodding acquaintances from the Jazz and Folk Club, the Amateur Theatre Group and the Rambler's Club. There were plenty of people to say hello to. She almost wished she lived in that area with so many more neighbours about and nowhere near the sites of Barney and Sadie's deaths or the cruelty of poor Growl-tiger's demise.

She felt much more cheerful since her lunch with DI Barker and interview with Clark Bodger. She was looking forward to meeting his brother.

She bought a ticket at the station and went to Grimpen Havell on the train, looking out on the suburban streets she had walked through to get to the station. She saw a large disused Victorian factory which was being converted into flats. There was a big advertisement on the outside of the building. "Coming soon, lofty apartments, sole agency, Bream."

*Why,* thought Margery, *did Denzil Bream not want to promote those in the article? Daft young man.* Well, he was in rehab now, maybe it would sober him up, eventually.

The train took her beyond Great Havell into open farmland, a wooded estate, paddocks and nature reserves. She knew she was close to Grimpen Havell when the serried rows of Victorian army barracks came into sight.

Clark Bodger had obligingly given Margery a map of the town which showed her the location of premises run by his brother, Grant.

The agency was at the end of Station Road, a long street of Victorian cottages from the station towards the town centre which were named Railway Terraces.

Margery found the Bodger's Commercial premises on the corner of Station Road and Victory Street. It had a shop window on both streets, advertising land, shops and offices. She had time for a good look before she went in. She also crossed Victory Street to take a picture of the agency from there. There was a muddy khaki two-seater 4x4, with a spare wheel on the bonnet, parked outside, she noticed. She was unable to avoid getting it in the picture.

In the windows of the agency, she had found there was nothing to suggest Bodgers of Grimpen Havell would be selling new homes on the Monks Thorpe estate. There were shops for sale and to rent, warehouses and storage units in the area and commercial premises to rent or buy. Farms were for sale or to rent. Farmland was available by the acre. There was building land for sale, but not anywhere near Home Farm, which Margery was specifically looking for.

When she entered the agency, she found, unlike the other agents she had visited, the staff were both men. She was surprised to see they were smartly, but casually dressed in V-neck jumpers over shirts and drill trousers. One of them, wearing all black and no tie, was a very good-looking man with longish dark hair. She was a bit disconcerted by the challenging look he gave her from his dark eyes when he came forward to shake hands. He introduced himself as Grant Bodger. She could see, from the resemblance, he was Clark's younger brother. His handshake was vigorous.

The other man, who seemed to be a little older, and taller, was also good looking. He was wearing a tie and dressed mainly in khaki. He appeared to be a bit reserved. He was introduced by Grant as Clint Westford, surveyor for all the Bodger agencies, and shook hands. Both men had tanned faces, Margery guessed their work took them outside a lot.

She asked Clint if he had been named after a film star like the Bodger family. The question seemed to embarrass him. It was Grant who answered: 'Clint is a nickname from army days, because he looks a bit like Clint Eastwood and has a similar surname. We were both in the army. We are in the territorials now. My name is Cary Grant Bodger, but I prefer Grant.'

Margery was expecting Grant to show her into an office at the back for the interview as Clark had done, but he pulled a chair from opposite a desk and invited her to sit on it. She realised the interview would take place there. He sent Clint to make coffee for them and tea for Margery. He sat opposite her at his ease, leaning back in his chair, almost as Denzil had done, although he stretched his legs out under the desk, rather than on it. He looked at her directly and put his hands up in front of him with the fingers spread and touching. She thought the look he was giving her from his dark eyes was slightly insolent. She was relieved when he asked her the same question his brother had done. 'What would you like to know?'

The invitation was too tempting for her.

'What I would like to know,' she answered, 'is whether you are going to be selling the new homes on the proposed Monks Thorpe estate?'

The question seemed to amuse him. Grant Bodger still looked straight at her, grinned and said: 'Of course! They are going to be a tremendous money-spinner. Did Clark tell you about those?'

'No. I first heard about them from Denzil Bream.'

'Denzil Bream! What's *he* got to do with it?' Margery was aware of a note of contempt in his voice.

'He's got sole agency for the executive homes which are to be built on the Home Farm part of the site.'

'Has he indeed!? That's what Denzil claims, is it, Miss Moore?'

Margery was a bit put out. 'Well… yes… Denzil gave me a map and a brochure. Haven't you seen them?'

She was relieved that he hadn't read the Weekender Gleaner and the article which was attributed to her.

'I've heard something about it. We are going to help the Farrells of Home Farm to buy their house. There are no plans for the farmland that I know of. I think they will still be renting it. That is the intention.'

*That's interesting,* Margery thought.

'What sort of houses will be built on the Monks Thorpe estate?' she asked.

'It's all dependent on the construction of the bypass. Nothing will be built until we know the money is in place from the developers for the road. That has to come first. I can see why Denzil has his eye on Home Farm. There is road access to that already. You say he has sole agency for homes on the land. Didn't you say they would be executive homes? Haven't you answered your own question?'

Clint came in carrying a tray with three steaming mugs of drinks which had the Royal Military Academy Sandhurst crest on them. With them was a plate of oat biscuits, which Grant said Clint had baked. Margery was surprised. *Were they more than colleagues in a commercial agency?* she wondered.

'Yes, that's what he said. Large, what Denzil described as executive houses,' she replied to Grant's question.

'I'm surprised Denzil is so sure he can build there,' remarked Grant.

Clint switched on more lights, as the sky was becoming dark.

'I was puzzled too,' she said. 'They've even designed the style of the houses.'

'Really? That's a presumption,' said Grant. 'Do you hear that, Clint?'

Clint joined the conversation, 'Perhaps they bought the land from the council?'

'I think if they had done that, we would have heard about it. We survey and handle land sales in the whole of the Hundreds. The council must offer land on the open market if they sell it. I am not sure how "right to buy" works in the case of farms. My guess is council-owned land would be offered to the tenants first, if they were farming there. But I am not up on the legislation.' At last Margery was being given snippets of information she could use. She noted it down in shorthand.

'Have you any particular aspect of your business you would like me to include in my article?' she asked. 'Or would you like to give me a few details of the commercial properties you are selling or letting at the moment? I could write an article which embraces all the Bodger agencies.'

'We sold an old Victorian clothing factory to a developer six months ago. It's being converted into flats.'

'There is a Victorian clothing factory being converted into flats between here and Great Havell,' she said. 'I saw it from the train on my way here. According to a huge advertisement hoarding outside. Bream has the sole agency for those.'

'Do they now!' exclaimed Grant, giving her a disconcerting, almost hostile, look from his dark eyes. 'What a mine of information you are, Miss Moore!'

Margery was a bit put out again, but nevertheless said: 'I thought you might tell me who had bought it and how much it sold for. I could include it in my article.'

'I'm not sure I want to do that.' Grant leaned forward, picked up a biscuit and dunked it into his coffee. Margery reddened with annoyance. The potentially long awkward silence was broken by a rumble of thunder and Clint. 'What about the building for the Brass Monkeys Brasserie Morris and Mack bought?'

'What about it?' asked Grant impatiently.

'We had great difficulty selling that, if you remember,' replied Clint. 'It was falling down and running with rats. We had to get the structural engineers in.'

'That's not likely to be the sort of thing Miss Moore is looking for,' said Grant dismissively.

'It's a good story,' said Margery, 'but I don't think Morris and Mack would want Gleaner readers to know about the rat aspect of it, even if they've got rid of them. But I'm interested.'

'When we got some floorboards up to see what was underneath,' explained Clint, 'the clay was pockmarked with rat holes.'

'OK Clint. That's enough about rats! We could tell you about the Victorian warehouses near the Old Granary Hotel and the Quay Marina.'

Clint went over to a filing cabinet, found a folder and took it over to Margery. 'Look, Miss Moore, they are four storey and built of local brick, with lime mortar and thoroughly sound and dry. They were no longer used as warehouses. The docks moved further down the estuary, where there is deeper water for the container ships.'

'And these are for sale?' asked Margery.

'Yes,' confirmed Grant, 'we will be advertising them locally in the Weekender Gleaner Property Supplement. In fact, they will be going on the market nationally and through specialist magazines and newspapers.'

'This is ideal, I'll pop into the local studies library tomorrow and find out the background.'

'No need.' Clint was grinning. 'Grant and I have done all that. Once we knew we could offer the property for development, we did all the research and I typed it up. I'll give you a photocopy.'

Margery laughed. 'You do make life easy for me, Clint, as well as delicious biscuits.' She helped herself to another one. 'I'm going to interview the branch at Little Havell tomorrow. Would you have any objection if I put all three agencies into one article?'

'What did Clark say about that?'

'He said he would leave it to me, you and your sister.'

'Ask Audrey then. Is there anything else you would like to know?'

Margery asked a few more questions about shops, business premises and farmland. She found Grant, impatient, unhelpful and evasive again when she asked if there had been any plots of land, or old factories, they'd had difficulty selling. He was only going to tell her what he wanted her to know. It was Clint who helped her with another angle. He took out two large black and white photographs, from a file, of what appeared to be farmland, and put them on the desk in front of Margery. 'I don't think the boss is going to object to you writing about these,' he said.

Grant laughed at Margery as she looked at the pictures, puzzled. One was a picture of horses in a field and the other of stables, with one or two horses looking over the doors.

'What did you sell?' she asked. 'A farm? The land? A field? The stables? Surely not the horses?'

Grant laughed again. 'Things like this make the job really worthwhile.' He didn't answer her question but continued to look very amused to find she didn't know what he was talking about. He expected her to puzzle it out. Clint was smiling as well, and he wasn't going to enlighten her either. So, she waited, trying to work it out.

'It's an equestrian centre,' explained Grant eventually. 'We have only sold that one so far, but I'm hoping there will be another one near the Grimpen Barracks which will come up for sale. I have made sure it will come our way when it does.'

Margery noted it all down and asked Grant and Clint to pose for a picture under the lights inside the building with a map of the Havell Hundreds in the background.

By this time, the sky was really dark, and it was pouring with rain. Margery looked out with apprehension. She put her camera, notebook and pencils into her bag, covering them with a plastic one.

'You surely don't intend to go out in this?' asked Grant, watching her.

'I don't really have a choice,' she replied.

'Haven't you got a waterproof?' asked Clint.

'Only this hat,' indicating the one she had bought recently from Fabb and putting it on.

Clint offered her a large umbrella. 'This will keep you dry, Miss Moore,' he said.

'I'll run you to the station in the Land Rover.' Grant jumped up and nodded towards the vehicle parked outside.

'Well, thank you, gentlemen,' she said as Clint shook her hand and said goodbye.

Grant picked up one of the black leather jackets from the coat stand near the door, put it on and took keys from the pocket. He took the umbrella and sheltered her out of the agency, not seeming to worry if he got wet himself. Margery noticed the heavy rain was washing the mud off the vehicle. The passenger door was unlocked for her and Grant handed her up the step to the seat. He jumped into the driver's seat and put the wet furled umbrella on the floor in front of her.

She discovered horses and riding was a subject Grant was happy to talk about as he drove her along Victory Street, turned left and drove up a street, parallel to

186

Station Road, which was lined with terraces of Victorian cottages and parked cars. He stopped almost outside the station entrance, jumped out, picked up the umbrella, unfurled it, held it up, handed her down from the passenger seat and asked her to keep it for her journey home. He waited long enough to see her into the station and drove off after she turned and waved.

Margery was grateful for the umbrella as she had to go over the open foot-bridge to the other platform, to wait for the train under the shelter of the station canopy.

She had a five-minute wait. The two interviews she had done that afternoon had been quite tiring. The older brother had been easier than the younger to talk to. Grant and Clint had been a sort of double act. Grant had been nearly as difficult as Denzil. Clint provided the drinks, the biscuits and most of the information. Yet Grant had taken her to the station and made sure she kept dry. But then, she thought, *he was probably keen to get rid of her.*

The train was crowded with people returning to their homes in Great Havell from work. She had to stand, but as it was only a short journey, she did not mind. The rain was so heavy the windows were misted up, she couldn't see much outside. She was looking forward to going home, putting her electric fire on, drying out and cooking a hot meal. The gossip in the morning at the Gleaner had been a shock for her. Meeting DI Barker at lunchtime had been reassuring. The interview with Clark Bodger had been pleasant, but the one with his brother had been difficult. Although he had been polite and pleasant enough when he drove her to the station, it had been hard work getting any information out of him. She was tired and not expecting to be involved in a further mystery or that she would be changing her plans for the following day.

# Chapter VII

## Documents Discovered

Margery stepped out of Great Havell Station and opened the large umbrella Bodgers had given her. She noticed "BODGER'S COMMERCIAL" was in big capital letters all over it, but, at least in this case, the firm was keeping her dry. As the rain splashed over her boots, she was glad she was wearing them and pleased they came up to her calves and helped to keep her legs and feet dry. She hurried down the road from the station, not noticing much, but sheltering from the rain under the large umbrella. She was just passing the turning to the market-place, when she saw Jonah rushing towards her in a plastic mac and holding an umbrella.

'Ah! Margery! I just went to your cottage, but, actually, you are not in!' he said breathlessly.

'I know,' said Margery amused. 'I'm here, on my way home.'

'I'm going to Hair today and Shorn Tomorrow.'

'What, for a haircut?' asked Margery, even more amused, because Jonah's comb over meant he didn't have much hair to cut. 'And won't they be closing and isn't it just a ladies' hairdressers?'

'I had someone called Tina in the library today. She says she knows you.'

'Yes, she does my hair. Why are you going to see Tina?'

'Actually, she thinks her boys might have found something that would interest me.'

'Does she? I'll come with you, Jonah.'

'In fact, Margery, I was hoping you would say that!'

She followed Jonah into the marketplace and round the corner to her hairdressers. The salon was still open, but there were no customers inside. Jonah opened the door for her, and they stood dripping on the doormat as Tina came to greet them. Margery put her large umbrella in the umbrella stand and Jonah took off the plastic mac he had over his suit and hung it up on the coat stand.

'Come in and sit down,' said Tina, taking them over to the chairs in front of the mirrors. She pulled them out so they could all face each other.

'I'll tell you what it's about,' she said. 'As I mentioned to Miss Moore the other day, Mr McKay, my boys are always pulling things out of skips and reusing them or making something out of them…any old rubbish. Yesterday they were packing really expensive looking files into their school bags. I asked them where they got them and they said they were from a skip and they'd found them in a bin bag, hidden under a broken plaster fire surround. There had been quite a lot of them, they said, with fairly thick clear plastic coverings inside with loads of old writing. I asked them what they had done with the contents of the files and they said they were still in the bin bag in the loft. I let them go to school and take the files in case they were late, but when they came home, I asked to see the bin bag. When they brought it down from the loft and showed me, I saw inside the cardboard files were clear plastic ones showing close, hand-written stuff, which was difficult to read. It was on paper which was rough and yellow and obviously old, brown at the edges. I put them all back in the bin bag and tucked them away on the shelf at the top of the broom cupboard. They are still there, no one will find or interfere with them there. I popped over in my lunch hour to tell you, Mr McKay, because I thought you might know what they were.'

'Could I come over and have a look?' asked Jonah. 'Would you mind, Tina?'

'Do you think you know what they might be?'

'Actually, I do. I know what they could be,' replied Jonah, quite excited. 'How soon can I come and have a look?'

'I really need to catch a bus home now after I've locked up,' replied Tina. I have a half day tomorrow, if you would like to come over about 2.30 pm before the boys are home from school. Would you like to come too, Miss Moore?'

Margery nodded enthusiastically.

'Where do you live, Tina?' asked Jonah.

'It's a short bus ride away in the suburbs,' said Tina, 'on the Glebe Estate. I live at 86, Hawfinch Road. I'd better lock up now.'

Jonah put his plastic mac back on and he and Margery picked up their umbrellas and stepped outside into the pouring rain, leaving Tina to lock up the salon.

'How do you fancy going to Feasta Pizza for a bite to eat, Margery?' said Jonah.

'Now that's a good idea; I've had a busy and fairly difficult day.'

They hastened across the marketplace to the little Italian restaurant in the opposite corner of the square near the town hall. It wasn't busy and the staff were pleased to see them in spite of their soggy umbrellas and Jonah's dripping mac.

They put the umbrellas in the stand, by the door, and Jonah's plastic mac on a peg. Gina showed them to a table for two with a gingham tablecloth and a Mateus Rosé bottle made into a lamp at the side.

Jonah ordered some Italian wine, bread and olives and they looked at the menu. The restaurant had a brick pizza oven and Margery knew the food was good. She ordered a pizza with extra mushrooms and Jonah ordered one with salami. They both had side salads.

Gina, part of the restauranteur's family, served them.

'I hope the demonstrations in the marketplace and outside the town hall on Friday didn't disturb you too much, Gina,' said Margery.

'It was noisy, but very good for business,' Gina replied, 'especially when the market was finished and there were still people in the square. We were so busy, we had to turn people away, but some of them came back on Saturday, because they fancied coming here and were disappointed on Friday.'

'So, you would like more demonstrations in the marketplace?' asked Margery, smiling.

'Well, I suppose things could have been a bit rough,' said Gina. 'But you know the family, we like to cook, the more the better. On Friday, we started something new, we cooked large Margherita pizzas, cut them up and sold them in slices outside the restaurant for 50 pence each. The children especially loved them. They came back on Saturday for more. We may do that on a regular basis at a weekend perhaps, but not every day.'

Gina brought the wine and opened it. Jonah tried some and Gina poured it out for Margery and topped up Jonah's glass. He raised it.

'Here's to Tina's boys and the return of the papers missing from Barney's house,' he said.

'You really think they are those?' asked Margery. 'Why didn't you tell Tina?'

'It's best she does not know. From what Barney and I read of them, they were quite sensitive and would overturn the verdict on those witches, although it is far too long ago to matter now. But from a historical point of view, they may prove to be a very valuable record. You know how Barney was a stickler for facts and getting things right. He wouldn't have kept quiet about any of it, once we had proved their authenticity. There were some intriguing notes about the backgrounds of the women too. There were some later documents with them as well. At least, Barney said there appeared to be, but he didn't remember finding them with the Tudor ones. He did say he was so excited about finding them, he might not have noticed, if there were some later ones.'

'That's interesting. It might mean the papers were known about and hidden at a later date, perhaps, so someone at least, in Great Havell, must have been aware there was a miscarriage of justice when those witches were hanged,' said Margery. 'What will you do when you get them back?'

'I'll…continue—' Jonah began, as the door opened, and a couple entered. Margery looked round and saw they belonged to the Moyen Circle. They greeted Jonah and Margery and sat down. Jonah made a warning signal for Margery to change the subject of conversation.

'There seemed to be an embargo on every subject at the moment, but the coroner's court was in the public domain.' Jonah praised Margery's accurate report on that.

It had been, just a case of typing up her shorthand notes into a readable form, she said.

'Not everyone could do that,' said Jonah.

Margery mentioned the Bodger family. She told Jonah they were all named after film stars, even Grant's surveyor had a film star nickname, she told him.

Jonah said he didn't often have any reason to go to Grimpen Havell. Margery said nor did she, but it was very easy to get there on the train. She mentioned the new flats in the old clothing factory and that Bream had the sole agency for that and she felt it was odd that Denzil had not promoted them.

Jonah agreed and said the whole business with the new homes at Monks Thorpe and Bream was odd.

Margery said they would not build there until the bypass was in place and that Grant Bodger was helping the tenants at Home Farm to buy their farmhouse on the right to buy scheme.

Jonah was interested. 'So, the scheme to sell the homes planned for land on Home Farm may not materialise after all?' he asked.

'It may not,' confirmed Margery. 'Did you know the Bodger grandparents and great grandparents were builders?'

'I did,' said Jonah. 'The family have been builders here much for longer than that. A lot of them emigrated to America in the 1630s to construct a new world there.'

'That's interesting,' said Margery. 'Are you planning any more trips to France Jonah?' she added.

'Yes, I'm going on Saturday, actually, with our Francophiles group. We're just hopping over for a day or two and we will have a meal out at Wimereux as we usually do. We will bring a few bottles of vin rouge back with us, in fact.'

'Did you see anything of the fracas after the Valentine's Ball Jonah?'

'No, I was home and tucked up in bed by then.'

'Was there any trouble inside the venue that you saw?'

'I don't think so, it was all very good humoured. The food was good.'

'I heard it was prepared by Morris and Mack from the Brass Monkeys.'

'They did a great job. The music was good, and I enjoyed watching the dancing. I saw Cheryl, but I didn't have much of a chance to talk to her, she was with a group of girls from the Gleaner. They were all queueing up to dance with Harry Grimes.'

'Were they really, Jonah?'

'It looked like it to me. He'd dance with one and then the next one took over and so on, it was quite amusing to watch. I don't think his wife was too pleased about it though.'

'I don't suppose she was. You didn't see Vlad on Saturday, did you?'

'No, I hadn't seen him all day. He wasn't at the ball. I don't think he would have anything to wear to go to something like that. But he met up with me on Friday night when I was on my way home after DI Barker and I had seen you home. Vlad said he had missed seeing us at the Arts Centre that evening.'

When they had finished their pizzas and half the bottle of wine, Margery and Jonah paid the bill and left. Jonah walked home with her, saying he would probably call in at the Amicable Anarchist for a quick pint before he went back to his house. She could keep the rest of the wine if she liked. The rain had eased off and they only needed to use the umbrellas. Jonah's plastic mac was dry, so he folded it up and put it in his bag.

Jonah left her at the gate, and Margery opened the door to her cottage. She noticed Alf's curtains twitching as she went in. She switched on her lamp and the electric fire. She had been expecting Vlad and thought he might be there waiting for her but wondered if he would now after all had been said about him.

She was keen to see him; it had been a hard day and she felt emotionally exhausted. She was not sure when she would be able to write up the story about the Bodger's estate agencies until she had been to the Little Havell branch and confirmed that Audrey Bodger would like it to be one article. It was time for a cocoa perhaps, listen to some music, read, have a shower, a hot water bottle and bed. She didn't know why, but she felt a bit lonely. It was an odd feeling for her. She was used to being on her own.

## Tuesday 18th February

Margery woke up in good time for a leisurely breakfast. When she dressed, she put a pair of black trousers with a black roll neck jumper and black jacket. She had her habitual breakfast of toast, marmalade and tea. She put on a pair of ankle boots and found a plastic cape, as it appeared to be drizzling. She put on the hat she had bought from Fabb as it was waterproof, and she could tie it under her chin. It was not really a suitable day for a bike ride to a client, but her notebook pencil and camera would stay dry under a plastic bag in her basket.

She extracted her bike from her shed and left by the back gate, cycling up the bridle path, past the back gardens of Priory Cottages, to turn at the end into the road, past the mound on the right and the market gardens and greenhouses, until she came to the fork in the road which led round the Glebe Mound. It ran along the boundary of the Glebe Park, until she reached the wall of the estate belonging to the Country Hotel. Over to her right, the Glebe Park extended to the Glebe Estate in the Great Havell suburbs. These were all 1960s and 1970s houses and had originally been built as council houses. It was a huge estate, on which many people were exercising their right to buy. Margery cycled past the Glebe Park and playing fields, the Little Havell Primary School, over the bridge spanning the tributary to the Cricklewater and past the parish church in the centre of a large walled churchyard. As she cycled into the village, rows of timber-framed cottages and Tudor domestic houses, similar to Barney's, lined the road on either side. They were painted in pastel colours, and some were white plaster with the timbers exposed. A few, near the river were thatched, but most had red tiled roofs which came into view higgledy-piggledy, crowded together, like an illustration in a nursery rhyme book, Margery thought, as she peddled up the market hill to the marketplace. Here the Little Havell branch of Bodgers occupied the whole of a fine timber-framed building, which had been a guildhall at the top of the hill.

Margery realised she was a little hot and bothered from her ride. She locked her bike on some railings nearby, took a mirror from her handbag, checked her make-up and refreshed it where she needed to. She removed her plastic cape and put it in her bike basket, took her bag out of its plastic covering, put her camera round her neck and took some distant shots of the agency. With the camera still round her neck, she, popped into the newsagents to buy a copy of the Gleaner, glancing briefly at the headline "DRUGS HAUL AT DEN" and walked into the agency.

Although Little Havell was only a village, the Bodgers branch was the largest she had been in. A hall from the entrance offered a choice of Tudor doors on either side with labels in Gothic letters on them. One was marked "Lettings" and the other was marked "Sales".

Margery knocked and opened the door to the sales.

She found three people behind desks. Audrey Bodger rose to her feet as soon as Margery entered. She had her hair in a neat French pleat and was as elegantly dressed as her film star namesake might have been. Margery noticed a family resemblance to her brothers. Audrey shared their good looks, although, with her large soulful brown eyes, Margery thought she had the look of a Madonna about her.

'Miss Moore, what a pleasure to meet you! May I introduce my assistants, Tracey Munson and Lenny Carter.'

Audrey Bodger shook hands with Margery and the two, younger people in the room stood up to shake hands too. Tracey, Margery knew, was Denzil Bream's girlfriend.

She had not met Lenny before, who, from his looks, she guessed, his parents were from the Caribbean.

'My goodness me,' said Margery, 'is that an original painting on your wall? I never knew Constable painted in Little Havell.'

Audrey Bodger laughed. 'No, he never came to the Havell Hundreds. That was painted by a very talented artist who has a studio in Little Havell. It's a Pricilla Buckler.'

'I've heard the name,' said Margery. 'She has her own distinctive style and paints local scenes like this one. This is amazing, I really thought it was a Constable.'

Audrey showed Margery another oil painting on the walls of the office. 'This is one of Pricilla's in her usual style, which you will probably recognise,' she said. 'Pricilla painted the other one for a bit of fun. I challenged her to see if she could do it.'

'This is a lovely painting of your offices,' said Margery. 'Did you commission it from the artist?'

'Yes, you might have noticed our agencies put on art exhibitions in the Great Havell guildhall sometimes, and Pricilla Buckler is one of the artists we sponsor. If you are interested, there is an exhibition arranged to launch at the guildhall this Friday, which will have some of Pricilla Buckler's work in it. Would you like an invitation to the private view?'

'If it's for Friday, I am already going out on Friday night, but I could go to the exhibition on Saturday.'

'I'll make sure I send you an invitation to our next exhibition launch.'

'Thank you, I would like that.' She made a note to go to the exhibition on Saturday.

'This is something Pricilla did for us,' said Audrey, taking Margery over to a framed hand-written legal document with a seal on it.

'Pricilla did that!' remarked Margery. 'That looks like an original. Even the paper looks old.'

'She's a very talented lady,' said Audrey. 'She also drew and painted this delightful map of Little Havell, which we give away to clients. Would you like one?'

'Yes please,' said Margery, as Audrey unfolded one of the firm's brochures to reveal a map of Little Havell with some of the village's historic buildings drawn in and delicately coloured with a watercolour wash.

'It's a work of art,' Margery was delighted.

'I think so,' agreed Audrey. 'At the studios we run in Little Havell, we have a little colony of talented writers and artists, Pricilla is one of them.'

Margery turned to Tracey.

'Tracey, your tan still looks good, how did you enjoy the Valentine's Ball?'

'We all went to the ball,' said Audrey, before Tracey had a chance to reply. 'It was a good event, but the aftermath was a bit unfortunate. Come and sit down, Miss Moore.'

Margery found she would be talking to all of them in the beamed room, which had an oriel window on to the marketplace.

When they were sitting down, Margery took her notebook and pencil out of her bag and looked up at them expectantly.

'Is it, domestic housing, you sell in here?' she asked.

'Yes,' said Audrey, 'we particularly specialise in historic houses, listed buildings, lettings and country estates. My brother Clark concentrates mainly on Victorian and Edwardian suburban houses, exclusively on sales and lettings. Many of them were built by our grandparents and great grandparents. My brother Grant, as you probably know, is on the commercial and surveying side of the business. He is a land agent. He sells properties for redevelopment and handles shop and industrial lettings. Grant also deals with the commercial properties and the surveying here in Little Havell. We try to specialise here. If anyone would like to rent or buy a listed or timber-framed cottage or house, they come to us. We handle most of the historic properties which come up for sale in Great Havell too. A lot of our clients are looking for a country retreat. We have cousins in development and civil engineering who work closely with the Ministry of Building and Works and the Society for the Protection of Ancient Buildings, when the historic properties we handle need refurbishment.

'Tracey lives in Great Havell, and Lenny lives nearer in the village. We all went to the Valentine's Ball together on Saturday because Tracey's boyfriend has been sent away by his family. She's been a bit traumatised about it since she couldn't wake him up after a party. We thought we would all go to give her support.'

'Yes, I heard about Tracey's boyfriend,' said Margery. 'It was in the Gleaner.'

'So was the story about your poor cat, wasn't it?' asked Audrey.

Margery had not expected that.

'Well… yes…' she said slowly, 'it was. I still don't know who did that or why. It was a horrible thing to happen.'

'It's possible Tracey might know something about it,' said Audrey.

Margery didn't know what to say. She looked from Audrey to Tracey and waited for an explanation.

'I am so, so sorry, Miss Moore,' said Tracey, 'I don't think it was ever intended to involve or hurt your cat.'

Margery turned towards Tracey in surprise, hoping for an explanation and saw a very troubled look on her tanned features.

'It was going to be a bit of fun,' Tracey explained. 'Denzil has such weird ideas at times. He decided to pinch the broomsticks from outside the Witches Cauldron after we'd had a wild night out at the Den, the nightclub near the Quay Marina. We'd all been to the Witches for coffee previously, and he'd noticed the broomsticks over the door and decided he wanted them. Denzil called it a "crazy jape". We were laughing about it all the way back to his flat. He never said what he intended to do with them. I thought he might put them back, because he had just taken them for a lark. I drove his car because he had been drinking heavily when he pinched the broomsticks. I thought no more about it until I saw the Gleaner headline. I was so shocked someone's pet cat had been killed, I mentioned to Audrey and Lenny what we had done. I only know Denzil took the broomsticks and they were probably used for that. I really don't know any more. Except, when we celebrated his birthday the following week, we had another wild night out at with our friends and they were laughing about the headline in the Gleaner. Some of them were saying it was the exactly what they wanted.'

'Thanks Tracey,' said Audrey. 'Miss Moore, we wanted Tracey to tell you this, because we understand it was your cat involved and we wanted you to know she has no idea who actually did that.'

'Well, thank you, Tracey, for being so honest. I have to admit it was a shock, but I'm getting over it now,' said Margery. 'My friends and relatives have taken a very poor view of it, but I can't believe I, or my cat were specifically targeted.' Margery decided it would not be diplomatic to mention the rag doll and twigs which had been pushed through her door.

After this, they discussed historic buildings, timber-framing, thatch, ornate chimneys and the sort of clients Audrey and her team had in Little Havell.

Audrey took her across the hall into the lettings department. Lenny came with them, as he worked mainly in lettings. He explained they had some houses in multiple occupation in Little Havell.

'It works very well, Miss Moore,' he said. 'We have some large Edwardian houses, built when there were plans to create a spa. These are now split into bed-sits. They can be let out at very reasonable rents. The tenants get to know each other. We have some students too, although they have a bus ride to go to university or college. It's mainly the mature students who choose to rent in Little Havell. The younger ones like to be nearer college, university and the night life in Great Havell.'

'We have a team of skilled people who live locally,' said Audrey. 'There are gardeners, decorators, cleaners, carpenters, locksmiths, plumbers, electricians and heating engineers. Some of them are lodged in these houses. We know we can call on them for maintenance and repairs at short notice.

'One of our tenants was rumoured to have been in a fight in Great Havell on Saturday night, but two of his flat mates knew he had been at home at the time and were able to vouch for him. He's a very sought-after electrician, plumbing and heating engineer. The ladies like him and always ask for him if something goes wrong with their plumbing. One of our tenants punctured her own ball cock recently just to get him round. He told us a hole that size could never have appeared in a ball cock, unless someone had pierced it deliberately. He had no idea why someone would have done that. But we did, didn't we, Lenny?'

'We had a pretty good idea,' agreed Lenny and laughed.

Margery laughed too. 'I don't think I can put that in my article,' she said. But the fact you have a good maintenance team nearby to sort out problems and they are also your tenants, is interesting. Your brothers asked me to check if you would want all branches of Bodgers to be in one article. If my editor wishes to split them up, would you have any objections?'

'We'll leave it up to you and your editor to decide,' replied Audrey.

Tracey came in with some tea and biscuits before Margery left. The phones had been on answerphone whilst she was there and there had been plenty of calls. It was a busy agency. Margery took some pictures inside the building, with the three staff. She included the beams, studs and pictures. She said her goodbyes and cycled home.

The drizzle was easing off on her homeward journey. She was looking forward to typing up her notes on the Bodger agencies. She took her bike through her back gate and put it in the shed. Relieved Alf was not hanging about waiting for her, as he usually was, she was surprised to see her other neighbour banging on her bedroom window. Margery indicated to her she would go round to her front door.

Wondering if Florence was all right, she put everything in her front room, left by her front door, went round to Florence's cottage and saw her looking out for her in the window. She opened the door as Margery walked up the path.

'Florence! Are you all right?' asked Margery. Florence turned her hearing aid up and she asked again, but louder.

Florence nodded and asked Margery to sit down. She took one of the armchairs in Florence's front room and her neighbour sat in the other one, which had an elaborate piece of knitting on the arm. Margery didn't often go into Florence's cottage. She usually saw her to wave to when she went out. Florence's white hair was tucked away in a bun, she had half-moon glasses on and was wearing a loose light-coloured housecoat over her clothes. She had put her knitting down and leaned forward to Margery earnestly.

She was alright, she told her, but had heard from her neighbours the other side, that the morning Barney Cobbler was found unconscious on the priory railings, they had seen a car drive slowly along the bridle path at the back of the cottages and stop outside Margery's. A man in a black leather jacket got out and went onto the Glebe Mound. The car had driven round the cottages and her neighbours saw it go along the lane at the front of them. It must have stopped for a while at the priory, then they saw it reverse back up with two people in it. They had mentioned it to the local police when they came round. But since then, they had read Margery's report on the inquests, so they had asked Florence, if she would pass the information on to her. They had seen different vehicles along both the bridle path and the lane on the following day, but they were only passing by and no one got out.

'Do you think it is important, Miss Moore?' asked Florence.

Margery nodded and asked slowly, distinctly and loudly what sort of car her neighbours had seen the morning Barney died.

Florence told her they said it was the sort of car farmers use, but they didn't know any more than that, except it was muddy and had a spare wheel on the bonnet.

Margery thanked Florence and hurried back home to get on with her story. She would have to break for a quick lunch but would need to catch the 2.00 pm Little Havell bus from the marketplace with Jonah to go to the Glebe Estate and Tina's house in Hawfinch Road.

She put her electric fire on to take the edge of the chill and realised she should really ring DI Barker with the latest information from her neighbour.

Margery went over to the phone, picked it up and dialled Great Havell police station. She recognised Sergeant Taylor's voice at the other end of the phone.

'Could I speak to DI Barker please? It's Margery Moore'

'I'll try and put you through, if I don't get you through, I'll page him and tell him you would like to speak to him, Miss Moore.'

Margery waited and waited on the phone, there was no reply from Barker's extension. Eventually, Sergeant Taylor came back on the phone.

No reply. I think he's out, but I'm not sure. I'll page him and tell you rang. Is it urgent?'

'Not really,' she replied, thinking she would like to get on with the Bodger article.

'All right,' said Sergeant Taylor, 'I'll tell him you were trying to contact him.'

Margery decided to read the lead story in the Gleaner before she started work. She sat in the small settee under the window and read.

"Great Havell police were alerted, by Dennis Williams, boss at the popular Den night club at the Quay Marina, to his discovery of a large stash of cocaine.

"'I have no idea how it got there, or who put it there,' said Mr Williams. 'This is a respectable nightclub and our bouncers are trained to check clients for any illicit drugs as they enter.

"'How this amount entered the club is a complete mystery to me. There is far too much for it to have been brought in at the door without one of the staff noticing.'"

"A substantial quantity of the drug, which is thought to be worth thousands of pounds on the black market, was discovered by Mr Williams under some toilet rolls and with some distinctive imported Valentine's Day decorations in a cupboard near his office.

"'At first I thought it was a small bag of plaster,' said the astonished Mr Williams, who explained he had purchased the toilet rolls in bulk from the cash and carry about four weeks ago. He stored them alongside boxes of tissues, paper towels, liquid soap dispenser refills and decorations for Valentine's Day.

"'The cupboard is not locked,' added Mr Williams, 'so any member of my staff with a key to the offices could access it. The drug could have been hidden at any time within the past four weeks and I would not have noticed.'"

"Great Havell police are questioning staff at the Den nightclub, but no arrests have been made."

*So, there is no mention of DI Barker or the drug squad,* thought Margery. All was being dealt with locally.

She put the paper aside, picked her note book out of her bag, put it on her desk next to her typewriter and started to write up her article about the Bodger family and their estate agencies. She realised she hadn't much time before she needed to leave the house and meet Jonah to go to the Glebe Estate. She got herself a glass of water, some cheese, biscuits and an apple and ate whilst she worked.

She was typing the article and it was going well, when there was a knock at the door. Margery finished the paragraph she was writing, and the knock came again, more urgently. She got up and answered the door. It was DI Barker.

'I'm sorry to disturb you, Miss Moore, may I come in?'

'Yes, of course, mind your head,' Margery reminded him. Feeling a bit annoyed she could not continue with her work.

'I understand you rang me earlier today.'

'Yes, I did.'

'I wasn't informed of your call.'

'But Sergeant Taylor said he would page you.'

'Yes, I heard him on the phone to you, that's why I am here. But he was unaware I was in the lobby when he took your call. He didn't page me or mention it when I walked in and he had put the phone down.'

'But why wouldn't he?' asked Margery, puzzled.

'Small town politics, my dear Miss Moore. What did you want to tell me?'

Margery told DI Barker everything Florence and Tracey had told her.

'And so, Florence's neighbours didn't want to tell you themselves and got Florence to do it?'

'Yes, that's right.'

'We know who was on the Glebe Mound with Barney and we know who the vehicle belongs to.'

'Does that mean you've solved the case?'

'In a sense, yes.'

'Have you had to make any arrests?'

'No. There won't be any arrests.'

'But…why?'

'Miss Moore, one of the reasons I came to see you is to advise you to keep a low profile. I think you are intelligent enough to realise Mr Cobbler's death was not due to the addiction to which it is still being attributed. I think you also realise there have been many attempts to incriminate people as being involved in the two deaths and the incident with your cat. We know whose Land Rover made the tracks you pointed out. We also know who buys the drugs. I am hoping the drug squad will be on the track of the source. But, from experience, that may not be the end of the problem. One source of supply may be closed, but the demand is still there and another one will open. I've walked here. This is an unofficial visit. Everything I tell you is off the record. It was not a coincidence there have been two deaths near where you live or the episode with your cat, which was attributed to you. I wanted to advise you to keep to your normal routine and avoid any controversy over the fair and the concert planned for the solstice. The inquests requested by Jonah McKay and Eric Bolton on the deaths of Barney Cobbler and Sadie Petal will be officially closed at the coroner's court on Thursday. The Gleaner may ask you to cover it. That's all I have to say. Thank you very much for all the help you have given me. Janine is coming to join me at the Palace Hotel in Havell-Next-the-Sea on Friday. We are going to the Arts Centre at Great Havell in the evening. I've suggested a few numbers for Andy Clarke and the local musicians to play. It should be a good evening. Goodbye Miss Moore, I'll see you there, if not at the coroner's court.'

Margery saw DI Barker out and watched him walk off in the direction of the old priory, pausing at her gate to wave to her and making sure he would be seen by her neighbours on both sides. She was beginning to see his point. She could easily have been incriminated in some way in Barney's death, she was often seen walking through the priory and had done so that morning. She went that way almost every day. Also, people might think she was involved in some way in Sadie's death. She had often spoken to and passed the time of day with her. She would have to wait until the reconvening of the coroner's court, on Thursday, to find out the verdict. The coroner would sum up on any evidence available. It would be interesting to see who would be called.

It was time to meet Jonah at the bus stop. After days of drizzle, the sun was out, so Margery wore her tartan cape and beret over her black slacks and jumper. She picked up her notebook and pencil and put them in her bag, out of habit, put her moccasins on and took the familiar walk down the lane, through the old priory, across the car park, across Priory Street, past the Amicable Anarchist, past the terrace of houses and into the marketplace.

Jonah was at the bus stop already. They only had a five-minute wait. Once on the bus, Margery mentioned her visit to Bodgers at Little Havell that morning.

Jonah was enthusiastic. 'Well, I've always been a great admirer of Audrey Bodger, actually. A real lady. She was at the Valentine's Ball. Brendon and I are going to have to consult her over the sale of Barney's house. As far as we know, he has left the property to the Moyen Circle. The circle has designated us to handle the transfer of the property. I'm going to have to ask Audrey for advice. I'm looking forward to that.' Margery smiled. She hadn't imagined Jonah would have such a strong admiration for someone like Audrey Bodger. The bus took them along suburban roads which backed on to the Glebe Park and playing fields. It stopped outside a sports centre and leisure pool where Jonah and Margery got off.

Jonah had a map. 'We need to cross the road,' he said. The crossing was outside the sports centre. They went over to the Glebe Estate and turned into Hawfinch Road. Margery noticed one or two houses in the road had pampas grass outside and remembered what Ruth Baldock had said about the extraordinary demand for the plant. So, she thought, it must be fashionable to put it in front gardens. There were 1960s semi-detached houses on one side, with open plan front gardens, and some older 1930s semis on the other. Number 86 was near the end of the road. It was a left-hand semi-detached house with a porch canopy, a fairly mature cherry tree and rose bushes in the front garden.

Tina responded quickly to their knock, she took Margery's cape and Jonah's coat and hung them on hooks in the hall.

'Thank you for coming,' she said. She led them into a long single room with picture windows at each end, which had a sitting area at the front and a pine dining table and chairs at the back. Tina opened a sliding door into the kitchen, with a window at the back over the sink and a glazed outside door on the side, near the cooker. The broom cupboard was just inside the kitchen. Tina spread some newspaper on her dining table, opened the cupboard, extracted a bin bag, which, Margery noticed, was dusted with dried mud, and put it on the dining table.

Jonah, Margery saw, could barely contain his excitement.

'Would you mind if I looked inside, actually, Tina?'

Tina said, 'No, Mr McKay, please go ahead.'

Jonah peered inside the bag tentatively and put his hand inside. He pulled out a thick file tied with document ribbon, which he undid and revealed a clear file inside with closely written handwriting on yellowed paper. He re-tied the ribbon and did the same with the other files.

There were two clear files on their own, with the same kind of handwriting on them.

'I would need to take these away to examine them properly,' said Jonah. 'They are historic archives and may belong to one of the local solicitors. They were likely disposed of in error. Your boys can keep the files they are using if they like. May I take these others away? Or would your boys like them back?'

'You may take them, Mr McKay, I don't think the boys will want them back,' said Tina. 'I expect they were thrown out for some reason, keep them and dispose of them, if they are of no interest.'

'Thank you, Tina, and thank you for alerting me to them. I had thought they were the papers missing from my late friend's house.'

'I hope you haven't had a wasted journey,' said Tina. 'Can I make you both a cup of tea?'

'No thanks, Tina,' replied Jonah. 'Margery may like to stay, but I took a late lunch to do this and I had better get back to the library.' He put everything back in the bin bag and held it as if it was so much rubbish. Tina found him a large plastic supermarket bag to carry it all in.

'Thank you, Tina, I would have loved a cup of tea, but I have to get back to get something written for deadline,' said Margery.

'Your hair is still looking good, Miss Moore,' remarked Tina.

'It certainly is,' agreed Jonah.

'You do a good job, Tina, I know when you've given me a perm, I don't have to worry too much about styling it for some time, just pop in regularly for a shampoo and set and no doubt I'll see you soon for that, thanks Tina.'

'Thank those boys of yours for finding these things,' said Jonah, 'I can tell you; I'm looking for documents stolen from a friend's house and I will be interested in any documents your boys might discover.'

'Oh, I'm sorry if you are disappointed,' said Tina. 'I thought you would know what to do with these.'

'I do. I think they look interesting. I shall study them carefully. Thank you, Tina. Tell those boys of yours to keep looking.'

'I most certainly will, Mr McKay.' Tina took his coat from the peg in the hall and Margery's cape. She waved from the door as they walked up the road and turned towards the bus stop opposite the sports centre and playing fields. Neither spoke, both were deep in thought. When they reached the stop, Margery was surprised to see Jonah carefully rearrange the documents inside the bin bag and the plastic bag, so they were neater and compact enough to fit in the briefcase he had brought with him.

'I'm sorry you were disappointed,' said Margery.

'Well, actually, I wasn't.'

'You weren't? I don't understand, why did you give Tina the impression you were?'

'I hope I didn't give Tina the impression I was entirely disappointed. When I ate fish and chips on the sea front at Sandy Reach with DI Barker, he suggested Barney was targeted because of these documents or one of two of them. Or there was something about them which was extremely interesting or valuable to someone. He said he thought Barney's death was probably accidental and he was wanted out of the way for a while and that it was intended to discredit him, because he was claiming he had seen proof the Grimes family did not have title to the land which will be sold for new homes and a bypass. He thinks Barney was supposed to be in a drug-induced coma, so these documents could be found and hidden or destroyed. If that is the case, I'm surprised they turned up in a skip and were not burned. Maybe DI Barker got that bit wrong. But he said enough last week to convince me it was best to give everyone the impression they were well and truly lost. Perhaps whoever took them couldn't bear to destroy them. Who knows? But then why would they turn up in a skip? It doesn't make sense.'

'No,' agreed Margery pensively, 'It doesn't make sense and I've never known you to be devious before, Jonah, you quite surprise me.'

Jonah laughed. 'It's not being devious, Margery. I was quite careful what I said at Tina's. I didn't want her boys to have them back, so I needed to say they were interesting and that I would like to study them. I thought the boys could keep the folders. After all, they are not unique and can be bought at the stationers. You might have noticed I said I had thought they were the papers missing from my late friend's house. I didn't say they weren't, I just tried to give the impression they might not be.'

'You fooled me, Jonah. I've never known you to be anything other than honest and straightforward.'

'Actually, I was honest, in a way. At least I hope I was. I just didn't let on what they were.'

'You know, DI Barker gave the same sort of warning to me,' said Margery. 'He also said the Great Havell police failed to give him a message from me, when they promised me, they would. I wonder if I can find out anything from the Gleaner when I go there in the morning.'

Just then the bus turned up and they got on.

Margery asked Jonah if he remembered the Glebe Estate being built. He did, he said, but now a lot of the houses were being sold on the "right to buy" scheme. She told Jonah, that, according to her uncle, the proceeds of right to buy were not being invested in more council stock. They agreed it was a pity.

Back in Great Havell marketplace, Jonah went back to the library and Margery walked to her cottage to continue her article on the Bodger Estate Agencies. She took a long look at the Glebe Mound on her way home when she crossed the road to the old priory from the Amicable Anarchist.

She hadn't made much progress on her articles to date. She had only started writing about the enthusiasm of the founders of the agency for films and the ancestors who were builders. This was general information on all the agencies. She decided to write about the specialisms of each location as separate articles.

Margery worked away for a couple of hours, with a pot of tea for refreshment. There had been no Alf looking out for her and all seemed to be quiet at Priory Cottages. It all looked peaceful in the late afternoon sun. She took another look from her kitchen window, when the kettle was on. The Glebe Mound was just a large grassy hill. She found it hard to believe Growltiger had been on the top, and harder still to imagine those six women hanging there and before them, the monks from the priory. She looked down and saw she still had her cat's beanbag on the floor near the boiler. It had some of his long gingery hairs on it. She sighed. She would have to take the outer bag off and take it to the laundrette. So much had happened recently. Not for the first time recently, she felt lonely. She went back to her notes and her typewriter.

When she was writing about the Little Havell branch of Bodgers, she noticed she had taken notes of the anecdote about the tenant who punctured her own ball cock to get the plumber in. Margery smiled to herself and then realised it was probably Vlad who was popular with the local housewives. She could understand that. She looked at the daffodils he had put on her desk for her. They were a bit droopy. Impulsively she picked them up and disposed of them in the compost bin. She washed out the milk bottle and put it outside the front door for the milkman.

After a cheese and onion omelette, peas and potatoes, washing up and work finished, she sat in her chair and put the radio on a music programme with a cup of tea. She was tired and wondered if she should get a television. Gill and Philippa were always on about that. They had given up asking her if she had seen particular episodes of Coronation Street or East Enders. She could hear both her neighbours' televisions faintly through the shared walls, but she didn't really mind, it reminded her they were there. In two days, DI Barker had said, the mystery of how Barney and Sadie died would be revealed. Well, everyone already knew how they died, they had both injected themselves or been injected with a large dose of cocaine which had proved fatal to them. Barney had been pushing for an extraordinary meeting of the council to discuss the cancellation of the fair. He had discovered a hand-written contemporary account of the witch trials in his house and these had been stolen when he was found unconscious on the railings of the priory. Margery thought Sadie had seen something and had wanted to tell her. Sadie had said something to Eric, and he had told Vlad, who had described a man in a leather jacket with military bearing with his arm round Barney. The same man Florence's neighbours had seen getting out of a farmer's car on the bridle path at the back of her cottage. Was this the same man who had arranged to meet Sadie on the Glebe Mound? He had been described as very smartly dressed. Why had she seen nothing when she was walking to and from the Gleaner on those days? And that horrible business with Growltiger, why target her cat and her with that rag doll? Was it meant as a threat? Did the person who administered the cocaine to Barney, perhaps Sadie as well, intend to pin it on her or someone connected with her…Vlad? And what was the significance of the drugs found among the Valentine's Day decorations in a cupboard in the Den Nightclub? The Quay Marina venue was popular with many young people in Great Havell. The mayor was in hospital, Denzil Bream had been sent away to a health farm and Gloria had a fur coat. Harry Grimes had been having a massive row with his wife, Rita, after the Valentine's Ball. Gloria had driven off in her company car in a huff on Monday.

Perhaps she would learn more about it all at the Gleaner. Margery decided to have a shower, make herself a cup of cocoa and read in bed.

There was no sign of Vlad, no note, nothing to say he had popped in. *Perhaps he was still spending a lot of his spare time with Eric, or with some Little Havell housewife who had punctured her own ball cock just to get him round,* Margery thought with a pang. Yet, she mused, they had become closer recently. She found it impossible to imagine Vlad would respond to another woman. They had been seeing each other regularly, for nearly a year now. She felt they had a special sort of understanding. He could melt her heart with a look. But, perhaps, hers was not the only heart he melted. Did he turn up in his grubby vest and army jacket regularly at some other woman's house? Was he there now? If she didn't see anything of him this week, perhaps he would turn up at the Jazz and Folk club at the Arts Centre on Friday? Whether he did or not, she would go as DI Barker said he would be there. The coroner's court would give the answers they were all looking for on Thursday. They could discuss it in the open… Except Jonah had rescued the Tudor documents he and Barney had been studying about the witch trials. Would Jonah inform the Great Havell police? They were supposed to be investigating the theft. It was not up to her to inform them. It was for Jonah to do.

Jonah was being secretive. Margery actually doubted he would tell the local police and that would be out of character for him. He was usually so honest. Even the chapbook Jonah had found for her described the gallows already built on the Glebe Mound, so the women could be hanged as soon as they were pronounced guilty. Two of them could read and write. Two of the young women were unable to talk comprehensively and may have had mental health problems and there was a girl and her grandmother. It had been decided all six were guilty before they were even tried. Even that, more than four hundred years ago, was a mystery. It looked as if the women were hounded to death for being poor and helpless.

### Wednesday 19th February

Margery awoke after a good sleep. In her dreams, she had been in houses she had lived in when she was a child, they merged into each other and into Hawfinch Road. She dreamt she wandered from room to familiar room and found people she used to know sitting in the rooms. They were places which were both familiar and unfamiliar. She was used to those dreams which, when she woke up, she was always pleased to find herself in her own cottage. A psychologist would probably say she was looking for answers in those rooms and with those people, but not finding them. It was certainly how she was feeling at the moment. She was also slightly unsettled because she had not seen Vlad, although he had said he would come back on Monday. She felt he had let her down.

She got up, washed and had her usual tea, toast and marmalade breakfast.

She changed her bedsheets and took the cover off Growltiger's beanbag, put them all in her shopping trolley to take to the laundrette. She decided to call in there on her way to the Gleaner, leave it with the manageress and pick it all up on the way back. She saw a few nodding acquaintances on her way. She popped into Hair Today Shorn Tomorrow and made a Friday appointment for a shampoo and set. Shopping trolley in tow, she looked over at Bream and noticed the agency was open. She imagined the older members of the family were fully in charge since Denzil had been packed away to sober up.

She had four articles, three of which could be made into one, and her camera with her. Gill and Philippa were on the phone as usual when she entered the office with her cheery 'Hello girls.' Gill seemed to be trying to placate an irate customer and put the call through for accounts to deal with. Margery picked up the Gleaner and looked at the headline.

"MORE PROTESTS PLANNED"

'Not more disruption in the marketplace,' remarked Margery. 'It looks like it's going to be a regular activity!'

'You tell her,' said Philippa.

'No, you tell her,' said Gill.

'OK, Margery, listen to this, you've missed quite a bit of drama. You remember Gloria walked out when you were here last?'

'Yes, it was only on Monday,' said Margery.

'Well, she never came back, she went off with her company car and Harry Grimes was absolutely furious. You knew he'd been knocking her off, didn't you?'

'No, I didn't know,' said Margery, surprised.

'Where do you think she got her fur coat?' asked Gill.

'Oh! I didn't think, I always saw her with Bill Walker from Moonlight Motors.'

'Oh, Bill's all right, he was just doing her a favour, so she didn't have to drink and drive. It's nothing to do with him. He's only interested in cars, not a lot else. Anyway, he's got a girlfriend who runs a gym, Sylph Self or something.'

'Oh yes, I've heard of that. It's down on the Quay Marina near the Den nightclub.'

'That's the one. Gloria used to go there. You know she was madly jealous of you, don't you?'

'Jealous of me!' Margery was surprised. 'But why should she be?'

'Because Harry Grimes makes no secret of fancying you, of course. He was always saying he liked a woman with plenty of curves.'

'I wish he could keep his hands to himself,' said Margery.

'Oh, you know what he's like! Flirts with everyone. He's always been a bit of a lad. He's got a roving eye. We don't mind him, do we, Gill?'

'We're safe behind our desks, aren't we?'

'I sometimes think I should be wearing armour when he's about,' joked Margery. 'So where is Gloria now?'

'We don't know, but we know where her company car is.'

'Where?'

'It was found abandoned on the Quay Marina, all locked up, no sign of Gloria, with all the soft toys on the back windowsill. We don't know, but we reckon she's gone home to the West Country with diamonds, fox fur coat and everything else Harry bought for her.'

Margery sat down.

'So, Gloria has left, and the company has got its car back, with the bonus of lots of soft toys. The soft toys could go to a charity. It would look good for the Gleaner to donate them. We could make a story out of it. Not out of the Gloria and Harry affair, but the donation of toys.'

'That's not all,' said Philippa as her phone rang.

'Oh, hi Cheryl, yes, she's here, she'll be along right away.'

Margery got up and told the girls she would see them later. She popped her camera into photographic for them to develop the film and put a new one in, telling them she would collect it before she left the office. The door of the office opposite was open, and she noticed it was empty. There was no one in there sorting through piles of dockets as she had seen last week.

The advertising sales offices were buzzing as usual, although she noticed Gloria's desk was empty and had been cleared of all her personal stuff. One or two of the salespeople said hello to her as she passed their desks.

Cheryl seemed really pleased to see her.

'Hello Margery, how are you?'

'Fine thanks. I've written all the assignments you asked for and here's my bill.'

'Thanks, and here's your cheque, I'm sorry you didn't have it earlier.'

Margery took it gratefully. She decided to pay it in to the bank and check her balance after she picked up her washing from the laundry.

'Sit down for a few minutes, I'll get a cup of tea for you,' said Cheryl, popping out of the office and asking one of the feature assistants to make tea for them both.

She shut the door when she returned.

'The shortfall in the advertising revenues has been found. We discovered a load of advertisements, which had not been charged. Accounts are on the case now. Everyone is sighing with relief.'

'But how did that happen?' asked Margery.

'They were all motors and property advertisements. Of course, the revenues have been boosted by all the features the sales teams have been selling, so, all being well, things are looking up.'

'Well, that's a relief, I thought my job here might be coming to an end.'

'Far from it,' said Cheryl. 'We are already planning some prime advertising around your report on the second inquest tomorrow. I presume you will be able to do that for us. We won't publish it until Monday. If you could get it written up on Friday, we could get it sub edited and persuade production to set it over the weekend.'

'I'm out on Friday evening. I'll have to get it done before then. And I've booked up at Hair Today and Shorn Tomorrow for a shampoo and set.'

That didn't seem to worry Cheryl. 'If it has to be published on Tuesday, we'll run with it then.'

Margery was surprised. 'So, everything is sorted, Cheryl? You've not anything for me apart from that?'

'Well, yes, would you mind finding out the exact route of this new bypass please, Margery?'

'Well, that's easy, it's been in the Gleaner house ads.'

'What!?'

'Look, Cheryl,' Margery, picked up a copy of the Gleaner from Cheryl's desk and turned to the full-page house advertisement for a property sales executive.

'These are the plans for new homes which Denzil Bream gave me, used as a background for the full-page house advertisement for a Gleaner property sales representative.'

'Did you provide the image for this house ad then, Margery?'

'No, I just noticed it was the same map as Denzil had given me and was published in the Weekender Gleaner. They won't be able to build the homes before the bypass, or so I am told. According to this map, it will skirt Great Havell entirely and run through the grounds of the Country Hotel at Little Havell over here. The only alternative route would be to run it by the Glebe Mound and through the Glebe Park. Or if it went on the priory side of the Glebe Mound it would have to run through the Great Havell suburbs and by the priory. If they are not so ambitious with the size of it, they could widen the existing road between the Glebe Park and the Glebe Estate.'

'I can't imagine any of those options would be acceptable to local people.'

'Nor can I.'

'I am amazed this had been published.'

'I'm surprised you didn't notice it.'

'I don't really look at house ads. They don't bring revenue in and they are rarely in features, so they are of no concern to me. I suppose I looked at it and thought it was just a generic map the studio had knocked up.'

'They are advertising new homes for sale from plan on this part of the site, which is Home Farm,' said Margery. 'Didn't you see the demonstrations last Friday?'

'I thought they were all about cancelling the fair.'

'There were some people demonstrating about the cancellation of the fair and there were also placards with "Hands off Home Farm" and "No to Bypass". They were demonstrating outside Bream estate agents which was all shut up.'

'We missed that story then.'

'You did. You can understand why people are angry. And you know it doesn't take much for the locals to go out and protest in the marketplace. It can be the slightest thing they perceive as an injustice. It's almost a tradition here!'

'Yes,' agreed Cheryl, 'I can understand why people are angry.'

'These new homes are dependent on the bypass being built, otherwise there is no access, except via Home Farm and the land belonging to it. This is why they are advertising the land there as the site of new homes. The Gleaner really should not have used this image. The land is council owned land. You'd better take it up with Harry Grimes. The rest of the land for the bypass and new homes belongs to the Grimes family. I can understand why the Gleaner didn't run with the story of the protests, especially if Harry Grimes had a word with the MD.'

'Harry Grimes is away on a cruise for a fortnight with his wife.'

'Oh, I see.' Margery was just beginning to understand.

'I suppose I had better tell you, Margery, Harry has taken his wife on a luxury cruise to Venice and the Aegean as a sort of apology for his affair with Gloria, which you will have heard about from the front office girls. Since it's been an open secret in the Gleaner, I didn't see why they needed to keep quiet about it anymore, especially since it is all over. Gloria had been very inefficient. There were a lot of motors advertisements which had not been charged for. I don't know what she was thinking of. You know she's left in disgrace and her car was found in the Quay Marina. But I don't understand how this map of the proposed new homes got into a house advertisement. I can't take it up with Harry, so I'll mention it to the MD as soon as I can. Are you doing anything tonight?

'No. Why?'

'I wondered if you fancied a bite to eat at Feasta Pizza and then we could go to the flicks together.'

'It sounds good to me,' said Margery. 'What's on?'

'The Jewel of the Nile, Kathleen Turner and Michael Douglas.'

'I would like that. Doesn't Nigel want to come?'

'No, you know him and going out. It's my turn for the free tickets at the Regal this week. That's great. It will be a break for us both, I'll see you in Feasta Pizza at 6.00. I'll book a table and bring my car in, so I can run you home.'

Margery walked home via the marketplace to go to the laundrette and pick up her washing. She went to her bank to pay in the cheque. She picked up a payment slip to fill in the amount and opened the envelope. She almost gasped, Cheryl had given her an extra £100 for her work on the Glebe Mound. It was actually itemised on the pay slip. Perhaps the Gleaner would publish it after all. She had the afternoon off now. She could pop into the library and see Jonah, to discuss the hasty dispatch of the six witches, more than four hundred years ago, and see if he had any idea why the gallows were built before the trial. She might even see if he would like to have lunch with her in Dewbury and Hicks.

Jonah and Margery enjoyed a soup and roll each in Dewbury and Hicks restaurant, whilst Margery said she was interested in finding out why the authorities in Great Havell had built the gallows, so the witches were hanged as soon as they were found guilty.

Jonah said he would help her all he could. It would make an interesting project.

Margery asked why he thought the six women were taken up the Glebe Mound and executed immediately. Jonah explained the magistrates and justices of the peace for the Hundreds would have to order the gallows to be erected and would only do that if the accused were known to be guilty already. It might be interesting to find out who the magistrates were. They were usually the local landowners and burghers. Was there any relationship between any of the women and the local gentry for instance, legitimate or illegitimate? There might be a link somewhere. Jonah was hoping the rescued documents might shed some light on that. He had the idea Barney had said something about it. There was also a legend of some missing gold or treasure, either to do with one of the Trincaster guilds or from the treasury of the priory. Gold and treasure could be just legend and could be a euphemism for something else in the broadsheets and folk songs.

It was best to have an open mind, he said and not to approach the stories and legends with preconceived ideas about them which could blind you to the truth.

Margery asked Jonah if he thought the account written by the London clerk would be helpful. Jonah nodded enthusiastically. 'From what Barney and I have already seen, it will be extremely helpful. It's an account from a young man coming to the area for the first time and watching events unfold, recording them and using them to print an account in chapbook form for the popular market. I think, Margery,' continued Jonah. 'It's not just what this young clerk put into the printed account, which is interesting, but what he noted just for his own information and that is the account Barney discovered hidden in the plaster in his walls.'

'Do you think,' asked Margery, 'at the time of the witch trials, the whole of the Great Havell population were convinced of the guilt of these women, that whatever the JP and magistrates might have thought, they could only deliver one verdict which would be guilty?'

'That's a good point. If the JPs hadn't come up with that verdict, the mob might have lynched the women anyway. I won't be able to look at the Tudor documents properly until I return from France after the weekend. As you know, I'm going with the Francophiles for a couple of days.'

After Jonah left to go back to the library, Margery had a look at some of the items in the store which had caught her eye when she was working on her feature.

She was on the first floor in the fashion department, looking at a dress when Emma Dewbury caught up with her.

'Try it on, Margery, I think it would suit you.'

'Hello, Emma, it certainly looks nice on the hanger, it's really pretty, but I'm not sure it's my style.'

'Do try it. I would like to see you in it.'

'I really was just looking, Emma, but I suppose I could try it on.'

In the changing room, Margery looked at herself in the dress. It was very different from her usual style, more flowing, less tailored, but it was a lovely dress. She looked at the label. She could just afford it and perhaps wear it to the Arts Centre on Friday with her calf length boots with the Cuban heels. She went on to the sales floor to show Emma.

'It really does look good on you, Margery, a perfect fit and it shows off your figure. I could let you have it on my staff discount if you would like to buy it.'

'It's very generous of you, Emma; yes, I should very much like to buy it.'

She walked home with her new dress packed in tissue paper in a Dewbury and Hicks bag. She hung it on a hook in her bedroom, so she could admire it from her bed. She decided to change into her jeans and an old jumper and spend a couple of hours on housework. It was about time she planted the herbs Ruth Baldock of Root and Branch had given her last week. After that, it was time to change again and go to meet Cheryl at Feasta Pizza.

Margery resisted the urge to wear her new dress and dressed in slacks and matching jacket with ankle boots. She left a light on in the cottage and took fifteen minutes to walk to Feasta Pizza to meet Cheryl.

Gina was pleased to see her back so soon. She recommended their homemade pastas for a change, perhaps ravioli? They studied the menu, Cheryl had Pizza and Margery chose ravioli. They shared a salad and a large bottle of Orangina between them.

'Tell me more about the Valentine's Ball,' said Margery. 'I presume Nigel didn't want to go.'

'Good Lord, no!' He dislikes any kind of do which involves my colleagues at the Gleaner. You've met him, Margery, you know what he is like. He's an intellectual, a professor. At home, he is passionate about his model railway and he's always listening to music. He has more time at home than I do and often cooks for us, which is great. We lead different lives, but, poor man, he really hasn't understood what has been getting me down for the past few weeks.'

'All that business is sorted now then?'

Cheryl lowered her voice, 'Yes, on the face of it, it is. You asked about the ball, there was a lot of antagonism between some people there, you could see it on their faces, you could sense it in the atmosphere and then, apparently, it boiled to a head outside in one almighty row and fight. It seemed to be all the Grimes family and friends involved. Look, Margery, I've heard things, but have not known what to do about them. Harry Grimes was desperate to have you at the ball, he thought you would bring Vladimir if he gave you an invitation. Berkley even delivered an invitation to your door after a night out at the Den last Friday. They felt sure you would fall for it and come. As you know Harry is popular at the Gleaner, he buys the drinks, he gives away party invitations. There was that rumour you strung your own cat up on that gallows. Someone was claiming you were seen on the Glebe Mound that night. One of the cub reporters wanted to go round to see you and confront you with it. I've never known anything like it. I was thinking, this is my friend they are talking about. It was said you didn't come to the ball, in spite of the invitation, personally delivered by Berkley Grimes, because you were so ashamed of your recent behaviour, you couldn't face them.'

'I can hardly believe what I am hearing,' said Margery. 'Why would anyone want to do something so horrible to my cat? Why would they want to accuse me of it? Why would they want me at the ball and to bring Vlad? I just don't get it.'

'Nor do I,' said Cheryl, 'but I must tell you the atmosphere in the office has been awful on occasions. They made a big thing of boosting the sales and we thought heads would roll over the losses in advertising.'

'Thanks for paying me for the Glebe Mound articles by the way,' said Margery. 'How did you manage that one?'

Cheryl laughed. 'I'd had instructions to spike your story, but it was such a ridiculous change of policy, I went to the MD to check it with him. He had not been aware of it and I now have directions to run with the article at some point, because, as he said, the pop group would be playing at the Glebe Park with the mound in the background. They have a national and even international profile and the images from the pictures taken at the concert, would put Great Havell well and truly on the map.'

'I see, I still don't understand why they were so keen for me to go to the Valentine's Ball, or why they expected me to bring Vlad.'

'This is how I see it,' said Cheryl, taking a sip of her drink.

# Chapter VIII
## The Mystery is Solved

Cheryl Francis leaned forward towards her friend Margery Moore as they dined in the Feasta Pizza Restaurant and lowered her voice in a confidential manner.

'Our friend Vlad has been seen regularly in the vicinity of the old priory, Margery. He's not really that well known in Great Havell, so people noticed him in the area on a regular basis. Of course, most people at the Jazz and Folk Club at the Arts Centre know him. Apart from that, only people where he lives and works in Little Havell are familiar with him. A rumour began to be spread around Great Havell he was a Russian spy, and that Barney Cobbler was on to him. I don't know when the rumour started. It could have been before or after Barney died. But it was pervasive. I tried to scotch the rumours in the office. I was laughed at and asked if I had a soft spot for the Russian. I gave up on it in the end. Then someone else died and the rumours included them. It was alleged they had been Vlad's contact. When Sadie's name was known, it was said her drinking had been a front and she was passing over secrets to the Russians. It was silly really, because everyone could see her sitting in the old priory day after day, drinking and smoking, so how she could have known anything which would have been useful to the Russians? It was all getting out of hand and more and more ridiculous. Then Eric Bolton was included in the rumours, because he was a bit of a recluse, it was suggested he was a spy as well and used Sadie to pass messages to Vlad. A lot of people began to believe the rumours and, inevitably, you were seen regularly talking to Sadie. Vlad was with you at the Arts Centre and putting his bike in your front garden, so you were involved too. People began to believe it was spy ring. Then when someone played that nasty prank on Growltiger, it completely involved you. People were saying it served you right for fraternising with the enemy in the Cold War. Others said you did it yourself because you were a witch and your cat had been a familiar and was no longer of any use to you. Others claimed to have seen you on the Glebe Mound that day.' Cheryl reached over the table to touch Margery's hand in sympathy.

'The rumours in the Gleaner offices were that you had done it yourself. I couldn't believe that. If I said anything in your defence, it seemed to make things worse, so I had to keep quiet and I just pointed out what a good job you were doing. Some of the younger reporters thought it was really funny and made sick jokes about it all the time. They even wanted to go round to see you and confront you with it. They had the idea of putting a toy cat on a gibbet in your garden one night, so you would wake up and see it in the morning and there would be another front-page story. It would involve you and you'd be forced to talk to them. They couldn't decide between them whether you were a witch, living in that little cottage of yours, with a view of the Glebe Mound, or a spy. One of them even went to talk to your neighbours when you were away. But he completely failed to be understood by Florence, who kept her hearing aid turned off and he had to give up asking questions. Alf was more forthcoming but carried on about all the things he didn't like about the town council or what he calls the "yoghurt people" and "born agains" who use the mound regularly. Alf kept emphasising he had nothing to do with the death of your cat. So, the reporter gave up in the end. It didn't stop the ideas becoming more and more bizarre. Fortunately, the editor put a stop to it. He sent them out to the marketplace to get reactions to the cancellation of the fair. Most people didn't believe it would be cancelled. They thought it would be rescheduled. So, in fact, a lot of those demonstrators, last Friday, had been stirred up by our reporters! Then they failed to report on it! As far as the sales staff were concerned, they were desperately trying to make up for lost revenues. Everything seemed to be completely mad.

'When I discussed it with Nigel one evening, he advised me strongly to keep out of it all and just go in to work and do the job. He also said, if I could, to advise you, Margery, to keep out of it as well, I should do so. I did realise, though, it was difficult for you living in the area where it all seemed to be happening. In the evenings, Nigel and I watched some films of the musical comedies we both enjoy. We'd recorded them on video. You know we even thought of inviting you over to come and watch them with us. You really should get a television.'

'I know, a lot of people say that, but I don't fancy watching those soap operas Philippa and Gill are always on about.'

'I think you would probably enjoy the dramatizations of classic books, Margery. I know you often work in the evenings and I'm grateful for the amount you have done recently, but you would probably like quite a few programmes on television. And if you had a video player, you could hire films and programmes to watch them at your leisure. You could rent one and see how you liked it.'

Margery laughed. 'Televisions, videos, it's all so sophisticated. What did you and Nigel watch on video?'

'You know how he's mad keen on opera and musical comedies. He'd recorded the whole of "Rigoletto", which was broadcast from Covent Garden. We had "Me and My Girl" on video as well. In the end, I watched them both twice. Well, no, that's not strictly true, I was reading while they were on and Nigel was making models for his railway, so I suppose we weren't actually watching them.'

Margery laughed again. 'You watched a couple of videos, but you weren't actually watching them?' she queried.

'Yes,' said Cheryl, 'I suppose that's it. I do enjoy the dramas though. It's a great luxury, especially in winter. I have a cosy fire and curl up with a pot of tea and watch a well-adapted piece of classic literature. It's great escapism. Much as I love my job, these past few weeks have been difficult to say the least. Production staff are touchy when we need changes made at the last minute and it's difficult to publish anything, however urgent, after deadline. Even the studio won't let anything go without a union stamp on the back. We can't publish any advertisements without one. The management have blamed the unions for our revenue problems. When I discussed it with Nigel, we couldn't understand how they could be at fault for not charging for advertising. That had to be down to the sales team for not raising dockets. I've even had Gloria pouring her heart out to me.'

'Gloria!' exclaimed Margery in surprise.

'You heard from Gill and Philippa she's been having an affair with Harry Grimes.'

'Yes, I did, but I had seen her with Bill Walker a lot and I thought she was having an affair with him.'

'Really? How do you mean you saw her with Bill Walker a lot?'

'He was always giving her a lift in his Porsche. Gill or Philippa said her company car was in Moonlight Motors for a respray. I can't count how many times I saw her with him in his car or getting out of his car. Whenever I saw him in his car, Gloria was with him.'

'I'm surprised,' said Cheryl. 'She always said to me she was "popping out for a bit". A bit of what? I'm beginning to wonder now. She was rarely in the office. Now, of course, she's gone. She came in to say goodbye to me. Harry had given her a fox fur coat as a farewell present. He gave her the coat and sacked her, just like that!'

'That's a bit callous, isn't it?'

'I should say so. As I say, she was always coming in my office to pour her heart out. I couldn't do or say anything or I might have got the sack as well. I used to tell Nigel all about it when I got home. The thing is, Margery, Harry is more popular than ever at the Gleaner. As far as they're concerned, he's just been behaving like a bit of a lad. He makes sure they get their bonuses. He even helps them achieve them. He gets them all tickets for the Valentines Ball. He introduces them to girls or blokes they fancy. He buys rounds of drinks for them when they all go out. He's untouchable, our Harry.'

'He and his wife are off on a cruise to Venice and the Aegean I think you said?'

'Yes, Gerald Smith, the MD, has packed them off. Harry identified where the shortfall in advertising revenue was and that's his reward. I think the idea of the board was they needed some time away together. I can tell you Margery, these last few weeks have been more than a nightmare for me, and I know they haven't been easy for you. The good news is Nigel is coming to the Arts Centre on Friday for the Jazz and Folk Club. I think he felt bad about not coming to the Valentine's Ball. I just hope we have a good evening.'

'So, do I, I've bought a new dress.'

'Really? What's it like?'

'It's not my usual dark colours, it's sort of purply pinks. Emma Dewbury let me buy it on her discount.'

'Ace,' said Cheryl. 'I'm longing to see it. Do you think Vlad will put his bike in your front garden and come with you as he usually does?'

'I don't know, I haven't seen him for days. I expect he's replacing ball cocks for housewives in Little Havell.'

'Pardon! Is that a euphemism for something? If it is, it's a new one on me!' said Cheryl laughing. Margery repeated what Audrey Bodger had told her on Tuesday and they both laughed.

'Audrey Bodger looked lovely at the Valentine's Ball on Saturday night. She was with her brother and sister-in-law, her staff and two very dishy blokes, I think one of them might have been a brother as well. He was dancing a lot.'

'Did he have longish dark hair?'

'It might have been long. If it was, it was tied back. I also noticed he was the only man who hadn't bothered to wear a tie.'

'I think that was Audrey's brother Grant. I interviewed him on Monday. I had the impression he would have been as truculent as Denzil Bream if his surveyor hadn't been there, who was much more helpful. It was pouring with rain and Grant gave me a lift to the station, which was nice of him. I thought afterwards he was probably keen to get rid of me. There'll be a picture of him to go with the Bodger's feature.'

'I felt I should have made more effort with my clothes and make up when I saw Audrey Bodger and Pricilla Dant. They looked fantastic, but then, they've got the money to do it.'

'Did you see anything of the aftermath?' asked Margery.

'No, I took a taxi home. I shared it with a couple of tele-ad girls who live near me. Nigel gave me a set time to go home. I heard about what happened outside the Assembly Rooms from Philippa and Gill on Monday.'

'I hear Berkley Grimes, Morris and Mack from the Brass Monkeys and their friends insisted Vlad was involved in that too. Audrey Bodger said one of her maintenance team had been said to be involved in a fracas, when I interviewed her yesterday. She said many of them rent flats in the same building and they were able to vouch for him. I realised that was Vlad when I thought about it later.'

'Well, that was ridiculous. It just shows you how damaging rumours and gossip can be.'

'I know I have to keep out of it, DI Barker and you have both advised me to do that. But I am still curious to know why all these disturbing events have occurred recently and why they are so near where I live, and why people are so keen to accuse Vlad of being a spy.'

'Perhaps all will be revealed at the coroner's inquest tomorrow,' said Cheryl.

They finished their meals, paid their bill and walked out of the marketplace into Thorpe Park Road to the Regal Cinema, where they took their seats. There was a cartoon first, after which they bought ice creams and enjoyed The Jewel of the Nile, which was the main feature.

Cheryl's car was in the car park near the Regal. She took Margery home and parked it on the grass verge in the lane outside the front gate of her cottage. Margery invited her in for a drink.

'I haven't been in really, since I came to pick up your report on the inquest. Gosh, you must miss Growltiger. I see you've washed his beanbag. Can I see your new dress?'

Margery put her electric fire on and invited Cheryl to sit down.

She went upstairs to bring the dress down. Cheryl loved it and decided to have a look for a new dress for herself in one of the boutiques near the market-place.

They both had cocoa. Margery offered Cheryl some oat biscuits.

'I couldn't resist buying these. Did you know Clint Westford the surveyor at Bodger's Commercial makes the most delicious oat biscuits?'

'Really? I can't imagine that!'

'I've met quite a few interesting people these past two weeks. Audrey Bodger has a lot of original paintings in her Little Havell agency. Many of them are by Pricilla Buckler.'

'She was at the Valentine's Ball,' said Cheryl. 'As I said, she looked fantastic.'

'I thought you said Pricilla Dant was at the ball.'

'That is Pricilla Buckler, she uses her maiden name for her art works. She has a studio in Little Havell and he has a house near us in Great Havell. They go out together for civic functions, Moyen Circle events and balls and things, but lead pretty separate lives otherwise. It seems to work.'

'Well, I never knew,' said Margery. 'Did I tell you about Eric Bolton's Honey Monster watch?' She repeated the story to Cheryl.

'How bizarre! I knew he was pretty eccentric. I heard the police let him go after they arrested him. How did you find DI Barker?'

'He was OK when I got to know him. He was a bit abrasive and sarcastic when I first met him. It's odd, he was giving me the same advice as you were, as if I was a target.'

'It was that horrible business with your cat, I think. And of course, people see you regularly walking near the Glebe Mound and through the old priory.'

'I've a pretty good idea who did that to Growltiger,' said Margery, 'but I still don't really understand why or how. DI Barker says the case Mayor Grimes invited him to investigate is sorted, so everything should be revealed at the inquest tomorrow. If you and Nigel are coming to the Arts Centre on Friday, I can fill you in then. I heard Gloria has abandoned the company car she went off with on the Marina Quay. Apparently, there were loads of soft toys on the back window-sill.'

'Oh, they were a little indulgence Gloria used to have. She was always buying them to put in the back of that car. I think some of them were gifts from Harry. I'm surprised she left them all in the back window. It's where she used to keep them, but I expected her to take them with her. I bet she took her Paddington Bear, though, that was always her favourite.'

Margery was beginning to feel sorry for Gloria. 'I can't believe all that missing revenue was all down to Gloria's inefficiency,' she said.

'Nor can I,' said Cheryl, 'but it's been sorted now, the money has been found and no one is worried about it. Harry Grimes is the hero of the hour and Gloria has been sacked in disgrace. That's it. I wonder if the coroner's verdict will be as conclusive at tomorrow's inquest?'

## Thursday 20th February

After her usual breakfast of tea, toast and marmalade, Margery dressed in black slacks, grey roll neck jumper, black jacket and ankle boots for the court. She put on her make up carefully, packed her notebook, sharpened up a couple of pencils and set off to walk to the courtroom in the guildhall. She was early and had her pick of seats but chose to sit where she had sat the week before. Again, she noticed a couple of reporters from the Gleaner and wondered why they were so keen for her to cover it as well. She decided to go home as soon as it was over, type it up and take it to the Gleaner on Friday for publication on Monday. She was pleased when Jonah came to sit next to her. 'I hope this will be an end to it, actually,' he said in his cheerful breathy tones.

'So, do I,' agreed Margery.

'In fact, Margery,' said Jonah, turning his head, 'just look over there!' She followed his eyes and saw Mayor Walter Grimes looking a bit pale and very serious but with no obvious wounds on his head accompanied by his son Berkley, looking equally serious. They nodded to Jonah and Margery and sat opposite them in the court. The family resemblance, which Harry Grimes shared, was clear to her. Father and son had similar wavy dark-brown hair, dark eyes and wide mouth. They were both very smart in pinstriped suits. She hadn't seen much of Berkley, but she had seen the mayor often and remembered he had the most charming smile. She guessed Berkley would have the same.

Everyone stood as the coroner entered and the proceedings began.

The coroner reminded the court of the findings of the previous inquest and said the unexpected deaths of Barney Cobbler and Sadie Petal, within twenty-four hours of each other, had been from an overdose of cocaine and that he had ordered a further investigation into the source of the cocaine by Great Havell police and the drugs squad. He called Sergeant Taylor of Great Havell police.

'A large amount of the drug has been discovered by Great Havell Police in a cupboard near the offices of the Den Nightclub,' said Sergeant Taylor. 'The package was found under some toilet rolls and among a box of distinctive decorations which had been made in the Netherlands. These decorations, Great Havell police had ascertained, were used by the nightclub on Valentine's night and had been borrowed from the nearby Old Granary Hotel. The drug was tested by forensics and it is believed to be from the same batch, an overdose of which had caused the deaths of Mr Cobbler and Miss Petal.

'May I thank Mayor Grimes for enlisting the assistance of DI Barker from Scotland Yard,' concluded Sergeant Taylor. The mayor nodded in acknowledgement.

Margery was surprised to see Gail Cooper was to testify. She introduced herself as reception manageress at the Old Granary Hotel.

'I would like to confirm some of the hotel's seasonal decorations have been found in the Den Nightclub. These had been imported from the Netherlands from the Christmas markets. They are distinctive. They are decorated heart shaped German spice biscuits of various sizes.

'We are grateful to members of the sailing club for bringing these over regularly.

'They have added to our festive scene every year. They give a unique atmosphere to the hotel. We keep them in a loft on a wing of the hotel. The only outside access to the loft,' explained Gail, 'is from double doors, which are kept bolted and can only be opened from the inside. They open to three flights of stairs up to the loft. The only other access is from a single door in the hotel at the other end of the loft. When the decorations are delivered, a member of the sailing club alerts me at reception. I take lift to the top floor, remove the coded padlock and open it with a key. I walk through the loft, down the three flights of stairs at the other end, unbolt and open the double doors at the bottom. The decorations are taken up to the loft ready for Christmas and other festivities. The deliverymen leave the same way. I go back to reception through the hotel and lock and padlock the loft door. I put the key back in the key safe and lock it up. This occurred about four weeks before Christmas. The decorations for Christmas and Valentine's Day are accessed from inside the hotel after that. I have no idea how some of our decorations came to be borrowed by the Den Nightclub without my knowledge and were stored in a cupboard near their offices. Great Havell police have searched our loft at the Old Granary Hotel. There were no illegal substances found there,' she concluded.

Margery was even more surprised to see Clint Westford called as a witness. She had more surprises in store when she heard what he had to say. He spoke in a commanding way and introduced himself as chief surveyor for all the branches of Bodger Estate Agencies. He was dressed less casually than she had seen him on Monday, in a suit and tie.

'I was with Grant Bodger in his Land Rover. We had been commissioned by the town council to explore options for the route of the Great Havell bypass,' he began.

'We left the road near Home Farm and took a bridle path round the Grimes' manor estates.' Clint looked at the mayor, who confirmed his statement with a nod.

'We joined a public road again at Little Havell and went across the grounds of the Country Hotel to join up with the road which runs from the docks towards Havell-Next-the-Sea and Sandy Reach. Because this route takes us through the grounds of the Country Hotel, we felt it would be unpopular with local people, especially those living in Little Havell. We had been asked to consider all possible options.

'One option would be, to dual the road between the Glebe Park, the sports centre and the Glebe Estate. This would be the least expensive choice. Another possible route would be to put the new bypass by the Glebe Mound and run it across the Glebe Park.'

There was an audible intake of breath in the court at this suggestion and a lot of whispering, so the coroner had to ask for silence. Margery was wondering why all this was relevant to the inquiry. Clint continued.

'We were asked by the council planning department and one or two members of the Moyen Circle to check a route for the bypass round the Cricklewater Estuary side of the town. We, therefore, went to check the viability of this. We realised the bypass would have to run close to the river and the old priory, the Glebe Mound and could possibly involve the demolition of Priory Cottages.'

It was Margery's turn to gasp now and she wasn't the only one to be shocked at the idea. Surely, they were not contemplating that. Jonah touched her arm reassuringly.

'When we were assessing this route,' continued Clint, 'on the bridle path which runs between the Glebe Mound and the back gardens of Priory Cottages, Mr Bodger was driving slowly along the path when we saw someone who looked distressed walking on the mound. I got out to see if I could help him. Mr Bodger said he would drive round the cottages and take the lane to the front of them, which comes to an end at the ruined priory, and pick me up there. I said I would see if I could help the individual down the mound and summon an ambulance if necessary. I am first aid trained. I hurried up the mound and caught up with the man. He was incoherent when I asked him if he was all right. I helped him down to the priory where he bent over the railings and started retching. I realised he needed urgent medical attention, but when I went over to the phone box next to the Amicable Anarchist it was already occupied by someone else, a man with a young girl. They had seen the man in distress and were calling an ambulance. I explained to the man, when he came off the phone, that I had helped a man down the mound, and he was now bent over the old priory railings. He said he had called an ambulance for him and he would wait for it. I now know the man I helped on to the railings was Mr Cobbler. I went back to Mr Cobbler, reassured him help was on the way. I don't think he heard me. He was still suspended over the railings. I took the footpath to the back of the old priory to where Mr Bodger had stopped at the end of the lane. By the time I got there, we heard the ambulance arrive for Mr Cobbler and went back to our office in Grimpen Havell to relieve the temp and write our reports.'

The coroner asked Clint if he had noticed anyone sitting on the old priory ruins.

'I was concerned with Mr Cobbler, he had a very bad colour and was making retching noises,' he replied. 'I can't say I noticed anything or anyone else in the area. The only other people I saw were those in Priory Street outside the Amicable Anarchist and the man and girl who were phoning for an ambulance. You can see Priory Cottages easily from where I caught up with Mr Cobbler and I think residents, some of whom are elderly, might have seen me and Mr Cobbler from their windows and could corroborate my account. Grant Bodger is in the court and will confirm everything I have said.'

The coroner accepted Mr Westford's account of events. There was no need to call Mr Grant Bodger to verify it. Margery looked round the court to see where Grant was sitting, but she couldn't locate him.

The solicitor, Brendon Dant, was called. Margery was surprised. He had given evidence a week ago, why call him again?

'I was telephoned by Cricklewater Sailing Club member Fenton Bradley's widow on Monday. I am dealing with the probate for her. He was knocked off his yacht by the boom, as he was sailing back to his mooring on the Quay Marina, on Tuesday last week. Although he was a strong swimmer, he drowned in the marina. Mrs Bradley is still in shock and very distressed. She asked me to check her husband's yacht, which, according to his will, he has left to his sister's family. She asked me to collect any food from the cabin and personal possessions, all of which I had instructions to remove. I needed the key for the hold. This was supplied by Mr Bradley's widow. I also required someone from the sailing club to come with me. Mr Berkley Grimes kindly volunteered. Mr Grimes and I walked along the jetty at the end of the marina, where Mr Bradley's yacht was tied to a capstan. Last week, on Tuesday, the secretary of the sailing club, who had rescued Mr Bradley from the marina, had signalled to another member, out sailing that day, to tow the yacht back to the marina. It was tied up and left there. No one had put it back on its mooring.

'When Mr Grimes and I boarded the yacht, we found we had no need of the key, the hold was not locked. We collected all the foodstuffs and personal possessions from the yacht and returned them in bin bags to Mrs Bradley. The following day, I had a phone call from Mrs Bradley. She asked me to go over to see her as a matter of urgency. When I arrived at her house, she handed me a pair of her late husband's deck shoes, which Mr Grimes and I had taken from his yacht. Sergeant Taylor will show you the shoes.'

There was a pause whilst Sergeant Taylor came back to reveal a pair of white deck shoes. He put them in front of the coroner, who told the court that each shoe contained a syringe. There was a surprised murmur in the court.

Berkley Grimes was next to speak. He corroborated everything Mr Dant had told the court. He said only Mr Dant had visited Mr Bradley's widow and taken the shoes to Great Havell police who had then fingerprinted Mr Bradley's yacht.

Sergeant Taylor was called again.

'I confirm a forensic team from Great Havell police examined the late Mr Bradley's yacht, the deck shoes and their contents. Fingerprints found on the yacht were only those of Mr Dant, Mr Grimes and Mr Bradley himself. The syringes were examined and found to have contained a cocaine solution. This, Great Havell Police suspect, is from same batch of the drug which was found in the cupboard in the Den nightclub. Great Havell police have also concluded that Barney Cobbler and Sadie Petal had taken a big enough dose of it to result in their deaths. The syringes,' said Sergeant Taylor, 'found by Mrs Bradley, had her and Fenton Bradley's fingerprints on them. Also,' said Sergeant Taylor, 'Barney Cobbler's fingerprints have been found on one of the syringes and Sadie Petal's on the other. It has been concluded by Great Havell Police and from the investigations of DI Barker from Scotland Yard, from this evidence, these syringes were used to administer the cocaine which was found in the bodies of Mr Cobbler and Miss Petal and contributed to their deaths.'

A member of the Great Havell ambulance service was then called to give evidence to the inquest. He said he had been summoned by a member of the public to attend Barney Cobbler who he and his colleague found suspended over the railings of the old priory and unconscious. They carried him to the ambulance and attempted to bring him round on the way to the General Hospital. He stopped breathing shortly after he arrived there and was put on a life support system immediately, but the medical team at the hospital were unable to save him. Another member of the ambulance team attended the Glebe Mound sinkhole, with him, the following day, from which they extracted the unconscious Sadie Petal. She was confirmed dead on arrival at the hospital. He also reported that the local ambulance service had been called to Quay Marina on the same day. He confirmed they had been unable to resuscitate Fenton Bradley, in spite of the fact two first aiders on the scene had attempted to revive him, before the ambulance team arrived, on Tuesday 4th February at 4.15 pm.'

Gail Cooper, reception manager of the Old Granary Hotel returned to the witness stand to confirm she and her assistant Debbie had watched the rescue of Mr Bradley from the marina in the afternoon of February 4th. They had both attempted to resuscitate Mr Bradley, as they had been trained in first aid, but were unable to revive him. It was, she said, very distressing. She and Debbie were both very upset by the incident. Mr Bradley had been a frequent customer at the hotel. He often dined at the Grain of Truth restaurant, sometimes with friends, other members of the yacht club and his wife. Debbie would come and corroborate her account, if the coroner wished. The coroner did not consider it to be necessary.

A member of the sailing club took the witness stand to say he was sailing on the Cricklewater on 4th February in his yacht and had seen and signalled to Mr Bradley. They had both been returning to their moorings at the Quay Marina, when he witnessed the accident with the boom. He saw a member of the club dive in and rescue Mr Bradley from the water. He answered signals, from the club, to tow Mr Bradley's yacht into the marina which he did. Another member of the sailing club had tied it to the capstan at the far end of the jetty where it remained. At that stage, he said, he was unaware Mr Bradley would not recover. No one had thought to shut and lock the hold. The whole episode, he said, had been a bit of a shock. There were other witnesses could be called to testify to this if necessary.

One of the solicitors from Lockhart and Upton then confirmed Mr Dant had been in their Great Havell premises from 9 am until 5 pm on both 3rd February and 4th February with clients. They had lunched together at the Grain of Truth restaurant at the Old Granary Hotel on both days. There would be other witnesses to this, if the coroner wished to call them. The coroner did not.

Mr Dant returned to testify. He said at the last meeting of the Moyen Circle, which had been held at the guildhall on Friday evening the 31st January, Barney Cobbler, the chairman, had informed members the sink hole cover in the Moyen Midden on the Glebe Mound had been vandalised. He and Mr Cobbler had walked up together the following morning with the keys for the grid over the top, to inspect it. When they arrived, they found there had been an attempt to wrench the cover off. He and Mr Cobbler undid the padlocks on both sides to remove the metal mesh cover and tried to flatten it to get it back into shape.

'Had it been lifted enough for someone to be able to get underneath?' asked the coroner.

Mr Dant replied that was their concern. An adult could not have done it, but a child could have wriggled underneath and fallen in. He and Mr Cobbler had tried to flatten it, to make it safer. When they left the mesh grid, he and Mr Cobbler had agreed it would have been impossible for even a small child to have got underneath it and into the sinkhole. They had both decided a more substantial grid was needed to avoid anyone entering and disturbing the archaeology or even hurting themselves. They decided they might order a new grid after the next full meeting of the Moyen Circle in a month's time. Mr Dant said that after that the unconscious Sadie Petal had been found under the partially opened grid on 4th February. As vice chairman of the Moyen Circle, he had been notified the grid had been partially forced open again. Forensics from Great Havell police had fingerprinted the grid, but they only found his and Barney's prints on it. He and another member of the Moyen Circle had been back to attempt to flatten the grid again. Mr Dant said they had taken delivery of a more substantial cover, because of the increase of visitor numbers expected in Great Havell this year at the solstice. He had taken it on himself as vice chairman to order it.

The coroner asked when this new cover would be in place and Mr Dant replied they received delivery of it at his solicitor's office a few days ago and that it would be in place at the beginning of next week.

The coroner then asked Mr Dant why he thought Miss Petal had been found caught under the grid to the sinkhole in such a position? Mr Dant replied it was most likely curiosity. 'Could Miss Petal,' the coroner asked, 'have had the strength to lift the padlocked grid herself so she could look down the sink hole?' Mr Dant confirmed that, although he and Barney had done their best with the grid, it was insubstantial, had been badly warped and could more easily have been partially lifted again in spite of the two padlocks. In hindsight, he said, which is a wonderful thing, he and Barney should have padlocked it back flatter and in a position which it would make it more difficult to lift.

After a few other eyewitnesses affirmed the events described, it was lunchtime. The coroner adjourned the inquest until the afternoon, when it would reconvene.

Jonah suggested to Margery they could go into the Amicable Anarchist for a swift half and their special floury soft bap rolls for lunch. Margery readily agreed and they set off for the pub.

They settled in the snug with a half of Falcon best bitter for Jonah and a shandy for Margery. Jonah ordered a cheese and pickle roll and Margery a prawn salad roll. Derek was not there, which was unusual. The pub wasn't as busy as she had expected, but then it was a Thursday lunchtime and people were more inclined to pop in there after work.

She began. 'It looks like nobody was responsible for the deaths of Barney and Sadie, Jonah.'

'Actually, Margery, I was thinking the same. I thought, poor Barney, as I was listening to it. All his knowledge of local history and work for charities ended with an overdose of cocaine. I still can't believe it. I still think of things I would like to discuss with him and ask him. It was so sudden.'

'No sign of DI Barker then? But Mayor Walter Grimes who enlisted his help is there.'

'I suppose our man from the Yard has gone home. Job done.'

'I think he has. I would have expected him to say goodbye at least. He said, in the last conversation I had with him, the case was all wrapped up and would be concluded at the coroner's court today. He did say he would come to the Arts Centre for the Jazz and Folk Club on Friday, but I'm not expecting to see him there now.'

'Actually, the way things are going, it looks as if there will be a final verdict today,' said Jonah.

'Unfortunately, it looks as if that verdict, from what we have heard this morning, will be the lethal doses of cocaine have been self-inflicted,' sighed Margery. 'I wasn't expecting to see Berkley Grimes there. I didn't realise he looked so like his father, until I saw them sitting next to each other, and then you can see it. How are you getting on with the files we picked up the other day?'

Jonah lowered his voice, 'Really, well, thanks Margery, there'll be plenty of interesting bits of information for you when I have finished going through them. There is one odd thing though. Barney had found some more recent documents among them. He was not sure if he had found them in his wall or not. I hadn't seen them, actually, but Barney had told me they were deeds, a marriage certificate, floor plans and maps. I don't even know how many there were. He said they were nothing to do with the witch trials and it was odd they were with the earlier ones. Did Barney say anything to you about them Margery? Do you think they were the documents Barney was on about when he had that row in here with the ex-mayor?'

'I suppose they could be. You say Barney had them with the Tudor documents?'

'Actually, yes, in fact, I think I've got that right, but I'm now beginning to doubt it. I've not been through everything yet. I'm trying to sort them out, so that they are in the same order as we were working through them. But they seem to have been messed about a bit, although most of them are still in the same files.'

'Well, I shouldn't worry about them. If they were causing Barney enough trouble to be kicked out of here and told not to come back, you are probably best without them. At least you've got those notes on the witch trials, which should be interesting. Barney never mentioned later documents to me.'

'As you know I'm off to France at the weekend, but I'll start sorting them in order when I return. It's going to be a marathon task without Barney's expertise and help.'

'I will type up my shorthand notes on the inquest and take them into the Gleaner as soon as I can. I'm not sure I will have time tonight, or that I particularly want to start on it. There are a couple of reporters who will give an account of the verdict, but my full report will be on Monday.'

'And will your article be word for word?'

'It could be. I noted it all down, although so much seems to be irrelevant, especially about the supply of drugs and witnesses corroborating witness statements. I wonder if we will have more information this afternoon. I suppose the person who supplied the drug is, in a sense, responsible for their deaths.'

'Actually, I was thinking that too. It doesn't seem possible my poor friend Barney should have died in that way, and by his own hand.'

'I've met a few people recently who have surprised me, so I suppose anything is possible. If he did inject himself with the stuff, was it because he was in pain in some way and was promised it would relieve the pain? It might have been given to him by someone he knew and trusted.'

'In fact, that's a good point,' said Jonah. 'Barney wasn't one to grumble, but he did tell me recently he was suffering from sciatica. He even took the train to Trincaster and was being treated at Berkley Grimes osteopath practice for it. I had forgotten that. Maybe that will be mentioned this afternoon.'

Back in the guildhall courtroom, Jonah and Margery were able to secure the same seats as before, opposite Walter Grimes and his son. The young Gleaner reporter was just behind them.

They all stood for the coroner and the afternoon proceedings began.

Derek from the Amicable Anarchist testified to seeing Barney Cobbler on his usual walk on the Glebe Mound, before the historian went into work at the tax office.

'Was there anything unusual in the way he walked?' asked the coroner. Derek replied he was holding his low back a lot and could have been in pain.

Berkley Grimes was called to witness again. 'I knew Mr Cobbler had been suffering from excruciating back pain, as he had recently begun treatment for it at my clinic in Trincaster. One of our chiropractors was treating him. He had been prescribed co-codamol, which has a small amount of cocaine in it. Mr Cobbler had been taking the drug regularly, although he had been warned not to take any other pain killer with it.'

The coroner asked Berkley Grimes if, in severe pain, he thought Mr Cobbler might be tempted to take a stronger form of cocaine if he were offered it. Berkley Grimes took a long time answering. He said he didn't think Mr Cobbler was the sort of man to do that, but, he supposed, in extreme agony, he might be tempted to, if it were offered. 'Sciatica is a very painful condition,' he said. 'Mr Cobbler was doing well. The treatment, my clinic was giving him, had been moderately successful. Mr Cobbler was not the sort of man to give in to pain. At the clinic, all agree it is best to keep moving and, indeed walking, with severe back pain. Mr Cobbler was in the habit of walking every morning before he went in to work. We advised him to continue this and to take painkillers beforehand if he needed them. There had been an incident recently, when Mr Cobbler had become very angry in the Amicable Anarchist. When someone of Mr Cobbler's temperament tenses up through extreme stress, as he probably did under these circumstances, it can exacerbate a painful condition and make it worse.'

Much to Margery's surprise, Derek Robinson from the Amicable Anarchist testified again. This time the coroner asked him if he often saw Sadie Petal.

'I used to see Miss Petal almost every day,' said Mr Robinson. Her habitual place in the old priory was in my line of vision from behind the bar, either through the windows of the pub or through the door if it was open.'

The coroner asked if she ever went into the Amicable Anarchist.

'Yes, she did. I supplied her with bottles of the strong cider she particularly liked.'

'Was he aware Miss Petal took drugs as well?' the coroner asked.

'Sadly, I was. She used to smoke roll-up cigarettes too and had boasted to me she would lace them occasionally with anything she could lay her hands on,' said Derek. 'Sometimes I would see her smoke a roll up and then sit almost like a statue at her habitual place, for hours on end. I guessed she might have smoked something dodgy under those circumstances. When that happened, I contacted her social worker. On the occasions I saw Miss Petal sitting and apparently staring into space, or for any other reason, I saw she was acting oddly, I knew she had taken something. Sadie was not a bad character, just misguided.'

'Had Mr Robinson seen Miss Petal on the day of her death?' asked the coroner.

'I had seen her,' answered Derek, 'I had seen her sitting in her usual place on the wall, briefly. She was looking at something in her hand. Then she rushed off up the Glebe Mound and went round the side where the Moyen Midden is. I can't see that from my pub. That was the last time I saw her, until the ambulance team brought her down and took her to hospital.'

Ruth Baldock took the witness stand. 'I run the Root and Branch Garden Centre and I employed Miss Petal. She was a good horticulturalist and a great asset to Root and Branch. Unfortunately, I had to let her go because she became unreliable. Also, she had been growing cannabis in one of the firms' greenhouses. I had to nip that practice in the bud. After that, I didn't see much of Miss Petal. On the morning of Tuesday 4th of February, I thought I saw her on the Moyen Midden side of the mound in the vicinity of the sinkhole, which is just visible from my nursery. I thought it was her, although she was in the distance. Since she has been identified as the person found in the sinkhole, I realise I must have seen her. She seemed to be looking for something. It was unusual to see her up there. I watched her for a while, until she disappeared completely. After that, I saw a dog walker stop and he went out of view. I now know, from the report on the first inquest, it was to call an ambulance for Miss Petal.'

There was a break in the proceedings whilst the coroner left the court to consider his verdict on the two deaths.

There was a buzz of whispering when he left, but complete silence in anticipation when he was ready to make his declaration.

'I have considered all the circumstances surrounding the tragic deaths of Barney Cobbler and Sadie Petal from overdoses of cocaine,' announced the coroner. 'Taking all into consideration, I have carefully examined the evidence submitted. My conclusion is these deaths were misadventure. Mr Cobbler and Miss Petal inadvertently took large amounts of cocaine which resulted in their deaths. I order the bodies of the two deceased to be released to their families or next of kin.'

He closed the court.

The reporter left the court in a hurry to get the verdict into the stop press section of the Weekender Gleaner.

Margery thought she detected relief on the faces of the mayor and his son, but then decided she might be imagining it from what she had heard of Berkley's involvement. Outside the court, there was a lot of shaking hands and Brendon Dant was particularly popular with the Grimes family. Agatha Grimes, who Margery noticed was slightly taller than her husband, joined him and her son. She looked at her as closely as she dared, expecting to see bruises on her carefully made-up face, but she had either disguised them cleverly or the gossip, Margery had heard about the aftermath of the ball, had been exaggerated.

She parted company with Jonah and started walking back to her cottage to begin her full account of the inquest for the Gleaner deep in thought.

*It followed Sadie could have taken drugs as well as drink,* she thought. It was possible Barney had been so desperately in pain, he had inadvertently overdosed on cocaine. But what Margery thought mostly unlikely, was that they had injected themselves with the stuff in the same part of the arm within a day of each other. *Anyway,* she thought, *how was the cocaine sold to them? Or was it given to them?* It didn't make a lot of sense. She had her shorthand notes and would type an account of the proceedings in a readable form. Walking out of the marketplace, she found Derek from the Amicable Anarchist had caught up with her. They turned into Priory Street together.

'It is odd not to see Sadie sitting on that wall anymore,' remarked Margery.

'It is,' agreed Derek, 'but she was on the road to ruin with her drink and drug habits.'

'I suppose she was, what a tragic waste of a life. From what I have seen of him, she and Eric Bolton were very fond of each other.'

'I wouldn't know about that. I saw him arrested though.'

'Yes, I saw that too, I was helping him look for his Honey Monster watch.'

'Is that why she was found in the sinkhole, do you think? Did she think she had dropped the watch down it or something?'

'I suppose she could have been looking for it down there. She could have dropped it through the cover of the grid. But Eric saw it in the priory car park, just as the police car which came to arrest him ran over it. I expect she dropped it when she was carried down from the Glebe Mound unconscious.'

'I shall miss Sadie coming in for her bottle of cider. She never interfered with visitors to the old priory. She even used to talk to them about the ruins and what she knew about them. She was good at naming the wild plants and flowers that grew there. Visitors used to tell me about it when they popped in for a drink after looking over the priory. I never thought I would say this, but she will really be missed. Poor Sadie.'

'Apparently, one of your regulars saw the fracas outside the Assembly Rooms on Saturday Night. What was all that about?' asked Margery.

Derek Robinson laughed. 'So, he says. I don't think he was anywhere near it. He's got the hump about the Russian at Little Havell over something. I think his wife is a bit of a problem for him. He's always carrying on about some bloke or other, who, he claims, has tried to take advantage of her.'

Margery said goodbye to Derek and crossed the zebra crossing to the old priory. Bill Walker of Moonlight Motors gave her a toot and a wave waiting for her to cross. There was no Gloria with him, of course. He was probably on his way to pick his girlfriend up from the Sylph Self gym on the Quay Marina, she thought. She walked through the old priory car park and looked over to where Sadie used to sit. There was no sign she had ever been there. She walked through the ruins and looked up at the Glebe Mound. It was empty, no dog walkers or ramblers on it today. A cool breeze blew up and Margery shivered as saw shadows of clouds waft across the mound in the fading light. It was easy to understand how legends grew up about it. She sighed, there was no fair to prepare for this year, but a pop concert instead. The fair had been the start of her romance with Vlad and probably many romances for other people over the centuries it had taken place. Perhaps the pop concert, which was planned instead, would be the same.

Alf was actually at his gate, waiting for her when she went up the lane to her cottage.

'Has the coroner sorted it all out then, Miss Moore?'

'He certainly has, Alf.'

'What was the verdict then?'

'Misadventure.'

'And what does that mean?'

'I'm not sure, Alf. You'll be able to read my full report in the Gleaner on Monday. I've all my notes of the proceedings in shorthand here. I'm going to type them up this evening.'

'Haven't they got anyone for it?'

'No.'

'Why not?'

'Because the coroner's verdict is that Mr Cobbler and Miss Petal inadvertently took an overdose of cocaine which killed them.'

Alf was quiet for a moment.

He looked at Margery, scratched his head, looked up at the darkening sky and scratched his head again.

'So, no one done it?' he asked flatly, disappointment in his voice.

'No, no one done it,' repeated Margery patiently.

Alf was silent for a while, so Margery started to open her gate and go up the path to her front door.

'So, no one done it. Police aren't going after anyone for it.'

Margery stopped, turned and looked at him.

'No Alf, the coroner has released the bodies for burial or cremation. The verdict was Mr Cobbler and Miss Petal took too much cocaine and it resulted in their deaths.'

'Who gave them the cocaine?'

'It could have been a man who drowned in the marina a couple of weeks ago. The rest of the drug has been found by the police and they have disposed of it. There's an end to it.' Margery was getting impatient.

'If the man's drowned, he can't go to trial.'

'No, he can't,' confirmed Margery.

'So, no one done it, but a drowned man might have done it.'

'Yes, that's exactly it.'

'What about that bloke Florence's neighbours saw with Mr Cobbler the day he died?'

'He's a surveyor. He said he was here because he was asked by the town council to look at the feasibility of putting the new bypass through here. He tried to give Mr Cobbler first aid when he saw him stumbling on the Glebe Mound.'

'They want to put the bypass though here!?'

'Yes, through here.'

'They can't do that, it's not wide enough on either side of our cottages.'

'They'd have to demolish our homes to do it.'

'They can't do that!'

'Well, let's hope not,' said Margery, 'but if you are worried about it, contact your local councillor and tell him. I'm only reporting what the surveyor, Florence's neighbours saw, said he was doing round here and why he was with Mr Cobbler on the Glebe Mound.'

Alf shook his head and started to grumble about the local council, so Margery walked up to her cottage door and let herself in, took off her hat, jacket and boots, switched on her angle poise lamp over the typewriter, filled the kettle and put it on the stove. She put her shorthand notes next to the Olympia typewriter and started to type her report on the inquest almost immediately.

She had made good progress, was drinking her tea and beginning to think about making an evening meal when the phone rang. It was Uncle Alec.

'Margery?'

'Yes, how are you?'

'Aunt Carrie and I are fine. We wondered how the inquest went. What was the verdict?'

'Misadventure.'

'Really! Both for Cobbler and Petal?'

'Yes really, for both Cobbler and Petal.'

'Are you free to come out for dinner tonight? I'll like to hear more. Shall I book us in at the Country Hotel in Little Havell?'

'That would be nice,' replied Margery. 'I can finish this tomorrow and take it to the Gleaner for Monday's deadline.'

'We'll pick you up in half an hour.'

*Just time to get changed,* thought Margery. She thought of wearing her new dress but decided to save it for the Arts Centre the following evening.

Instead, she put on a silver/grey jumper, black skirt, a maroon silk scarf her mother had given her, black stockings and moccasins.

Looking in the mirror and brushing her hair, Margery was glad she had booked shampoo and set with Tina the next day, after she had delivered her copy to the Gleaner. She carefully refreshed her make-up and was ready just in time to see her uncle and aunt pull up in the lane outside her front garden.

Margery left a lamp on, locked up and got into a back seat of the car. Alec reversed to the end of the cottages and turned into the lane in the direction of the coast, past the market gardens and the turning to Heathlands and to the fork in the road past the Glebe Mound. They were taking the same route Margery took on her bike a few days ago. It was much quicker by car. They soon turned into the parkland which surrounded the Country Hotel, they drove past the ornate towers in the grounds, where there was an afternoon tea tent in the summer, the golf pavilion, sports pavilion and up to the wide car park at the front of the hotel.

Margery, Alec and Carrie walked into the reception and round to the Orangery Restaurant, where Alec had booked a table near one of the tall windows which overlooked the landscaped grounds.

A waiter took their coats and jackets and they sat down to look at the menu. Margery realised how hungry she was. She hadn't eaten since that floury roll with Jonah in the Amicable Anarchist at lunchtime.

It was all typical English fare. A choice of tomato soup, prawn cocktail or duck pate and toast to start. Fish and chips, roast chicken or mushroom risotto for a main course. Apple pie, lemon mousse, fruit salad or ice cream for dessert.

They all chose something different, ordered a glass of wine each for Carrie and Margery and a large bottle of Little Havell sparkling mineral water. Alec and Carrie asked Margery what the coroner's verdict was.

As she had said to Alf, she told her aunt and uncle, the coroner had decided Barney and Sadie had both died from an overdose of cocaine, which they had probably taken voluntarily. As Alf had done, both Alec and Carrie wanted to know why there wasn't a prosecution at least for the supplier. Margery explained about the sailor who drowned in the marina, the syringes found in his deck shoes by his wife. The surveyor who tried to help Barney, the cocaine found in the nightclub among some imported decorations from the Old Granary Hotel. The verdict had been misadventure. In other words, Barney and Sadie had been the authors of their own demise but they had not necessarily intended to do it.

Margery's aunt and uncle listened in amazement.

They were all quiet for a while as the first course was served.

'So, the probable source of the cocaine drowned in the marina the day Sadie died?' asked Alec.

'You say they found the actual syringes used to inject the cocaine?' asked Carrie.

'Yes, and they had the fingerprints of victims and the owner of the yacht and his wife on them.'

'Well, I'm shocked!' exclaimed Alec.

'I'm amazed!' remarked Carrie.

'It exonerates everyone neatly, doesn't it?' asked Alec. 'What did your Inspector Barker have to say? He must have seen other possibilities at least, even if the evidence given at the inquest pointed to that verdict.'

'Barker said nothing. He wasn't even there. Last time I saw him, he said the case was all sorted and he was going back to London.'

'Well, I never expected that,' said Carrie slowly. 'You say they found the syringes, earlier this week, in the yacht belonging to the man who had drowned the day Sadie died from an overdose of cocaine?'

'Yes, and they were examined by Great Havell police who found they had Mr and Mrs Bradley's fingerprints on both, because, Mrs Bradley had found them in a pair of his deck shoes. Barney's fingerprints were on one, and Sadie's fingerprints were on the other.'

'So, who represented Great Havell Police?'

'It was Sergeant Taylor.'

'And who reported the discovery of the syringes?'

'Brendon Dant, he is the solicitor acting for the sailor's widow. He was vice chairman of the Moyen Circle and has taken over from Barney as chairman. His story was backed up by Berkley Grimes who was in court with his father, the mayor. They had been asked by the widow of Fenton Bradley to rescue perishables and personal property from the hold of the yacht. It was the widow who found the syringes in the shoes from the things they had found in the yacht and delivered to her. Forensics found Dant and Grimes fingerprints all over the yacht.'

'Were any reasons given why Barney and Sadie might have taken the cocaine voluntarily?' asked Alec.

'Yes, Barney was suffering from acute pain with sciatica, which was being treated in Trincaster, by a chiropractor, in Berkley Grimes' clinic. Berkley Grimes said they had prescribed co-codamol for him to relieve the pain, so Barney could continue his usual walks and go to work. He explained there was cocaine in that painkiller. He suggested Barney could have been in such acute pain he might have been tempted to take cocaine to relieve it, if it were offered.'

'What about Sadie?'

'There were two witnesses, Derek, from the Amicable Anarchist and Ruth Baldock, her former employer. Derek said Sadie used to put cannabis and sometimes other drugs into those roll ups she used to smoke. Ruth Baldock had to sack her because she discovered Sadie was growing cannabis plants at the nursery.'

'Well, well, very neat,' remarked Alec. 'How did Barney Cobbler get suspended over the railings? How was that explained?'

'Clint Westford, the surveyor, testified he and Grant Bodger were in the lane at the end of the back gardens of Priory Cottages. He said they were assessing the feasibility of putting the Great Havell bypass through there. They saw Barney in distress and Clint went to help him down the mound and give him first aid if he needed it. He said he left him retching over the railings and went to call for help, but found someone else was already doing that in the phone box next to the pub.'

'So, the vexed question of the bypass and where it will be sited is involved as well! How did you feel when Westford suggested the bypass went round the east side of the Glebe Mound, close to your home?'

'He even suggested Priory Cottages could be demolished for it. That worried me for a moment. But then, I thought, they just looked at all possibilities.'

'So how did Sadie get her head down the sinkhole in the Moyen Midden?'

'It's thought she was looking for something. Brendon Dant said he and Barney had un-padlocked the grill and taken it off because it had been vandalised a few days before. They thought they had got it back into place and secured it again, but obviously Sadie was able to get underneath it somehow.'

'It looks as if there is an explanation for everything!' remarked Carrie.

'So, it does,' agreed Alec thoughtfully. 'Margery, I advise you to keep your actual thoughts about all this to yourself. My guess is, they could be similar to mine, in that, those in the court, and possibly testifying, know a good deal more about what actually happened, than they were prepared to admit. This bypass will be built and the new homes too. I don't think Priory Cottages would be demolished, or that the bypass would go on that side of the town. It's impractical. It will be suggested so fewer people object when it goes elsewhere. I can't see it going through the Glebe Park by the Glebe Mound either. This leaves the option of widening the existing road between the sports centre and fields on the edge of the Glebe Park and the Glebe Estate. The only other alternative is to run it through here.' Alec waved his hand at the view of the parkland.

As he did so, Margery and Carrie cried out 'Nooooooo!' simultaneously and rather loudly. Everyone in the restaurant looked round, including, Margery noticed, Audrey Bodger, who was in the restaurant, sitting nearby.

'I'm sorry about that, Audrey,' said Margery. 'My uncle Alec is winding my aunt and myself up. He's an awful tease.'

'Of course, Miss Moore, I didn't realise Alec Moore was your uncle, although I should have guessed he was from the name.'

'Good evening, Miss Bodger,' said Alec cheerfully, 'I've been retired to Havell-Next-the-Sea for a few years now. It's good to see you again and looking so well.'

Audrey Bodger raised a glass to Alec, Carrie and Margery. 'I'm delighted to see you all here. I hope this will be the first of many visits. I'm here with my cousin Terrence Wilkins. Good health to you all.'

Audrey, her cousin, Margery, Alec and Carrie all raised their glasses to each other.

In a low voice, Alec said, 'Terrence Wilkins is a civil engineer.' Both Margery and Carrie heard him. They continued smiling at Audrey and her cousin as their main courses were served so they turned back to the table. Margery found her smile was still on her face, but she felt it had gone from her eyes. Yes, she promised herself, I shall keep quiet about what I actually think from now on. Keep my head down and get on with the job.

When Carrie and Alec dropped her back to her cottage, they said they would be going to Orkney for a week to stay with her parents and taking Bobby with them. They would miss seeing her at the weekend and hoped she would come back and stay on a Saturday night again soon. Margery asked them to give her love to her parents and she would look forward to staying with them again.

## Friday 21st February

Margery woke up, rose, had a shower and her usual breakfast. She finished her account of the coroner's court, using just the main points the witnesses made. She made all the statements factual and was vague about the reason the surveyor gave for being between Priory Cottages and the Glebe mound.

That done, she put it in her shopping trolley and walked down the lane, through the old priory, across the car park and across the road by the Amicable Anarchist. She continued down Priory Street to the Gleaner Offices.

Picking up the Weekender Gleaner and glancing at the headline "VERDICT AT INQUEST", she popped it in her shopping trolley. She said a cheery 'Hello girls' and walked through the doors into the offices to find Cheryl. There was the usual buzz of salespeople and tele ads on the phone and Gloria's desk was clear.

Cheryl gave her a friendly smile when Margery extracted her full report on the inquest and gave it to her.

'Thanks, Margery, have you looked at the Weekender today?'

'Only the headline.'

'Look again,' said Cheryl.

Margery took her copy of the Gleaner out of her shopping trolley. She read out the front-page splash.

'This year's Moyen Midden Fayre set to be bigger and better than ever. Turn to page three.'

Margery turned to page three. She read, 'Mayor Walter Grimes announced from the balcony of the Town Hall, early yesterday morning, to some delighted reporters, the Moyen Midden Fayre will not only take place at the solstice, but he is determined this year's event will be bigger and better than ever. Mayor Grimes proposes the return of the popular 1940s style tea tent. He hopes the medieval fair will sit alongside the pop concert which will headline Gary Hogan and the Fly by Night Boys.'

Margery looked at Cheryl. 'So, the fair will go ahead this year and it's all back to normal. Will the Gleaner be publishing my articles on the Glebe Mound, the Moyen Midden and the Havell-on-the-Marsh witches?'

'We most certainly will. There is enough there for three articles in the Week-ender Gleaner with plenty of advertising for the local businesses involved with the fair. It certainly is, all back to normal, thank goodness.'

'Yes indeed. Here's my bill for the inquest report, Cheryl. The editor and the subs will probably cut it down and will want to leave some bits out. The witness statements go round the houses a bit.'

'Who were the witnesses then?'

'The main ones were Sergeant Taylor of Great Havell police, Gail Cooper from the Old Granary Hotel, Clint Westford, surveyor for Bodgers, Berkley Grimes, the osteopath, Derek Robinson from the Amicable Anarchist and Ruth Baldock of Root and Branch. They were from various walks of life. The chief and most important witness was the solicitor, Brendon Dant.'

'Isn't he vice-chairman of the Moyen Circle?'

'He was. He is chairman since Barney Cobbler died.'

'So how do Berkley Grimes and Brendon Dant fit into all this?'

'They were asked by the widow of Fenton Bradley to board his yacht, to recover any perishables and personal effects he might have left on it. Brendon Dant is her solicitor and dealing with the probate. Berkley Grimes is a member of the sailing club. They returned everything they found on the yacht to her. The following day, she phoned Dant and got him to go round to her house because she had found two syringes in a pair of her husband's deck shoes. Barney's fin-gerprints were on one and Sadie's on the other. Mr and Mrs Bradley's finger-prints were on both.'

'Goodness me! And it's all here,' said Cheryl, putting her hand on the article Margery had submitted. 'I have some more work for you. Would you like it now, or shall we wait until Monday?'

'Wait until Monday, I've an appointment with Hair Today, Shorn Tomorrow for a shampoo and set and later I'll be at the Arts Centre for the Jazz and Folk Club.'

'By the way, before you go, was DI Barker at the inquest?'

Margery smiled. 'There was no sign of him. I guess he's gone home. The last time I spoke to him he said the case was all sorted. I think he's letting the Great Havell police take all the credit for it.'

'I see. So, Barker was up the right tree in the end!'

They both laughed and Margery left, saying goodbye to Philippa and Gill on her way out. She had time to pop home for a quick lunch before going out for her appointment with Tina.

'The perm has kept its shape well,' said Tina. 'I'd like to set your hair, so it frames the face a bit more, like this, she said, taking the curls at the front in both hands and illustrating what she meant.'

'Go on then,' said Margery. Tina washed Margery's hair and then put the rollers in to re-shape it.

'Thank you for alerting Jonah to those files your boys found, Tina. He was most grateful. He finds that sort of thing so interesting. I think he has put them in the library and will make them accessible to researchers.'

'Oh, that's excellent, I'll tell the boys. You know they didn't actually find those old papers in a skip.'

'Really? I would be very interested to know where they did find them.'

'They confessed to me they had been a bit naughty when I explained Mr McKay, the librarian, thought they might be important documents which had been thrown away inadvertently. I must say, as long as they are honest with me, I don't get angry with them. They confessed to me they were on the Glebe Mound and looked down the sinkhole in the Moyen Midden. They saw a black bin bag hanging on the metal steps under the mesh grill. They were curious to find out what was in it. The mesh grill had been partially lifted, although it was still padlocked, so they tried to reach it, by getting underneath. They attempted to pull the bin bag out, but it had too much in it to go through the narrow gap they made. They gave up at that point. They went back the next day to see if it was still there. I warned them, when they told me, anything could have been left in that bin bag, even poison. The boys said they were intrigued, because it looked as if it had books in it. They took a plank of wood with them the next day. They said they wedged it under the grill so they could stand on the end of it and force the grill

244

open. They tied the end of the bin bag with string and one of them hung on to it. They then both stood on the plank until they raised it enough to be able to pull out the bag.'

Margery smiled to herself. *So that's where the Tudor documents had gone. For some reason they had been hidden in the sinkhole*, she thought.

'All credit to your boys for coming clean about it. I hope you've thanked them from Jonah and myself. I must admit they are most resourceful and enterprising. You should be proud of them.'

'Yes, I have thanked them for it, and I've encouraged them to keep looking. But I have asked them to involve me in anything which might be a bit dodgy, because, I have pointed out, they could get themselves into trouble or even hurt themselves doing things like that.'

'That's true,' said Margery, smiling.

'There is just one other thing,' said Tina. 'The boys said they had made a bit of a mess of the grill on top of the sinkhole. You will not tell anyone it was them, will you?'

'Most certainly not. Of course not,' replied Margery. She went home wondering who had put the bin bag with the documents in the sink hole; why and when they put them there? It did seem most peculiar.

After cooking herself some pasta for an evening meal, Margery decided to get ready to go out. She wondered if Vlad would put his bike in her front garden as he usually did, and they could walk together to the Arts Centre. She also wondered where he was. She hadn't seen him since Monday morning and she hadn't really seen him then, because he had left before she was up. She supposed, because of all the rumours about him being a Russian spy, he was not keen on coming in to Great Havell at the moment. She went upstairs and put on her new dress. It looked really nice with the way Tina had styled her hair. She put on a pair of black tights and her calf length boots with the Cuban heels. Not for the first time, she wished she had a full-length mirror, but she felt she looked good in it all. She refreshed her make up carefully and decided to leave her glasses off. She put them in a case in her bag to take with her.

She put on her black jacket and maroon scarf with a black beret to finish. Feeling sorry she had to walk to the Arts Centre on her own, she contemplated taking her bike, but decided not to. She stepped outside, shut and locked her front door and opened the front gate.

Looking up the lane before she turned towards the old priory, she was surprised to see Vlad wheeling his bike walking towards her with Eric. Vlad was wearing what looked, to Margery, like an air force blue bomber jacket over a white t-shirt and neatly pressed jeans. She was so surprised, she stopped in her tracks. Eric Bolton had his long hair tied back, his battered fedora on his head and his usual greatcoat and long scarf.

When Vlad came up to her gate, he stopped and looked at her with admiration. 'You look beautiful!' he said.

Margery blushed, thanked him for the complement and noticed Eric was looking away. Unable to contain her pleasure in seeing Vlad, she grabbed his hand and said how pleased she was to see him. 'And you, Eric,' she said. Eric mumbled something she couldn't hear, but at least he replied.

Vlad put his bike in Margery's front garden and the three of them walked down the lane through the old priory and car park, then across the road to the Amicable Anarchist, where Derek gave Margery a cheerful wave from behind the bar through the open door. When he saw Eric with them, he was so surprised, he came out from behind the bar and watched them from the doorstep as they walked along Priory Street and turned into the marketplace towards the Arts Centre. The large former converted chapel, in a side street, had been fitted out as a hall with a stage.

Margery realised the music had started already. She heard a local folk group singing Chas and Dave's "Rabbit".

'Not fucking bad,' said Eric appreciatively, after they climbed the steps to the door, paid their entrance fees and found seats with Jonah. He had saved them a table near the edge of the stage with plenty of extra stacked seats against the wall nearby if they needed them. Eric bought them all drinks, a beer for Jonah, a shandy for Margery, a lager for Vlad and a large whisky for himself. Margery marvelled Vlad had actually persuaded Eric to come out. He sat there in his hat coat and scarf and didn't seem to feel too hot. He was an odd character, thought Margery, they must look quite a strange assortment of people to the other regulars. Jonah started to chat to Eric, saying he hadn't seen him for a long time and how sorry he was to hear about Sadie.

Margery noticed Eric did not check his tears and took a dirty cotton handkerchief out of his pocket to blow his nose noisily. Andy Clarke and the others who ran the Arts Centre knew Eric. He and Sadie had even been there regularly when Sadie was still working at Root and Branch.

Vlad had taken his jacket off. Margery smiled at him. She was still smiling at a happy Vlad when Cheryl's voice asked, 'Can we join you?' Without waiting for a reply, Cheryl and Nigel picked up chairs from the stack and sat with them.

Nigel had met Vlad before. He shook hands with Eric who just grunted an acknowledgement but got up and asked them gruffly what they would like to drink. Their little group had been receiving some odd looks from the regulars, but Eric became more acceptable as he was seen to be buying the drinks and Cheryl and Nigel didn't seem to mind him.

When the local folk group launched into the Ian Drury number "There aint 'arf been some clever bastards", a couple walked in who turned heads. Margery followed their look and gasped in surprise. It was DI Barker in his wide lapel double-breasted suit, trousers with turn-ups and two-tone shoes with his wife, Janine, looking glamorous in a thirties style black georgette dress topped with a fake fur cape. Her hair was in a marcel wave. Vlad, Jonah, Margery, Cheryl and Nigel immediately got up and Margery made the introductions. Vlad found chairs for DI Barker and Janine. Eric went to buy them drinks. A black coffee for the DI and a gin and tonic for Janine. When Eric came back with the drinks, he tried to pour some of his whiskey into Barker's coffee, but the DI was too quick for him, put his hand over his cup saying, 'No, thanks very much, mate. I appreciate the thought though.'

Margery thought the Ian Drury song was most appropriate for the DI. When the group finished the song, they all clapped and Eric surprised them by saying a loud 'Hey, hey, man, woof, woof!' Vlad looked at Margery raising his eyebrows in query. Margery whispered to him. 'It's Eric's way of saying he really liked the song.'

She started chatting to Janine on her other side who said, 'We're staying at the Palace Hotel in Havell-Next-the-Sea. I love walking along the sea front and Gerry doesn't mind the antique and second-hand shops.'

Margery asked Janine where she had bought her dress.

'There are some fantastic bargains in the charity shops along Marylebone High Street,' said Janine. 'We found we could buy handmade and couture clothes for ridiculously low prices. It was such fun looking for them too.'

The folk band was taking a break and Margery, still chatting to Janine about style and clothes, didn't notice Eric's seat was empty until she heard the beginnings of Gershwin's "Rhapsody in Blue" being played on the piano on the stage. Everyone in the room turned their heads to look, the buzz of conversation ceased, and all went quiet as Eric played the piece through, following it with more Gershwin. Andy, of the arts centre got his instrument and started to play rhythm guitar alongside Eric, who launched into a ragtime medley. He was still in his hat, scarf and greatcoat draped over the piano stool. His audience was amazed. The folk group were surprised too.

Margery saw Gerry Barker mount the stage, go over to Eric, when he paused for a moment. Then, to her surprise and everyone else's Gerry Barker sang "When the Clouds Roll By" in a strong baritone voice, with Eric on the piano and Andy on rhythm guitar. They all stood up and clapped. Everyone was delighted and called for more. The ad hoc trio followed it up with "Painting the Clouds with Sunshine", to more rapturous applause. The local folk group asked if Gerry Barker would like to sing with them, but he declined and came back to their table to sit down. Eric stayed at the piano and continued to play with the folk group, who found they could follow him easily embellishing the medleys he played.

'I didn't expect to see you again, Detective Inspector,' said Margery. She added a little wickedly. 'I heard at the inquest yesterday Great Havell Police have sorted everything out, all out by themselves.'

Gerry Barker grinned. 'That is exactly what Great Havell Police have done. Goodness knows what I was dragged down here for,' he added.

'I thought you had left Great Havell,' said Margery, determined to pursue it.

'I have.'

'We came back to the Palace Hotel because I was keen to stay there again, and explore more of the area,' explained Janine.

'Back to London tomorrow,' said Gerry Barker. 'The grandparents only allowed us one night away.'

'Why didn't you go to the inquest yesterday?'

'No need. It was all sorted as Mayor Grimes had requested when he asked the Yard send someone down to assist the local police.'

'So that's it then,' pursued Margery, 'you go home tomorrow and don't come back?'

'There is no doubt in my mind,' said Gerry Barker. 'I shall be called back to the Havell Hundreds before too long.'

Margery was thinking in terms of months or even years. She had no idea how soon it would be, or how glad she would be to see him.

# Chapter IX
## Loose Ends

Margery, the Barkers, Eric and Vladimir said goodbye to Cheryl, Nigel and Jonah, who was going to France the following day. They walked together to the old priory car park, where the detective inspector's BMW was parked. They lingered for a while, as Gerry Barker played a piece from one of his tapes in the car to Eric. Janine told Margery how much she liked the area and she hoped they would be back. They intended to go home via Trincaster, she said, which had some antique shops they wanted to visit and there was a bygones fair at the weekend. Margery went back to her cottage and Vlad took his bike to walk to Heathlands with Eric. He said he would soon be back.

It had been a lovely evening, but there was something niggling at the back of Margery's mind worrying her. There was a loose end or two which had not been tied up, something which was not mentioned in either the first or the second inquest, but she wasn't quite sure what it was.

She forgot all about it when Vlad came back. She asked him if he had met the artist Pricilla Buckler who lived at Little Havell.

'Oh yes, I've unblocked her toilet for her. She is a nice lady,' said Vlad cheerfully.

Margery was highly amused at the idea of this rather unglamorous encounter.

'I wonder what it was, the acclaimed artist managed to block her toilet up with? Did you only see her toilet, or have you seen any of her paintings?' she asked.

'She said I had to go into her studio to see them. There were a lot of them, and I thought they were very nice. I only went into her studio to do jobs for her when she requested for me to do them. There are other heating and electrical engineers and plumbers in Little Havell, but some people always ask for me. They are usually women. She is one of them. Her toilet was blocked with thick paper all torn up! I put it on the compost heap when I got it out. I instructed her not to put any more, thick paper down her toilet.'

'Do you often find you are asked to do trivial things like that, which people could easily do for themselves?' asked Margery.

'All the time,' replied Vlad. 'It keeps me in a job. It surprises me how late some English women stay in bed.'

'Really? what do you mean?' she was intrigued.

'I am sometimes called out in the morning, it could be 10 or 11 o'clock, and they answer the door in their night clothes, or at least clothes which looked to me very much like night clothes. Some of them hardly have any clothes on. I mentioned it to Miss Bodger, and she said she would try to make sure it didn't happen again. She knows I find it embarrassing. I went to sort out a tank overflow in a loft and found a huge hole in the ball cock, so it didn't float. I had no idea how the ball cock was punctured. I thought the tenants must have done it themselves. I went to the ironmongers in Little Havell and bought a new one to replace it. When I got back the woman was in her dressing gown, she said she had been having a shower whilst I was out. She said she was fed up with hearing the overflow going and thought she would use some of the water for a shower. It was late afternoon, and her husband came home whilst I was fitting the new ball cock into the tank. When I came down from the loft her husband was quite angry with me and I didn't know why. I left as soon as I could and told Miss Bodger about it, the next time I saw her. She seemed to think it was quite a joke and I didn't understand that either.'

Margery laughed. 'It's because the women in Little Havell fancy you, Vlad. They think up excuses to get you round, hoping you might like them too.'

'What do you mean fancy me? They are always teasing me about women fancying me at my flats. Whenever we have a call at odd hours, if I am there, they always say I must go because the housewife fancies me.'

'They like the look of you. They want to flirt with you. They want to get involved with you.'

'Why would I want to get involved with them?'

'I hope you wouldn't want to. Would you?'

'No, I don't think I would.'

'I know someone who probably wouldn't take that attitude though,' said Margery.

'Who is that?'

'You wouldn't know him, it's one of the bosses at the newspaper. He flirts with women all the time.'

'Does he flirt with you?'

'Yes, he does. He had an affair with one of the salesgirls and it's all over now. The company have paid for him to go on a cruise with his wife for a fortnight to Venice.'

'On the submarines, some of the men used to boast about the women they'd had. Others were not interested in women at all. But they kept quiet about it or made up their boasts. I used to think, perhaps it was not a woman they were talking about. It was best to make things up to be one of them, rather than appear not to be interested at all. When I said the other day there could be violence, that's what I meant. It was usually when men were arguing about women and whether the men were telling the truth about it, especially when they tried to outdo each other with their stories of the women they knew. It was difficult to keep out of those arguments, because they would think there was something wrong with you, if you didn't join in. It could be much worse when we were on shore leave and very difficult not to be involved in disputes, especially in foreign ports.'

Margery found the rest of the wine she and Jonah had shared at Feasta Pizza and poured a glass each for them. They had some apples, cheese and biscuits for a light supper.

'There's an art exhibition in the guildhall I am going to tomorrow,' she said. 'There are some Pricilla Bucklers in it. I'll probably have a lunch out somewhere and go afterwards. Would you like to come with me, Vlad?'

'I would like to come, but I still have to avoid Great Havell if I can. I think you know the stories which have been spread. I'll go to Eric's tomorrow and stay here at the weekend, if it is all right with you. I wanted to come back on Monday night as I had promised, but I heard people thought I was the centre of a spy ring with that woman who used to sit in the old priory and you and Eric. I didn't even know Eric until last Saturday. That is why I kept away. I didn't want to. I felt I was letting you down. I missed being with you.'

'And I missed you,' said Margery, smiling at him, so his face lit up.

'Did you miss me?' he asked. 'Did you really?'

'I did, I really did. I don't mind that you live in Little Havell, and the women there, fancy you. I don't blame them. I'm glad you came into my life.'

Later, hungry, they finished the food and the wine.

## Saturday 22nd February

Margery woke up warm and happy. There was no hurry. It was Saturday. Vlad had some oats which he put in a two-handled saucepan he had brought. He put it over one of her saucepans with water in. It was porridge and tea for breakfast. Vlad said he would go over to Eric's as he had promised, but he would be back that evening. Margery decided to do some housework and a little gardening before she went out to lunch. She put the radio on and found herself singing along to the music. Her heart was very light. Life was good. She had forgotten all about the deaths of Barney and Sadie, or the one mystery which had been bugging her. She still missed Growltiger and looked wistfully at his beanbag by the boiler in the kitchen. Outside, she found the herbs Ruth Baldock had given her were doing well, and she weeded the bed they were planted in.

Housework and gardening completed, she changed out of her jeans and jumper into a black dress, black stockings, boots, tartan cape and beret for the exhibition. Walking along the front of Priory Cottages, there was no sign of Alf, although the students at the cottage near the end were playing music loudly. Margery thought it was a blessing the cottage in between theirs and Alf's was just used occasionally for weekends. She walked through the old priory and looked, as it was her habit, at the place on the wall where Sadie used to sit. She crossed the car park, which was full of cars and the hot food van was back in place. She thought she would rather a sandwich from the bakery than a hot dog or a burger. She crossed Priory Street to the Amicable Anarchist, looked to see if she could see Derek, but he was busy behind the bar with plenty of Saturday customers and didn't appear to be looking out. She looked at some of the food stalls in the marketplace and then had the idea of going to Feasta Pizza to see if they were offering pizzas by the slice. If not, she would be passing Dewbury and Hicks, she could treat herself to a light lunch there. Her aunt and uncle were on their way to Orkney, Jonah was on his way to France. Cheryl had said she and Nigel were spending the day in Trincaster at the antiques fair, where Gerry and Janine Barker would also be. Margery wondered if they would meet up. She thought with affection of all of them and how supportive they had been over the past three weeks, which had been very difficult in so many ways. But there was something which was still disturbing her, she was not sure what or why. She didn't feel threatened any more. The source of the cocaine which had killed Barney and Sadie had been found and the drug had been disposed. The likely person who supplied it, if he had not administered it, was dead. But there was something. Then Margery remembered what it was. But it she would try and work it out later, first, there was lunch and an exhibition.

Gina was offering slices of pizza. Margery asked if she could sit in the restaurant to eat hers with some salad. Of course, she could, said Gina, she could sit in the little corner table by the back window.

After her lunch, Margery made her way to the guildhall in the marketplace. At one time, the guildhall had been in the centre of a row of low-grade cottages, which had been swept away to widen the marketplace earlier in the century. Historians from Trincaster disputed it was a guildhall at all. They contended the people of Great Havell had never been skilled enough in making cloth, pottery, leatherwork, cutlery, metalwork, beer, carpentry, or anything else which would have made it important enough to have guilds, let alone a guildhall. There had been more than four guildhalls in Trincaster, as the Blue Badge guides in the city never failed to point out to visitors.

The Great Havell guildhall was a long rambling building which showed the architecture of many centuries. The oldest part was timber framed and sat on a high brick plinth, part of which was the public toilets, which effectively heightened the building to three storeys. Above the public toilets were two large timber-framed rooms which acted as meeting rooms or, when there was an art exhibition on, an art gallery. The courtroom was the other end of the building the whole of that end was brick faced, had a vaulted ceiling and took two floors, with galleried seating in the courtroom. Below it, were the holding cells for those on a charge when the magistrates' court sat. In the days of the witch trials, the assizes had been in this courtroom. The six women had been in the cells beforehand.

In the middle of the two wings of the guildhall was the museum which was under a series of four gabled sections, or bays. It was longer and higher than each of the ends of the long range of buildings. It was on four floors. The ground floor of the museum, in the brick plinth, was devoted to the priory, the witches and the legends of the Glebe Mound. The first floor held the Moyen Midden exhibition and the story of how antiquarian Walter Wilkes had fallen into the sinkhole and found the pottery. This was all on display together with the objects found in the pots. It was a microcosm of local medieval life.

The second floor dealt with the history of the area, from the time of the dinosaurs up to the WW2 coastal defences and the RAF and USAAF airfields between Great Havell and Trincaster. The top floor was a permanent gallery of historic pictures.

Margery made her way to the southern end of the guildhall above the public toilets, where the exhibition was on two floors.

She picked up a catalogue inside the Tudor entrance door and looked at the prices. There was no way she would be able to afford anything, but she still thought she would enjoy the exhibition. She was particularly keen on seeing the Pricilla Buckler pictures. There were other artists exhibiting, but Margery particularly liked Pricilla Buckler's style. It was clever, she thought. What looked like blocks of flat coloured brushwork close up, shaped people, plants, buildings and landscapes. It was a style, she thought, which would lend itself to promotional posters of the Havell Hundreds. She thought the town council should commission some from the artist as Audrey Bodger in Little Havell had done.

'Enjoying the exhibition,' said a cultured voice in her ear.

Margery turned round to see Brendon Dant beside her.

'Very much, Mr Dant,' she enthused. 'I was just thinking the town council should commission some of these for promotional posters for the town.'

'I agree,' he replied. 'They could be done specifically for the purpose. But I'm not sure the town council is in a position financially to do that.'

'Why do you say that?' asked Margery, surprised.

'They are complaining the Moyen Midden Fayre will take too much of their budget, now it has been put back on the agenda.'

'I heard that. I can't understand how that would happen. I suppose once the upkeep of the church and the alms houses have been paid for, there is not much left.'

'No, sadly there isn't. And this is the problem we have. Now documents have gone missing which might have made a difference to Great Havell financially.'

'Really?' asked Margery. 'I heard about the Tudor witch trial notes, but I wasn't aware there were others. I can't see how a trial which took place more than four hundred years ago, even if it was a miscarriage of justice, could possibly make any difference financially to Great Havell or to anyone who lived here. Unless of course, the documents themselves were very valuable in some way.'

'There were other documents,' said Brendon Dant. 'Do you not know about those?'

'I don't,' replied Margery, thinking that Jonah had hinted there were, but like her, had not seen them. 'Were they found in the plaster of Mr Cobbler's walls as well as the witch trial ones?'

'No. Barney Cobbler was keeping them safe in with the Tudor ones.'

'Where are they now then, Mr Dant?'

'I was hoping you might tell me that, Miss Moore.'

Margery felt her stomach suddenly churn with dread. Jonah had the witch trial documents. Jonah was away. He too talked of other documents but hadn't found them. Her aunt and uncle were away in Orkney, Vlad was with Eric, Cheryl and Nigel were in Trincaster for the day and the Barkers were probably on their way back to London by now.

She tried to keep her voice steady, but it sounded high pitched and nervous to her. Perhaps Brendon Dant would not notice.

'I haven't seen any of these documents, Mr Dant. I heard Barney had a row with one of the council officers in the Amicable Anarchist over some documents. He said they would challenge the ownership of land in Great Havell. Barney thought he could force the council to hold an extraordinary meeting about the cancellation of the fair, but I thought it was all something to do with the witch trial documents.'

Brendon Dant came closer and looked Margery in the eyes, so she blinked.

'Miss Moore, you are an intelligent young lady and know when to keep your mouth shut. But you need not keep your silence with me on any matter. You know you can trust me. Barney did not know when to keep silent and, as you say, had that ridiculous row with the councillor and former mayor in the Amicable Anarchist. I'm sure you know where these documents are, and I feel sure you will be able to tell me.'

'Mr Dant, I really do not know of any others than those which the clerk of the witch trials made and hid in the walls of Barney's house. I have only heard about them from Jonah. It has puzzled me to know how the witch trial documents could change the ownership of land locally. Jonah lent me a chapbook which was printed from some of the notes the clerk made at the time of the trials and published the same year. At least, he didn't lend me an original chapbook, it was a facsimile.'

'These deeds, maps, plans and marriage certificates are nothing to do with the witch trials,' said Brendon Dant.

255

'I know nothing about them,' Margery was genuinely puzzled and beginning to feel a little relieved.

'Odd,' said Brendon Dant, 'I felt sure you did.'

'I should think,' said Margery, 'there are copies of the documents you are talking about somewhere. There must be. There might even be copies in the museum, we could have a look.'

'That's a good idea,' said Brendon Dant enthusiastically. 'We could start at the bottom and work up. We can access the museum from here.'

Margery followed Brendon Dant through a Tudor doorway into the museum, where all the pots from the Moyen Midden were displayed.

'How old are these documents?' asked Margery.

'Are you sure you haven't seen them?'

'Quite sure, who would have shown them to me?'

'Barney perhaps, or Jonah?'

'As you well know, Mr Dant, Barney was only ever interested in correcting my journalism. He used to give me a hard time. I have to say, I was always very grateful to you when you met up with us in the marketplace and took his attention away from me. I never had the chance to say thank you, so I say it now. Thank you.'

Brendon Dant laughed. 'Yes, Barney was very good at giving people a hard time. He could be a difficult person to deal with.'

'You always seemed to manage him well,' said Margery, relieved that Brendon Dant was friendlier and less inclined to accuse her of knowing more than she did. At the back of her mind, though, was her complicity with Jonah in retrieving the documents from Hawfinch Road. She was feeling a little uncomfortable, knowing that Jonah was keeping them safe somewhere. It was up to him to tell Brendon Dant about them. After all, they were both members of the Moyen Circle, and had the interests of Great Havell traditions in common.

Brendon Dant led the way through the open Tudor door down the narrow stairs to the ground floor, where the documents and artefacts from the Tudor period were displayed alongside the stories of the priory and the witches.

Margery made a straight for the documents. Copies of the Great Havell charter and legal documents from the trials of the monks and the witches were on display and interpreted.

She put her bag down so she could use both hands to open the drawers under one of the display cases, where she knew other documents were kept under glass.

She looked in a few of them and then found an old map of Great Havell in one of the lower drawers.

'This is a good starting point. Here is one of the best historic maps of the Havell Hundreds I know of,' she said, turning round to Brendon Dant, to find he was nowhere to be seen.

'Mr Dant!' she called. 'This is a good section to start in. This is where most of the maps of Great Havell are kept. Mr Dant! Mr Dant! Mr Dant!' she called, but there was no reply.

Margery was puzzled. She looked for a door in the brick walls he might have gone through, but there was not one. The door, which connected the museum with the public toilets was firmly locked. She realised it was probably never opened, as people could get in and out of the museum that way without being seen by the staff. She rattled the handle, hoping someone might hear her. She looked through the keyhole and realised the door led to a little lobby and a further door which was most likely locked, so he couldn't have gone out that way.

She looked under display cabinets and wandered all around the brick floor wondering where he had gone. Eventually, she decided to go upstairs and back on to the first floor, where they had started. At the top of the stairs, she found the door firmly shut and even locked. Margery rattled the door and called out, hoping someone in the museum would hear her. But no one came. For some reason or other, Brendon Dant had left her on the ground floor of the museum without a word, and shut her in.

She rattled the door at the top of the stairs again and called out. But still no one came. It was Saturday, surely there would be visitors to the museum, who would want to come downstairs to see the displays on the ground floor and open the door at the top.

She went down the stairs deep in thought. It occurred to her Brendon Dant might have locked her in deliberately. But why? It was Saturday afternoon. The museum would be shut on Sunday. It wouldn't open again until Tuesday. There would be no one to miss her except Vlad tonight and he would probably think she had gone to her uncle and aunt's in Havell-Next-the-Sea and go back to his flat in Little Havell.

Brendon Dant must have been caught short or something and shut the door at the top of the stairs by mistake. *He'll be back,* she thought. Or did Brendon Dant think she knew where the documents which had gone missing were? He had told her they existed and what they were. Jonah had not said anything about other documents in those files, but then, it was possible there were. Jonah had said he was trying to sort them into the order he and Barney had been studying them. Perhaps only Barney knew about them. Barney wasn't one to keep quiet about things like that, especially if the documents were authentic and they challenged local land ownership. As far as she knew, no one else had seen these other documents, except Barney, until she and Jonah had possibly collected them from Tina's. It was a puzzle. It was exactly this which had been puzzling her since the last inquest.

Everyone was focussed on the drugs, the source and the dealer and then there had been the vandalism to the grid on the sinkhole of the Moyen Midden. Brendon Dant had a key to the mesh grid on the sinkhole. He was the only holder of the key since Barney had died. Barney seemed to think the documents he found in his wall would question the ownership of a lot of the land in Great Havell. But that had never made sense to Margery. It was too long ago. There were alternative possibilities though, if there were other documents, perhaps added to the ones in Barney's walls, later ones. *Or,* she thought, *information on the witch trial notes might have challenged land ownership or the identities of the women.* Were there other documents found to confirm the information on the witch trial notes perhaps?

According to Jonah, Barney was insisting the documents he had found, or seen, not only questioned the legal ownership of local land, but also proved it would be illegal to cancel the fair. Barney had also been questioning the legitimacy of the ownership of the Grimes family land. *But, if that were the case,* thought Margery, *why were these documents not revealed by anyone other than Barney?* Had Jonah known about them before they went missing from Barney's house? Were they hidden in the bin bag Tina's boys found the sinkhole with the Tudor witch trial notes? And if so, why? Why would they be valuable to Dant, who seemed to think she knew about them? *He* knew about them, otherwise he wouldn't accuse her of concealing them.

She still didn't understand any of it. In the meantime, she was stuck in the museum, possibly locked in by Dant. Why would he do that? She'd have to find a way out. Margery looked at the windows which were long, narrow and high up. She might be able to open one if she climbed up on one of the display cases. But surely the museum staff would shut the museum and come and check the door before they did and be surprised to find it locked. She would go up to the top of the steps and wait.

Time was marching on. It was a quarter to four already, the lights were still on. Margery didn't fancy being shut down there in the dark. She found her mouth was dry and she wasn't sure if she hoped or feared Brendan Dant would come back. If he did, would he apologise for shutting her in by mistake? She hadn't let on Jonah had found the files which went missing when Barney died, but then she remembered Brendon had been to Barney's house that day, on his own admission at the first inquest, to collect the Moyen Circle files. He said he'd taken them to his offices at Lockhart and Upton for safekeeping.

Sitting at the top of the steps, Margery tried to piece together Brendon Dant's part in all this and tried to work out why he would assume she knew about, had seen, or even knew where these documents were. Had Jonah said something? No. Jonah was being uncharacteristically secretive about the rediscovery of the files. It was a puzzle.

She wished Uncle Alec had not gone away. She wished she had asked Cheryl to come with her to the exhibition, or that she had left coming to see the exhibition until Jonah came back from France or even that Vlad felt able to come with her. But no, people probably still thought he was a Russian spy and until that all died down, it was not a good idea for him to come into Great Havell except to go to the Arts Centre, where he was known, and to his English evening classes at the institute. And, of course, when he came to stay with her.

Apart from the Amicable Anarchist regular, who Derek Robinson clearly thought, had an agenda of his own and was probably one of the husbands whose wives called Vlad in for some trivial repair, it had been Berkley Grimes and his friends Morris and Mack who had implicated Vlad in the fight outside the Assembly Rooms, according to Philippa and Gill. Why would anyone be so keen to involve Vlad, unless it was to deflect blame or suspicion from themselves?

Berkley Grimes was also friendly with Denzil Bream who had taken the cocaine which had put him in a coma. Denzil and his girlfriend Tracey had pinched the broomsticks which made a gibbet for her cat. Was Grimes in on that too? Did he take cocaine as well? He was treating Barney, or at least his osteopath practice was treating him, for severe back pain. Could Grimes have persuaded him to take the cocaine to ease the pain? It was possible. Could Grimes have supplied the syringe to Sadie as well? The description Sadie gave Eric, who mentioned it to Vlad, would fit Berkley Grimes. But there were many people that would fit. Perhaps it had been Berkley Grimes who put the rag doll and the twigs through her door. He had put the invitation to the Valentine's Ball through the door, so she would bring Vlad and he could more easily be accused of being a spy or starting a fight or something. Margery's mind was beginning to spin with it all. Berkley Grimes was supposedly arguing with his father outside the Assembly Rooms too. What was that about? Berkley Grimes had been on Fenton Bradley's yacht and may have put the syringes into a pair of the man's deck shoes. *He didn't look like a criminal,* Margery thought, but then, she wasn't sure what a criminal looked like.

It was getting late, it was 4.30 pm, the museum would close at 5.00 pm. Margery banged on the door, hoping there would be a museum assistant or visitor who would hear her.

She banged on the door again and waited.

She called out: 'Is anyone there?' and waited. Nothing. Her mouth was getting very dry. She had visions of staying in the dark overnight and then only with the windows for light, all day on Sunday. She wouldn't be free until they opened the museum on Tuesday. Perhaps she could climb on the display cases and open one of the small narrow windows at the top and attract the attention of someone outside.

Then she had an idea and wondered why she had not thought of it before. Going over to the display case with the documents in, she tried to break into it, hoping it would trigger an alarm. She picked up her bag thinking she might be able to set off the alarm using her keys as a lever on the case but found she hadn't put them in the usual handy pocket at the side. Looking in the other pockets for them, she found a metal nail file in her make up bag. She used it to try to lever one of the display cases open through the lock and trigger the alarm. Nothing happened and Margery was beginning to wonder if any of the cases were actually alarmed.

She tried some others and then picked up her bag and went back up the stairs and banged, shouted and tried rattling the door. She was still doing that and becoming frantic as her watch showed the time approaching 5.00 pm, when the door was opened, and she fell through it.

'Whatever possessed you to take the Yale off the latch and shut that door? That door should never be shut when the museum is open,' a woman's angry voice railed at her.

'You really should not have done that. You would have been shut in there until Tuesday. Get up, I want to close the museum.'

Margery, in a daze, stood up as quickly as she could and was ushered out through the door to the exhibition, which she heard closed firmly behind her. She stumbled frantically down the stairs, out into the street; she was vaguely aware of someone dropping something into her bag as she went round to the public toilets to relieve herself.

She looked in the mirror as she washed her hands. She saw her dishevelled and anxious reflection. She looked in her bag but couldn't see anything unusual in there. Perhaps she had imagined someone had dropped something in it. At least she was out.

Margery didn't even stop to refresh her make-up, as she normally would or even put her beret on straight. She started running home, out of the marketplace and along Priory Street as far as the Amicable Anarchist, where Derek Robinson came out of the pub, stopped her and said:

'Ah, Miss Moore, we've been wondering where you were; there's someone waiting to talk to you in here.' He led the disorientated dishevelled Margery into the pub to the snug, where she would normally sit with Jonah.

'Goodness me!' exclaimed Berkley Grimes. 'Are you alright, Miss Moore? Let me get you a drink.' Margery nodded wordlessly. She noticed Berkley Grimes looked entirely different from when she had seen him in court. He was dressed in jeans, a white open neck shirt and a pale blue sweater, with Great Havell Yacht Club embroidered on it in white.

Berkley went over to the bar. 'I'll have whatever Miss Moore usually has, please Derek.' He came back with a half pint of shandy for Margery, which she took in her two shaking hands and drank thirstily.

'I went to your cottage. Your neighbour said you had gone out, but he didn't know where. I guessed you were shopping somewhere, so I came into the pub, because I thought you would have to come back this way to go home. Derek said he had seen you go out, but he didn't think you had come back. He said he would keep an eye out for you.'

Margery took another long drink. She was sitting opposite a man who seemed to be in thick of everything that had happened in the past three weeks, possibly even a murderer. She didn't know what to say. She took another long drink.

'Brendon Dant shut me in the museum,' she announced eventually.

'Dant shut you in the museum? Why on earth would he do that? He goes too far that man, he always goes too far.'

'He certainly went too far doing that,' she said angrily. 'I was talking to him and I turned round, looked for him, and discovered he had gone upstairs to the first floor and shut me in.'

'But why would he?'

Margery looked at Berkley Grimes. She looked round to the open door. She was in a public place with him. She decided she would have to give him the slip and get home somehow without him seeing. Make the excuse to go to the Ladies and not come back. He must have noticed she was edgy.

'I see Dant has given you a bit of a shock. He's too much than man. He really is. He's got these documents he claims will dispossess our family of all the land the new bypass is likely to be built on, but he won't show them to us, so we don't know if they even exist. He's been using them as a hold over us.

'I was the member of the sailing club, as you know, who helped him empty poor Bradley's yacht after he drowned. He asked for me specifically. At the inquest he said I had volunteered. After Dant had returned everything to the widow, she called him back. He finds there were syringes in a pair of deck shoes. I think I would have noticed them when we were collecting stuff to take to her, don't you? I don't think they were there when we cleared the yacht.'

Berkley took a long drink from his pint. Margery was too interested in what he was telling her to take the opportunity to escape.

Berkley continued his narrative: 'Dant was up on the Glebe Mound when Bream did that ridiculous jape involving your cat. Bream had unintentionally run the cat over, by the way, it didn't suffer. Bream had a rag doll he was going to put on the gallows. He is insane at times and insisted on putting the cat up there instead.

'Dant was up on the mound at that time and seemed to think it was a good idea to alert the police and the press to the whole thing. He took the rag doll.'

Berkley took another long drink from his pint.

'It was also Dant who insisted the Russian from Little Havell was involved in the fracas outside the Assembly Rooms after the Valentine's Ball. Dant was just behind Dad when he stepped backwards and fell. Mum nearly broke his fall and got a bit of black eye in the process, but Dad hit his head on a low wall and was concussed so had to go to hospital. I was having a go at Dad at the time. I was at the end of my tether with it all.' Berkley paused. Margery was fascinated.

'Dad was telling me these documents, which we hadn't seen, would cost us all our land and I was telling him let them do just that. I said, if it was going to cause that much trouble, he and Mum should just sell up and move out into some-thing smaller in the Great Havell suburbs. After all, they are rattling around in that old manor house, and Mum does all the housework herself. It's costing them a fortune to keep up. Every time they have to repair something, they must consult all sorts of heritage groups about how to do it.'

Berkley was overturning all Margery's preconceptions about his family. She listened fascinated.

'We'd all had too much to drink at the Valentine's Ball and so had all the Gleaner journalists. Mum was furious with the report about it in the paper. I never saw the Russian, but Dant insisted he was there and managed to convince Morris and Mack they had seen him too. To top it all, Uncle Harry was having a row with Aunt Rita, because, as usual, he couldn't keep his hands to himself.

'Dant is always in the middle of everything. He appears to try to calm things down, but when I think about it, maybe he stirs things up!' Margery noticed Berkley was quite angry with the man as he continued:

'That is why I suggested to Dad he just sell up the manor house and have done with it. Any documents which contest his ownership of the manor would then have to be produced. It's all causing Mum and Dad too much hassle and I haven't any patience with them over it. Sell up, move out and have done with it, I say. But that didn't go down very well with either Mum or Dad and, as I say, we'd all been drinking too much.'

Margery could hardly believe what she was hearing. Berkley was contradict-ing everything she had thought about him. He was even confessing to have been involved with poor Growltiger's demise. She finished her shandy and said:

'These documents, Mr Grimes, are you telling me you haven't seen them?'

'No, I haven't. Nor has my father.'

'But Barney Cobbler, before he died, was insisting they would dispossess your family, wasn't he?'

'Yes, Barney Cobbler, was very excited about them.'

'But neither you, nor your father have seen them?'

'No, we haven't seen them.'

'Well... Perhaps they don't exist then?'

'Those are my thoughts exactly. How can you take anything seriously if you have never actually seen it? Except for one thing and that was Barney Cobbler, who was such a stickler for facts. They had to exist if he had seen them. It didn't make sense to me. I have to assume they do exist. I think the best thing is for

263

Mum and Dad to sell the manor house. That way they can't have the likes of Dant or anyone else holding these documents over them, like some sort of threat. And, by the way, please call me Berkley.'

Margery was thinking hard. She had finished her shandy and Berkley got up to get her another one and came back from the bar with another pint for himself too.

'My goodness me! You are thirsty, although I'm not surprised if you've been locked in a museum for a couple of hours. I bet you didn't think you would get out until it opened again on Tuesday!'

'That's exactly what I thought. I tried to set the alarms off, but I don't think they were working or switched on. I tried to do it without vandalising the display cases. I tried them all. I even thought I might be able to get out of one of those long narrow windows, or at least attract someone's attention from them.' Berkley's serious face broke into a smile. It was, as Margery had guessed, as charming as his father's.

'I've heard you are pretty feisty and resourceful from my uncle Harry.'

'The museum assistant, who let me out, thought I had shut myself in, by mistake, or even deliberately, I don't know which. She was pretty cross. I noticed when I was banging on the door to be let out there was a Yale lock on it, so it would have been easy to shut myself in. I hope Mr Dant did it by mistake and didn't intend it.'

'I wouldn't like to say what Mr Dant does and does not intend.' Margery watched as Berkley's serious expression changed to one of delight. 'Look! Here's Bodhi, I said I would be in here, when she'd finished her yoga class.'

Margery followed his gaze and saw his girlfriend walk into the pub, looking very beautiful in a silky pinky-beige long tunic over matching trousers.

Beginning to get over her panic at being shut in the museum for two hours, Margery got up as Bodhi entered the pub and so did Berkley. The beautiful Indian girl was turning heads, as she always did, her long wavy dark hair tied back in a silk ribbon which matched her clothes and a delighted smile on her face as she saw Margery and Berkley in the snug.

Margery knew her by sight as she took the yoga sessions on the Glebe Mound and she had seen her with Berkley at the opening of the Brass Monkeys Brasserie.

Berkley introduced Bodhi formerly to Margery as his fiancée and bought her a bottle of Little Havell sparkling mineral water at the bar. The three of them sat down again with their drinks.

'Are you all right, Miss Moore?' asked Bodhi. 'Only you look as if you've had a bit of a shock.'

'I'm recovering from being locked in the museum for two hours.'

'Would you like us to take you home when we've finished our drinks?' asked Bodhi. 'I've parked Berkley's car in the old priory car park, so it will be on our way.'

Home! Margery had sudden idea. She picked up her bag and looked into it. Her house keys were in there, she saw them immediately, they were sitting on top of her make-up bag. She usually kept them in a little pocket on the outside of the bag, which was empty. She hadn't seen them there when she was locked in the museum and had hoped to use them to trigger the alarms.

'Are you all right?' asked Berkley Grimes, watching her.

'I think someone may have been in the cottage, whilst I was out, Berkley. I think I may have been locked in the museum so my keys could be borrowed and then they were dropped in my bag when I came out.'

'I've been over to your cottage and I didn't see anyone except your neighbour.'

'When did you go there?'

'I suppose about an hour ago, I waited for a while. Your neighbour thought you would be back. But I didn't stay there long, I'm not a very patient person.'

Bodhi smiled at this, she caught Berkley's hand. 'As I try to tell you, darling, things are not going to be sorted out overnight. Take one thing at a time and relax more. Everything will fall into place, eventually. Just be patient.' She turned to Margery. 'He won't do yoga, he won't make time for it, but it would do him so much good Miss Moore.'

'Call me Margery please, both of you,' she said.

She was beginning to have a new idea of what might have been happening. She was beginning to find answers to the things which had been puzzling her after the second inquest. She was still feeling hot and bothered and she was sorry she had not taken the time to neaten her hair and refresh her makeup. It seemed to her Berkley had no clue about what he may have been involved in, but Margery was beginning to have a very good idea about it all. She was now expecting to find something in her house. She was starting to realise the person who put it there, would say he had a perfectly good reason to have a key to her cottage, if either of her neighbours had challenged him. But it was quite possible that even if Alf was in his garden, the person was seen so often in the area, for various reasons, he might not even be noticed. He was clever enough to watch and wait for an opportunity to pop in and out of her cottage and look as if he was just taking a walk on the Glebe Mound, along the bridle path or along the lane at the front. He was in the market place every day, he often used to be seen with Barney. He even talked to Sadie in the old priory, he was often in the Amicable Anarchist, he was a key member of the Moyen Circle. Why hadn't she realised all this before?

'I would very much like you and Bodhi to come with me to my cottage, Berkley. I would like you to witness me finding whatever has been planted in it.'

'Now you are talking in riddles, Margery, whatever do you mean?'

'I think, Berkley and Bodhi, I may have found a solution to these recent mysteries.'

'And you are expecting to find it in your cottage?' asked Bodhi.

'Yes, I think there could be something planted somewhere. It might take some looking for, but I think I know what it might be.'

'Now you really are puzzling me, Margery. I'm looking forward to going to your cottage to find out what you are on about.'

'I'm sorry to be a bit mysterious about this, but I have only just realised what could be behind it all. What was it you came to see me about anyway, Berkley?'

'It was Bodhi and I who came to see you earlier today, because Bodhi said I really needed to tell you exactly what happened to your cat. She said it was only fair.'

'Well, thank you. And thank you for telling me it was an accident.'

'Denzil is a very good friend of mine, but he always goes over the top about things and he was as high as a kite that afternoon. Tracey, Bodhi and I have all tried to sort him out and get him out of his bad habits, but so far, without success. Dant saw us and wanted to know what we were doing up there, but he didn't stop us. He even helped. I don't know why. I don't know what *he* was doing up there. I wouldn't put it past him to encourage us and then blame us for doing something entirely different. He usually has a different version of events to everyone else.'

*I probably know what he was doing up there*, thought Margery, but didn't say anything. They finished their drinks and left the pub.

She, Berkley and Bodhi crossed Priory Street to the old priory car park. Bodhi took a key out of her bag and opened the boot of a Ford Escort to get her jacket out. It was a thick multi-coloured knitted jacket and the three of them walked on through the old priory, into the lane at the back and to Margery's cottage. Although it was dark by then, Alf was looking out for her.

He seemed a bit put out to see she was with Berkley and the 'yoghurt lady' and said so.

'Alf, have you seen anyone let themselves into my cottage this afternoon?' asked Margery.

'I've only seen this young man and the yoghurt lady go up to your door this afternoon, Miss Moore. But I can't be watching your place for you all day you know. I have things to do. Your fancy man hasn't been in, if that's who you mean.'

'Thank you, Alf,' said Margery and opened her door.

She turned to warn Berkley of the low lintel and then realised she had no need. Like all the Grimes family, he was medium height.

Margery invited them to sit down and, out of habit, she put the kettle on.

'Would you like a cup of tea?' she asked.

They both said, thank you they would, and sat down on her small settee.

'Do you mind, while the kettle is boiling, if I have a look round to see if there is anything missing, or if, indeed, as I suspect, there might be something hidden here?'

'Not at all,' said Berkley, looking a bit puzzled.

Margery took her time to look all over her small cottage. There weren't many places where something could be hidden. She also felt she should check there was nothing missing.

Her desk, her telephone and her typewriter were all in their usual places. She looked in the desk draws, nothing seemed to have changed. She looked in all the kitchen and bathroom cupboards. Upstairs in the wardrobes and dressing table, nothing either seemed to be disturbed or taken. She was beginning to think she was completely mistaken in her theory and went downstairs, when the kettle whistled, to make the tea. She used mugs and brought in the tin with the biscuits.

'I'm beginning to think I was mistaken about someone coming in here when I was locked in the museum,' she said, 'maybe I've got it all wrong after all.'

'I'm intrigued to know who you think might have been in here and what they might have put in your cottage,' remarked Berkley.

'Since I'm beginning to have my doubts and since I think whoever it is, may be very clever and calculating indeed, I don't think it would be a good idea to say at the moment,' replied Margery, offering them oat biscuits. 'I'm really glad you came back with me, though, sorry about my neighbour, Bodhi. He is always describing yoga as yoghurt and winding me up by calling it some sort of diet fad which puts on weight. He's like that. He's always grumbling.'

Bodhi laughed. 'It's taken some time for local people to accept yoga. It's very beneficial, not just for fitness and flexibility. At first, I only took classes in Trincaster. That was how Berkley and I met. He started referring patients from his practice to me. The ones he felt were suffering chronic pain and, he had the idea yoga might be beneficial for them. It is. I've been able to help quite a few of his patients. Sometimes it is a case of relaxation and posture to relieve chronic pain. I can't get him to practice it himself, though, can I darling?'

Margery was treated to another of Berkley Grimes charming smiles. She began to think, if she was wrong about one person, could she have been right about Berkley after all? She gave an involuntary shiver as she contemplated that she might have the charming mastermind of it all in her room.

Berkley Grimes noticed. 'Are you all right, Margery, would you like us to go?'

'I'm fine,' she replied, 'and it's really nice to meet you both properly and have you here.' She found she meant it. She liked this couple who were a few years younger than her. She had found out they were engaged to be married. She wondered what sort of wedding they would have. She had a sudden thought.

'Are you both warm enough in here? I have the storage heaters on very low to take the edge off the chill, but I can easily put the electric fire on if you would like?'

'I'm OK, thanks Margery, what about you, Bodhi?'

'I'm warm enough also, thanks. Do you ever have an open fire?'

'Very rarely, sometimes at Christmas if family are staying. It's a very small chimney and needs sweeping regularly, if I make a habit of having an open fire.'

Margery looked towards the fireplace and noticed something. The sampler on the stand she kept in front of the grate and behind the electric fire had been moved.

She had an idea and got up out of her chair.

'I think I know where it's been put.'

'Where what's been put?' asked Berkley in surprise.

'I'm not sure what it is, but I think something has been put in here and my guess is, it has been tucked up my chimney.'

Berkley and Bodhi looked at each other puzzled. Berkley shrugged.

Margery went to get her torch from the windowsill in the kitchen, removed the electric fire from the grate and put the sampler aside. She moved her small coffee table out of the way and spread a copy of the Gleaner on the floor. She lay down on it with her head in the grate and shone the torch up the chimney moving it around and turning her head with it.

'Would you like me to look?' asked Berkley, a bit alarmed, as she pushed her head further into the grate and seemed to be craning it backwards.

'Would you mind taking the torch and shining it in this position?' asked Margery, holding it so that it shone on the room side of the inside of the chimney.

Berkley got down on the floor close to Margery and carefully took the torch from her keeping it in the exact position she had asked for.

'Thanks,' she said. 'This is what I need to do now.' She stretched both her arms into the chimney as far as they would go. With a little more effort, she caught the corner of something with her right hand, gave it a little tug, which caused a bit of soot to fall on her face. She pulled the object down with both hands and handed it to Berkley.

'There you are, I knew there would be something.' Margery got up and brushed the soot off her face and her clothes onto the newspaper and went to the bathroom to wash her face. She looked in the mirror and saw she still looked quite dishevelled but was pleased her theory had been right. What a pity DI Barker was not staying in the area anymore.

When she went back into her front room, she saw Berkley and Bodhi shining the torch on the object she had extracted from the chimney, so they could see it clearly. It was an old map. It was almost exactly what Margery had hoped to find, although she hadn't been quite sure what it would turn out to be.

'Well! Your hunch was right after all!' exclaimed Berkley. 'You've found an old map of Great Havell with the monastery, the priory and all the Glebe Lands marked on it. Over here is where Dad's manor house is today. There's another grand house marked too. It looks as if it is the area the Home Farm is on. According to this map, it's called Thorpe Castle and has a lot of land, all around it, stretching to the monastic buildings where the manor is today. Does that mean Home Farm isn't council owned do you think? Does it mean this other estate owns that and most of the land up to the manor house?'

'I think that is the intention of the map,' replied Margery.

'I don't understand.' Berkley was puzzled.

'What Margery means is she doesn't think the map is genuine,' explained Bodhi.

Berkley shook his head. 'It looks genuine,' he said. 'Why would anyone go to the trouble of producing a map with this amount of detail and make it look old?'

'For money?' suggested Margery. 'To get a bypass and new developments built where they want them?'

'You've lost me,' said Berkley, 'Do you mean old maps are very valuable?'

'Yes, I'm sure they are. But why, if it is genuine, would someone hide it up my chimney? It doesn't make sense. But if it is a genuine map and shows someone might have a claim to land. Anyone intending to buy it, live on it, put a road across it or even build on it, would have to buy that land off the owner.'

'I still don't get it,' said Berkley. 'I remember Denzil was boasting about some council land which was going to be developed, which he expected to make a lot of money from. I wasn't really interested, I must admit. It was one of the things I was arguing with Dad about after the ball, but we'd all had a bit too much to drink and I should have known better. I've apologised to Bodhi and Mum about that, haven't I, darling?'

'Berkley is delightfully naive about some things,' remarked Bodhi, smiling.

'If I can explain,' said Margery. 'Here is your parents' and ancestors' manor house and some of the land which goes with it. It's all where the former monastery was. This is where the new bypass and some new homes will go. But, until the bypass is built, with a slip road to the new homes, there will not be any access to them. So, the developers are looking at this land here, which is occupied by Home Farm today. It has road access to it. It belongs to the council. They let it to a farmer who farms the land and has done for years. It can't be developed unless the farmer ceases to rent it and the council approves it for development. What this map does, is to show the land, historically, was privately owned and may still be, if there is someone living who can lay claim to it. The deeds would be needed of course, but I'm sure they are in existence.'

'What makes you so sure about that?' asked Berkley, puzzled by Margery's certainty.

Bodhi spoke up again. 'Margery thinks this map is a forgery, Berkley, and there will be other forged documents to back it up.'

'But why? ... Oh! I see what you are getting at. If the land can be proved to be privately owned and the descendants of the owners are still living, they can approve plans for the bypass and new homes and the tenant farmer would have to be evicted from his farm. The council could do nothing to stop it.'

'Yes, that is probably what would happen,' said Margery.

'But why are you so sure these are not genuine? They look as if they are.'

'For many reasons. One is that they are being talked about but kept secret. Also, there may be actual documents in existence which might contradict these. My guess is there are some clever people behind this. They could make a lot of money out of it. Maybe they have done so already. They use people. They've used you, Berkley, me, Barney, poor man, Denzil and, probably, all the Bodger family of estate agents. Because people are always looking for answers, these people are skilled at providing those answers, plausible answers. In the process of providing them, they find others, such as ourselves, to put the blame on.'

'But who?'

'I don't think I should say,' replied Margery, 'but I now understand why your father wanted DI Barker on the case. It had puzzled me before, but now it makes sense. Sometimes, people become essential to others. They are always so obliging, helpful, friendly and talented, they are never thought, or considered be anything other than what they appear to be. There is always some other, clever explanation for what happens. For instance, I shut myself into the museum, or Barney needed the cocaine, because he was in such severe pain. I don't think he was intended to die from the overdose, but I think he was intended to be discredited and out of the way, until some documents which were in his house were extracted.'

'Would you like me to ask Dad if he can get DI Barker back?' asked Berkley.

Margery nodded, 'I would. Yes, I think that would be a good idea. I'm not sure what the next move would be. It could involve my house in some way, so this map would be "accidentally" discovered here. I am beginning to see how these minds work, but I can't predict what they would do next.'

'Do you mind if I use your phone, Margery?'

'Not at all, please do. I'm glad to have you both here, actually.'

Bodhi smiled at Margery reassuringly and Berkley phoned his father.

'Dad? It's Berkley, Bodhi and I are at Margery Moore's cottage, she had a bit of a scare in the museum earlier and Bodhi wanted me to confess about that business with her cat. The point is, she is wondering how to get in touch with DI Barker…

271

'What's that? Ring the Palace Hotel at Havell-Next-the-Sea? Have you got the number? Thanks Dad.'

Berkley rang the Palace Hotel, who said Barker was out for a walk, but they would page him. He left a message for him to get in touch with or come round to see Margery Moore as soon as possible.

When Berkley put the phone down, there was the sound of a key in the door, which opened, and Vlad walked in. He looked surprised and disconcerted to see Berkley and Bodhi and even more alarmed to see Margery in her dishevelled state. Then he and Bodhi greeted each other as old friends and gave each other a hug, Margery and Berkley looked on in surprise.

'Vlad rearranges a meeting room for my yoga class at the Country Hotel every week and puts the room back to how it was afterwards,' explained Bodhi.

Margery introduced him as the "Russian spy" to Berkley Grimes, who was a bit taken aback at first. He looked from Bodhi to Vlad to Margery with a bit of a frown until he realised that someone who had a key to Margery's cottage must be pretty close to her. There was a lot to be explained to Vlad and Berkley undertook to do it, with Bodhi attempting to help recount what was turning out to be a complicated story.

Margery realised it was getting late and suggested she look in her store cupboards for something for them all to eat. Bodhi suggested they ordered a takeaway from her cousins' Indian restaurant in Priory Street. She even suggested a menu they would probably all like. Vlad offered to go and collect it on his bike. Berkley insisted on paying for it. Margery looked around her small front room and wondered how they would manage with a takeaway Indian in there. Eventually she thought of using her picnic blanket.

Bodhi organised it. She put the picnic blanket on the floor. She put the coffee table over to one side and put Growltiger's beanbag and cushions from the chair and the settee on the floor for them to sit on.

It was a lively Indian supper party in Margery's cottage. Bodhi showed Margery the best way to sit cross-legged for her back. They all ate their share of the *dahls, curries* and *kormas* Bodhi had ordered, on plates with forks, sitting cross-legged on the floor, when DI Barker knocked on the door. Margery let him in, supplied him with a plate and fork and Berkley invited him to 'get stuck in', which he did, sitting on Margery's button back chair.

When they were having mugs of tea from the large pot Vlad had made, they all took a hand in clearing the plates and empty take-away dishes. Vlad volunteered to wash up, shutting the kitchen door, so the others could fill in DI Barker with recent developments.

Margery began by telling him about the exhibition of Philippa Buckler paintings, where she met Brendon Dant and they had started talking about documents he knew about, which had gone missing and which he thought she might know where they were. She told Barker how she then suggested they went to look at the ones in the museum and he said they could start on the ground floor. Margery had turned to talk to him, to find he was not there. Further, she found the door at the top of the stairs had been shut and there was no way she could open the Yale lock from the inside. Effectively, Brendon Dant had gone, and she had been shut in for a couple of hours. She panicked a bit, thinking she would have to stay there until the museum re-opened on Tuesday. She described how she got out, falling flat on her face, just before the museum was due to close and museum assistant had been extremely cross with her. As she left, she thought something was dropped into her bag.

'And had there been something dropped into your bag?' asked Barker.

'Yes. My keys. I had missed them when I was considering using them to put them in the display case locks to set off the museum alarms. I think they had been taken out of the little pocket I keep them in, whilst I was looking at the exhibition or after I followed Brendon Dant down the stairs to the ground floor.'

'So, whoever took them would have a chance to come here and do whatever they intended, whilst you were locked up in the museum?'

'Yes, that is what I think happened,' said Margery.

'When I left the toilets in the guildhall, I started to hurry home, almost running, but Derek at the Amicable Anarchist waylaid me and said that Berkley Grimes had been trying to find me and was in the pub, so I went in. He has apologised for, and explained, his part in Growltiger's fate. He explained Denzil had run my cat over and had decided to use him instead of the rag doll they had for their so-called jape. Brendon Dant was on the Glebe Mound that afternoon and had even suggested they use my poor cat and helped them do what they did.'

Berkley Grimes affirmed that: 'Bodhi wanted me to come and explain to Margery what had happened. She said we owed it to her. It had not been fair, the way it had turned out. I was concerned when Margery came in the pub, she was anxious, hot and bothered. We had a few drinks until Bodhi finished her yoga class and joined us. In the course of our conversation, I think Margery realised something, which I still don't quite follow, but she will explain.

'As usual, with anything Brendon Dant is concerned with, I was not sure if I had inadvertently shut myself in the museum. I thought something was dropped in my bag, but I wasn't sure about that either. Something Berkley said made me realise that sometimes, people you see regularly in a certain place in a certain way, make it all acceptable, whilst the unusual makes you sit up and take notice. I realised too, the source of a lot of the accusations and gossip, which involved Berkley and myself in these events, was probably traceable to one or possibly two people.

'I realised the Tudor documents found in Barney's wall had not been stolen but had probably been taken alongside the Moyen Circle papers, when it was known Barney was in hospital and had died. I think there could be some later documents among them, which Barney had seen. He had effectively authenti-cated them and had even used threatening behaviour to a former mayor in the Amicable Anarchist over them. He had been aggressive enough to be banned from the pub.

'These documents had been hidden somewhere to which only Barney and this one other person had a key. They are now missing from the place where they were hidden. Only the person who hid them would know that which is why, I think, Brendon Dant shut me in the museum. He had probably taken the key to my house from my bag, once he had found out I didn't know where the docu-ments he had lost were. He probably took my keys when I was looking round the exhibition and I think he dropped them back again, when I came out and hurried off to the toilets.

'I came to the conclusion he wanted me out of the way long enough to search my cottage or to plant something in it. So, when Berkley, Bodhi and I came back here, I started looking. I was really pleased to have them here, in case Mr Dant decided to come back for any reason. Initially we didn't find anything and then we were talking about open fires and I realised I hadn't looked up the chimney. We spread an old Gleaner on the floor, and I stuck my head in the grate. Berkley held the torch, whilst I looked in a most inaccessible spot and found this.'

Margery showed DI Barker the map which she had wrapped in newspaper.

'May I take this?' he asked.

'Yes, please do, I think you will find it's a forgery.'

'What makes you say that?'

'It shows land was privately owned which now belongs to the council and is tenanted by a farmer. This land is to have expensive homes built on it and they are already being offered for deposit by one of the local estate agents.'

'But you would need deeds and marriage certificates or birth certificates to show there are descendants of the owners still living, to prove it,' said DI Barker.

'There are other documents. Barney Cobbler may have kept them with the Tudor ones in his house. I guess Brendon Dant took them when he collected the Moyen Circle files. I think they were taken to conceal them. He was the only person with a key to the padlocks on the sinkhole. The witch trials were probably too long ago to be relevant to land ownership, so Barney had to be talking about another document, probably a later one. Maybe it was the deeds to some land on this map.'

'But then,' said Berkley, 'if there are deeds and my family doesn't have any title to the property, I'm right to advise them to sell up and move.'

DI Barker looked at Berkley. 'I think what Margery is suggesting, is that this map and any deeds in existence are both forgeries.'

'Oh! I see! You think the map you found in your chimney was set to be discovered and it would link you to the theft of the documents in Barney's house. It would be claimed, as you had the map, you were also concealing other documents.

'Because of the circumstances, no one would consider authenticating the documents. The item Barney was talking so much about in the Amicable Anarchist and even quarrelling with an ex-mayor, might have been a forgery, but because the most eminent historian in the area and had authenticated it, everyone would accept it as an original.'

'I think that was intended,' said Margery. 'I think Dant wanted Barney out of the way so he could take the document back. It would then be "discovered" hidden with this map. No one would know which documents Barney had seen, but because he was so sure about them, there would be less chance they would be questioned or need to be authenticated. But the place Dant chose to hide them, with the Tudor documents, which are probably genuine, was somewhere to which he was the only key holder, since Barney died. There is also the possibility there is something in with the Tudor documents which these people would rather was kept hidden.'

'Such as deeds, for example,' remarked DI Barker. 'They were discovered among Tudor documents and are now with the fraud squad at the Yard.'

Margery smiled. She was relieved she was not the only person who was on the track of forgeries.

Barker continued, 'Thank you for this and the Indian, I wasn't expecting that. I'll collect my things from the Palace Hotel and go home tonight. I'll say good-bye to Vlad and suggest he stays in your spare room tonight.'

Margery blushed and hoped Berkley and Bodhi didn't notice, but they both looked amused.

'I think you will be the envy of every woman in Little Havell tonight,' said Bodhi, smiling.

'I can see Uncle Harry has no chance now,' added Berkley, chuckling.

'Your uncle Harry is in Venice, mending his marriage, as if you didn't know. And I have a bone to pick with you too, Berkley, delivering Uncle Harry's Valentine's Ball invitation through my door in the early hours of last Saturday morning and scaring the life out of me. You also upset my nosy neighbour. But I guess you've made up for it since.'

Berkley looked a bit rueful.

'I'm sorry, Margery, it wasn't very clever. I realise now I've been a bit stupid over a few things.'

Vlad had finished in the kitchen and shook hands with Barker who suggested he stayed in Margery's spare room and left with the map.

'Vlad, DI Barker asks if you can stay in my spare room tonight?' said Margery.

'I will if you insist,' Vlad sounded slightly petulant. With a roguish smile, he sat down on the beanbag next to Margery's chair opposite Berkley and Bodhi.

In answer to Margery's question, Bodhi said she and her parents had fled Uganda in 1972. They, and other members of the family, had been found a place to live on the Glebe Estate by the Ugandan Asian Resettlement Board. It had been difficult at first for her parents, but, as a six-year-old, she had attended the local school and made friends with the children. She trained as an alternative therapist at the Institute. Through family contacts in India, she studied yoga under a master for a year. She met Vlad every week when she took a weekly yoga class in Little Havell at the Country Hotel. When she heard the fracas outside the Assembly Rooms, was being blamed on a Russian spy from Little Havell, she guessed they were talking about Vlad. She was able to say to Berkley, if they were talking about Vlad, they were almost certainly making a mistake.

Vlad repeated his story to Berkley and Bodhi, leaving out the bit about defection, but telling them about the nuclear disaster and the devastating affect it had on his life. It was late when the younger couple left the cottage. They all agreed it had been a good evening and they would like to meet up again.

Vlad took a very dim view of Margery being locked in the museum for a couple of hours. He felt he should have been with her at the exhibition. But she said she had no idea what would happen. She said Bodhi had encouraged Berkley to explain her cat had been run over and not hurt deliberately. It had been a long and trying day, but she felt reassured. The map and the deeds were with the police and being investigated by the fraud squad. Vlad was there to make sure she was all right.

## Sunday 23rd February

Vlad and Margery had porridge and a pot of tea for breakfast, the morning sun was shining through the cottage window and through the open kitchen door into the room. He was keen for her to go and see Eric with him. He said he had tidied the place up and she could listen to Eric playing the piano and perhaps play cards with them. But Margery wanted some time at home. A little housework, a little gardening, she would take a walk on the Glebe Mound and prepare something for an evening meal for them both. She had a feeling of relief and was looking forward to sorting things out, after the visitors of the previous evening.

Vlad cycled to Heathlands and Margery put some music on the radio. She found herself singing along to it.

After vacuuming, dusting, cleaning the kitchen and the bathroom in her small cottage, Margery turned the radio off and went outside to tidy up the garden. She was delighted to find the primroses were in bud and there were wild violets all over the garden, even in the lawn. Some of the flowerbeds needed a bit of weeding. She was doing that when she thought she heard someone open her front door with a key. Vlad wouldn't be back until the evening. Maybe he had forgotten something, she thought. Well, if it had been her door she heard, he would probably come and find her outside.

Margery finished weeding her herb bed, took her shoes off inside the kitchen and decided it was time for some lunch. She had the sense someone was in her cottage, so walked into the front room and had a sudden shock to find a stranger sitting in her chair.

The stranger was a woman dressed in loose flowing clothes with very fair hair tied back in a long loose plait. Margery had seen her before, but not often.

'How did *you* get in?' she asked so surprised she realised she was being rather rude.

'You left the door open,' replied Pricilla Buckler in a rather imperious tone of voice. 'I walked in. I have been sketching your cottage. I have decided I would like to sketch the interior too, but I want to do it with a fire in the grate.'

*So that's it,* thought Margery, *she's after the map and, probably still trying to find out what has happened to other documents.* She knew perfectly well she had not left the front door open.

'If you are cold, I can put the electric fire on for you.'

'No, I'm not cold. But I would like to see a fire in your grate.'

'I'd have to have the chimney swept before I did that.'

'Well, you'll do that for me then, won't you?' asked Pricilla Buckler.

*What a cheek this woman has,* thought Margery. *She might be a clever artist, but it was her cottage, her fireplace and she wasn't going to be dictated to.*

'I might,' she answered. 'What has possessed you to suddenly take an interest in my cottage? There are others along here you could sketch just as easily.'

I think you know why I have an interest in your cottage,' replied Pricilla, looking at Margery directly through her pale-blue eyes.

'You tell me,' said Margery defiantly. She was thinking this woman had the audacity to let herself into her home with a key her husband had copied when he locked her in the museum.

Pricilla kept her unblinking blue eyes on Margery. The affect was mesmerising.

'Don't pretend you don't know. You've hidden it all very well in here. I've had a look. Brendon had a look yesterday. Concealing important documents is a criminal offence! You should know that.'

'It's not a criminal offence I've committed,' Margery was more defiant.

'My goodness me! You're brazen, aren't you? I say again, concealing important documents is a criminal offence and we will see you are prosecuted for it once they are found.'

'You say you've had a look. You know there is nothing here. You say Brendon intruded in my home yesterday and had a look. If you've both looked for them and not found them, whatever they are, they can't be here. That is logic. You must have the wrong cottage. Now, I would be obliged if you would leave.

I didn't leave my door open. Your husband must have taken my key when he locked me in the museum yesterday and made a copy.'

Pricilla Buckler didn't move. She looked angry. 'You'll find those documents for me while I wait,' she said. Her gaze was powerful, steady, unblinking.

'I'm not wasting my time looking for something I haven't got.' Margery was becoming angry. 'And if the documents, you pretend I am concealing, are so important, why don't you ask the local police to look for them and get them round here?'

'The police are already looking for them. Jonah McKay has reported their loss to the police.'

'Well, perhaps they will find them then. But I can tell you with complete confidence, they won't find them here,' said Margery.

'Why? Where have you hidden them?'

Margery went red with annoyance. She was also beginning to be frightened. How long had this woman been in her cottage? Had Pricilla or her husband planted something else to involve her in their schemes? She began to feel uneasy but didn't want to show it.

'I'm flattered you are going to sketch my cottage and I would like to sketch the interior,' she said. 'I'm a great admirer of your work. I enjoyed looking round the exhibition in the guildhall yesterday. Did you sell many paintings?'

'You are beginning to get tedious now. You think you are so clever, don't you? Margery Moore, photojournalist, feature writer, with your "Take a Pew at the Pollux" column. You write "oh so" precise reports on inquests. You have your precious by-line in the newspaper for articles and photographs. You have your hunky Russian lover in your bed whenever you want him. Are you going to tell me where you've hidden those documents, or am I going to have to put pressure on you? I warn you. I expect you to find them, or I will have to make you.'

Margery was beginning to be alarmed. She would play for time.

'I don't have and have not seen any documents. I'd like to remind you, you are in my home, my guest, but uninvited. If you have, in fact, come here to sketch my cottage, you can do that from the outside, which I suggest you do.'

'Oh no! I'm staying here until you find the documents which I know you have hidden in your house. I want to witness you finding them, so I can turn you into the authorities and have you prosecuted for concealing them.'

'If you are so sure I am hiding documents here, you must know what they are and where they are,' she said, realising that, as clever as Pricilla Buckler might be, she was unaware Margery had already found one document and had turned it over to DI Barker. She was beginning to wonder if there were another one. But, if there were, then Pricilla would know where that one was too.

'Please tell me where they are, because I don't know.'

That angered Pricilla. 'The least you could do is look for them. Someone took them from Barney Cobbler's House and Jonah McKay reported the theft. I know they have been found and that you were involved in the discovery. I, therefore, expect you have hidden them in this cottage. I demand you find them!'

'If you know they have been found, perhaps you would be kind enough to tell me where they were found.'

'I think you know where they were found.'

'And what makes you think that?'

'Never mind how I know. Just tell me where they are.'

'If you are so sure documents are here, perhaps you can tell me what they are, and where they are, because I certainly don't know.'

'I suggest you start looking.'

Margery had an idea. 'Why don't we look together?' she suggested. 'We could start with my shed in the garden. Come on.'

But Pricilla wasn't moving. Margery realised she wanted to be in control of the situation. It was stalemate. Pricilla knew there was one, possibly two documents concealed in Margery's cottage, because her husband had planted them there. She didn't know Margery had guessed he had done that, found one and handed it over to DI Barker.

She sat down opposite Pricilla on the settee and looked straight at her.

'If you are determined to stay, I'm making a cup of tea. I came in for some lunch. I'm going to make a Tuna sandwich; would you like me to make you one?'

'You can make a cup of tea and have some lunch when you've found the documents.'

*This woman, this artist, this forger*, Margery thought, *was telling her what she could and couldn't do in her own home. It was insufferable.* She had a sudden idea. *Alf was in his garden.*

'Whatever you are going to do, I'm putting the kettle on and making myself a sandwich for lunch. I'll ask my neighbour to come and help me look for the documents you are so sure are here; he's just outside, I'm sure he won't mind.'

'Make yourself a sandwich if you must. But you will not involve your neighbour in this.'

Margery went into the kitchen to make herself a pot of tea and a sandwich. She wasn't feeling particularly hungry, but it was good to get away, even for a few minutes from the glare of those piercing blue eyes and the constant attempts to control her.

She left the door open and kept an eye on Pricilla sitting in her chair. She hadn't moved. She heard the front door open again and saw Brendon Dant had entered the room. He must have been the one with the key to her cottage. She closed the door a little so he could not see her. She heard them talking about her as if she was not there.

'Has she found them?'

'No. She claims she knows nothing about them.'

'We're going to have to use pressure.'

'I know. She'll have to find them. This business can't wait any longer. The whole development depends on it. Everything else is in place. The Grimes family are prepared to cede ownership.'

'The easiest way to deal with the woman is to put her out. Find the documents ourselves and claim she was concealing them to prevent the development of the bypass and the housing.'

'There's only one way to deal with people who stand in our way. You know that. We've come too far to be set back by this obstinate woman.'

# Chapter X
## Run to Ground

Margery had heard enough. She felt momentarily unable to move. Her heart was pounding. It was like a bad dream, a nightmare. The kettle began to whistle. She opened her back door whilst it was whistling and quickly turned the hob off. Moving stiffly, almost paralysed with fear, she left her cottage as quietly as she could and locked the door behind her.

Once outside, she knew she could shout for help if she needed to. It gave her confidence. She found she could run down the garden and out of the back gate, along the bridle path. She ran past some Sunday walkers who looked surprised to see someone running with no shoes on. She turned right and ran along Priory Street. She was about to cross the road to the Amicable Anarchist when she heard music she now recognised as "Wang Wang Blues" faintly playing in the car park. She turned and found DI Barker sitting in his BMW with another man. He turned the music off and got out of his car when he saw her.

'Miss Moore! Are you all right?'

'I've got the Dants in my cottage insisting I'm concealing valuable documents. They are threatening to sue me for it and dispose of me in some way. While they were arguing between them about how they could force me to find them and how to put the blame on me…what to do with me. I ran out of the back door.'

'So, we've managed to run them to ground between us. Detective Sergeant Francis and I will come back with you. I guessed they would be likely to act sooner or later. It's as well Jonah is in France. When that map turned up in your chimney, it seemed likely they were involving you. I stayed in the area. I thought after the second inquest, they would be confident to carry on. They must have been here already. We are watching all approaches to Priory Cottages. We've even someone on the Glebe Mound. I don't know how he missed them.'

Margery, Barker and Francis ran through the old priory and along the lane in front of Priory Cottages. Margery opened her front door with caution, expecting to see the Dants. She let DI Barker and DS Francis, go in before her, warning the latter to mind his head, but a little bit too late.

There was no sign of the Dants in her cottage, nor much sign of disturbance. In the fifteen minutes it had taken her to run to the car park, inform DI Barker and DS Francis that the Dants were in her cottage, and run back again with them, the Dants had gone. There was little trace they had been in there. Margery began to worry the two detectives would think she was making it up. DS Francis went up her stairs and she managed to warn him to mind his head, this time, before he got to the top. She heard him looking about upstairs. DI Barker looked into the kitchen, the bathroom, outside in the garden and in the shed, but there was no sign of either of the Dants.

They all met up again in Margery's front room.

'I'll go next door and see if Alf has seen them,' she said quickly, before they had a chance to cross-examine her and ask whether the couple had really been in her cottage. She slipped her moccasins on and went out, leaving the door open.

Alf came out of his house when he saw her.

'How did you do that?' he asked.

'How did I do what?'

'You left a few minutes ago, dressed all smart and got in a taxi. How did you to get back so quickly and change?'

'But I didn't. I went out of the back door and I ran along the bridle path to the street and then into the priory car park. There were two people in my cottage when I left. Did you see them?'

'That's odd. I could have sworn I saw you come out of your front door and get into a taxi. The taxi driver held the door open for you. A real gentleman he was. Very smartly dressed.'

Margery had a sudden thought. 'What was I wearing Alf? Did you notice?'

'Yes, you had your black jacket on, one of your hats and a nice dress. I've seen you in it before.'

'Thank you, Alf, you have been really helpful,' she said quickly and left him looking even more puzzled as she ran back into her cottage. DI Barker was still looking round. DS Francis had gone outside to ask the policeman on the Glebe Mound if he had seen anything. Margery dashed up the stairs to her bedroom and checked which of her clothes were missing.

'Well! What a cheek!' she said loudly, coming down the stairs really angry.

'What is it, Miss Moore?' asked DI Barker.

'That woman has taken *my* new dress, *my* black jacket and *my* new hat. My thinking is, Dant was driving a taxi, he was dressed like a taxi driver. I only heard his voice. I didn't see what he was wearing. He has picked her up in my clothes outside my cottage. My neighbour thought it was me.'

Margery also noticed her poker had been left in her hearth and the wood-framed sampler which was usually kept in the fireplace had been pushed to one side. There was soot and brick dust in the grate, where the Dants had scraped around trying to find the map which Margery had found and removed previously. There was one other sign of disturbance. Her wild-flower picture, which normally hung over the mantelpiece had been completely removed from its frame. The paper at the back of it was missing. 'That's where another document was hidden!' she said showing DI Barker. She had never considered looking there.

He asked to use her phone. He called Scotland Yard: '"wild-flower" is on the move.'

'I don't hold out much hope,' he said to Margery, when he had put the phone down.

'Do you think they'll come back?' she asked.

'No, they will probably have changed their image already. We'll find the house in Great Havell and the cottage in Little Havell belongs to some holding company or is rented in the name of an elderly maiden aunt or some other obscure untraceable relative. They've probably got a place in London or another part of the country, where they are known and accepted under different names. These two are clever. They may even carry this off. I don't think this is the end of it, if we do catch up with them. They are unlikely to come back here for the immediate future. They've got part of what they wanted, but thanks to you realising what Dant was up to yesterday we've got a map and one of the deeds from Jonah. Another one, perhaps a marriage certificate, birth certificate or floor plan, was, after all, hidden behind this picture. They probably had a couple of so-called experts lined up, apart from the late Barney Cobbler, to authenticate the documents.'

'So Dant hid the map in my chimney and something else behind the picture, when he locked me in the museum?'

'Some kind of document could have been in the picture longer than that. This has probably been years in the planning.'

'It may always have been there? Surely not. But how come? I don't understand.'

'Look at the initials "P B" on your picture. It's the same initials as Pricilla Buckler. We probably don't know what her real name is. She's a very talented artist and also skilled at copying and forgery. A very clever woman. I hope we will be catching up with her this time, but neither DS Francis, nor I, saw them go into your cottage. They didn't come from Priory Street and there is no sign of their car. Dant was almost certainly driving a taxi. It wouldn't be noticed. I don't think we saw it, but there are other approaches he could have used, or it was parked at the end of the row of cottages. There was often one there, but I had not associated it with the Dants.

'People don't notice the Dants either. Pricilla Buckler was often sketching or painting in the area and he was constantly walking about and talking to people he knows. They have been thoroughly accepted by local people in many ways. He is vice chairman, now chairman of a local charitable group and a well-respected local solicitor. She is a well-known and sought-after artist. They mix with all the influential people and not just in this area. I have no doubt they will be in the same sort of groups elsewhere. But I am hopeful we will catch up with them this time. If we do, Miss Moore, you may have to be a witness.'

Margery's phone rang. She answered it.

'Miss Moore. Could I speak to DI Barker please, it's Sergeant Taylor.'

'Yes, of course, he's just here,' Margery handed the phone over to Barker, 'Sergeant Taylor for you.'

DI Barker listened. 'The Quay Marina. Good. Can the sailing club stop them from leaving? Excellent. We're on our way. You might like to come with us, Miss Moore.'

DI Barker went into her back garden and called out, 'Francis, we're in business!' DS Francis came running down from the Glebe Mound and round the end of the terrace in time to meet Margery and DI Barker at her front gate.

She slipped her moccasins on and locked her cottage up. They all ran through the old priory to DI Barker's BMW and got in. The engine started and the sound of it was accompanied by 1920s dance band music. Gerry Barker turned the sound down. They were at the Quay Marina within minutes.

When they all got out of the car, they saw many members of the Cricklewater Sailing Club were on their yachts in the marina. Every available member had untied their boats from the berths, switched on their outboard motors and were regimenting themselves across the channel from the marina into the estuary in time to prevent a luxury motor yacht from leaving. It didn't appear anyone was on the motor yacht. They watched as the RNLI from the nearby Cricklewater Harbour and the coast guard entered the Marina. The flotilla of sailing club yachts made just enough room for them and closed ranks.

They watched as the coast guard went alongside the motor yacht and two uniformed men boarded it. The RLNI were there, Margery thought, as a precaution, in case anyone decided to jump overboard, or the people in the motor yacht tried to force their way through the barrage of yachts and caused damage, or one capsized.

The coastguard officers steered the motor yacht towards the jetty when they had control of it. It was tied up alongside Bradley's yacht, which was still at the end of the jetty. They secured the sailing yacht and the motor yacht together.

Margery watched DI Barker, DS Francis, Sergeant Taylor and a police constable run along the jetty and board Bradley's yacht. For a while, the coast guards disappeared. They emerged with a couple of people. She couldn't see very well what they looked like, but they didn't look much like the Dants. She was expecting to see Pricilla in her clothes and Brendon in a suit and tie, perhaps with a peaked cap also, but it looked, from where she was standing, as if two women had been found on the motor yacht. She was puzzled.

The couple were herded over Bradley's yacht and handcuffed at the end of the jetty. They were escorted by the two detectives and two police officers. A detective and uniformed policeman flanked each handcuffed person. As they approached the end of the jetty, Margery was surprised to see someone who was dressed like Mrs Smith from number seven Priory Cottages. She was walking upright without a stick. One of her daughters, who she thought she had seen in the past, doing Mrs Smith's shopping for her and using a tartan shopping trolley like hers was also in handcuffs. They were taken by the four policemen to two waiting squad cars, where the police drivers had started the engines ready to take them to Great Havell police station. They left with their sirens going and blue lights flashing. The little crowd from the Old Granary Hotel dispersed when the police cars had gone. Margery didn't see anyone she knew amongst the crowd, although some of them had probably left their dinners on the tables in the Grain of Truth Restaurant, to come out and watch the drama. They still had their napkins in their hands or tucked into their collars.

DI Barker came over to Margery and rubbed his hands with glee.

'That's what I call a result!' he said. 'I'm hoping we can find enough evidence to charge them with murder, forgery and attempted fraud and have them tried at the Old Bailey. Let's get you back home!'

At home, Margery was having difficulty settling, even to finish making herself a sandwich. She found she wasn't hungry. DI Barker had taken her wildflower picture for finger printing, although he said it was likely Dant had been wearing driving gloves. He said he would return it as soon as possible. She took a walk into the marketplace to see if the Foo Kin restaurant was open on a Sunday evening. She discovered it would be open and booked a table for two. She went home, got her bike out of the shed and cycled up the lane and along the road to Heathlands.

Vlad answered the door after she pulled the bell and was very surprised to see her. 'Are you all right, Margery? Come in. You decided to come after all. I'm glad.'

Margery noticed he had tidied up the hall.

He led her into the back of the house into the large room with the grand piano, the clocks, which could be heard ticking, the old furniture and all the books. The piano was still piled with all sorts of stuff, but there was room to sit down on the sofa and chairs. A game of chess was in progress on one of the low tables. Eric gave her a mumbled greeting and Vlad said he would make her a cup of tea. She followed him into the kitchen. She noticed he was able to use an electric kettle. Either Eric had paid his electricity bill or Vlad had used his skills as an electrical engineer to connect Heathlands up again. Margery wasn't going to ask. There were serried rows of full bin bags at one end of the kitchen. She explained to Vlad she had booked them a table at the Foo Kin Chinese restaurant that evening, because the events of the day had been so exciting, she felt she couldn't settle down to cook.

She said she would cook the pot roast, she was keeping in the fridge, tomorrow evening, when he got back from work. Vlad looked in his jeans pocket, with a frown in his face, to see what cash he had with him. Margery said not to worry about it, she'd had a bonus payment from articles she had written. The Foo Kin wasn't expensive, and she would either use her bonus or they could go halves on the meal, if he wanted to.

They all sat down in the large, long room at the back of the house. There was tea for Margery and Vlad and black coffee with a generous helping of malt whisky for Eric. Margery related the events of the day. She was not sure if either of them actually understood exactly what the Dants had been up to, or how they had tried to involve, and put the blame on anyone and everyone they could, including her. Vlad took a dim view of the danger she might have been in, when both of them were in her cottage. Margery described the map which Dant had planted in her chimney and the fact her wild-flower picture had been taken out of its frame and lost its backing. She said the map looked genuinely old, and the paper it was on, seemed to be antique as well. Eric was interested and taking notice as she was describing how the detective on the case thought there may have been more than one, possibly two or three documents concealed in her cottage or elsewhere. He was beginning to realise how much Sadie had, unwittingly, been involved. It was dawning on him how her bad habits and dependencies had been utilised and taken advantage of. Eric asked Margery to describe the colour and the size of the map she had found in her chimney. At one point in Margery's narration, Eric even went over to his bookcase and took out some of the larger old leather-bound books he kept there. He brought them over to show Margery. They had the blank flyleaf pages missing. He looked at them wistfully and shook his head over them.

'Oh Sadie, Sadie, Sadie!' exclaimed Eric sadly. 'What a fucking silly cow you have been.' He sat down and had a good cry, blowing his nose noisily on his filthy handkerchief. As he did so, Margery realised where the paper had come from for the map which she had found up her chimney. The fraud squad could probably prove that the paper had been extracted from one or two of Eric's books. She asked Eric if he would mind if his books, with the pages missing, were used in evidence by the police. She said they would make an appointment to see him and asked Vlad if he could make sure he was with Eric when they came, as he had met DI Barker. Perhaps the police constable who had ensured he kept his bail condition could come back. She said she would put DI Barker or DS Francis on to it as soon as she could if Eric didn't mind. She found Eric was keen to cooperate with the police in any way he could for Sadie's sake. Although he felt she had been very foolish, he nevertheless had loved her enough and was, in his way, as alcohol dependent as she had been. Margery reflected if two people loved each other, as Eric and Sadie had, they had accepted each other, with all their faults, just as they were.

For Margery, it was a novelty having a meal out with Vlad. It was something they had never done before. Fortunately, he had a clean vest in his rucksack and put that on under his air force blue jacket before they both cycled over to the marketplace on their bikes. People she knew in Great Havell were quite surprised to see them together, but she was past caring. They locked their bikes on railings near the Foo Kin restaurant. The staff remembered her from when she went there to interview them to write an article. They made a fuss of them both.

Margery found she was very shaken up by her earlier experiences and it took her a while to get her appetite back. They had the teapot refilled several times because, once again, she had become very thirsty.

Vlad found it hard to believe Pricilla Buckler, who he knew from visits to her home and her studio, to do odd jobs, and to unblock her toilet, had been so threatening to Margery. He thought she must have been bullied by her husband into doing it. Margery was not so sure about that. She had been alone with both the Dants in the past two days. She had found Pricilla far more menacing than Brendon. It was difficult to know which of them was the main instigator, had planned it all and was the most intelligent.

'Pricilla has stolen my new dress, my black jacket and my new hat?' she said. 'Why did she do that?'

'To make it look as if it was me going out of my cottage and not her.'

'How do you know she did that?'

'Alf said he had seen me, smartly dressed in those clothes, getting into a taxi not long before I went round to ask him if he had seen the Dants. He thought I had returned and changed quickly. I went upstairs and found my dress was missing from its hanger.'

'I can't image Pricilla doing anything like that. She is always such friendly, pleasant lady.'

'Do you remember seeing Mrs Smith and any of her family from the cottage at the end?'

'When I cycle round that way from Little Havell, I have very occasionally seen an elderly lady bent over a stick. She walks very slowly.'

'Yes, that's Mrs Smith. Have you ever seen anyone else go into that cottage?'

'I may have seen a woman taking some shopping in. I noticed, because she uses a shopping trolley like yours.'

'Did you ever see a taxi at the end of the cottage when you came that way on your bike?'

'Yes, I have seen a taxi. Quite often, now I think about it. There is usually one parked at the end of the cottages on a Friday night when I cycle over.'

'When DI Barker and DS Francis took me to the Quay Marina, I saw Mrs Smith, standing up straight and with no stick and the other woman, the one with the shopping trolley like mine, taken off a motor yacht, handcuffed and taken away in a couple of police cars.'

Vlad was quiet, taking it all in. He'd never met Brendon Dant, so didn't know him. He didn't come into Great Havell enough or at the right times of day to have seen him regularly in the marketplace as Margery had. He'd seen Mrs Smith. He'd seen a younger woman. He'd seen a taxi. They all came and went regularly, and he just accepted they were an elderly lady and a younger relative or friend with her shopping. He looked a bit puzzled. Eventually he asked, 'What are you telling me, Margery?'

'I'm saying that Pricilla Buckler took my clothes so that she looked like me and then went off in a taxi, probably the one which you sometimes saw parked at the end of Priory Cottages and often took Mrs Smith out and brought her home. Mrs Smith from the end cottage and the younger woman, who used to do her shopping for her, using a shopping trolley like mine, were arrested and put in handcuffs at the Quay Marina this afternoon.'

Vlad was very quiet for a long time, taking it in. Margery watched his face as his expression changed from puzzled to apparent understanding and then puzzled again.

He shook his head in disbelief. *'Nepostizhimiy, nepostizhimiy,'* he said eventually.

'I don't like to think of Pricilla taking your clothes. I didn't think she would be the sort of person to do something like that. She has very nice clothes of her own. Are you sure it was Pricilla who did this?'

Margery then understood it would not only be Vlad who would have difficulty believing Pricilla Buckler, if that was her real name, was anything other than a highly talented artist. All her friends and acquaintances in Little Havell and beyond would be unlikely to think she could be anything other than the person they believed her to be.

She thought of Audrey Bodger and her pride in her friendship with the artist, and the pictures Pricilla had painted, and the document she had copied, especially for her. She realised, if she tried to spread it around that Pricilla Buckler was PB the wild-flower artist and had been involved in forgery, drug dealing and even, perhaps, manslaughter, it would be likely Margery herself would become discredited rather than the artist. She decided that except for Cheryl, Jonah, her aunt and uncle, it was best not to talk about either of the Dants and what she now knew about them. Vlad was quiet, taking it all in. It appeared he was trying to work it all out in his own mind. It was probably best to change the subject and talk about other things. They discussed Chinese cooking and cooking utensils and how the distinct flavours were achieved. Margery wondered whether it was worth buying a wok and if she would have room for it in her small kitchen. She decided she wouldn't have room. Her kitchen and cooking facilities were all geared to typically English food.

They lingered over their rice and noodles, both enjoying the novelty of having a meal out together.

Margery eventually managed to get the events of the past few days off her mind.

'Here is some good news,' she said, 'the solstice fair had been reinstated this summer. I am expecting Agatha Grimes, chair of the Women's Institute to ask me to help to serve teas the 1940s-style tea tent again.'

She saw the thoughtful look leave Vlad's face. He looked pleased with the idea.

'Would you like to help me with it this year? Would you like to help me serve the cream teas, sandwiches and cakes in the summer?'

'Yes, I would really like to do that. But is that for one day or longer?'

'It is to be held over three days this year, so I would volunteer to serve the teas in the tea tent every afternoon on the Friday, Saturday and Sunday. Would you be available to help me for all those days?'

'I should be able to take the Friday off. I will make sure I am not on maintenance or emergency call with Bodger's that weekend. I think Miss Bodger would like me to volunteer for the fair. I will ask her as soon I can, to make sure I will be available for all the days of the fair to help you.'

Margery was pleased. She began to put the events of the past few days behind her and plan for the future. This was something she was really looking forward to doing. It was something they would enjoy doing together.


## Monday 24th February

Vlad cycled off to work and Margery went to the Gleaner to relate her adventures. She was careful not to name too many names to the front office girls, except she said she had Berkley Grimes, his girlfriend Bodhi and her Russian friend round for an Indian on Saturday evening. The front office girls were both surprised and impressed with those dinner party guests. Margery didn't mention they had all been dining on a picnic blanket cross-legged on cushions on the floor. She left those details out. She said Bodhi and Berkley were engaged to be married and that Bodhi had got him to apologise to Margery for his involvement in the incident with her cat. Berkley had confessed to her that Denzil Bream had accidentally run Growltiger over.

They also heard that Margery had got herself locked into the museum and thought she would be stuck there until it re-opened on Tuesday. She also related, how, with the help of Berkley, she had found a forged map which had been planted in her fireplace when she escaped from the museum and got home. Philippa and Gill were in wonder and reluctant to let her go into the offices to see Cheryl. They wanted more details.

Margery felt able to tell her friend Cheryl the whole story. She now guessed Cheryl's brother-in-law, DS Francis, had been involved in the investigation all along and wondered how much he had said to Cheryl and Nigel about it.

Margery asked Cheryl to tell her brother-in-law the books with the blank end pages missing, which Eric had on his shelves, would provide the evidence needed the map, she found up her chimney, was a forgery and possibly the deeds Jonah had given to DI Barker as well. She said Eric was ready and willing for the police to use the books for evidence, although she had promised him the police constable, who ensured he kept the terms of his bail, would come over when the police borrowed Eric's damaged books for evidence. Margery explained Eric had been devoted to Sadie and was only too keen to help incriminate those who had taken advantage of her. The discussion of how much DS Francis had been involved with DI Barker's investigations and for how long, would be left for another day.

Cheryl advised Margery not to talk about what she knew.

'I have to say this in complete confidence to you,' she said. 'There is a group of ex-Grammar School friends who may be involved in all this. I know a few of them. Please keep this completely to yourself. Brendon Dant, as you might guess, is one. Our own Harry Grimes is another. Bill Walker of Moonlight Motors is also one of them. Another is the master of the hunt at Trincaster Hall, but I can't remember his name. The late Fenton Bradley was also part of the group. They have stayed friends since they were at school together. They look after each other. They do each other favours. They scratch each other's backs, you could say. There may be more in the group, but those are the ones Jonathan knows.

'You've met Nigel's brother, DS Jonathan Francis, haven't you? He's based at Grimpen, but he has been able to give Barker this type of local information, which you wouldn't know about. I've been to our managing director Gerald Smith with it, but he thinks the support of Harry Grimes' old school network has been beneficial rather than detrimental to the Gleaner and therefore didn't really want to know what they got up to. Dant, for instance, is well known to him in the Moyen Circle and it looks as if, even if he is prosecuted and convicted, it probably won't be reported by the Gleaner. Gerald Smith will insist we go with the Moyen Circle's agreed and accepted version of events to avoid discrediting the charity and their philanthropic aims.

'Harry Grimes and Brendon Dant shone in most of the Grammar School's sports teams. If they were playing football, rugby or cricket, they were the ones to score. When they played opposite each other, the games were very competitive. They were popular and successful at the school. This is the reputation they have locally. Dant has a lot of friends and supporters. The Grimes family has a lot of influence. The late Fenton Bradley has a widow and a grown-up son. The Fulton-Hides at Trincaster Hall have the master of the hunt and gamekeeper, who is loyal to them and part of the group. As I say, I can't remember his name. Last, but not least, Bill Walker is a loyal friend to them all and is willing to help the group in all sorts of ways. You said, for instance, you saw Gloria with him a lot in his car, no doubt it was at the behest of Harry Grimes.

'The MD, Gerald Smith, got quite cross with me when I first went to see him about all this. I had to back track completely and I said I must have made a mis-take. It was after that he asked me to sit down and his secretary gave me a cup of coffee. Otherwise, he left me standing up, didn't offer me a chair and looked at me as if he thought I was a fantasist. I realised then he knew about the group and their friendships, but felt they were of benefit to the newspaper, particularly with Harry Grimes contacts.'

'I had no idea about any of this. I begin to see what people meant when they said I should stay in my "cosy little world" and not trouble myself about any of it. I'm a bit shocked in fact. Before I started working as a freelance, I had to cover all sorts, as you know, including sudden deaths and bereaved parents. That sort of thing could be difficult, but in some ways, it was straightforward. This sort of deviousness, this kind of corruption, I can't think of better words to de-scribe it, is different. It's the sort of thing my uncle came up against as town clerk. He put it all behind him when he retired. It's the reason my parents retired to Orkney. They both spent most of their working lives in Westminster and are happy now they live well away from it all.'

'Yes, I supposed you are not the sort of person who would easily understand how devious some people can be. You've been brought up to be very straight-forward and strait-laced about things. You probably expect everyone else to be the same. I had a similar upbringing. I've had most of that knocked out of me working here. I do enjoy the job though. It's the people and the constant buzz of activity which I particularly like. I even enjoy the daft things they do when they celebrate targets in advertising. You and I had a good night out at the cinema last week, didn't we? We'll have to do it again. I'm hoping Nigel will come more often to the Arts Centre too. He enjoys the jazz and the folk. I've got some more features for you. They all need a bit of research. You should find them interesting.

'I also wondered whether you might find out a bit more about the background stories of the witches and the witch trials. Not necessarily for immediate publi-cation, but as an ongoing project, which we could run with in the Weekender Gleaner around the time of this year's fair and at Halloween. Local people are very interested, especially the Wicca and the Pagan groups. It's also local histo-rians and archaeologists who are keen to know more. I know the documents, which went missing from Barney's home, have been found, but only a few peo-ple know about that. You could use those, with Jonah's help perhaps, and we could publish the stories without revealing the source. What do you think?'

'Yes, Jonah had the same idea; it would be interesting to find out more about the six witches and why they ended up together on the gallows. It's something I would enjoy doing in my spare time.'

'That's if you have any spare time. I've had a special request from Gerald Smith to ask you if you would like to extend your freelance services for the Gleaner by giving regular reports on the coroner's inquests held in Great Havell and sometimes, perhaps, further away the Crown Court cases at Trincaster? He would like you to report on those cases too, if they are particularly interesting. You would have travel expenses, of course. Between you and me he prefers your court reports to our cub reporters. He likes the fact they are thorough and factual. I sometimes wonder if our younger reporters can read their own shorthand.'

'It's nice to know I am appreciated. I must admit, I would like to do that, Cheryl. It uses shorthand and the reports are easy and straightforward to write, because the inquests and cases follow a set procedure. I'll give it some thought and let you have a definite answer in a day or two. My further investigations into the lives of the witches might have to wait, if I am going to do that.'

That evening Margery cooked the pot roast and vegetables she had intended to prepare the previous evening, when they had gone to the Foo Kin restaurant instead. Everything was ticking over nicely on her stove when they heard police sirens.

The sirens became louder and louder. There were blue flashing lights outside the front of Priory Cottages. The police were also at the back of the terrace in the path by the Glebe Mound. The cars were in pincer movement around the end of the cottages. There were three police squad cars outside. Margery turned down the stove and she and Vlad put coats, jackets, shoes and boots on and went outside into the lane to see what was going on. Three police cars, their blue lights still flashing, nearly all the Great Havell police fleet, were surrounding Mrs Smith's cottage.

They joined Florence, Alf, his neighbours, who happened to be staying in their holiday home, the students at the end and even Florence's neighbours, to watch the drama. People walking down Priory Street and regulars from the Amicable Anarchist left their pints half-drunk, walked through the priory ruins, and into the lane to see what was happening. They made up a little crowd watching, as the police with powerful torches, since it was nearly dark, broke into Mrs Smith's house and surrounded it. There was silence, except for the sound of the police searching the property inside. Then the forensic team went in. The electricity had been cut off. Torches were being used inside the property as well as outside.

Eventually, Sergeant Taylor came out. He recognised Margery in the crowd and came over to her.

'What did you find in there?' she asked.

'The place is empty,' he replied. 'Completely empty. There is nothing in there at all. It's been stripped. We've scoured the cottage. There is no indication anyone ever lived there. The shed is empty too. We'll fingerprint everything, but that's all we can do. That's what the forensic team are doing now. I have never been in a place so devoid of any clues to someone living in there. It's extraordinary. We would usually find a paper clip, a hair clip, a nail, a curtain hook or a drawing pin. Even in places which have been empty for years, we find something, but here, there is nothing. We are even looking carefully at the floorboards to see if any appear to be loose and may have been raised.'

Margery thought of what Cheryl had said about the group of friends. The Dants had tried to leave in a hurry and been arrested disguised as Mrs Smith who had lived, or at least, appeared to live in the end cottage and the relative who used to visit her. How many other members of the group, she wondered, had a key or access to the cottage? It could have been any one of them or a group clearing it out at any time of night, and it would probably not be noticed or even heard, right at the end of the terrace of cottages. The Dants had been arrested two days previously. The police could have raided the cottage anytime since then, but chose that night to do it, making sure all the neighbourhood noticed them. No wonder mayor Walter Grimes had asked for outside help to investigate the deaths of Barney and Sadie. It looked as if Dant and his cartel of former Grammar School friends had influence over the local police force as well. There had been time to clear the property completely before it was raided.

Margery and Vlad went back to her cottage and enjoyed the pot roast after all the excitement. They had the spring and summer to look forward to.

It seemed to Margery, the last few days of February to the beginning of March were all about funerals. Fenton Bradley's had been arranged by Brendon Dant who was not able to attend the occasion, but Bradley's family and many other friends were all there. She heard it was a burial in the local cemetery. The main beneficiary of his will, apparently, was his only son who would be starting an estate agency with his inheritance. She expected to be commissioned to do an article on that, when it was up and running.

Margery and Cheryl went together to Barney Cobbler's funeral which had been organised by the Moyen Circle and was a celebration of the distinguished historian's life. The church was packed with mourners. The church hall was open to everyone who attended for non-alcoholic drinks and snacks. In the absence of Brendon Dant, it was Jonah who talked about his friend, in the service, and did a good, if slightly breathless, job, Margery thought. Jonah emphasised the loss to the locality of someone, his friend, who had devoted his time to researching and recording local history. They all owed a tremendous debt to him for that and his death was a loss to the community.

They didn't go to Sadie's funeral. Her family had arranged that in Hertfordshire, where she came from. Sadie's family didn't even invite Eric to go. He might not have gone, even if invited, thought Margery, but he had cared for her, so it was unfair on him. Sadie's family hadn't tried to help her when she was alive and was now claiming her back and saying, according to Ruth Baldock, who went to the funeral in Stevenage, that moving to Great Havell had been the biggest mistake Sadie had ever made in her life.

Ruth confided in Margery and Cheryl, when they met her at Barney Cobbler's funeral, the Petal family were blaming Eric for Sadie's addiction and death. Margery didn't think that was fair on Eric. She remembered Eric had loved Sadie enough to lend her his treasured Honey Monster watch. She mentioned it to Ruth who said she had met Sadie's mother at her daughter's funeral. Ruth said she thought that if anyone was to blame for Sadie's addiction, it was probably the very controlling, even abusive, mother she had. Ruth said Sadie had mentioned difficulties with her mother when she worked for her, but it wasn't until she met her at her daughter's funeral, she realised exactly what a negative influence this highly controlling, very critical mother could have on her daughter.

Ruth informed Margery and Cheryl that Sadie had been growing cannabis secretly at her nursery long before she met Eric. Since Sadie met him, Ruth had not felt so bad about sacking her, because she knew he wouldn't charge Sadie any rent and she wouldn't be on the streets with no job. Ruth told them she had pointed all this out to Mrs Petal at the funeral, but the mother had turned on her and blamed her for Sadie's addiction and death. Margery mentioned to Ruth she thought Eric had been genuinely fond of Sadie. He still cried when he talked about her. It was sad to reflect he might have been the only person who had truly loved her, and he wasn't even invited to her funeral.

*It was very disheartening*, Margery thought, *to reflect on the three funerals which had taken place.* There was a father mourned by a widow and son. A highly distinguished historian whose local knowledge could not be matched and was a loss to the whole community. A botanist whose life had been messed up by a controlling parent, but who had been appreciated by many of the people she met, when they visited the old priory and was truly loved by the eccentric Eric. *Had they all been victims?* She thought. The idea didn't bear thinking about.

The Moyen Midden Fayre in 1986 was one of the most successful ever, according to the Gleaner. Margery attended the whole event. The newspaper had been packed full of pictures and stories. It carried pages of advertising and there was even a special souvenir colour supplement, which was free with the Gleaner and given away at the fair. The editorials, written by Margery Moore, on Gary and the Fly by Night Boys, the origins of the fair and the witches of Havell-on-the-Marsh, attracted pages of lucrative advertising. The rival Advertiser had no presence at the fair at all, much to the satisfaction of all the staff at the Gleaner.

Berkley Grimes had organised an exclusive interview, for the paper and the colour supplement, with his cousin Gary Hogan, together with all the Fly by Night Boys. He particularly requested for Margery to come to interview the pop group and write the article. Gary Hogan and his musicians were staying at the Little Havell Country Hotel. Berkley took Margery over there to meet them. They insisted on being photographed outside one of the Palladian towers in the grounds. She couldn't get any of them to smile, when she pointed her camera at them. They all wanted to look moody and aggressive. She wasn't too pleased with the result, but they were delighted with her pictures. They were so pleased with Margery's photographs, they used one of them on their latest album cover. They told Margery they were looking forward to their first open air performance in the Glebe Park.

The ground floor of one of the Palladian towers in the grounds of the Country Hotel had been cleared out by the hotel maintenance team for the band to practice in. There were some concerns raised about the volume of the amplifiers possibly weakening the structure of the tower. The vibrations from the bass drums and the sound system could be felt underfoot by people walking in the Country Hotel parkland on the golf course. Golfers complained the earth tremors, from the band rehearsing, deflected their best shots from the holes and the noise put them off. Gary Hogan, a golfer, who won a very competitive game against his cousin Harry Grimes, dismissed the complaints. He said members of the golf club were using his band practice as an excuse for playing badly and losing.

For all three days of the fair, Vlad helped Margery serve the sandwiches, scones, cakes and tea every afternoon in the 1940s-themed tea tent in the Glebe Park. The tent was decorated with red, white and blue bunting inside and out. Vlad even wore a pair of khaki drill trousers with his khaki jacket to serve the teas. It was often hot in the tent and Margery had a job persuading him to keep his jacket on the first afternoon. She managed to explain it wouldn't be appropriate for him to serve teas in a vest, even if it was a clean one. For that first afternoon he wore a t-shirt. Margery solved the problem that day. Agatha Grimes took over from her to give her time to go into Great Havell. Margery bought Vlad a short sleeved khaki shirt in a charity shop, which he wore on the Saturday and Sunday. There was a generator nearby which they used for boiling the water. It was also used for a tape machine which played World War Two songs and music.

Over the three days, the tea tent was always busy, often with queues. Margery found she had to get used to seeing a steady stream of Vlad's female admirers, mostly from Little Havell and the Glebe Estate. They came every day the fair was on to have afternoon tea in the tent. Margery called them his fan club. She found Gill and Philippa, the front office girls from the Gleaner, became enthusiastic members of his fan club. They were very giggly when Margery introduced Vlad as the Russian spy. He winked at them both, put his finger to his mouth and asked them to keep his spying activities secret.

'You are welcome to come and spy on us any time you like,' they said.

Morris and Mack from the Brass Monkeys Brasserie supplemented the quantities of scones made by Agatha Grimes and other ladies from the W.I. They helped in the tea tent as well, particularly with replenishing supplies. Margery and Vlad were happy to be serving the teas most of the afternoons, with occasional breaks. The tea they served in the tent was Dewbury and Hicks "Wartime Blend", some of which the store had donated to the event, so there would be additional profits for the charities. There were also specially packaged Dewbury and Hicks shortcake biscuits and fruit cake available for sale.

Alec and Carrie Moore brought Neil and Bobby to the fair. If they hadn't had an inkling before, her aunt and uncle were pretty quick at noticing a rapport between Margery and Vlad. After watching the pair of them serving teas together, both looking happy, there was no doubt in their minds that he had been the 'friend' who had come to stay with her in February. Margery left Vlad in charge for fifteen minutes whilst they were there and joined them for a cup of tea. She had brought one of Growltiger's bowls to fill with water for Bobby and other visiting dogs.

Harry and Rita Grimes came in for tea with their two lively boys. Margery made a point of asking Vlad to serve Harry with the tea. She was glad she was behind the table and he couldn't get anywhere near her. His 'hello honey,' was not, therefore, accompanied by the usual pat on her bottom, but he managed to extract a sharp look from both Rita and Vlad when he said it. Margery served the Grimes boys with generous slices of the carrot cake they had their eyes on and earned an appreciative 'thank you' from them and their mother.

Berkley, Bodhi, Tracey and a pale, rather subdued Denzil came into the tea tent together. Margery noticed Berkley was managing to extract a few weak smiles from his friend, whilst the girls were making a fuss of him and trying to cheer him up.

When the twins from the Witches Cauldron came in for tea, Margery greeted them and said to them it was a pleasure for her to serve them with tea for a change. They wanted the recipe for the cheese scones they bought, so she referred them to the W.I. and found out from Agatha Grimes the secret ingredient was a pinch of paprika pepper in the mix.

Elsewhere at the fair, Tina's boys had organised a sand pit "midden archaeological dig" which was very popular with children. They used various strange objects and bits of toys they had found in skips, which they had cleaned and buried in a sand pit. They offered prizes (usually other things they had found and cleaned up) if the children were able to identify what they were.

The Moyen Circle had an exhibition of old photographs and postcards of the Havell Hundreds. Many of them had belonged to their late chairman Barney Cobbler. They were mounted on card and displayed on folding cork boards on tables. Barney Cobbler's many publications on local history were also available for sale. All profits went to the Moyen Circle charities.

Great Havell pottery had made some "1986 Fayre" souvenir pots, based on one of the urns found in the Moyen Midden. They had a treadle-powered potter's wheel with plenty of clay, so people could have a go at making their own pots for a donation to the charity. This proved very popular, although it also increased the sale of the souvenir pots as visitors found casting their own was more difficult than it looked, when demonstrated by an expert.

Root and Branch were doing a tremendous trade with their broomsticks and the collection of six herbs named after the witches of Havell-on-the-Marsh. It was a complete sell out for Ruth Baldock. She was taking orders which people could collect in a few weeks, when stocks had been replenished.

Gerry and Janine Barker brought their children with them from London. They looked round the fair, scoured the second-hand stalls for 78 records and had tea in the tea tent. Morris and Mack had taken over serving the teas. Vlad and Eric were looking at the second-hand book stalls together, and Gerry Barker asked Margery to walk round the fair with him, whilst Janine took the children to explore the other attractions.

Gerry Barker informed Margery that thanks to Eric's antique books, which had the missing blank pages, the police were likely to get a successful prosecution for forgery and attempted fraud against both the Dants. They would try for a murder or manslaughter charge too, but he didn't hold out much hope of getting a conviction on that. Gerry Barker told Margery, in confidence, that Brendon would probably serve time for forgery, attempted fraud and possibly manslaughter, but that Pricilla had an exceptionally clever solicitor and would probably get off all charges completely. He said he could now predict it would be argued she had been Brendon's victim. Pricilla only spent one night in the cells. Her friends had put up bail for her and guaranteed her appearance in court. If Margery and Jonah had not alerted the police to the existence of the forged deeds and map, they would never have got as far with the case.

The evidence from Eric was crucial as well. He realised he had been foolish to let Sadie take the end papers from his antique books. After her death, when Eric discovered they were being used to make forgeries, he was not only co-operative, but positively helpful. The amount of end papers missing from Eric's books did point to the existence of other, yet undiscovered documents. He had accepted a fireproof metal cabinet to keep the damaged books in, so they would be available, if they were needed by the police at some future date.

The Dants' occupation of the end terrace of Priory Cottages and their appearance in different guises had allowed them to manipulate the situation to their advantage. Brendon had the local historian, Barney, to authenticate the forgeries and Pricilla was able to use the paper supplied by Sadie to create documents which appeared to be genuinely antique and authentic. They thought they had it all going their way. Barney, however, was too keen on talking about it. Persuading Mayor Grimes to cancel the fair had backfired. They needed Sadie out of the way because she was the source of the antique paper they used for the deeds, the map and any other documents needed to authenticate the existence of Thorpe Castle. In spite of her addictions, she could still have given them away and they couldn't risk that.

Brendon had not calculated on Barney finding genuine documents in the walls of his Tudor home either. His idea of integrating the forgeries with them only served to make Barney so confident they were all genuine, he talked about them. Brendon had not expected Barney to be so vociferous about the map either. He must have realised when Barney was thrown out of the Amicable Anarchist the distinguished historian's reputation would be damaged locally and he would have to be prevented from doing, or saying anything else which would jeopardise their plans. The Dants had not expected Fenton Bradley to drown in the Marina either. Gerry Barker said he wondered why there had not been a post-mortem requested by the widow until he came to the conclusion, Bradley could have been a drug smuggler and may have taken something himself. Neither Bradley's family, nor his friends, would want that revealed from a post-mortem, or inquest, and reported in the Gleaner.

Gerry Barker also thought some of the circumstances such as the presence of the surveyor and land agent from Bodger's Commercial, the incident with her cat and the fracas outside the Assembly Rooms had been planned, or even engineered to stir up gossip and deflect people from realising what was actually going on. Such things, he concluded, are relatively easily done in a semi-rural area, especially when there are so many legends and superstitions which local people persist on taking seriously.

Margery felt it was not for her to mention what she knew about the network of former Grammar School boys who could have worked together on aspects of these plans, to buy cooperation with hard drugs, plant forged documents in the homes of local historians and stir up public feeling and interest in local history and traditions by having the fair cancelled. She had only heard about these people from Cheryl in confidence and it wasn't for her to point fingers or name names. Besides, Cheryl's brother-in-law probably knew about the group of former school friends and would have tipped DI Barker off about them.

Margery and Gerry Barker collected Janine and their children from the Root and Branch tent. They had bought a set of the witches' herbs with the artist's drawings on the labels. Janine said she was looking forward to planting them in their garden in the north London suburbs.

They all met up with Jonah in the beer tent, where one of the most popular pints was the special Falcon Fayre brew, which Margery had tried earlier in the year, when she wrote a feature on the Brewery. It was being served in pint and half pint glasses with "Moyen Midden Fayre 1986" printed on them. These could be bought for £1. Gerry Barker managed to persuade Vlad to try it, teasing him about his preference for cold lager. He thanked Gerry Barker for the pint, but complained it was a little warm. Margery noticed a twinkle in his eye when he said it. He delighted her by winking at her too. *Perhaps he was beginning to understand the English and their sense of humour*, she thought.

The Barker children, a serious boy, George, who Margery guessed must be about ten, and a lively talkative little girl, Laura, aged six or seven, had powerful magnifying glasses with them. They were finding tiny bugs and spiders in the grass on the floor of the beer tent. Laura climbed on her father's lap and inspected his pint with her magnifying glass. She insisted there was a tiny spider in it. Gerry

Barker appeared to take no notice at all and drank it all up in one go. He then said, holding her tightly so she couldn't get away, that if his drink had a spider in it, he had drunk it, and it was a money spider, which would make him very rich. His small daughter put her magnifying glass up to one of his eyes, made him look really grotesque and told him he looked like a one-eyed giant.

Janine asked George what he had done with his pocket money and whether he had spent it. He claimed he still had it and rifled his pockets which revealed a collection of things, including a water pistol and a conker on a string, which he boasted had been the champion at school the previous year. He found his pocket money eventually but said he would be saving it for his model railway.

The three-day fair was such a success, the Gleaner reported the Moyen Circle were able to pay for the upkeep of the church and the alms houses with the proceeds. The council also announced, with pride, there was money to spare to invest in the following year's event, which was now certain to go ahead.

After the fair, Jonah said to Margery, over a beer in the Amicable Anarchist, that neither the new chairman nor the new vice chairman of the Moyen Circle could understand how the event had made a loss in recent years. The committee had come to the conclusion, Jonah said, that nice Mr Dant must have made some miscalculations somewhere.

It was more of a puzzle, how Barney could have made mistakes over the figures, though. That he could have got his calculations wrong, or condoned mistakes, didn't make any sense to Jonah at all. Barney had always been meticulously accurate with his figures in the past. He was known and respected for it in his job at the tax office. Jonah thought that perhaps, his friend had been so obsessed with the documents he had discovered in his walls and the other documents which had come to light, he had neglected to see the errors which were being made in the Moyen Circle accounts. Brendon Dant had produced spread sheets rather than the double entry book-keeping which Barney had used for the Moyen Circle accounts. The figures had not been accurately transferred from the books to the spread sheets in the past two years. This meant large amounts of money, which were still held for the fair in the bank account, had not been transferred or taken into account on the spread sheets. How his friend Barney could have allowed this to happen was a mystery to Jonah.

Other members of the Moyen Circle said it was a such pity Mr Dant and Mr Cobbler, who had both put so much effort and work into making the Moyen

Circle and the annual fair a success, could not have enjoyed this year's event. Poor Mr Cobbler, who could have predicted he would have died in such a way?

Poor Mr Dant too. It was a tragedy he'd ended up in intensive care in a London hospital in February. His employers Lockhart and Upton had received notification from a very concerned family member, who asked for all communications to Mr Dant be directed through him. Mr Dant had only been seen in the marketplace and enjoying the exhibition in the guildhall the day before. Poor man. You never knew what was going to happen. It was such a pity, so awful, for his wife who, they heard, was being comforted and looked after by friends and family in London.

The town council did not make a loss on the fair either. The Gleaner reported the council meeting which discussed the costs of policing, stewarding and tidying up after the fair and the pop concert. The councillors apparently were unable to understand where the figures had come from, earlier in the year, which showed this annual event cost the council more money than it made. It was such a popular event people were clamouring, falling over each other, even, to volunteer, to keep the Glebe Park free of litter, for car park duties and as wardens. The whole town boomed over those few days and they decided that was a good thing for everyone in Great Havell, including the council.

Shortly after the fair, Margery, wearing the wrap-over polka dot dress she made to serve the teas in the tea tent and her 1940s style sandals, was shopping in the market on a Saturday morning. She was buying some strawberries from a stall when she looked across the marketplace towards the shops and something caught her eye. She finished her purchase and went over to the Hospice Shop to look in the window where she had seen a dress. It was on sale for a few pounds. She went inside the shop and bought it. The Dewbury and Hicks label was still inside it. She was pleased to get it back and she felt the money went to a good cause.

When she looked round inside the shop, she saw a tartan cape, and hat for sale identical to hers. She bought them as well. She took a further look, found and bought her black jacket back, and the hat she had purchased from William Fabb's.

She asked the staff where the items had come from? Who had brought them in? Apparently, Gail Cooper from the Old Granary Hotel had delivered them whilst the fair was on. They had been packed in a tartan shopping trolley, which was also for sale. When she gave them to the shop, Gail said they were all items which guests had left and had been in lost property. The hotel had tried to trace the owners, but without success. They kept the items in storage in the loft for a long time, expecting the owners to reclaim them. By the summer, Gail decided it was time for a clear out. She thought it best to bring them to the hospice charity shop, so they could benefit from selling them.

Pleased to have her waterproof hat, dress and jacket back. Margery also bought the spare tartan cape and hat and the tartan shopping trolley, which she said she would come back for after she had taken hers home. She thought another one would come in handy and she could keep it in her bike shed. She put all her purchases in her shopping trolley to take back to her cottage.

She had not heard any more from DI Barker and did not know if the Dants had yet been prosecuted. She had found out from Audrey Bodger, Pricilla Buckler had sublet her studio in Little Havell to a sculptor. It took the locals a little while to become used to his work. He cast nude figures with exaggerated genitals in bronze. The sculptor, Anton Bijou, was recognised and acclaimed internationally according to the Gleaner, which carried pictures of his work, with certain parts blanked out. Margery had taken the pictures when she went to interview him on Audrey Bodger's request.

The sculptor made of point of telling her that his reputation was far-reaching and he didn't expect people in the provinces to be sophisticated enough to understand his work. He insisted on sitting opposite Margery, for the interview, with one of his larger sculptures behind him. The exaggerated male genitals were directly behind his head, so that it looked as if he had a pair of huge bulbous ears and a penis growing out of his head. She took a picture of him, but they decided in the Gleaner it could not be used, even with certain parts blanked out. Photographic were delighted with the picture when they developed it. An enlarged print of it appeared on their office wall and there was also a print of it on Gleaner's studio wall, where the graphic artists worked.

Even after Margery's carefully worded article, Great Havell folk decided collectively they had no time at all for Anton Bijou, or his sculptures. The general opinion in the town was that he was just out to shock. His work, most people in Great Havell said was, "a load of bollocks" which was a pretty accurate description, Margery thought. After that, Little Havell residents became quite proud and defensive of him. His work became sought after for major exhibitions at the City of Trincaster, where his sponsors said people were more discerning, more sophisticated and there was greater appreciation of fine art. Vlad found the sculptor was as keen to have him round for odd jobs at the studio as Pricilla Buckler had been. Vlad confided in Margery he had difficulty understanding the sculptor's English, especially when he had asked him to pose for one of his art works. He said he'd had to rush off to an urgent job on the Glebe Estate.

Audrey Bodger invited Margery to dine with her at the Country Hotel after her interview with Anton Bijou. She wanted to tell her about her poor friend Pricilla Buckler. Margery was shocked when Audrey said Pricilla's husband had beaten her to force her do his bidding. Apparently, Audrey said, in complete confidence, Pricilla's husband had abused her so horrifically she had scars. When Audrey had met up with Pricilla in London, her talented artist friend had just had an appointment with a Harley Street specialist for a rare, as yet undiagnosed, but very painful and debilitating nervous condition.

These things were running through Margery's mind, as she walked home to Priory Cottages from the Hospice Shop. She did wonder how an abusive relationship as bad as the Dants reportedly had, could have occurred when the couple lived apart. *They had only ever been seen together at public events*, she thought, according to Cheryl. It was possible Cheryl had made a mistake.

Margery was pleased she had bought back the clothes Pricilla Dant had taken when she escaped from her cottage. Also, in her tartan trolley were the duplicates of her tartan cape and hat, which had probably been used to make it look as if she was somewhere or doing something that she never was and never did. She could go back to the Hospice Shop and collect the other tartan trolley when she had taken everything else home in hers. As she reached the door of her cottage, she had an idea. *Yes*, she thought, *that's a really good idea, it will take a bit of thought and planning, but I'll do that.*